The Story of Q.

♑ ♋ ♌ ♈ ♏ ♓ ♒ ♑ ♐ ♎ ♍ ♉

"Beautifully, lyrically, and powerfully written, this book reminds us that it is divine to simply be alive …"
-C.Hart (Canada)

"The last book that left me with such awe was The Alchemist."
-E.Conroy (UK)

"A wonderful read. Delicious truths written with such compassion that even those who find the book a bitter pill to swallow will surely have their hearts and minds opened. Here's to you, Walt Whitman and Saul Williams …"
-L.Barrington (New Zealand)

"Extraordinary. A powerful, courageous debut."
Dr. Pauline Wolf, author of The Healing Cook (Canada)

"N.M.Freeman is a powerful, poetic writer … unique …"
K. Sheean, artist (Australia)

"Remarkable."
Don Garry, The Don Garry Literary Award (Canada)

"One of those rare books where you can feel the truth of the works resonating in your own heart …"
P.Howells (New Zealand)

"Captivating … Everything about The Story of Q. is unique and a triumph."
C.Battersby (New Zealand)

"What you've written here is huge. Intense, huge, and wonderful. So, so wonderful …"
Esther, Esther Mitchell Music (New Zealand)

the story of Q.

INSPIRED BY ACTUAL EVENTS

"Deeply moving and fearlessly controversial.
A story resonating with profound truths."
—Dr. David Owen

N.M. FREEMAN

iUniverse, Inc.
Bloomington

the story of Q.
Inspired by Actual Events

iUniverse books may be ordered through booksellers or by contacting:

iUniverse
1663 Liberty Drive
Bloomington, IN 47403
www.iuniverse.com
1-800-Authors (1-800-288-4677)

ISBN: 978-1-4502-7698-6 (sc)
ISBN: 978-1-4502-7702-0 (hc)
ISBN: 978-1-4502-7703-7 (ebk)

Printed in the United States of America

iUniverse rev. date: 10/02/2012

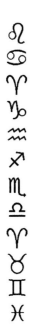

For Jonathan

Contents

Prologue

There was once a vast, rocky wilderness, void of all vegetation but the hardiest thorns and briars. Through the middle of the desert stretched a rough highway along which the whole of humanity was making its pilgrimage. They straggled along footsore and thirsty, tired and frightened by a myriad of nameless fears.

But at one point along the way a clear spring of running water bubbled up out of the naked rock. No one knows who first discovered it; that secret has long since been lost. Yet for countless generations the people journeying along the road stopped to refresh themselves there. And as they did so, found to their surprise and delight that the waters not only slaked their thirst, but satisfied deeper needs as well. Somehow, in drinking at that source, they found their minds and bodies healed, their hopes and courage growing stronger again. Life became rich and fresh with meaning. They found they could pick up their various burdens and take to the way once more with new hearts. They called the spot "the place of living waters" and the spring itself, "the water of life."

Now, as time went on, various people began to roll up boulders around the spring as monuments of gratitude. As the generations and centuries passed, these monuments became more elaborate and ornate, until at last the spring was totally enclosed, arched over by a great fortress-like building and protected by high, stone walls. A special caste of men who wore special robes declared themselves deliverers and caretakers and began to set rules for preserving the purity of the well. Access was no longer free to all, and disagreements as to who could drink there, and when, and how, sometimes grew so bitter that wars were fought over them.

The victors always put up more monuments and safeguards in gratitude for winning, and so it was that as the years rolled by, the spring itself was bricked over and lost from view. No one remembered when exactly it was done or by whom. But when the pilgrims complained about the loss, and many were found fainting or even near death on the road, those now in charge simply ignored them or said sternly that "This is the way things are." Beautiful ceremonies were carried out inside the holy place to celebrate what the well had done for pilgrims many years before, while at the very gates people were dying of thirst.

Eventually, the vast majority of people avoided the now-sacred "place of living waters" and survived whatever way they could. But sometimes, in the night, when all the chanting and ceremonies were stilled, those few pilgrims still searching were sure they could hear an almost miraculous sound. From somewhere deep under the foundations of the great rock structure there came the faint echo of running water. And their eyes would brim with tears.

Parable of Living Waters graciously provided by Tom Harpur

My people are destroyed for lack of knowledge.

~God

DAY ONE

MATEO

Some of what you learn here will seem familiar.

Cappadocia, 255 BCE

♈

Mateo paused briefly on his descent of the stairwell, smiling as the sound of familiar voices wafted up toward him. This is where he learned what it meant to be human. It was a place of secrets and revelations and was alive as a beating heart.

And even though Mateo knew what he would see when he rounded the corner at the base of the stairwell, even though he knew what he would smell—incense and fresh air, sunshine and earth, linen and cotton, prayers and papyrus, wood, woven carpets, and moonlight—none of this familiarity could placate his emotions, and Mateo arrived at the Sanctuary as he always did—with eager anticipation undulating beneath his skin, trailing in scintillating waves behind him.

Older now, he took the steps one at a time, stirring up small clouds of dust that puffed around his ankles. Behind him, the sun broke the top of the stairwell, and he smiled. It was fitting, he thought, that The Way should be lit by early morning sunlight. Appropriate, somehow. For what lay ahead was the Truth That Never Perished—that which was true, had always been true, and would forever be so: *ab aeterno, ad vitam aeternam—from the beginning of time, for all time.*

What lay ahead, was the truth about God …

♌

FARAH

And the Lord said, 'When thou passest through the waters,
I will be with thee; and through the rivers, they shall not
overflow thee: when thou walkest through the fire, thou shalt
not be burned; neither shall the flame kindle upon thee.'

~Isaiah 43:2

Right now. Not far from where you live.

♌

Farah wasn't dramatic; she was desperate.

For months now, the thought of suicide had crept in on her and again, on this day, she pushed vigorously at it with her hands and feet, away with her might and her mind watching helplessly as her will stood aside. She saw it there … her will … held in the shackles of her fear, gripped by her panic attacks, distracted by the same confusion that made her skin crawl and her spirit heave with alarm. Slowly, she was being dominated by the thing she had desperately sought relief from these last several years: this nervous energy in her chest, these pinpricks of questions.

The suicide, or "Mephistopheles," as she had named it, cajoled her from normality at times when she least expected, and because of this began to own more of Farah's life than she thought she could handle. Like now: He whispered horribly at the edges of her mind. In maleficent tones he irritated, scraped his nail repeatedly over the same spot on her skin, tugged at her attention, and began to dictate her heartbeat into irregular rhythms. This time he dropped by while Farah waited in line to buy a cup of coffee.

The queue hadn't moved for some minutes, and when Farah looked to see why, a woman near the front leaned forward. Only moments before, Farah had been inhaling ocean air on the small deck of the ferry, watching a retreating mainland, wondering whether *he* and all of her worry could be left behind. Wrapped in the late winter weather, her face bathed in the sinking afternoon sun, Farah had stood. Still. Quiet. Contemplative. And only a little afraid.

But then the wind changed. Faces were suddenly sprayed by water, jackets zipped to the collar. Passengers bunched together for the doors and huddled into the cafeteria where they queued, stamping feet and rubbing hands. Children stood in small groups or hugged between parents legs, friends laughed, and men made jokes about shrinking willies all with the same thought in mind: hot drink. Farah, among them, tucked her hands under her arms and thought the same thing. And it was this insidious cool, this want for warmth that motivated Farah to peek to the front of the line. If she had known, in that very moment, that the last of the days sunlight—one giant ray streaking through a cloud-filled sky—would reach boldly through a tiny west facing window, or that as the woman leaned forward her necklace would emerge. If Farah had known the tiny gold cross was about to glint brightly and make her blink, she mightn't have bothered. In fact, she would have kept her eyes averted, would have remained on the ferry deck, wind bursting through her jacket zipper, barreling down the nape of her neck. Because the tiny gold cross was what did it—triggered everything—brought Mephistopheles skipping to her side. That tiny little cross. That Christian bane.

Farah fidgeted, irritated that she had seen it, but more irritated because something so *small* had done it this time. Brought on her panic attack. Triggered the feeling of what she thought was anxiety but feared was insanity. It used to take bigger, more substantial, more overtly influential or invasive religious things: a sermon, a church bell ringing, a glimpse of an early-morning television evangelist before Farah's frantic fumbling fingers could change the channel. But *now* ... a *hint* of religious symbolism, a breath of the word Jesus, a cross around a stranger's neck ... and before the queue moved one more step, before the necklace could disappear again between the folds of the woman's clothing, before Farah could exhale her aversion to the cross, Mephistopheles had arrived. On the edge of her consciousness he instantly began to seep. Like black ink, like oil, or venom. And work as he always did, with such enthusiastic vigor, taking over her thoughts and her physiology. When it happened like this, Farah imagined him thrilled—like a vampire invited across their unwitting victim's threshold, and, like that unwitting victim, Farah didn't know how to un-invite him. She could only wait for the inevitable: Death. Or—as suicide began to seem—relief.

Five minutes passed. Six. Farah's skin swirled with anxiety, and the deepest breath she could take wasn't deep enough. It felt as if her lungs had stopped working; it felt like going crazy might. She shifted back and forth uncomfortably and cracked her knuckles, chewed a bit on her nails, wiggled her toes in her shoes, and rubbed her arms ... waiting. Hoping Mephistopheles would depart so that her mind, her body, could settle back into homeostasis. But instead he prodded and pushed her, poked and sneered, reminding her over and over that she was damaged, that God didn't want her, that she was forgotten, and as good as dead—like road kill in periphery vision, like a body after suicide. *Why put it off?* he would say. *You know you can't live like this: tortured, anxious; you'll give yourself cancer by thirty-five at this rate. The body/mind connection isn't a myth you know*, he would lecture, wagging his finger. *All this worrying. Come on*, he would prod, *do yourself a favour   end it*. She could feel him delighting, especially in moments like these where he and the cross could, together, remind her that she was fundamentally un-right.

Seven minutes passed ... *finally*, a choice.

Caramel, mocha, vanilla cappuccino. Farah scanned the coffee instamatic for a button that said *just plain coffee*. There wasn't one. So she opted for a hot chocolate instead, figuring the caffeine wouldn't help her rattled nerves anyway. She dug in her bag for money and found some trapped beneath her Bible, handed it to the cashier, and willed her hands to stop trembling as she waited for her change. And that was when it happened. Something big. Incandescent. That would eventually lead Farah to a place she didn't know existed. A place that had been waiting, all along.

At the other end of the cafeteria, a souvenir shop buzzed with tourists and ferry-goers, and there in the small crowd of people, under the fluorescent lights, it glittered: silvery and fluid, blue-green and deep. Water. It was a tiny floating patch of … water? Farah blinked and squinted through hands perusing tacky keychains, between arms marveling over picture postcards, over children's voices shouting "Mommy, can I …" to see if she was hallucinating—surely she had to be. But there *it* still was. Shimmering a quiet mystery that no one else seemed to notice.

Farah dropped her change into a charity box and then walked—without taking her eyes off of it—toward the shop, leaving Mephistopheles, her hot chocolate, and her panic attack behind without even noticing.

As she got closer, the water became matte and stilled in the painting that housed it. Rocks, a blue cape that looked like velvet, skin that glowed in ethereal tones, and water flowing forward into a cave from a deep-set background. It was Leonardo da Vinci's *Madonna on the Rocks*, impressed pristinely on the front cover of a large leather-bound book. Farah crouched and reached forward to pick it up: thick, title-less, she turned the book over in her hands and felt its weight rest in her palms. Mesmerized, she traced her fingers over the images. This used to be her favourite painting: Mother Mary, John the Baptist, Jesus, and Uriel, the angel of fire and prophecy, the Light of God.

Familiarity wrapped itself around her like comfort, and the faintest smile began to warm Farah's lips until suddenly, sharply, she realized what she was holding. *Religion.* And it hit her like the sound of dropping glass—instantly—with a reverberation that didn't echo but threatened to cut her—on the inside. And it began to do what it always did. Choke. Words and images flashed like lightning.

Jesus.

The cross.

Blood.

Flesh and blood.

Pews and hymns and downcast eyes and stained glass shattering over her.

Eyes that bore in.

A gold cross. … Farah glanced fearfully toward the cafeteria for any sign of him there, for any sign of him coming. She closed her eyes, held her breath, and sat.

Waiting.

Waiting.

Waiting.

"Amazing," she whispered, too afraid to look up in case he was actually standing there, but right then, suicide felt nowhere near. Tentatively, Farah squinted her eyes open, and through the fuzzy vision of half-closed lids noticed that there seemed to be no shadow looming, no figure creeping forward. *Incredible*, she thought, just as the water in the painting again seemed to sparkle and swish like a tide right below her lower lids; a trick of the light, she was sure, but one that stoked Farah's curiosity into flame. She could no longer wait. Slowly she opened the cover, and with the scent of leather and paper wafting into the air, smiled at what lay open before her.

♋

ROSE

And ye shall know the truth,
and the truth shall make you free.

~John 8:32

Rose sat in her car, not shaking her knee like most people did when they were nervous, not smoking a cigarette, or snacking mindlessly on food. Her thumbs, instead, rubbed the top corners of her Bible, right and left corners respectively with right and left thumbs. The Good Book was her subconscious comfort; reading it, looking at it, holding it, just knowing it was near brought Rose some kind of solace. Today however, was different. Today her hands gripped instead of cradled, clung instead of held. Today, her fingers and palms rubbing persistently were doing more than working to create a soothing friction … today they were asking. Begging. Silently pleading as they pressed, hoping to squeeze out any extra ounces of the Book's ready-made remedies. The ones meant to calm, soothe, fix, or simply cure by default because they came from a Book that was what it was: the Bible.

Again, Rose glanced furtively toward the house she was parked in front of. She wasn't clock-watching but she knew she had been sitting there for a reasonably lengthy time—or rather, unreasonably, she thought, biting her lip. Her hands gripped, her thumbs rubbed, she glanced at the key to her son's house on the passenger seat beside her and asked herself again, *what are you waiting for? He's gone for three days! That gives you more than enough time to do what you have to do.* But still her body wouldn't budge because Rose knew: Going into the house would change everything. For as long as she remained in the car, Rose's son would still be who she had always hoped he would be, still be all the good things, still be … saved. But once she went inside, started searching through his things, *finding out*—all of that would change. Rose hoped in vain that it wouldn't, but she knew that it would. And it was this very worry—the loss of what she hoped was true—that kept Rose relatively immobile, relatively afraid of picking up the key, relatively content not to enter the house, just yet. Instead, her hands continued to beg and wait for comfort or the power of God, for the Book and its contents to fix everything.

Alvin Boyd Massey Harpur III (or "Alvin", as Rose preferred to call him), however, was oblivious to all this. He only knew that he was hungry, and that Rose (who usually fed him when Roger was away) was *still* sitting in the car instead of organizing his dinner. He sat large, orange, and purring on the grass, curious as to what the holdup might be before deducing that a closer look might be in order; in particular, Rose needed to get a closer look at *him*. Perhaps that would stir her into action. So he hopped his furry, tubby, tummy-wagging body onto the hood of the car, and blinked affectionately when Rose let out a startled shriek.

"Oh, for goodness sake, Alvin!" she said, holding her hand to her heart. She looked at the cat with exasperated adoration. He purred back at her through the windshield and pressed his paw upon it. Rose realized what he wanted, but could only manage a hesitant, apologetic smile. A moment later, Alvin hopped onto the roof of the car, and sauntered toward the sunsoaked rear of it. If he was going to have to wait, he wanted to do it in the sunshine. "Where are you off to?" Rose turned in her seat with a guilty chuckle. But as soon as she had, she wished she hadn't. Taped to the rear window was a piece of paper. Behind it, Alvin's shadow made itself more comfortable.

It was a note. But the writing was illegible, the paper too thick. All Rose could make out was the colour of the ink. Red. She swallowed and shifted in her seat uncomfortably. *Please*, she whispered desperately to God, *Not more to worry about.*

She wanted the note to have nothing to do with what had happened that morning, with what brought her here, but Rose knew very well that wasn't the case. Stress laboured her breathing and successfully rimmed her eyes with tears. She didn't want to read the note. She didn't even want to look at it.

She didn't want to go outside or into the house. She didn't want any of it to be happening at all. She wanted Roger to be good, and Rose wished then with all the devotion she put into prayer, that this whole horrible mess would go away.

Her knee shook with frustration and she wondered in that moment if the inevitable was ever avoidable. Could God make it so? Rose closed her eyes and took a deep breath with that very hope filling her lungs.

And she sat—still—like that, for as long as she could, repeating a summary of Luke 18:27 in her head.

Anything is possible with God.
Anything is possible with God.
Anything is possible with God.

The Bible said so, and Rose believed it. Anything *was* possible: the parting of the Red Sea, the Virgin Birth, the Resurrection, even miracles for regular people. Rose didn't have leprosy or demons under her skin, she didn't even need to be raised from the dead, but she prayed now to Jesus to heal her life, to change things so that she didn't have to be sitting there in that car not wanting to get out. Rose prayed for Jesus to bring Roger back to God so that none of this would have to go any farther. She prayed for all those not on the right path (especially Muslims and Jews and irreligious people) to find their way *to* Jesus. Around that time, her oxygen began to run out.

Her breath shot out between pursed lips, and Rose's chest heaved while her breathing returned to normal. Slowly, she opened her eyes. Slowly, she looked around and then grimaced. The note was still there, Alvin still needed to be fed, and the reality of what she didn't want to face hadn't changed at all. Clearly, God was not in the mood to perform a miracle in her life that day.

Just then a breeze caught an untaped corner of the note and lifted it; the sunlight on the white paper blinded Rose briefly. She watched, hopeful, but the paper wasn't torn free, wasn't blown away by an easterly wind. It stayed put instead, beckoning her to come and read it. Reluctantly, she let go of her Bible. Reluctantly, her hands fumbled with the door before grasping for each other, wringing and clenching as she stepped out, until worry began to fall in big, invisible drops to the ground, soaking the tops of her shoes.

The words, blazoned in red ink, were not scrawled, but written meticulously. Not a work of passion, but one that was calculated, meant to mean every word. The last sentence was underlined.

> Woe to that man who betrays the Son of Man!
> <u>It would be better for him if he had not been born.</u>
> Mark 14:21

Rose's chest tightened, she felt sick. She shook her head as if in attempt to rearrange the words on the page; surely they did not say what she had just read—it seemed impossible.

She recognized the writing immediately, but did not want to believe that someone from her church, someone who knew her well, whom she had known for decades, could write such a thing about her son. She frowned deeply. Things were much worse than she thought, and she glanced up again at the house. With trembling hands and a heart heavy with not knowing what to do, Rose removed the note, unconsciously crumpling it between her worry-soaked palms.

Wherever she went, she carried a deck of cards. Not playing cards, but cards with scripture written on them. She used them in a multitude of circumstances: when she needed inspiration, when she hoped to offer inspiration to others as to why they should turn to Jesus, but also in times when she didn't know quite what to do. Like now. So as quickly as she could, Rose returned to the driver's side door and dug the deck from her handbag, praying, "Lord, tell me what to do and I will do it," before spreading the cards and choosing one blindly.

The card read:

> For the Son of Man came to seek and to save what was lost.
> Luke 19:10

She repeated the words to herself, waiting for something to happen, some kind of recognition or message to arrive. "To save what was lost—" she whispered. "To save what was lost—"

Meanwhile Alvin, peeping in the back window, seriously wondered what was going on. Why had Rose gone back *inside* the car? His meow was a bit more demanding this time.

Rose held up a trembling hand, begging one more minute. She continued to repeat the words, staring hard at the card at first, and then closing her eyes, *For the Son of Man came to seek and ...* her eyes flew open. "To save what was lost!" That was it! *That* was what God was telling her to do! She was sure of it. Unfortunately, that meant doing the last thing she wanted to—go inside the house—but who was she to question? God did, after all, work in mysterious ways.

"It's all right, Alvin," Rose called to the cat, gathering her jacket and purse, grabbing Roger's spare key from the passenger seat. "I'm coming."

♑

ROGER

Everything that is now hidden or secret will eventually be brought to light.

~Mark 4:22

♑

About a hundred people streamed into the library and made their way down the dimly lit corridor; their footsteps echoed off the gray ceiling and bounced back toward them from the bare walls. The group moved in a loose jumble, some wanting to rush ahead to get a good seat while others less concerned with that avoided the bother of trying to rush at all.

The brochure had said to turn right at the end of the corridor before they reached the large wooden doors. If they ended up in the library, they had gone too far. If they turned right as instructed they would find a classroom. This would be the location of the three-day seminar they were there to attend.

And so the group did. They turned right where they were told and trickled in singles and pairs into a small, rarely used auditorium-style classroom, so rarely used that a light film of dust lay on the seats and desktops (not that many people noticed this; generally, they were more concerned with where they wanted to sit: if they would be uncomfortable in the front row, if the back row would be *too* far back to hear the lecturer, among other things). Some people wondered if they had made the right decision not to bring a pen and paper because, they noticed in a small panic, so many others had.

Before they took their seats, many in the group began to shed their outdoor layers: hats, sweaters, even some shoes came off, and jackets unzipped into the air various degrees of nervousness and trepidation that floated invisibly but palpably, like whispering pulses of energy. Curiosity too tumbled out; suspicion, defensiveness, excitement, all began to hover and lilt a quiet noise about the room.

Some Bibles, more pens, and additional pads of paper emerged, pulled out of backpacks and satchels by hands tied by myriad things—racial definitions, cultural constraints, religions, condescension, and even anger. Some hands were only there to fight—the world, the teacher, the topic—and several others were held in slipknots by ignorance; but most of the hands in the room that day were tied by the same thing: Questions. All of them there for the same reason: Roger Erskine, who was about to walk in the door behind them.

He hated being late, and this morning Roger almost was. Normally, he equated being late with a lack of respect for others, but in the case of these three-day seminars, Roger's concern about being tardy was for a far more practical reason: three days wasn't a lot of time to get through the material he wanted to cover. He glanced at his watch as he entered the room and took the stairs to the front of it two at a time, oblivious to the stares, gapes, and glares directed at him. It was 8:00 am on the dot; introductions and niceties would have to be exchanged later.

He dropped his leather bag on the makeshift desk—a bald and lonely-looking table at the front of the room—and from his pocket pulled a well-worn piece of chalk. He wrote his name on the board in hurried block letters while simultaneously trying to shake off his jacket. When he turned around to face a sea of myriad expressions he thought, *and so it begins.*

♈

MATEO

The Sanctuary lay open as it had for millennia, a reflection of the world above it, alive and stirring with miracles.

The air there was filled with a multitude of tangible but invisible things: the gentle susurrations of angels, the quiet of humility, voltaic streams of curiosity and revelation. Hope sparkled fresh like the colour of lime, bright and undeterred. Gratitude (so deep there were no words, only a feeling between the self and God) rippled and surged in small breezes. Prayers, asking God to fix or reconcile, begging God for change, floated in quiet shimmers like unseen but felt aurora borealis, flickering like invisible fireflies all hours of the day of night.

Mateo stepped beneath the giant archway entrance. A meeting of this magnitude was rare, which left him and the others who had already arrived wondering why it had been summoned.

Before him, sandaled feet stirred up pebbles along rock-lined paths as people walked carefully but socially between the giant floor murals. Friends and strangers mingled in plush, carpeted seating areas, catching up on old news, hugging or bowing hellos. The kindness in the air, the congeniality, made Mateo's heart ache with quiet appreciation, for he knew there were few places in the world one could go where acceptance and the feeling of being welcome—of being loved despite cultural differences—was absolute, but this was one of them. All around him, voices mixed in the beautiful sound of people coming together: languages, skins, and tongues gathered *in nomine Domini,* in the name of the Lord, to *emitte lucem et veritatem,* send out light and truth.

Mateo loved this. His father had taught him from a young age that in order to really be a part of humanity, he had to learn more about the world. And there was no better place to do so than here, gathering in the place where it all began—where hundreds of torches cast a golden glow, where the rising sun far above streamed down in columns through ancient skylights bore through the rocky ceiling.

It had been well over half a century since Mateo's father first brought him here. The cave to his five-year-old eyes had looked behemoth, which wasn't really a far cry from the truth. The Sanctuary was very significant in size (it had to be) but it wasn't illimitable in size, as it appeared. An inadvertent trick of the light had left portions of the back wall unlit, making it appear as if the cave opened into a magical infinity, a place that contained the secrets of humankind and all things that existed before the memory of man. This, of course, was not true; the cave *did* have a back wall, and it opened into what Mateo considered reality's version of that rumoured magical infinity: libraries. Six of them. With archway entrances that framed intriguing views of oil-lamp chandeliers hung low over reading tables, with smaller torches illuminating bookshelves, casting texts, scrolls, and fine drawings in a golden glow. The six were the libraries of practical, geographical, political, and astrological history: the histories of health, herbs, plants, the human body, and the animal world. They were rooms that contained history waiting to be learned about, history waiting to be remembered, and life in the process of being recorded. The information contained within them was considered invaluable, but only when the contents of the *seventh* library were fully understood.

The seventh library, where Mateo now stood, was the most sacred, for it was the root from which all things grew. The knowledge contained therein put all other aspects of human life into perspective and helped, if perspective was ever lost, to draw attention back to where it was always most important to look. The seventh was the library of the great Gospel. It was the library of Spirit. It was not, however, a place of books and scrolls. The floor instead was the focal point, for upon it lay a reflection of what Mateo's father called "God's Wisdom." Stories. Spreading from east to west, linked by a gigantic sun, whose richly painted rays touched each artistic focal point. They were stories about the secrets of existence and the truth at the center of every human heart.

Because of the Gathering, the seventh library was quite full, its paths relatively congested, but if Mateo stood on his tiptoes, he could make out the gleam of the cross through hands shaking hello, through acquaintances bowing Namaste. If he crouched a little, he could make out the green of the palm fronds in the Jerusalem mosaic, and if he crouched even further, his hands on his knees, he could see the shadow of the mound at the base of the Zodiac—the place where his first lesson began all those years ago. A day he remembered so clearly, as if it really had only happened the day before, as if he had only just turned twelve, and his father had only just said to him, "Come, let's take a closer walk with God …"

♌

FARAH

The book wasn't what Farah thought it might be … what every religious book always seemed to feel like to her. It wasn't a book of confusing evangelical ramblings, or one hell-bent on convincing her why she needed to worship Jesus or someone or other. It wouldn't preach or tell her how to pray. It wouldn't dictate. And it didn't look back at her with sympathetic, condescending eyes—eyes that judged or pleaded for her to "just believe," to reconcile, to get baptized. No, this book was something else entirely. It was a book of empty pages: crisp, white, comely pages, waiting to be found, waiting for thoughts to be imparted via hand and pen, for imperfect cursive to display an emotional reality. It was perfect, and just what she needed, what she had been considering acquiring only the night before: a journal.

Farah fanned the pages and breathed in deeply. The smell of blank paper like that, of the potential of sorting through thoughts, had always been wonderful to her. She had kept a journal her entire life, until recently, when the panic attacks became so often that she was afraid to pen them into her experience. As if writing about her fear and the terror of Mephistopheles' whispers would somehow make them real, concrete in the world, potentially available for others to see, to judge, to institutionalize her over. But here, now, surrounded by strangers, the urge to take a pen and write struck Farah again. At this point she figured she had nothing to lose. So she hugged the large leather-bound book to her chest and made her way to the till. Mephistopheles, standing right beside her, seethed a whisper into her ear, "Where do you think you're going?" But Farah focused straight ahead.

As quickly as she could she found an empty table and dug a pen out of the side pocket of her bag. She gripped the pen tightly, but couldn't stop her hand trembling. Every journal entry Farah had ever written began with the same word: *Diary*. But this time, things were different. With her knee shaking, the skin on her fingertips pressed white, Farah titled the page.

And wrote:

Religion plays God in my life.

> *It hangs like a slackened noose around my neck. Heavy and uncomfortable. A cumbersome albatross with a twine that scrapes like a hair shirt at my soul. It takes deep breaths, presses its antediluvian lips to my mouth, and inhales the air from my lungs   leaving me left with so little oxygen   not enough to breathe, not enough to whisper conjecture, but only enough to exhale submission.*

> *Instead of lifting my spirit and "Saving" me, religion holds me by my collar over the great schism it creates in my heart. The crevice = what I am told to feel, the ground beneath my feet = how I <u>really</u> feel   and everything swirling around below and above me is my mind and my heart wondering why none of it ever makes sense. Why am I never left sighing in the relief of recognition   saying, "Ah ha, I completely understand," and then hugged in the open arms of God?*

She tapped the pen thoughtfully on her teeth; over her shoulder, Mephistopheles kept trying to grab it. With tears in her eyes Farah continued:

> *My thoughts   they have been picked raw by faith. And now, any hope I had left in myself and my ability to know God no longer lives, but simply hovers in the back of my mind, scratched and trembling with anxiety. And   and I catch myself fearing that at any moment, I might cause the slackened noose to cinch   if only to experience relief from all the doubt and confusion.*

Farah wiped at her tears gently. Over the loudspeaker, a ferry attendant's voice announced the boat would be docking shortly, asked that all passengers with vehicles please return to disembark. Farah and Mephistopheles looked up at the speaker as the other passengers began to pack up their things. Farah ended her entry not with *xo* and the letter *F.*, but with,

> *I never thought the search for God would bring me so much anguish.*

♋

ROSE

Rose turned the key and the back door to Roger's house swung open.

Alvin purred like a locomotive at her feet and entwined himself between and around her ankles as much as his tubbiness would allow. The cat's affection calmed her slightly, but Rose's hands still trembled when she poured his biscuits. "To save what was lost—", she whispered. "To save what was lost—"

She continued to repeat the words God had sent her, not because she was afraid of forgetting them, but because she hoped doing so would cement her motivation in place. Dislodge her fear and replace it completely with God's will (which she imagined pouring out of heaven and filling up her body). She shivered; even now she didn't want to believe that Roger needed her to save him, but not wanting to believe something didn't mean it wasn't true, and Rose knew: If she wanted to help her son and redeem him in the eyes of the church (God), she had to put her fears aside. Besides, she reminded herself with self-motivating aplomb, as a Christian, she was committed to helping those whom she believed needed spiritual help; Matthew 28:18–20 said it was what God required. The benefits of this undertaking (poring through her son's research material, and using it against scripture to show him how wrong he really was) would be many—not the least of which would be saving her son's soul. It was a big responsibility, Rose knew, but she loved her son enough to want to take it on, and at the end of it all, she would be welcomed back with open arms by the congregation, clean again in the eyes of God.

"Right," she said, with an air of determination. "Seeing as how I've lost my appetite, I might as well have a cup of tea." She really didn't want to start this journey on an empty stomach, and a cup of milky, sweet tea seemed the perfect remedy. She turned on the kettle and opened the cupboard above it, Teas abounded: chai, green tea, jasmine, rooibos and something called Zen. *Oh why couldn't Roger have normal tea like everyone else?* she thought fretfully, before her hand froze mid-air. Had *that* been a sign all along? Was not having normal tea a sign that there was something suspicious … even sinister … about the person who didn't have it? Her eyes widened at the thought of the congregation seeing these strange teas in her son's cupboard. She imagined what they would think. How they would *tsk* suspiciously and then murmur that they were right about him, before looking at *her* with traces of fearful disgust in their eyes. The image bred tribes of disquiet inside of her. *But …* Rose thought frantically … *What if he has normal tea? What could they or* anyone *say then?*

Suddenly, boxes were flying. "Come on," Rose pleaded. "There's got to be some normal tea in here!"

There was a lot riding on it. Rose had deduced that if there were indeed a box of normal tea in Roger's cupboard, it meant he wasn't so far gone; the devil's grip was not held fast. *But* if the only teas were those unfamiliar … well, then it would mean the note was justified. Normal tea meant things could still be normal, that Roger could still be good, that he was familiar … that he wasn't lost. And there it was.

"Oh, thank you, Lord Jesus!" she shouted, collapsing onto the counter.

A tiny box of Red Rose tea was tucked behind the honey. She snatched it to her chest and let go a little laugh. She had never been so relieved to see that big red rose in her life. Alvin looked up from his post-dinner bathing session to see what all the fuss was about, but all he saw was Rose giving a cardboard box an oddly enthusiastic amount of affection. She was hugging it and smiling at it like it was a prized possession before placing it fondly on the counter top.

"To save what was lost …" she whispered, smiling. She knew she still had a job to do there (God's will and such) but Rose savoured the moment anyway, because for her, *that moment* allowed her to be completely on her son's side, free of doubt, like the moment he was born and all Rose saw in her arms was a miracle of God. Her tiny, breathing, beautiful baby boy. This moment was her relationship with her son *before* all of the doubt, before the crumpled note in her peripheral vision, before all of his thoughts that seemed to usurp his belief. And so Rose lingered there until the echoing words, the presence of the *other* teas brought her back to reality, forcing her to blink back her memories. Alvin got back to his bath and Rose pulled the milk from the fridge, the sugar bowl from the tea cupboard. She slid onto a kitchen stool and drummed her fingers on the counter, fidgety with anticipation, waiting for the kettle to boil. In a minute, the real work would begin. (God's will pouring out of heaven.)

She scanned the open-plan room for anything obviously maleficent or sacrilegious. Around the kitchen there wasn't much. A piece of textile fabric that looked like it was from South America hung by the refrigerator, the window ledge was occupied by parsley and an aloe vera plant. That seemed normal enough. She turned on her stool to face the rest of the room.

Diagonally across from her was a bookshelf crammed with books, but also dappled with ornaments and statues.

Rose looked and judged quickly; at least from this angle she didn't see any multi-armed, goddess-esque, blue-skinned figures or elephants, no grinning pot-bellied Buddhas, no upside-down crosses or tarot cards, so was thrilled. A quick scan of the books revealed no Book of Mormon, another great relief. Of course, the rest of the book titles she would have to peruse at greater length later, of that she was sure.

A collection of photographs on the wall closest to Rose were of Roger in various parts of the world—Egypt, Rome, Jerusalem, Turkey, South America, and what she thought looked like England or Scotland. Her heart swelled when she looked at the images. There he was, her son, her darling Roger—all windblown in some, looking official and academic in others, always grinning broadly. She sighed heavily. He just *looked* so normal. How was it possible that her boy had grown into what he had? Or—something caught Rose's eye—had he?

On the other side of the bookshelf, a print of a very famous painting shimmered. Rose recognized it immediately, not only for what it was, but because she herself had given it as a gift. She rushed to it. Sure enough, there it was: *The Last Supper*. A gloriously religious, gloriously Christian image—and it adorned her son's wall.

She laughed. Maybe all of this would be for nothing. Between the box of regular tea, the Last Supper, *and* there was no book of Mormon, maybe, just maybe—Rose glanced toward the crumpled note beside her purse—they had been wrong. Her smiling eyes wandered happily toward the living room, and just as quickly as it came, her smile disappeared. There, on the wall above the television were a few ethnic-looking masks. (Rose generally disapproved of these kinds of things because most of the cultures they came from weren't Christian, and you never knew what kind of evil non-Christian cultures harboured; the suicide-bombing Muslims were a perfect example of that.)

Beside the masks, there was another wall hanging that looked like it was from India. There were no images on it, but that didn't matter; Rose definitely disapproved. *Those* people believed in very strange gods and practiced yoga—which her church did not approve of at all. Rose had become so frightened by what the ministers had preached about yoga that she was afraid she was inadvertently worshipping some strange god by doing her morning stretches and had stopped doing them immediately. If having a stiff body meant going to heaven, then she would suffer it! Compared to what Jesus had suffered on the cross, it was nothing.

Rose grasped the cross pendant Roger had given her all those years ago (before he went to university, before he stopped talking to her about his work, before any of this) and made her way toward the masks for a closer look. She turned on the lamp by the couch and squinted at an intricate drawing Roger had framed. It was just as she feared. A diagram of the Zodiac—an undeniable tool of witchcraft. "*To save what was lost*," she whispered. It appeared she had a lot of work to do indeed. (God's will. Down over her. Like anointing oil.) Anxious, Rose did then what she knew was the cure for all things.

She prayed.

Starting with the *Pater Noster*.

"Our Father, who art in heaven, hallowed be thy name—," behind her the kettle boiled to a whistle.

She walked to the kitchen.

"Thy Kingdom come, thy will be done—," and made a cup of tea, "on Earth as it is in heaven."

She stepped up to the kitchen sink.

"Give us this day, our daily bread—," and pulled back the curtain to the right of it, "Forgive us our debts as we forgive our debtors." Roger had taken down the gift she taped there for him (another bad sign). She closed her eyes and delivered the next line of the prayer loudly to increase its power.

"Lead us not into temptation but deliver us (*deliver my son*, she thought) from evil. For thine is the Kingdom, the power, and the glory forever. Amen."

Cup of tea in hand, Rose made her way back to the living room, her hands rattling the cup and saucer so badly, she didn't trust herself not to spill. A moment later, she stood at Roger's desk empty-handed, scanning spare bits of paper, piles of books, and essays. A collection of Bibles, several different translations, were piled on the corner of the desk to her left: the King James Version, the New Living Testament, the Young's Literal Translation, the New Life Version, and many others. Some looked older than any book she'd ever seen. Atop them lay a series of photocopied pages with text written in a completely foreign language. Scrawled across the top page in Roger's hand was, "compare to the Coptic and Hebrew."

Further down, highlighted in blue, two words: *Iam Suph*. A large, penciled arrow led from these to the margin, pointing to more notes titled: *Green/Reedy Sea*.

Her eyes skimmed. She reached for a series of stapled pages but hesitated when, again, she saw they weren't written in English. A series of unrecognizable symbols scrawled in the margin also put her off. She scanned the symbols individually— ♌ ♋ ♑ ♈ —and then drew her hand back. Was she ready for this? Unconsciously, Rose tucked her hands under her arms. And then there they were. Beside the keyboard. Three folders. Rose lifted them gently, one by one; each was titled respectively, Day One, Day Two, Day Three. Her heart fluttered. *This was it.* These were Roger's notes for the seminar he was teaching *right now*. And this was the start of everything Rose had been dreading, what God wanted her to come inside and deal with, the beginning of the end of things she thought she knew, everything she wanted to hold onto believing about her son. Rose held her breath as she opened the top folder; on the inside cover Roger had written:

Ignorance is the root and stem of every evil.
~Plato

Rose looked up as if toward God. *I can handle this*, she thought, *I can handle this.* But wondered if she could.

♑

ROGER

When he met their gazes, Roger could feel the people in the room trying to assess his demeanor. Was it steely resolve, arrogant defiance, irascible maleficence?

He could feel their eyes trying to look *into* his. Was there a visible darkness there? Would they see it, if they looked close enough? Would *that* be what evil looked like, looking back out at them?

And then, of course, there were the faces of those whom Roger knew wondered *why*. Why any of this at all? Was it because Roger was angry … an attention getter … was he molested by a priest? Was there a demon under his skin?

Or, was it something else entirely?

None of them knew really, which was part of the reason Roger expected they came—to find out who he was, what all the fuss was about, and most importantly, to see if any of it was true.

The room waited.

He complied by starting with the same question he always did. "What is the Bible?" He tossed his chalk in the air and turned to face the board. "Feel free to call out your answers," he said over his shoulder.

"The word of God."

"A bunch of bollocks!"

"The infallible word of God." This person aimed a dirty look at the person who shouted 'bollocks'.

Roger started a list. After Infallible he wrote: (100% error free—inspired from heaven in such a way that it is considered the actual word of God.)

A pause followed; of people thinking or too afraid to speak. Roger waited, breathing up against the chalkboard, his hand in the air, chalk poised to write.

"It's a story," someone called from the back.

Roger nodded. He wondered if that one would come out.

"The greatest story ever told!" someone added gleefully.

Then another pause. Roger waited. Surely they weren't finished yet. It never ended there. Still no one spoke.

"It's a lie. A myth. Not a single word of it is true."

The words dropped with the heavy thud of controversy and Roger thought, there it is. The fire waiting to spread. The glowing embers in the back of so many people's minds, lying in wait for the oxygen of brazenness or audacity or courage or blasphemy to flame them.

Was the Bible really the infallible word of God? Or was it a collection of mythological stories expressed through the vehicle of an ancient culture? Roger knew the truth lay in neither answer. He also knew that the Bible contained a secret so ancient, so universal, that it could never be a lie. He added to the list and then turned like a firefighter to stop the argument he knew was about to burst into flame.

As he made his way through the crowd, stopping here and there to say hello or be introduced, pausing now and then for a hug or a chat, Mateo's mind continued to drift back to that first lesson. How, on the walk to the Sanctuary, his father had explained that today would be the first of three days of lessons (more would come if Mateo wanted to learn about the Gospel in greater detail). How, when they descended the stairs that led to the Sanctuary entrance, his feet had tingled—from the rough sandstone, or from the energy of the room he was about to enter emanating up the steps toward him in welcome, he wasn't sure, but the closer he got, the more Mateo's body seemed to tingle. It was the first time he felt Providence coursing through his body: a sensation of anticipation and a great sense of purpose, a feeling of instinct, of somehow knowing *within* that what lay ahead was good, even though it was unknown.

Mateo also remembered arriving at the entrance, his breath had caught in his throat with an excitement so hardly containable he didn't know if he was about to laugh or burst into tears. He stood, head tilted back, eyes drinking in the words on the bottom of the arch, reading the ones he could actually understand; they all said the same thing. In Latin it read:

Veritas numquam perit

"*The Truth Never Perishes*," he whispered, and his father's eyes had sparkled. "Not *this* truth."

Mateo even remembered the feeling of his father's hand on his back—that steady comfort—as they stepped forward and made their way, just like Mateo did now, past burning torches, tables ornamented with candles and ink pots, scrolls and texts, carving tools and paper weights. Artisans, teachers, students, and scribes then had occupied the tables, but today they were covered with baskets, themselves overflowing with tightly bound scrolls. *Curious*, Mateo thought, raising an eyebrow. *That's new.*

A few more hellos. The odd bow. A hearty handshake. A familiar nod.

"Why now, Papa?" Mateo had asked, reaching for his father's hand. All the legends about the Sanctuary, the passion-filled rumours (and maybe even the truth) echoed in his head that first day. As a boy, Mateo had heard that the Sanctuary was a room overseen by God, that it housed the most accurate history of humankind, and that it was a meeting point of angels. His eyes had drifted up toward the ceiling in hopes of seeing them. Of course, now, all these years later, Mateo knew that he didn't have to look.

"Because twelve is a sacred age," his father said. "It is the age when *how* you understand the world begins to change. When growing up begins."

"But I've always been growing up," Mateo answered distractedly.

"Ah, your body, yes, but from a certain age, the *intellectual* aspect of your spiritual journey begins. From this age, you begin to turn from a child that observes the world, into a person who is learning to self-reflect about the world and your place in it—about *God*. You start to think more about what it means to … Mateo?"

But Mateo had stopped listening.

His eyes, having drifted down from searching the air for angels, had come to rest on something that when he looked upon it made him feel, as if only for a moment, that time stood still. That the passing of it only happened around him; that it was only him, the cross, and everything he couldn't wait to learn about it.

The scene was gloriously mysterious, and as they approached, Mateo went from squeezing his father's hand tighter to letting go of it, to walking forward alone. A giant wooden cross, lambent in shades of ebony and night-sky, lay on the ground, its glory visually amplified by a gentle, illuminating glow emerging from beneath it. Instinctually, Mateo had thought *this cross means something*. And he had been right. The cross meant everything. It was a secret waiting to be told. A bank of great truths.

"All these years and still the same," Mateo whispered as he arrived in that same spot again, where as a twelve-year-old boy he had only wanted to kneel and press his cheek against the invisible mystery that seemed contained within the rich, dark wood. It looked the same now, as it had then—shining, alive with something ancient, something true. He sat on the bench closest to the cross and looked upon it, fondness abounding in his heart.

He had been overcome the first time he stood there, had wanted to touch the wood, smell it, kneel alongside it and inhale the spiritual profundity of the cross's silent language. He had looked back to his father, who nodded permission.

Without hesitation Mateo had moved in, bent gently as he had in his mind's eye only a moment ago, and then placed his hands on the ground beside the wood. He closed his eyes, inhaled deeply, and with the scent of wood in his nose and throat, Mateo had smiled. He couldn't put it into words back then, but now he could. The cross had the scent of something deeply relevant to every human being, distinct and indisputably arcane: The cross smelled of the human knowledge of God.

"Shalom," someone said, breaking Mateo's reverie.

"Shalom aleichem,"[1] Mateo returned the greeting.

It was almost uncanny how the contents of his morning mirrored those of when he was a boy; only back then it wasn't a stranger that broke his enchantment with the cross, it was his father's shoe poking him persistently in the bottom. When he turned around Mateo saw not one pair of feet but two. Oh, how he had panicked and jumped to his feet when he realized who the other pair belonged to! As quickly as he could, he brushed the dust from his knees and wiped his hands on his robe before bowing a respectful hello to the man he knew his own father loved as a father. Master Lael received Mateo's greeting and returned it.

It was then that Mateo found out Master Lael would be his teacher.

Mateo remembered, in that moment, feeling honoured and terrified at the same time. He had hope that his father would be his teacher, someone with whom he was familiar, with whom felt safe. And yet, even as a boy, Mateo knew this was foolish. Master Lael was of the wisest of his generation, and to be his student, even only for three days, was an honour not to be disregarded simply from fear of the unfamiliar. To turn away would be an opportunity wasted, and so, when Master Lael motioned for Mateo to join him, Mateo took a deep breath and let go of his father's hand.

As they walked, Master Lael motioned to their surroundings. "What you are about to learn is older than the memory of man. At the center of this story is a truth; within this truth lies the meaning of life. This that surrounds you is the Gospel of Life, the good news of the Journey of Souls and within it," the teacher looked at the boy smilingly, "is the story of *you*."

Mateo shivered at the memory of those words.

The Gospel was about *him*. But how could that be? It was thousands of years old and he was only twelve. It seemed impossible. "Me?" he had replied dramatically. "All of this … the Gospel … is about *me?*"

"Yes," Master Lael smiled. "The Gospel is about you, which of course means that it is the story of everyone—every girl and boy, every woman and man, everyone who is born and everyone who dies. So of course, this also means you." The old man's eyes sparkled. "Everything here is about you because this is the story of the truth at the center of human existence. It is what you are here to learn, and yet, you will find, it is what you already know, which is why, Mateo, some of what you learn here will seem familiar."

Mateo looked around in curious awe.

"Understanding all of this," Master Lael opened his arms to the contents of the cave, "is the key to comprehending *who* it is that you are, which in turn, allows you to better discover who it is you were born to become. This same understanding is what the world needs know, in order to become what God begs of it."

"Jerusalem," Mateo whispered, translating the ancient concept

"Yes," Master Lael nodded, impressed. "A community of peace."

And that was the start of it. The start of everything. Of learning not just how but why it was that the words *A Cruce Salus* were true. Mateo whispered the ancient translation to himself: "From the cross comes salvation."

"Namaste," another woman bowed as she walked by, hands pressed in prayer in front of her heart.

Again Mateo returned the gesture, bowing in mutual veneration. He watched as she turned onto another path, toward the second largest mural in the cave: the Sun.

Several people chatted in the seating area there, as what looked like old friends beckoned excitedly to the woman. It was a wonderful thing, Mateo thought, to be in the company of people who understood their true identity. People that understood *who* they are—these *treasures in earthen vessels*. Because that was the ultimate question, the question Master Lael asked Mateo that very first day.

"*Who are you?*"

"Who are you," Mateo chuckled at the memory.

It was a question people rarely asked themselves, and if they did, the answers were always superficial: I am a mother, a father, a farmer, a wife, a husband, a teacher, a sister, a brother, a theologian, a politician, a man of the cloth. But did people *really* know who they were? What they were capable of achieving? What they were capable of succeeding through, of suffering, of fighting for, of *being*? Did they understand that so much of who they thought they were was based on perceptions of the world and reactions to those perceptions? That their perceptions were flexible, their reactions changeable? Did people understand that what they didn't like about themselves, they were born with the power to change?

Who are you?

It was the most important question a person could ask themselves in their lifetime, Mateo knew, because within the answer was a womb, a womb that housed everything taught by the contents of the seventh library, everything the murals were saying in whispers, everything wonderful about being human. But of course, when Mateo was twelve years old, he did not yet know these things and his answer then had been a very shaky, "I—I am Mateo"; his answer sounding more like a question.

Master Lael scrunched up his face in deliberation, "Hmm," he said, and then reached forward with both hands. "You are Mateo here," he tapped Mateo once on the head, quite hard Mateo thought. "You are Mateo here," he tapped Mateo on the shoulders. "You are Mateo here and here," taps on the hips and knees, "and here." Finally Master Lael knocked the tops of Mateo's feet respectively with his walking stick. "This is the body of Mateo, yes." The old man sat back and looked hard at the boy. "But what *else* is there? What *else* makes you Mateo?"

Mateo remembered thinking then of all the things he thought defined him: his name, he was a boy, he was a son, he was from Alexandria, he was a good student, he was a bit messy, he liked to read and draw, he preferred bare feet to wearing shoes (except on cold mornings). But surely these were not the things Master Lael was talking about. *What else?* He remembered thinking very hard. *I have a body … I have a body …* and then his face brightened … *and a soul! That is the other part of me!* And so he answered, "My soul—I am Mateo: made up of my body and my soul."

"Aha," Master Lael smiled. "Yes! You are made of your body and your soul. *Together* they make you Mateo!" He tapped his walking stick as applause. "Now come," he said, motioning for them to continue walking, "so the rest of your story can be revealed …"

♌

A modest highway ran the length of the island, lined thick with trees, grass, and bush waving myriad shades of green and shadow in the last of the day's light. With everything anticipating evening and the world quietly turning, Farah drove, looking for a roadside rest area where she might spend the night. The point of her trip was to get away, to leave all the things that were killing her behind. This, she realized quickly, was a fantasy.

Of course, she thought bitterly.

In the distance she could see it coming: a country church, hidden just back off the road, with a short drive that led to its polished railings and a daunting spire that cast an enormous dark shadow, two intersecting lines, across the highway. Farah's heartbeat skittered. It was like a worst nightmare: everything she wanted to get away from, forcing itself into her path. Frantically, she scanned the ditch for a place to avoid driving through it, but the trees were lined thick to the edge of the road. There was no detour. No other way around. It was then, in that instant, with the taste of fear in the back of her throat, that normal things began to appear differently. The clouds went from beautiful, thick white plumes hovering high above, to thick white plumes closing in. Farah's lungs tightened, her eyes darted from the cross to the clouds and back again. She tried to calm herself, calm the cold sweat, tried to remember that breathing was a natural, inexplicable phenomenon, not something her body would suddenly stop doing. And now he was there … rubbing her back soothingly. Gently, Mephistopheles began to whisper to her options that would bring comfort and relief. Friendly suggestions, a genuine attempt to help her out, so that she never had to feel this way, this fear, this state of dishevelment, this out of control … again. If panic attacks were how the rest of her life would feel, then how could life be worth living? Mephistopheles peered at Farah over her shoulder and grinned in her peripheral vision, his teeth dark and stained with malice, his breath hot, spiritual corruption on her cheek.

Farah stared ahead and pressed harder on the accelerator. This was it then: the cross, Mephistopheles, and her. She wanted to scream. Terrified and furious about everything that had brought her to this moment. Furious about the church, about heaven and hell, about the fact that understanding was so damn difficult! She was exhausted with trying to comprehend. Farah hit her hand angrily on the steering wheel. "Fuck you," she said to the fast-approaching church. "And fuck you too," she told Mephistopheles in her rearview mirror. He just laughed. "And fuck you the most!" Farah shouted at the cross, and closed her eyes as she sped through its shadow.

When she opened her eyes, he was gone. In disbelief, she looked from the road to the passenger seat, the road to the floor, the road to the rearview mirror, but nothing. He had disappeared. *Impossible*, she thought, the scene and her cursing receding quickly in the rearview mirror. Suddenly, her lungs filled again with oxygen, and the clouds became themselves. Somehow, her mind began to settle, and shortly thereafter, barely visible in the evening light, a rest area sign appeared. Farah turned on her headlights to make out the approach, and signaled to turn off the road.

The rest area was a natural clearing between trees that loomed centuries old. Patches of moss softened the ground into carpet, and hidden dollops of mycelium popped white and brown mushrooms out of the ground in the wet spring weather. As she turned, her headlights sparkled thick drops of sap and stirred an owl into flight. She parked beside the picnic table, and stepping out into the nightfall, inhaled the coolness of it deeply into her lungs. Just then, the moon broke the tree line and everything was illuminated in blue. Farah closed her eyes then and felt something she hadn't felt in some time: peaceful, in the moment, appreciative of the very existence of times such as these when serenity in the company of nature was tangible. She could feel the calm of evening settle around her, and for the briefest moment every thought ceased. She wished she could stay like this forever. Quiet. With nothing wrong. Not aching inside. Not terrified. Not searching.

In front, slightly to the right, a few trees in from where Farah stood, a branch drooped. Six pine needles sprinkled to the ground. She didn't hear it, but she felt him arrive; except this time, Farah couldn't tell if her fear had invited him or followed. Did it even matter anymore? When she opened her eyes, he stared back at her, half hidden behind the tree as if he were playing a game, grinning rancid thoughts, exhaling them in her direction.

She gazed steadily back at him, not blinking. Her heartbeat quickened. Her mind fought to steady it. *Go away*, Farah thought, and he disappeared into a shadow. She looked skyward to distract herself. The Big Dipper, Aries, the North Star. It wasn't working. She closed her eyes again and listened, but heard nothing. Her body trembled then, shook with a fight between her love of things only experienced by being alive and his poison. A long moment passed, and then she risked it. When Farah opened her eyes, he was inches from her face. Breathing. Chuckling in low bursts with domination in his cavernous eyes. He blinked slowly, and when he lifted his lids, she saw herself in the blackness there, bound and gagged, a crucifix about her head, suicide upon her skin. *Ha*! The syllable escaped playfully from his lips, taunting, as if he had right of possession and there was nothing she could do about it. She didn't flinch but her skin crawled. She watched him disappear, and Farah knew that if nothing changed, she wouldn't last the weekend. Silent tears dropped from her eyes, wetting the ground. She crawled into the back of her van, unrolled her sleeping bag and shivered fully clothed as the dark of night closed in around her. "Oh God," she wept, covering her face with her hands. "Why have you forsaken me?"

♋

Which creature in the morning goes on four feet, at noon on two, and in the evening upon three?
~The Riddle of the Sphinx: *Oedipus*

For since there are four zones in the world in which we live, and four principle winds … it is fitting that she [the Church] should have four pillars …
~Irenaeus, Bishop of Lyons, 180 AD

It is not by chance that the foundation of the higher life, the gate to heaven that is to be reached on earth, is placed not in emotion, not in feeling, but in knowledge: in the victory over delusions.
~Rhys Davids, Hibbert Lectures, 1881

Rose had no idea what any of these quotes was about. She turned a few more pages.

Nothing can impost better on the people than verbiage; the less they understand, the more they admire. Our Fathers and Doctors have often said, not what they thought, but what circumstance and necessity forced them to.
~St. Gregory of Nazianzus, *The Theologian* (329–389) in a letter to St. Jerome

This was just what Rose hated about academia—everything she couldn't understand, and all the things she had no frame of reference for. Not only did these quotes make no sense, they made Rose nervous because of it. Made her want to look away.

And she would have. Any other time she absolutely would have, but this time Rose was sent here for a greater purpose (to save what was lost). This time, she would *have* to look at the things she didn't want to. Directly at them, and *try* to understand for her son's sake, for the sake of his life, but especially for the sake of his life after death.

She turned a few more pages.

Christians prey on the ignorance of others; their injunctions are like this: Let no one educated, no one wise, no one sensible draw near. For these abilities are thought by us to be evils. But as for anyone ignorant, anyone stupid, anyone uneducated, anyone who is a child, let him come boldly.

~Celsus, *The True Word*, via Origen's *Against Celsus* 3:44

Rose slammed the folder shut and threw it on the desk. Anti-Christian. Anti-Christ. It was as if Satan himself were sitting among the pages reaching out to strangle the Holy Spirit out of her. Her hands went to her throat to protect it; her pulse fluttered in heavy, fast beats against her palms. *Lord Jesus, give me strength*, she prayed, and then realized she had only been looking at a *section* of the first folder—one aptly titled "Quotes"—that was now hanging by a broken staple from the cover. The rest of the Day One lecture notes were still fastened neatly, waiting. Rose lowered her head and took a few deep breaths; she reach for the folder again and thought, *Now it will really begin.* These were her son's very words she held in her hands.

Again, scripture floated into her mind, it was John 8:32: *And ye shall know the truth, and the truth shall set you free.*

And Rose hoped that it would, or at least take all of this fear out of her heart.

♑

The Bible was the most influential book in the history of Western civilization, which was why Roger found it so surprising how little people actually knew about it. They took for granted what religion told them it was, often without lifting a finger to find out if any of the claims were true. Roger's journey in this regard had been life altering. His study of the ancient book was the most fascinating on-going experience of his life, and what he had discovered was far too important not to reveal. Especially now.

Was the Bible a myth?

A load of rubbish?

Was it really the infallible word of God?

"In order to know which of these options is closest to the truth, we need to start—" Roger circled the word *Infallible* "—right here." It would come hard and fast now: the unfolding, the arguments, the controversy. Heartbeats quickened as Roger pulled his Day One file from his bag. Some people shifted uncomfortably, many leaned forward in their seats. A handful thought, *Infallible isn't up for discussion*, just before the world, and everything in it, began to look different.

"The doctrine that teaches the Bible as an inerrant, infallible document is interesting for two reasons," Roger said. "Firstly, because it is not at all traditional to Christianity;[2] in fact, to quote one of the greatest Biblical scholars of our time, Bart Ehrman, the views of inerrancy held by evangelical and fundamentalist Christians today, were developed less than a century ago and are a modern invention of fundamentalist theologians, largely from the United States. The second reason the doctrine of infallibility is interesting, is because the Bible *itself* tells us it isn't true. The Bible itself, tells us it isn't infallible …" Roger just dove right in; there was no other way to do it, he thought. Besides, right now he had everyone's attention, and who knew how long that would last. He pulled a transparency sheet out of his Day One folder, placed it on the projector then turned down the lights.

There on the wall, larger than life, was a list:

Examples of New Testament verses not original to the Bible[3]

There are three that bear witness in heaven, the Father, the Word,
and the Holy Spirit, and these three are one.
1 John 5:7

And in the same way after supper Jesus took the cup and said,
"This cup that is poured out for you is the new covenant in my
blood."
Luke 22:20

In his anguish Jesus began to pray more earnestly, and his sweat
became like great drops of blood falling to the ground.
Luke 22:44

And he said unto them,
Go ye into all the world, and preach the gospel to every creature.
Mark 16:15

He that believeth and is baptized shall be saved; but he that
believeth not shall be damned.
Mark 16:16

Roger watched as the students reacted or didn't react, as jaws dropped open or lips pursed, as breathing changed from stopping altogether in shock to exhaling in sharp puffs of disbelief. Some people just sat, silent, surprised. Others, not so much by what they had read. "I knew it!" a fervent whisper came out of the darkness. Someone else placed a hand on a Bible and said, "I don't believe it." But all of them, those that spoke and those that didn't, those whose cheeks burned with anger at Roger's audacity or anger at feeling deceived (even those who suddenly felt nauseous), were waiting for Roger to speak. He had some serious explaining to do, which Roger knew very well.

"How do we know this?" Roger asked, placing his hand over the list. "How do we know that these particular verses were not originally part of the New Testament, but were added to the Bible over the years, even centuries after the original gospels to which they were added, were written?" It was a rhetorical question that Roger didn't expect anyone to know the answer to. "We know this because the Bible itself has revealed it to be true." He turned up the lights slightly, leaving the room dark enough to keep the list illuminated, but light enough that everyone could see.

"To date," Roger said, "we have over sixteen thousand New Testament manuscripts spanning a time period of eighteen hundred years.[4] Some fifty-seven hundred of these manuscripts are written in Greek, some ten thousand of them are Latin Vulgate. The rest are written in Syriac, Coptic, Armenian, Old Gregorian,[5] and a heap of other languages that don't really concern us here today. What does concern us about these sixteen thousand copies, however, are the differences between them. To date more than two hundred thousand[6] variations and discrepancies have been found. Some completely insignificant, but others such as these," Roger motioned to the list, "extremely *significant*. Verses such as these have altered or influenced the meaning of the text into which they have been written, and have in turn influenced the formulation of church doctrine, ritual, and practice. Of course, the fact that these discrepancies exist at all is proof that the Bible is not the inerrant, nor the infallible word of God."

In the middle of the room a woman began packing up her things, "I can't … I just can't listen to this!" She was head down, putting on her jacket, shoving her things in her bag as quickly as she could. Everyone turned to watch. One mitten on, the other half hanging out of her pocket, the woman was struggling to put her bag over her shoulder and stomping one foot hard on the ground as she tried to put on her boot (which she had slipped half-off because it felt too tight with her thick socks on). The woman then bumped her way through the aisle toward the door (still stomping one foot, still trying to shove her notebook into her shoulder bag), made her way up the stairs, swung the door open wide, and left without another word.

All eyes swung from the woman and the door closing behind her to see what Roger was going to do. What happened next took even him by surprise. Maybe it was because the lecture had barely begun; maybe it was because she had reminded him of his mother, but Roger found himself holding up his hand asking for "one minute," as he bound up the stairs. He had seen the list of verses hit the woman with force, and he wanted to make sure she was all right, because some people, when they learned these kinds of things, were not—at least not at first. It was the shock of it all; the emotion that truth not commonly known invoked.

He found the woman stopped not far from the classroom door, hunched over, still trying to get her boot on properly while simultaneously yanking her other mitten from her pocket. Her breathing sounded laboured, as if she were trying to get control of it. She kept shaking her head, as if she were angry, or trying to shake something out of it.

Roger was glad he didn't have to run or call out. He took a few tentative steps forward and leaned on the wall behind her, before asking softly whether she was all right.

There were many things in the woman's eyes when she looked up, including, as she spoke, the arrival of tears that weren't quite falling. "No, I'm not all right. *This*," she motioned angrily to the classroom, "is *not all right*." She refocused her attention on buttoning up her jacket before adding, "At least it's not all right with me."

Roger listened, head down, before lifting his eyes to look at her. He rubbed his chalk pensively between his fingers. Finally, he decided to just ask. "What are you so afraid of?"

The woman stopped mid-button, but kept her gaze on her hands. When she looked up again, determination replaced angry desperation. "Afraid? Does it mean that I'm afraid just because I don't want to hear what you have to say?"

Roger shrugged, "I don't know, does it?"

The woman pursed her lips; her tears all but vanished, her voice came back hard and fast. "I don't need to know the history of the Bible. It is the word of God, and that is all that matters to me." She held her bag tightly to her chest and patted a book inside it defensively. "If the King James Bible was good enough for Jesus," she said, "then it is good enough for me!" And with that, she turned on her heel and stormed toward the exit.

Roger watched her walk away, and knew the woman wouldn't be back. He sighed, not in surprise or disappointment, but feeling that the circumstances were unfortunate. Especially her thinking Jesus used any Christian Bible, let alone the King James Version, which only came into existence a few centuries ago,[7] and whose translation was based on a notoriously error-ridden Greek manuscript—in fact, one of the worst and most erroneous manuscripts ever catalogued.[8] The King James Bible was, famously, one of the worst translations of the Bible ever to circulate among the masses.

But you can't blame people for what they don't know, Roger thought, as the woman pushed her way out the front doors of the building. "It would just be nice if they would sometimes allow themselves to know better," he muttered.

Just then, a man's voice reading from the Gospel of John trickled out the classroom door down the hallway. *Uh-oh,* Roger thought, and turned on his heel, hoping to get back before what he knew was about to start, could.

The Bible Reader read, "Jesus said, 'I am the way, and the truth and the life'."

He paused.

Pages shuffled.

"Jesus said, 'I am the light of the world'."

Another pause.

More shuffling.

"Jesus said, 'I am the Bread of Life'."

"But did he *really?*" someone smirked, clearly delighted by the controversy.

The Bible Reader ignored the Smirker and continued his conversation with a very worried-looking man behind him. "Jesus said that *no one* can get to the Father except through *Him*." The Reader then motioned to Roger's list of verses and said of it dismissively, "Don't worry. The Bible is older than *any* of his research—but it is good to know what Christians are up against. We'll see who gets to heaven on Judgment Day."

The Smirker shook his head and rolled his eyes before asking everyone sardonically, "Why is it that religious people are always so irrational?"

Oops, Roger thought, about to reach the doorway.

The Bible Reader's cheeks flushed and he slammed the Good Book shut on his desk. "Who are you to decide what is rational or true?"

Which caused someone else to comment, "Maybe that list bothers you more than you'd like to admit?"

Now red with emotion, the Bible Reader turned to face the class, "You think you, or some academic—" he pointed angrily to the front of the room where Roger usually stood, "—are more knowledgeable than God? I mean, come on! The Bible is filled with things far too complicated and holy for the human mind to comprehend. We—" he made a swooping motion with his hands to indicate the entire class or humans in general, "—could never fully understand what the Bible is saying to us, and I'm supposed to believe that this guy—" he jerked his thumb in the direction of the hallway, "—suddenly has some insight that two thousand years of church scholars never figured out? Now *that* sounds irrational. This is the *Bible* we are talking about, people, not some history text or contentious piece of literature."

A young man in a blue hat covered his face with his hands in complete exasperation. "Are you kidding me? *He*—" he now jerked his thumb in the direction of the hallway, "—is not trying to say he is more knowledgeable than *God*. All he's said so far is that the Bible has a history that proves it *isn't* infallible, and when, I'm guessing, pretty much everyone in here," he said, looking around, "is basing their *entire* interpretation of the world and of life and death on the Bible, it bloody well matters whether or not it actually is or isn't infallible. And as a Christian, I want to know!"

"He's right," a woman said. "*Every single one of us*, whether we go to church or not, whether we are religious or not, has been affected by the Bible. For that reason alone, we should want to know everything about it, whether we like what we hear or not."

The Bible Reader had his head down and was shaking it in passionate disagreement. He lifted his eyes to meet first those of the young man in the blue hat, then those of the others. His tone was one of disgust. "The Bible is the *word of God*. It doesn't matter how it came to be what it is. It isn't there to be figured out. It is there to be *accepted*. Jesus isn't there to be figured out. He is there to be *accepted*. And I," the man said, firmly, getting up out of his seat, "will no longer accept any of this." He didn't have a bag of things, nor had the Bible Reader slipped his boot half-off. He hadn't even removed his jacket. So when he stood to go, it was quickly and with the authority of his convictions. He didn't look back either when he exited the room or after he, upon encountering Roger in the hallway (who had taken a step back from the door when he heard the Bible Reader coming), pushed aggressively past him.

Roger took the knock with grace and simply half-turned under the force of it, keeping his eyes down. It wasn't up to him to tell people what to do, nor to carry their burdens. When he stepped back into the classroom he encountered a barrage of facial expressions: entertained, concerned, worried, nervous, thrilled. Roger had seen all of these expressions before. Certain things about teaching these courses were predictable. He might not know who would react, but the how was always the same: Someone always stormed out, many always argued, and almost everyone, every time, thanked him in the end.

*

"Now where was I?" Roger asked, as he made his way to the front of the room.

Someone pointed, "You were explaining the list of verses."

"Ah, that's right."

"Wait," a man turned and called out to Roger from the front row. "Can I just ask a simple question?"

"By all means," Roger nodded.

"Are you going to try and tell us that Jesus wasn't real?" The man's gaze followed Roger's every move. "Because if that's the case, I'll save myself the trouble and leave now too—there is absolutely nothing you could ever say, full stop, that would ever convince me of that."

A woman in Roger's periphery curtly nodded her agreement. The man smiled, garrisoned by her support. Every head in the room turned in anticipation of Roger's answer.

"Well," Roger tossed his chalk thoughtfully in the air before taking a deep breath. "When you consider that there is no evidence outside of the Bible that a historical Jesus ever existed, it seems quite possible that I would *want* to do a three-day seminar on that topic." He glanced in the man's direction before tossing his chalk in the air again. "*Or* when you consider that no contemporary non-Christian writer or historian even knew of Jesus' existence—"

"That's not true," the garrison woman interrupted, shaking her hand in the air. "That's *not* true! Josephus the *Jewish* historian mentions Jesus in *The Antiquities of the Jews*. Twice." She crossed her arms over her chest matter-of-factly, triumphantly.

Roger caught his chalk and pursed his lips with regret. "Unfortunately, it has been proven that the Josephus documents were tampered with, and that those two mentions of Jesus were actually inserted at a later date by Christians well after Josephus had died." Roger's tone was sensitive but also matter-of-fact. The garrison woman's face registered a stubborn suspicion.

"*Of all recorded history,* outside the Bible," Roger continued, now pacing the length of the room at the rate of a stroll, "there are only twenty-four lines that refer to Jesus. *Twenty-four.* And of those twenty-four every single one has been proven forged, interpolated, or to have been tampered with in some way: Pliny, Tacitus, Suetonius, Josephus, take your pick." Roger tossed his chalk again, catching it high this time. "Even the early Christian apologists—an apologist is someone who defends their religion to non-believers—make *no mention whatsoever* of a historical Jesus: Theophilius of Antioch, Athenagoras of Athens, Tatian, Minucius Felix in Rome—all revered defenders of the early Christian church, yet not a single one of them makes any reference to a human Jesus who was crucified for atonement, who was resurrected, or who was God, for that matter, when defending Christianity to the 'opposition'." Roger turned on his heel and walked to the opposite side of the room. "*And* when you consider that not a single New Testament author ever knew or even met Jesus—their books were all written seventy to one hundred and twenty years after Jesus' death—or the fact that each individual version of Jesus' story *constantly* contradicts the other, these facts alone might motivate one to *want* to discuss at length the curious nature of Jesus' existence or nonexistence. Never mind that the earliest Christian writings, those of St. Paul, fail to mention any of the most memorable moments in Jesus' life—the Virgin Birth, his raising Lazarus from the dead, his betrayal by Judas, the famous cleansing of the temple, or even Jesus' triumphant entry into Jerusalem. Paul doesn't even mention Mary, Joseph, or Pontius Pilate."

Many people in the room looked shocked. How was it possible that the founder of Christianity, *St. Paul*, did not mention any of the most well-known details of the birth, life, and death of Jesus Christ—the person upon which the entire Christian religion was founded—in any of his writings? It seemed surreal, and yet, it was true.

"But Paul lived in Jerusalem when Jesus cleansed the Temple," a perplexed student spoke. "And I thought that not a single person in the city didn't know about it." Several people nodded in agreement, many of them flipping through their Bibles to find the story in Mark.

Roger looked up and nodded, "An interesting contradiction of facts." He turned and walked back to the man in the front row, nodding pensively. "Yes," he said, turning his chalk between his fingers, "someone wanting to teach a three-day seminar about such things, would have to admit that Paul's silence about a historical Jesus is actually quite deafening."[9] He paused in front of the man's desk. "And you might think that I too would find such things motivation enough to *want* to tell you that Jesus wasn't real—but that in fact is not the case. Even though," Roger held his finger in the air, "the bottom line is there is *no* reputable evidence whatsoever outside the Bible that Jesus was indeed a historical person, that is *not* the reason I am here." Roger dropped his finger. "I am not here to tell you that Jesus isn't real. That is not what this seminar is about."

Someone stifled a laugh.

Another whispered "Far out."

But everyone else in the room was silent, as in the deepest part of night.

The man in the front row's jaw had dropped after hearing the Josephus documents were tampered with, and it remained open now.

"So you'll stay then?" Roger asked him.

The man closed his mouth with a click. He stared at Roger in wide disbelief. Within his eyes there swirled a shock, a slippery consternation, as if the man didn't know where to place his distress, where to focus it, or what to say. He glanced awkwardly at the garrison woman, whose face reflected his own expression. She gave him an unsure shrug. When he spoke, the man in the front row lengthened his words, as if they too were trying to sort through his thoughts, "Ye-e-s ... I will stay." He paused awkwardly and then shook his finger in a suspicious threat, "As long as you don't say anything else about all those things you just finished saying!" It was all he could do. The man said he would leave if the seminar was an attempt to convince people why Jesus wasn't real, and Roger had just said it wasn't about that at all.

"Great!" Roger gave the man's desk an enthusiastic tap before turning back to the board. "And I'm glad you mentioned the Josephus reference," he called back over his shoulder to the garrison woman as he wrote, "because it's a perfect example of this." He tapped the chalkboard beside the words he had just written: *Pious Fraud*.

"Pious Fraud was the permissible alteration of documents—Holy Scripture or otherwise—under the guise of something known as *Justa Causa*, which said that: "if the cause was just, an untruth need not be a lie."[10] What this meant was that the church and its scribes or scriptural copyists were allowed to take liberties with documents: to edit, delete, change, or forge whenever it was deemed necessary. 'Necessity,' of course, was defined by how well the action or the changes served the glory of the church. For your viewing pleasure, some famous quotes in this regard." Roger pulled the list of verses from the projector, and replaced them with a list of quotes.

"Great is the force of deceit
provided it is not excited by treacherous intention."
John Chrysostom, 347–407 CE
(Bishop of Constantinople, Doctor of the Church)

"There are many things that are true which it is not useful for the vulgar
crowd to know, and certain things which although they are false,
it is expedient for the people to believe otherwise."
St. Augustine, 354–430 CE
(Most revered Christian theologian, upon whose work
much of Catholic and Protestant theological belief and
practice are based, early Doctor of the Church)

How It May Be Lawful to Use Falsehood as a Medicine and
for the Benefit of Those Who Want To Be Deceived.
(Chapter title in the *Twelfth Book of Anselm*, *Evangelical Preparation*,
written by Anselm, Archbishop of Canterbury from 1033–1109)

"It was the reason historical documents like those belonging to Josephus were tampered with, and the reason why every act committed was done so with the perpetrator believing that they were doing it for the glory of the church, or the good of the people." Roger gave a small wink, "At least, that's what we like to think." He leaned over and stretched to remove the quotes from the projector, replacing them once again with the original list of verses.

"Pious Fraud is the reason these verses and many more are now thought of as originally part of the Bible, when the truth of the matter is that two thousand years ago, they were not." [11] Roger's eyes skimmed the page again with everyone else. "Every change on that list," he said, "is a result of a deliberate alteration of an original scriptural text."

"But why?" a voice, shocked, in a semi-whisper, wondered aloud.

It was the same tone Roger had, when he first learned of Pious Fraud. One that could not believe something so ludicrously blasphemous could take place on a regular basis, that something so ludicrously blasphemous was responsible for espousing so many apparently unjustified Christian doctrines (baptism, Communion, missionary conversion of non-Christian cultures). That something like Pious Fraud was an integral part of the history of the Bible, and the very foundation upon which the Christian religion was built … one that could not believe the gravity of what they were hearing.

Roger often wondered if the *why* would ever be satisfactory enough, when the past couldn't be changed or the event itself altered. He supposed the relief of knowing *why* came out of gaining some kind of understanding. If ignorance was the root and stem of every evil—the exotic, invasive species— then understanding must be the indigenous part of self, aching to break through into sunlight so that it can thrive on "knowing better."

"In order to understand 'why'," Roger began, "we have to look back to the days before the Bible was the Bible, before the New Testament even existed. Back to the days when documents were circulating throughout the Roman Empire—the Mediterranean, the Middle East, and Northern Africa. These documents contained stories, gospel stories, about a man who said and did certain things, and who had a spiritual message of 'Good News' for humanity. Back then almost all of these documents, except for a few letters written by a man named Paul, were written anonymously.[12] And there were dozens of them.[13] Different versions, different interpretations of the one story, different expressions of what the authors believed the spiritual message was trying to say. As word of the Good News spread, certain documents that explained it gained favour over others. Naturally, those with copies of the more popular documents wanted others to have copies, in order that others too might spread the word of these particular 'versions' of the stories of the man and the 'Good News.' But two thousand years ago there was no printing press, so the only way to distribute literature, spread it throughout the land, was to make copies. As many as possible. And it was through the process of copying that the variations we study today made their way into the documents that came to be known as scripture and eventually came to be called the Bible."

"Except for Matthew, Mark, Luke, and John you mean," a nervous woman, holding her Bible tightly, patting its cover protectively, interrupted. She looked up, "All of the documents were anonymous except for the gospels of Matthew, Mark, Luke, and John. Right?"

Roger could no longer sigh over the tragedy that was this particular question.

"Actually, no," he replied, softly shaking his head, genuinely sorry for contributing to the woman's distress. "Matthew, Mark, Luke, and John were also originally anonymous. No one really knows who wrote them or even how old their stories really are. It was only decades after those four 'versions' became popular that they were attributed to either a follower of Jesus, such as Matthew and John, or to a companion of the apostles, such as Mark and Luke."[14]

The woman stiffened. Roger could see her struggling with what to do with that kind of information.

Did it matter?

Did she want to subject herself further to learning more about the Bible—this thing she held so dear, this thing she had always believed was a particular thing: the infallible word of God.

Have faith, Roger thought at her, and then took out his proverbial catcher's mitt because the questions were suddenly flying.

"What about the other books?"

"Revelations?"

"Also anonymous. Attributed to someone named John, but John was a pretty common name back then, as was James.[15] Neither the author of Revelations or James identify themselves as a particular John or the brother of Jesus–Pious Fraud simply identified them as such."

"I heard Peter was forged too."

"It is."[16]

"And the epistles?"

"Yes, yes! What of Paul's letters?"

Roger knew that these people shouting out—so fascinated, so interested—were already looking for answers outside of religion. This information to them was like breathing fresh air after spending an extended period of time in a stifling room.

But the practicing Christians felt otherwise, and Roger knew it.

The practicing Christians were the ones now sitting quietly, trying to decide whether or not they believed anything Roger was saying at all.

But that was just it: Roger wasn't just teaching some theory about the history of the Bible; he was teaching things that were part of the *actual* history of the most influential book in the history of Western civilization, and therefore of the *actual* Christianity, which inevitably made everything he said in that room part of the history of the human condition up to that point in time. Which was exactly why he was there—because he knew a terrible mistake had been made, and he knew things didn't have to carry on anymore as they had for over two thousand years.

"Of the thirteen letters attributed to Paul in the New Testament, only seven were actually written by him." Roger wrote the authentic seven on the board: 1 Thessalonians, Galatians, 1 Corinthians, 2 Corinthians, Romans, Philippians, and Philemon. "The other six are complete forgeries."[17]

There were actually a few gasps.

"This means that in our generation, we are sometimes taking the motivations of a scribe or a forger as the word of God—even the motivations of a personal opinion, pious as it may have been—as the original words that God intended for us."

Again, the same person as earlier whispered, "Far out."

"The official line of the church is that the other six of Paul's letters were written 'epononymously' which means 'in place of'; but the truth of the matter is that those additional six letters were forged, and Paul's name signed to them to give them authority. The truth of the matter is that those additional six letters were written well after Paul's death. Of the forged letters, the women might be interested to know, for example, that 1 and 2 Timothy were not written by Paul but were penned by an apprentice some two hundred years *after* Paul's death."

At this point a woman in the back row put up a shaky hand, but Roger didn't notice.

"As well as that famous verse in Corinthians," Roger said, "the one that commands women be in subjugation—also not written by Paul[18] but by someone else, long after Paul had died. Again, the simple act of attributing the words to Paul gave them holy authority, and holy authority they have had since. The treatment of women in churches for millennia has been influenced greatly by these phrases alone. Imagine if they were never inserted into the Bible, nor ever attributed to Paul? It's a good example because it's one that affects every single one of us, men and women alike."

The woman in the back put down her trembling hand and tuned out as 1 Corinthians 14:34–35, then 1 Timothy 2:12–15 sounded in her head.

Let the women be silent in the churches, for they are not permitted to speak; but let them be in subjection, just as the law says; but if they want to learn anything, let them ask their husbands at home. For it is shameful for a woman to speak in church.[19]

I do not allow a woman to teach, nor to exercise authority over a man; they are to be quiet. For Adam was formed first, and then Eve. And Adam was not deceived, but the woman was deceived and fell into a transgression. But she will be saved through bearing children—if they remain in faith, love, and holiness, with moderation.[20]

She knew these verses well.

They were practically branded onto her skin.

But something else began to happen when Roger spoke these fascinating truths. His words infiltrated, melded with her body, and she began to think, *But if Paul didn't write the verses … then it wasn't really his command … or Jesus' command,* she looked up at Roger's list of verses on the wall, *Or God's command, after all.* The woman's heart pounded. The cells in her body stirred. An awakening peeked curiously out from behind the place it had been told to sit quietly, submissively. Anger tried to rear, but the calm of the woman's breath oxidized it into reason, itself a balm. Her pulse began to race with everything she might learn there, all the new ways in which her life could grow. Her attention dropped back into the lesson.

"And the church just accepted that?" An angry voice.

Roger held up his hand for calm.

"The church accepted it under the auspices of Pious Fraud. You must remember that the church, as much as the forgers, believed wholeheartedly that what they were doing was for the glory of the church, and by default for the good of all people under God. They were ensuring the scriptures reinforced what they thought the scriptures meant. As for how they were able to get away with it, well, this was easy considering that mass literacy is a modern phenomenon. The majority of early Christians—the majority of any population for that matter—was illiterate, which meant that unlike today, people couldn't read the gospel documents for themselves. If they wanted to know what the documents said, they had to attend a gathering and wait for the gospels or letters to be read to them, or to be told what the documents said or meant."[21]

"I still think it's shocking," the angry person retorted.

Fair enough, Roger thought.

"So what we had two thousand years ago," he continued, "was an atmosphere in which many documents, some gaining the status of scripture, were circulated through generally illiterate communities from which there were garnered different interpretations of what the spiritual message of the documents meant. This of course led to the formation of different sects of belief, in particular about the man in the stories and exactly what it was he was on about—exactly what it was his 'Good News' meant.

"Inevitably, a certain degree of conflict and competition developed between these sects, and recruiting people to the 'right belief' became a priority. Of course, the cogs in the wheel of all of this activity were the documents themselves. In order for the word to be spread, copies needed to be made. Lots and lots of copies."

Roger made his way back to the board now, pulling another sheet from his Day One folder.

"As you can imagine, all of this copying—coupled with opinions, coupled with varying interpretations, coupled with the belief that one interpretation was better than another—created an atmosphere in which plenty of mistakes were made: accidental and intentional. Not to mention that the copying process was a difficult one. It was a mentally arduous task, an incredibly tedious process, to say the least. Combine this with the reality that many early copyists were illiterate, and you have an atmosphere in which accidental mistakes proliferate. Accidental mistakes were caused by anything from a slip of the pen or tired eyes, to accidentally skipping a line that starts with the same word as a previous line.[22]

"For example, in John 17:15, the author writes of Jesus praying:

> I do not ask that you keep them from the world, but that
> you keep them from the evil one.

"But in the fourth century *Codex Vaticus*[23] —one of our best and most accurate manuscripts—the second line is completely omitted, leaving Jesus praying to God of his followers: I do not ask that you keep them from the evil one.'"

A few people laughed.

Some frowned.

"But how could a copyist not notice that?" someone asked. "Surely a Christian would know that Jesus would never say such a thing."

"Would they?" Roger asked. "The opinions about who Jesus was and what he may or may not have said were by no means uniform. There was no majority opinion, and the circulating gospels did not lay it out for certain."

"Wait!" A hand shot into the air, shaking in a *stop* motion. "What do you mean, 'majority' opinion?" The young man was sharp and listening on the edge of his seat. Roger could feel his thoughts scrutinizing every word, his body and mind in demand of answers and sense. "I thought there was only ever one belief about who Jesus was."

And so the history of the Bible begins to be known, Roger thought.

"Actually, no," he said. "There were many different opinions about who Jesus was, or if Jesus was at all.

"The arguments of course were fueled by the fact that every gospel account of Jesus' life claimed to have been written by an apostle of Jesus.[24] And yet between the many firsthand accounts, an incredibly diverse and conflicting range of opinions was undeniably apparent. At times, the authors went so far as to not only disagree about who Jesus was and what he came to say, but some even disagreed about God. For example, while some groups argued that God created the world, others said it was an impossibility—because the world is an evil place.[25] Some people believed that Jesus was wholly divine: basically, God in human clothing. Others believed he was 'merely' human, and still others believed that Jesus was human *and* divine. Even more argued that because Jesus was the Son of God, he was therefore subservient to God, while further opposition believed that Jesus was the Son of God, of God, and therefore equal to God, and should be worshipped as such.

"Was Jesus of God or created by God?

"Was Jesus Christ even real?

"Many very respected theologians argued that the concept of the 'Christ' or 'Logos'—the aspect of God that lives and mediates between God and Earth—could never be embodied in one man, and to suggest such a thing was complete blasphemy.

"And then there was the issue of polytheism: Some argued that worshipping Jesus was akin to idolatry, that religion should be about God, not worshipping a man. The debates then were heated and plenty, and bred a volatile atmosphere to which the scriptures themselves eventually fell victim." Roger motioned again to the list of verses.

"I'm sorry, but when did you say all of this was taking place?" A skeptical voice that sounded like arms were crossing over a chest rang out from the back of the room.

Roger looked up. The sound of a suspicious voice didn't surprise him. "Well," he said, "these debates were rife before the inception of the religion, until well after Paul founded the first Christian church."

"So in the first couple of centuries then."

"Yes, that would be correct—the first to fourth centuries CE."

"See, I told you," the Skeptic looked at her friend, who responded with an acquiescent shrug. They both began to pack up their things.

"I'm sorry?" Roger said. "Have I missed something?"

"It's quite simple really," the Skeptic retorted. "We've just figured out what you're up to." Her tone was caustic but cautionary. "Our church told us that we don't need to learn about the first couple of centuries, because they were a time of great confusion in Christian history. An 'evil' time, if you will, when many heathens tried to say different things about who Jesus was to trick people off the right path."

"The right path?" Roger was curious as to which path was deemed 'right' according to the Skeptic.

"Yes. The path of the church," the Skeptic replied, as if it were obvious.

"And which church is that?" Roger enquired.

"Pentecostal."

Roger opened the floor to the class. "Is there anyone else here that believes the way of *their* church is the right way?"

About 75 percent of the people put up their hands. "And what church are you from?" Roger asked, pointing to one man.

"Baptist."

"And you?" Roger asked a young woman with her hand held high.

"Anglican."

"And you?"

"Methodist."

"Born-again Christian."

"Assemblies of God."

"Jehovah's Witness."

"Lutheran."

"Catholic."

"Mormon."

"Christian Scientist."

"Islam."

One person in the middle of the room put up her hand and said, 'I'm Jewish.'

Roger stopped there. The Skeptic's cheeks were flushed—with what, Roger was unsure—but he hoped the she could see that there were many minds and opinions and ideologies to consider when one was talking about the 'only' right way.

There were thousands, millions, billions of people who believed different things, and all of them, *every single one,* thought that their belief was the right one. Roger wondered if the Skeptic would pay those opinions different from hers the respect she demanded for her own. Or would she choose willful ignorance toward all of those things she didn't want—or was perhaps too afraid to try to understand?

Roger watched—the entire class watched—and waited to see.

With all eyes on them, the friend fidgeted uncomfortably, but the Skeptic didn't; discomfort only showed in wisps behind her eyes. It was she who spoke first. "The early centuries of the church were a time of evil and blasphemy, and I am not willing to be exposed to it. All of *you*," she said, "can do what you like, but I am a *good* Christian, and I am going to listen to my church. My way lies with God, and that is exactly the way I am going to go."

And that was it. The Skeptic walked out.

Her friend, however, remained, shrugged sheepishly, and said, "I'm curious," before returning to her seat.

"The thing about the history of the Bible," Roger said, to the sound of departing footfalls, "is that we are so far removed from it, we don't think it has one. But it *does*. And it's not an evil history, or one that by any means should be kept a secret. It is one that is *real*, and that, by knowing, could reveal more about the scriptures than you might have ever thought you could know."

Roger spoke earnestly to everyone, from every background, from every faith. "Unfortunately, we are set up in this era to think that learning any truth about the Bible—like that it isn't inerrant, or that it isn't the infallible word of God—makes its spiritual message null and void. When the reality is, this could not be further from the truth. Learning about the history of the Bible does more for us than closing our eyes to it ever could, and whether we like it or not, that history is there … and there is no reason to avert your eyes from it, or be afraid. History is what it is: *real* … there to teach us about our present, and in the case of religious texts, there to teach us about ourselves."

♈

As they walked, Mateo learned many things.

He learned then that when life was born, not just human life, but *all* life, even the stars and the sun, the moon, the ocean, and everything that exists, invisible laws were born with it. These laws were the laws of God. The laws that fuel the perpetual motion and meaning of the universe; that fuel the state of being of all things.

The first—the law of action and consequence. Karma.

The second—the law of growth and change. Evolution.

And the third—the law of harmony of existence, of mutuality, of human synchronicity with God— was the law of grace.

The laws, Mateo learned, were God's divine mathematics in action, God's mathematical karma, based on the physics of all creation. Karma, of course, was the law of "action begets action." By this law, positive action created a positive reaction or positive energy that physically emanated from the action, and spread throughout the world. The same went for negative action: It begot a negative reaction or negative energy that would also physically emanate and spread, invisibly but tangibly, reverberating near and far.

The energy created by action was karma: the unwritten word that what one reaps one sows, what one puts out into the world, one gets back. Positive or negative, the karmic energy one created would manifest itself in the life of the person who created it: physically, psychologically, emotionally—fruit from the tree and all that kind of thing.

The second of God's laws, of course, worked completely in conjunction with the first. Evolution was the inevitable force that pushed the contents of existence forward in time, the force that created circumstances out of which growth and change inevitably occurred—which was exactly why it was the most feared of God's laws: *because* of its inevitability, because of the way it demanded recognition, because it forced people to grow—often when they didn't want to.

"Resisting growth and change is futile," Master Lael said. "Whatever lesson evolution wants you to learn will be placed in front of you again and again until you learn it." Evolution and change were the only constants in the universe; they ensured the movement of all things forward and would not be denied. "Of course you can choose not to grow," Master Lael said, "not to evolve; but let me assure you that in doing so you are moving against the physics of the universe—life will become harder. Besides, stagnancy smothers all the wonderful gifts that evolution of life can bring. And who would want to miss out on that?" He winked.

The law of grace placed compassion and morality in the world, and because of this was one of the most powerful laws in existence. It was invisible, but integral, and worked with the force of bringing dysfunction back to harmony. Grace, kindness, love was the common language shared between all humans the world over; it was even shared between species. "It is the mutuality between humans," Master Lael said. "The inherent kindness that you are born to share. Your inherent sense of morality. Grace is love in action." Animals and humans bonded because of grace; wars could be stopped because of it; broken hearts healed; darkness made light. Grace made anything possible, and gave humans the power to make anything possible. It had the power to heal the world.

"These are the heartbeat of God's creation, eternally present in the universe: Action and consequence—karma; evolution—growth and change; grace—mutuality, inherent morality, harmony."

Mateo then learned that when existence was conceived, there emerged from the mind of God a movement of thoughts and energy that stirred in the universe and created an environment out of which life could grow. "And the entire world became impregnated with this energy, which is, in its most raw form, the energy of *Life*." Master Lael whispered the word "Life" as if it held some delicious secret.

He led them farther into the cave. "This energy is the fuel that brings a flower to bloom, the pull that causes tides to ebb and flow, the lift that sends a plant reaching up toward sunlight—" he reached for Mateo's hand, "—the force that shaped the lines of your fingerprints. It is what creates lands and continents; the force of forward movement, evolution, and all the things that make the cycle of life possible. It is what beats your heart … God in your heartbeat." The teacher gave Mateo a small smile.

Mateo had listened, fascinated. In his mind he saw energy and love from the mind of God, swirling and thinking and becoming things. He saw God's thoughts emerge into possibilities, and evolution force them forward into action: action resulting in consequence and the creation of all Life. He could see the Beginning, and he felt the magic of it in his fingertips.

"But creation—plants, animals, the motion of the universe—is not the only way God is in the world." Finally, Master Lael motioned for them to stop walking. He had led them to a large, carpeted mound, itself hugged from behind by a lush seating area: carpet, pillows, a collection of small padded benches, and, poking out from behind a few cushions, a mysterious, ornately carved marble box. The designs on the box looked like hieroglyphs, mixed with some ancient form of Mesopotamian art. Lapis lazuli shimmered in waves that sparkled like water along its base; hematite rimmed its lid.

"God, Mateo, exists in the world in *you*."

Mateo looked up at his teacher then. His heartbeat fluttered. From recognition? From the thrill of discovering something so incredible about himself? Or from the excitement of knowing he was about to learn more, he wasn't sure, but Mateo watched in amazement as from a small box beneath the bench where they now sat, Master Lael pulled an intricate carving—one that Mateo would revere as the most beautiful piece of art he had ever seen.

♌

In Farah's dream he didn't speak. His mouth instead gaped open and closed like a fish, as if words should come out … but they didn't. His hand was wrapped tightly around her wrist but when she tried to push him away, her arm simply fell through him, whooshed through his limbs, disappeared into his chest. This sent Mephistopheles into gales of silent laughter.

The song in the background was the same, always the same: *Je-sus walk. Je-sus walk with me* in the voices of a staccato choir. *Je-sus walk. Je-sus walk with me.*

Farah's subconscious yanked and pulled, struggled in a desperate attempt to disentangle her mind from its dreaming state … to wake her up.

And that was when the tapping began.

Click. Click. Click. Tap. Tap. Tap. Tap.
Click. Click. Click. Tap. Tap. Tap. Tap.
Click. Click. Click. Tap. Tap. Tap. Tap.

The consistency of the small sound worked, and slowly Farah, whose fists were clenched, began to rouse. *Click. Click. Click. Tap. Tap. Tap. Tap.* Slowly, inch by inch, her body began to relax into consciousness, until eventually Farah opened her eyes to the gray of early morning, the dream tingling cool sweat on her skin.

Then it came again.

A tapping on the driver's side window.

Frightened, Farah pushed up onto her elbows—in her mind she saw Mephistopheles' fingernail tapping. Her heart actually stopped. And it felt as if time stood still, as if, for a moment, everything around her ceased, and all that was left was the only thing she could see: her fear—and everything that she was so afraid of. Was this it? Was this how death came? Scratching, hinting, tapping? Was this how Satan worked? Until little by little you handed yourself over? Or you were weak enough to be taken?

Tap. Tap. Tap.

Her hands had turned to iron, and she was terrified, but Farah pulled back the curtain anyway.

There on the driver's side mirror was a bird, its head tilting to and fro, its eyes glistening with the wakefulness of morning. It clicked its beak and fluttered its feathers before tapping on the window at what Farah was sure was its reflection. The relief that fell from her skin was palpable; the bird saw it. Farah smiled, suddenly deeply grateful for nature's idiosyncrasies. She laughed as she sat up wearily, struggling in the clothes that had twisted around her in the night. Click. Click. Tap. Tap. She thanked the bird gratefully for waking her and then wiped the window of condensation, pleased to see it wasn't raining. Perfect, Farah thought, *fresh air*. She wormed her way out of her sleeping bag, grabbed her jacket and slipped on her boots before stumbling out the van door into dawn on the cusp of morning. Around her, the air was misty at the tree tops and cool where she stood, crisp on her skin and minty in her lungs.

The bird flew, fluttered around her and then disappeared into the forest. Farah went to look after it, but became distracted by what she saw twinkling through the trees. Something that made her heart swell with fondness—just beyond the forest beckoned the beautiful blue-green of sea. The deep soulful movement of water. Hoping to make the sunrise, Farah grabbed her journal, locked up her van and started on a path she noticed winding its way through the forest floor. She hurried along, removing her dream-damp clothes: her hat and mittens, unbuttoning her jacket, unwrapping her scarf; hoping the sea breeze would dislodge the flaky crust of ill-at-ease the dream had left on her skin—blow it away, dissipate it from her body … and take the suicide with it.

Stepping out of the forest, Farah balanced her way down piles of sun-bleached driftwood onto the boulder- and pebble-strewn beach. The tide was out, and the scent of cool Pacific Ocean, seaweed, and sea life, no longer diluted by the foliage and bark of forest, rushed toward her, filling her nostrils with a pungent, salty-sweet familiarity. She smiled and dropped her things into a pile on the large rock beside her, turned to face the sea and stood still, arms outstretched, skin rippling shivers—and there, she waited. *Jesus, walk. Jesus, walk with me.*

Waited to begin to feel free.

Mephistopheles emerged from the forest behind her, tripping over a log and then kicking it for being in his way. He spotted Farah and wanted to laugh. He knew what she was doing: hoping something would set her free. She just didn't get it. He shook his head, smiling, delighted, shrugging as it was of no consequence to him. Her delusion only made things easier.

Jesus, walk. Jesus, walk with me.

As much as Farah tried to block it out, the dream came again; the song echoing in her head, as her body began to feel uncomfortable, began to ask for a jacket, a sweater, a scarf, for comfort.

Jesus, walk. Jesus, walk with me.

With a skip and jump, Mephistopheles arrived. Now he hovered in the air above Farah's head, turning backward somersaults, gesturing that he was first digging and then lying in a grave. He grinned wildly and tugged the invisible strings that extended from his fingertips into Farah's mind. He was trickster, iniquitous, maleficent puppeteer. And he was loving it. He hung upside down in front of Farah's face like Spiderman, and looked eagerly into her eyes. They weren't quite empty yet; way down in there he saw a pinprick of light.

Farah couldn't see him, but she knew that he was there, and that even if not by choice, she felt as if she were about to lose … *Jesus, walk. Jesus, walk with me.* Even getting away to this island hadn't made a difference—he had followed. The cleansing breeze of sea, the distraction of nature, the cool temperatures of morning as the earth turned into spring, even the impending sunrise—the promise of the warmth of the sun on her skin, even music played loudly—nothing could get her out of her head, or away from what seemed to now permanently occupy it: her thoughts, his presence. Mephistopheles was here, and any form of relief was not. *Jesus, walk. Jesus, walk with me.*

Beside Farah, Mephistopheles held his finger up in the air as if he were about to dance the Charleston, or at the very least had just come up with a great idea. Clearly he was thrilled. He turned his back to Farah, winked up at the sky, and did a little victory dance. At this point it didn't matter if he was facing her; he didn't have to be to know what was happening. This was the best part. Mephistopheles felt it floating up from inside of her, and he rubbed his hands together in anticipation before pumping them in the air and marching on the spot like a band leader. He waited until the last second and then whirled around to face her. "Ahhh. Yesss," he said, his arms opening like a conductor in the ecstasy of crescendo, his black eyes lighting up—for *there it was*, incandescent and perfect, floating fluid and beautiful, practically breathing: Farah's will. She was giving it up, choosing hopelessness and despair. Farah was giving up.

"Ha!" Mephistopheles shouted. One syllable, vicious and triumphant. His breath gray ash, he exhaled his impending conquest, dark and manipulative, into the air and onto her, onto the rocks around her. It settled like an oil spill on the water, came to rest on pine needles and in the grooves of pinecones, suffocating out light and encouraging the demise of living things. He was negative energy incarnate and Farah felt him like a weight pulling her spirit down.

Mephistopheles leered menacingly at it hovering silvery blue, lifted his leg and smoothly, with the force of wanting everyone in the world to fail, kicked. Hard. When he did, Farah's will shattered into a thousand tiny pieces that hovered in the air before they fell twinkling onto her hair in the waxing sunlight, in sprinkles upon her shoulders, and to the ground; onto the backs of her hands, and into the cuffs of her jeans they fell. In that instant

Farah's chest heaved—with panic, with the force of feeling out of control; she squeezed her eyes shut thinking she really couldn't handle this anymore, and Mephistopheles laughed a gale into the air, he danced a little jig. Today, he would have her, and he would cover her aura in complete darkness so that she could no longer see with rationality or reason past herself and into the world—or at least make her think that's what he had done to her.

Far away, Farah thought she heard someone sit down beside her. And then the oddest question rang in her ears. "Did you know that 'glamour' is a derivative of the word 'grammar'?"

Farah blinked. And when she turned her head, found an elderly woman sitting beside her.

"It's true," the woman said. "I just recently found out."

So used to Mephistopheles playing games with her, Farah didn't respond. She only blinked again, slightly confused. Mephistopheles, on the other hand, did respond. He crossed his arms and looked hard at Farah; the black shadows that swirled on his skin floated in dark tendrils toward her. What had just happened? Where had her attention gone? Confused and furious, Mephistopheles rushed toward Farah and grabbed her by the shoulders—he had never touched the girl before, but she was so close to being his that he felt entitled to this liberty; he'd invested so much time in breaking her down. He shook Farah and sneered into her face; saliva dripped from the corner of his mouth and landed with a sizzle on the rocks below. And for the first time, with her will settled in pieces on her skin, Farah's eyes focused on him. Instead of trying to look away, she looked Mephistopheles right in the eye. She was a bit surprised to find him so close to her face, but she didn't show it. Instead, she faced him with a mundane expression, as if she was bored with his raucousness, with his intimidation.

They both knew it would be over soon. Your bravado is no longer necessary, she thought at him. On her skin, her shattered will twinkled. The woman beside Farah then said something about how this was her favourite time of day, and that was when Farah told Mephistopheles that he could leave. That she would see him later. That he should well know it wasn't in her nature to be rude to people who were trying to make conversation, and that she deserved one last peaceful day. In her mind, Farah lifted her hands and pushed Mephistopheles' arms away—his grip let go like breaking through rice paper.

His jaw dropped, and a giddy grin slowly overtook Mephistopheles' face as he watched Farah talk to the empty air beside her. To him this was a bonus, when people let him play so much with their minds that they actually thought they were losing them. *It's just too easy*, he smirked and chuckled. She had asked for *his* permission for a last day in peace. *Too easy,* he said, and then sat back to watch his near-conquest lose her mind.

On the rocks, the woman was wafting the morning air toward her in big whooshing motions. Between deep inhalations, she peeked through her whooshing arms and smiled, "I'm Sophia."

Amused and curious, Farah grinned. "Farah."

"So, did you?" Sophia said, a little out of breath now, getting a bit more comfortable on the rocks.

Farah thought for a moment, *Did I what*? But before she could speak the woman asked again,

"—know the word 'glamour' is a derivative of the word 'grammar'?" Her gaze was transfixed on the horizon.

Farah found the statement so random, she couldn't help but laugh. "No, I did not know that." Laughing, she noticed, felt like a foreign country. Above her, Mephistopheles shook his head and twirled his finger in a *she's loony* motion by his ear. He had no idea what Farah could possibly think was funny about any of this.

Sitting cross-legged, the woman pulled her knitted cap a little further down over her ears and rested her hands comfortably on her knees. "That's the thing about language," she said, "it's so *fascinating*. The history of language, the history of words—often they end up meaning more than you think they mean when you learn where they came from," she nodded pedagogically. "Take 'glamour' for example. Now this history goes *way* back. You'd never know it today, but through the ages a great sense of mystery and wonder has been attached to words. In ancient times, reading and writing was so rare a skill, required such 'special knowledge,' that it was often regarded with superstitious awe. So much so, that by the sixteenth century England, literacy was associated with black magic."

"Really?" Farah was genuinely interested, the relief of distraction settled gently around her.

"Oh yes," Sophia said. "Because Latin was the language of a very cultured few—mostly intellectuals and religious leaders deemed to have different forms of power over the illiterate masses—the masses themselves, unable to read or comprehend the written words, became suspicious and accredited those who were fluent in Latin with occult or devilish powers. As a result, the ignorant masses began to associate the word 'grammar' with magic or sorcery. Now," Sophia winked, "'glamour' from 'grammar' right? As with everything else in the world, with the passing of time comes change. And as the word 'grammar' trundled its way through history, it fell victim to varied pronunciations—the letter *r* became mispronounced often enough to become an *l*, for example, as often happens with cultural transliteration. Before long, other modifications occurred, and a new word was born: glamour, which carried the original cabalistic undertones once attached to grammar. Which is why *today,* 'glamour' means 'enchanting, compelling, or something you can put under a spell.'"

Sophia smiled and wiggled her fingers mysteriously.

"Wow," Farah shook her head, honestly fascinated. 'Glamour' from 'grammar.' Who would have thought? I had no idea."

"Most people don't," the old woman said, slipping her feet back into her sandals. "But I always say, knowing things about the world helps you understand it better." Sophia got to her feet. "Just like knowing more about who Mephistopheles really is, will help you."

Farah's body lurched. She looked up. Sophia, bathed in the light of early morning, kept her gaze on the horizon. Farah's words bundled in her throat; she whispered hoarsely, "Excuse me?"

Sophia looked back at the girl casually, but in her eyes was a sense that she knew things, knew *everything.* "You heard me. Now, I don't bake very well, but I make a lovely loaf of bread. I'll be expecting you for breakfast in half an hour. Edyn Cottage, just up the road toward town. Come, and I'll tell you what Portmanteau words are, before letting you know the actual truth about life after death, and why suicide won't give you the relief you are looking for." She looked at her watch. "After we eat, I'll tell you the truth about *him.*"

Farah, stiffened by shock, wondered if her heart was still beating. She watched Sophia retreat over the boulders and disappear back into the forest, so comfortably familiar with the surroundings she hardly made a sound.

Farah, on the other hand, was everything but comfortable. Her body was tense with a hundred things, mostly astonishment. *Had that just happened*? She stared forward, looked over her shoulder in the direction Sophia had walked, then stared forward again. *Had any of that just happened*? She reached for her pen and scribbled *Edyn Cottage* on the inside cover of her journal. If it was real, there was only one way to find out. If it wasn't—well then, the worst had already happened: She had officially lost her mind.

As quickly as she could, Farah gathered her things, tottered her way over the boulders, and rushed back to her van—

—her will shimmering on her skin, like mercury in the sunlight.

♋

Rose sat frozen, Roger's list of verses open on the table in front of her. Behind her eyes, confusion, incredulity, doubt, and hot, fiery suspicion formed tornados.

She skimmed some notes about Judaism and how it was the first "religion of the book" in Western civilization.

She read about things she never realized, that Christianity was the child of Judaism, and the only religion in the world that includes in its Bible the entire religious scriptures of *another* religion.

When she read this, she thought *Jesus was the light that came to shine through the old Jewish way, hence the New Testament—the teachings of Jesus— usurping the old ways of religious or Mosaic Law. The New Testament usurped the Old Testament. That was why Jesus came.*

She read about something called the "Theological Interpretation of History." And how

> The Old Testament writers appeared more concerned with the theological meaning of the past, than with accurately depicting the history of a region. This accounts for historical, political, and geological disparities between what the Bible said happened, versus what the actual study of the regions in question show to be true. In this vein, it is important to distinguish between the Old Testament's interpretation of what happened and critical history …[26]

Rose skimmed these notes as quickly as possible, generally making a conscious effort to ignore anything she deemed critical of her faith. When she arrived at the pages discussing Pious Fraud though, she stopped—because they made her feel frozen.

Changes.
Mistakes.
Copies of copies of copies
Verses added. Verses changed.

Rose fumbled for her Bible.

When her fingers touched the cool leather, relief escaped her lips. She pressed her palm against the cover, and felt her church warning her like a pulse in her cells. An evangelist echoed out from her mitochondria and filled the pores of her skin until it came to her suddenly. *Of course*! Why hadn't she thought of it before? She picked up Roger's pages. This was anti-Christian sentiment. Propaganda! No more. Her hands shaking, Rose put the pages down and, smoothing her skirt with her palms, looked at them sideways. *Anti-Christian propaganda*. Her hands kept smoothing. It had to be.

"The mistranslation of words was another reason accidental mistakes made their way into the Bible." Roger enjoyed this part. "For example, in 1 Corinthians 5:8, Paul tells Christians that they should not eat the 'old leaven of wickedness and evil.' *Evil* in Greek is spelled *poneras*—" he wrote the Greek word on the board "—which looks an awful lot like the word for 'sexual immorality,' which is—*porneias.* And so it happens that in a few surviving manuscripts, Paul ends up warning his readers not against evil in general, but against sexual immorality.[27]

"Other mistakes happened when words sounded alike. For example, in Revelations 1:5 the author prays to 'the one who released us from our sins.' The word for 'released,' which is *lusanti,* sounds *exactly* like the word for 'washed' which is *lousanti.*" Roger scribbled the words on the board. "And so in some manuscripts the author prays to the one 'who washed us from our sins.'"[28]

A ripple of chuckles.

"Often accidental mistakes become evident because they tend not to make sense when you read them. For example, in John 5:39, Jesus declares to his opponents that they should 'search the scriptures … for they bear witness to me.' However, in one early manuscript the scribe changed the final verb to another word that sounded similar, but made no sense in the context of the verse. As a result, Jesus ends up telling his opponents to 'search the scriptures … for they are sinning against me.'"[29]

Everyone always found that one amusing.

"The errors we have reviewed so far are generally minor," Roger said, "but what of the mistakes that make a greater difference? That can significantly influence the way a religion is interpreted or practiced? Like the error found in Romans 5:1 when Paul states 'since we have been justified by faith, we have peace with God.' The word for 'we have peace,' which is a statement, sounded exactly like the word for 'let us have peace,' an exhortation.[30] As a result, in some of the earliest manuscripts, Paul doesn't actually say that he and his followers have peace with God; he instead urges himself and others to *seek* peace.[31]

"Which one is correct?

"For those hearing Paul's words for the first time, the difference between being told you will automatically have peace if you follow God the way that

Paul instructs, versus being told that the path to seeking peace with God is the one that Paul is on, are two very different things."

Just then, two voices came barreling down the hall. Roger could only assume they belonged to the two that slipped out a few minutes earlier, presumably to use the toilet. What happened while they were gone would remain a mystery, but its result would not. The two were engaged in a full-fledged argument, loud enough to make everyone look up.

"Didn't you hear me the first time? They weren't *real* Christians. They were heathens and pagans trying to confuse the true Christianity of Jesus with their own ungodly ways. Eusebius was *the* historian of the church, so if anyone is going to know what really happened back then, it was him."

The opposition could be heard stifling a sardonic snort. His reply came in a velvety, scornful tone. "You mean *the* Eusebius? The documented liar? Is that the Eusebius you are talking about?"

Silence. Not even the sound of footfall. Roger imagined the Christian Defender and the opposition—whom he had dubbed the Stirrer—staring at each other angrily. Suddenly, one set of footsteps resumed, this time more hurriedly, back toward the room.

"It's okay," the Stirrer's voice echoed. "You're a *Christian*. Why would you know anything about your religion? But FYI anyway: Eusebius was responsible for the historical record of your church up to 250 AD. He was *famous* for being a liar of convenience, of falsifying historical records to glorify the church, *and* of *suppressing historical evidence* that would in any way disgrace the Christian religion. *So*, in *actuality*, what you think you know is only a revised version of history that actually touts the vested interests of a religio-political empire!"

They were right outside the door now. Everyone waited.

"You can walk away from it, but that doesn't stop it from being true!"

First the Christian then the Stirrer stormed in. Both took their seats furiously, crossed arms, and turned away from the direction the other was sitting.

"Is everything all right?" Roger asked, feeling their level of malcontent far too elevated to ignore.

The Christian turned his head abruptly toward Roger. "Oh, no problem, no problem," then jerked his thumb in the direction of the Stirrer. "*He's* just being an idiot—trying as hard as he can to convince me that Christianity's greatest early historian was a liar."

"Ah yes," Roger's tone was regrettable. "Eusebius."

The Christian's jaw all but dropped. "What do you mean, 'Ah yes, Eusebius'?"

Roger pressed his lips together pensively and debated what to do with the kettle of fish this interruption had just opened. Whether now or later, the topic would have to be dealt with. Could he use the Eusebius information to open the next part of the lecture? He looked at his watch and muttered, "Getting the Bible to say what people believed it meant," under his breath, and then made a decision. "Eusebius," he said, "lived from 260 to 340 CE. He was a scholar, a theologian, and a church historian. He held great favour with Constantine I—the first Christian Roman Emperor—and was considered one of the most learned men of his time." Roger flipped through his Day One folder as he spoke. "Eusebius' *Ecclesiastical History* is the principle data source for the history of Christianity from the apostolic age until his own age—ah, here it is." From the folder, he pulled a sheet of quotes and placed it under the projector. "Unfortunately, while he maintained a great reputation for loyalty to the church, Eusebius' reputation as a reliable historian was not so great." Roger motioned to the quotes now projected on the wall. "The following has been said about Eusebius by contemporary historians who were able to cross reference Eusebius' claims with other historical documents and evidence."[32]

No one has contributed more to Christian history, and no one is guilty of more errors. The statements of this historian are made, not only carelessly and blunderingly, but in many instances in falsification of the facts of history. Not only the most unblushing falsehood, but literary forgeries of vilest character darken the pages of his ... writing.
(Charles B. Waite, *History of Christian Religion to the Year 200*)

Eusebius was the gravest of the ecclesiastical historians ... [he] indirectly confesses that he has related whatever might redound to the glory, and that he has suppressed all that could tend to the disgrace, of religion.
(Sir Edwin Gibbon, *Decline and Fall of the Roman Empire*)

Irenaeus, Epiphanius, and Eusebius—all early Christian apologists— have transmitted to posterity a reputation for such untruth and dishonest practices that the heart sickens at the story of the crimes of that period ... the duplicity is all the worse since the whole Christian outline rests upon it.
(Alexander Wilder, *Catholic Encyclopedia*: Evolution)

Eusebius was always ready to supply by fabrication what was wanting in the historical record.
(Tom Harpur, *The Pagan Christ*)

Roger watched the Christian Defender's reaction out the corner of his eye, how his face bore a multitude of expressions, distress being the first and most obvious, then confusion, suspicion, betrayal.

Upset.

But what could Roger do?

Whose fault was it?

Roger's for teaching an actuality?

Eusebius' for altering the documents at all?

Or the church's for misleading people about what its authorities have known was true all along? Who was to blame for the emotional upheaval, the confusion and distress, the anger and the inevitable feelings of betrayal that the religious and nonreligious alike would feel when they found out these things? When they found out that they, *right now*, in their homes, minds, and in their churches were living the effects of Pious Fraud? As far as Roger was concerned, blame for unchangeable pasts was as irrelevant as anger over the unchangeable. To him, the past was a place from which to learn and step forward on the way to creating a better future.

He watched the Christian rub his face with his hands, shake his head in disbelief, try to comprehend, to make sense of it in his own mind and heart. If anyone knew that feeling of displaced anguish, it was Roger, and growth through it was never easy. Personal growth never was—it meant facing things you not only didn't want to face, but that sometimes never thought you would have to. *This discomfort*, Roger wanted the Christian to know, *this ill at ease, is only transitory. It is not all that will be left.*

The silence of contemplation, of waiting, hung in the air. "As you can see," Roger said, acknowledging the quotes, "Eusebius did not have such a great reputation. By his own admission he altered documents and embellished history in favour of the church to make things 'all square' for the Christians."[33]

It was a good segue, Roger realized, and it brought him to the next group of pages in his folder.

"The second category of changes made to the Bible fall under a more dubious umbrella." He wrote the words *Intentional Changes*, and could feel it right away, rippling through people's minds, the question that had driven him incessantly when he first learned that scripture had been changed to intentionally alter their meaning. Why? Why commit such a wildly blasphemous and deceitful act, to gospels that were holy to millions?

The question kept Roger up nights, but the answer had him awake at dawn, reading, researching, comparing notes, piles of them, until suddenly, it all began to come clear. He hopped up to sit on his desk, leaned forward, hands beside his thighs, and began to explain.

"As mentioned, two thousand years ago debate over the nature of Jesus was heated and plentiful. Not everyone agreed on who exactly Jesus was, but by the third century two arguments in particular seemed to stand out. The Arians believed that Jesus was the Son of God, and therefore subservient to the Father. They did not put Jesus on a pedestal next to God, and they were adamant the scriptures said nothing of the sort. Their opposition, whom I have called the Literalists based on their interpretation of scriptures, disagreed. The Literalists believed Jesus as the Son of God was of God, therefore equal to God, and should be worshipped as such. Basically the Arians believed Jesus was a son of God, a messenger of God, while the Literalists believed Jesus was God in human clothing. Each sect of belief, of course, thought the other was committing blasphemy, and heated arguments between the two groups dominated the religio-political landscape of the Middle-Eastern Roman Empire until 325. At that time, sick of all the squabbling, Constantine[34]— who desired an empire united under one religion, demanded an end to the theological arguments. He commanded a conclusion be drawn, a consensus as to the details of the nature and identity of Jesus, so that a homogenized doctrine and dogma could be established, and the Christian church could become a stable religion with *one* belief practice.

"And so in 325 CE, some three hundred and eighteen[35] bishops arrived at Nicea for the first Ecumenical Council,[36] where the issues of semantics and the metaphysical distinction of Jesus were decided by way of a vote. The vote (by a majority of one, twenty, or fifty; no one knows), as you may have guessed, went the way of the Literalists, and by way of the Literalist interpretation of the doctrine of the Trinity, Jesus' metaphysical distinction was formalized as 'God.' From that point in history the foundation for the first official, politically supported and financed Christian church was laid. It was also from that point in time that the Literalist interpretation of scriptures became called 'orthodox' or 'of the right belief.'

"It was the self-proclaimed 'orthodox' then, who decided which books would become the New Testament, which books would be considered scripture, what documents or gospels would be considered heretical, and what the doctrine and creed of Christianity would be for future Christians."[37]

"I think I'm going to be sick," someone said, and made for the door.

Roger watched, not surprised. He too had felt nauseous for days when he learned of the terrible mistake, the truth, and when he considered the impact of it all.

"It's important to note at this time that any opinion that opposed the newly proclaimed orthodox interpretation, from that point on, was considered heretical. And any literature or material that didn't fully support Literalism— the same. Any bishop, theologian, teacher, philosopher that disagreed with the orthodox interpretation—including all Arians—were eliminated, destroyed, exiled, excommunicated, or tried as heretics.[38] Which brings us to the very heart of the reason intentional changes were made to scripture at all …"

There was a certain point in a lecture series when everyone seemed to be hanging on the words that were about to come next. This was one of them … when everyone was wondering which changes were intentional and what effect those changes might have had on not just a developing religion, but on themselves personally as a result. Did what was changed affect them? Did it affect what they thought about themselves? Did it affect who Jesus was or even who they thought Jesus was? Did it mean that something inside of them would be different as a result of finding out? Would it hurt to know? "It's okay," Roger said to the vomiting student who slipped quietly into his seat, "you've returned just in time."

Sun streamed through the skylights, making mobile columns of light that tilted and shifted over various murals, brightening corners of the Sanctuary with the passing of the day. Mateo knew it was lunch above ground. He detected the faint smell of bread and imagined children biting gleefully into moist, fresh figs between the games be heard them playing—children under the age of twelve. His lunch would come soon enough, Mateo knew, but for now, he couldn't imagine being anywhere else, doing any other thing, wanting to hear any words more than those his elderly teacher was about to speak.

In his hands Master Lael held an olive tree, carved from bronze, with greenstone and onyx for olives, the leaves randomly bejeweled with emeralds and amber. The base was solid, marked with different versions of the symbol that had captured Mateo's heart—the cross.

"Look at this olive tree." Master Lael had held the tree up in front of them; the sun twinkled through its branches. "It bears fruit." He carefully plucked one of the olives from a hook that held it in place. "And within each fruit is a seed …" Just as carefully, Master Lael unlatched the smallest latch Mateo had ever seen, and then opened the tiny olive.

The inner chamber of the tiny jade fruit was painted a rich dark green and at its center, catching the light, sparkling in a way that left one intrigued by its beauty, was a diamond. "The seed itself," Master Lael said, "is a living progeny of its parent. This is just like God and you. In creating you, God multiplied himself, so that you would be born implanted with the seed of your parent—just as the olive fruit is implanted with the seed of the tree that bore it—only instead of a diamond, inside of you is a fragment of the divine, a fiery spark from the great Being of Life that is God. This is how you, and every person in the world, are begotten of God. This is how you and every person in the world are invisibly connected—you see, Mateo, we are all siblings of Spirit. Because we are all *of* the spirit of God." It was how God multiplied by dividing … more of God's mathematics in action.

Mateo remembered unconsciously raising his hand to his heart then, partially to feel his body alive, partially from wonderment and awe. Inside of *him* there was an actual piece of God. Divinity. *He* was part divine.

"Every human in the world is born a child of God in this way," Master Lael said. "Every child, every woman, every man …"

Planting a garden of divinity in the world. Those were Master Lael's words.

"This is the reason we bow to each other and say 'Namaste'. Out of respect, out of mutual veneration—it means 'I recognize the divinity in you, that is also in me'. *This* is the root of the common language that every human speaks—that of knowing God and that of recognizing God in each other."

Mateo pressed his hand to his chest now. Still, all these years later, his emotions swelled with a feeling of amazement. Every human. Alive with godliness. A *literal* child of God ...

♌

Farah drove the road slowly, thinking if she went any faster she might miss the turnoff, but also thinking that the longer she took to find Edyn Cottage was the same amount of time she was away from discovering that there was no such thing. She gripped the steering wheel tightly with what felt like her last shred of hope—a shred that held her will twinkling in place, like fireflies in Farah's hair, like fairy dust in the folds of her clothes, like phosphorescence on her skin. And then she saw it. A piece of driftwood jutting out from a bush, four ornately carved letters made visible to the road: *Edyn*. The van rolled to a stop. "It's real," Farah repeated in light, astonished breaths. "*She's* real. *It's* real." Her heartbeat fluttered as she turned into the driveway, beat in grateful disbelief. She didn't know what all of this meant; there seemed no explanation for it—the idea that Sophia *knew* her, knew about Mephistopheles.

What she did know, however, as she drove the narrow drive, past trees and typical island bush, was that none of this felt anything like the whispering evangelist in her head, like Mephistopheles, or the pit of dark fear in her stomach. All of *this*, for some inexplicable reason named Sophia, felt like she could trust it. When the cottage came into view, Farah tingled from head to toe.

Draped by some sort of flowering vine, and wrapped by a small covered deck, the cottage was hugged by greenery: rambling roses, bushes, flowers, and herbs, all growing together in a chaotic beauty. A small section of well-kept lawn spilled to the edge of the forest itself, leading to the sea just beyond. Farah parked, grabbed her bag, tucked her journal under her arm, and walked from her van up the cobblestone path, noticing the smell of mint lift up from beneath her feet as she walked.

But the scent of lavender that followed, the three steps she took to the front door, her being called through the open-plan living room and kitchen out through the French doors to the back garden, all felt like it happened in a blur. Even being greeted by Sophia's hands squeezing hers, sitting down at a table decorated with a brightly coloured cloth, flowers, herbs, and fruit, being offered a piece of warm bread and saying thank you to a cup of spicy sweet tea, even her noticing a large branch bowing in the forest at the edge of the lawn behind Sophia, and Mephistopheles climbing to the ground, craning his neck to make sure he could get a good look at Farah—even his disquieting stare,

75

the look of patient derision on his face, the canopy of white sheets billowing over their heads—*all* of it seemed clouded, to be happening in slow motion, until the moment Sophia spoke. Her voice burned through Farah's haze, like a bold sunrise.

"Tell me," she asked, matter of factly. "What will committing suicide do for your life?"

And just like that, the slow motion returned. A feeling of detachment from reality.

Farah's breathing slowed. Her expression blanked before it went to shameful introspection. How does one answer a question like that? A question about suicide? How does one account to another the depth of their existential angst with *complete* honesty? Relate their innermost thoughts? Their deathly fear that meaning is lost in all things. … How does one account the confusion, despair, the lack of security or knowledge that everything really *will* be all right—even though nothing seems controllable or able to change? How does one begin to say the end of life seems the only relief?

How could Farah justify what she knew would sound irrational, as soon as she said it?

Especially when she could hardly explain the feelings to herself? All Farah knew was that if she took her life, all of it would end—the emotional and psychological pain, the anxiety, the panic attacks, the despair, the *fight* would end. No longer would she feel rejected by the life that surrounded her—by the religion she could not be honest in—by God, who had turned His back to her and ignored her desperation …

What about hell?

What about it?

She was living a version of it anyway. Evil under and in her skin, woven between her fingerprints, that no stitch-ripper could set free.

Farah took a sip of tea. When she spoke her voice sounded as if it wasn't coming from her own body, like she was listening to herself talk from somewhere else. Her words dropped flat in the air, like stone hitting tin. What would dying do for her life?

"It will end it."

The words hovered in the air between them, before tumbling to the ground.

"That!" Sophia said, "*Right there*, is exactly the problem. That is the *exact* mistake people make."

Again, the voice came as if an eyedropper of clarity had let go above Farah's head, like liquid washing something away and the blur lifted.

Farah looked up at the woman then, took her in: the smile lines around her eyes, the small dangling earrings, the pulse in her neck, the wrinkles that formed on the back of her hand when she broke her bread into pieces. *Are you sure that this is happening?* she asked herself. On the edge of the garden, Mephistopheles crossed his arms and tapped his foot impatiently.

"All right then," Sophia saw Farah watching him, noticed the girl's neck muscles tighten, felt her body tingle with fight or flight, "ask God to send him away." She took a bite of bread and waved her hand dismissively in Mephistopheles' direction. "Go ahead. Pray right now with all your might for God to take him away, and see what happens."

Farah looked from Mephistopheles to Sophia, and back again. Once, twice, three times. Sophia nodded, *Come on then.*

After the mysterious events of the entire morning, Farah wasn't sure that a miracle couldn't happen, and so she did: She closed her eyes and prayed aloud. "Lord God, I beg you, please take Mephistopheles away. Please send him away, out of my life forever. Please, Lord Jesus, free me from this demon, let me be pure of spirit. Fill me instead with your love and with the Holy Spirit. Please, God, take Mephistopheles away, I beg of you. In Jesus' name, amen." Her was voice urgent, strained, hopeful.

A moment passed.

Another.

"Now look," Sophia said, adding a smidgen more butter to her bread. "What do you see?"

Slowly, Farah squinted her eyes open and looked toward the trees where Mephistopheles had been standing. Her shoulders slumped. He was still there, grinning, shaking his head. Was he actually *tut-tutting* her?

"Is he still there?"

"Yes." Misery glistened on the girl's skin.

"Hmm," Sophia said, pressing her lips together in an expression of "just what I thought." "Do you know what that tells me you know about God?"

Farah blinked. What *did* she know about God? Only one thing for certain—that in her he was not well pleased.

"Nothing," Sophia said. "It tells me you know nothing." She slapped her hand on the table. "Here! Look at me now! You sit there shrouded in your misery and you expect *God* to fix your problems? Problems that *you* are responsible for creating?"

She felt as if she had been slapped. Misery *she* was responsible for creating? Inside, Farah shook her head vehemently. *No*, this was wrong. Sophia was wrong! Mephistopheles had come to *her*. Farah remembered it clearly: In whispers and scratches at first, but then one day, full bodied, waiting for her. She *remembered*, and she hadn't invited him. In fact, she had vomited on the spot when she saw him there in the passenger seat of her van, grinning, whispering that everything Farah feared about herself and God was true.

He had wiggled his fingers at her in a puppeteer's wave, and she had felt that something *that* real could not be exorcised.

"People do this all the time," Sophia said, adding sugar to her tea. "They pray to God to fix their problems as if He's some kind of magician, as if they had nothing to do with creating their own mess in the first place."

Slowly, but then more emphatically Farah began to shake her head. Her eyes darted from Mephistopheles to Sophia. "N-no," she said. "Y-you've got it wrong. I didn't create him." She wagged her finger at Mephistopheles, who looked affronted and gave her the finger back. "He *invaded* me." Inside, Farah's heart was screaming. *Why would I ever want any of this to happen to me?*

Sophia raised a dubious eyebrow, as if the girl's answer was nothing more than an excuse, an aversion from responsibility.

Farah knew then that she needed to explain. She needed to *show* Sophia that the devil was insidious, powerful, that she had tried, but in the end, had failed. The devil ruled over the earth and caused suffering, and Farah was a perfect example of that. Humans couldn't help who and what they were—just as she couldn't.

So Farah made a decision. She bent then, over the deep well of memories in her mind, and with trembling hands began to draw from its content in armfuls.

♋

Fear moved through Rose's body in small, sickly waves. With insistent tendrils it infected her organs. She could no longer read full paragraphs; she was barely reading full sentences. Instead, her eyes traced words, slid over paragraphs, took in only what they had to. Sentences stood out in bold, before her eyes blurred over and moved down the page. A question she didn't want to contemplate thudded inside of her.

Did accidental mistakes   did intentional changes   change who Jesus was?

Christians went from being a periphery cult of social outcasts to the most powerful religion in the Roman Empire.

Even Eusebius didn't agree on arguing over the semantics of the metaphysical details of who and what Jesus was.[39]

Origen too, one of the church's most revered Fathers and most pious leaders, suffered. His works became banned after he refused to agree with developing doctrine …

In 529, Emperor Justinian succeeded in closing the doors to Plato's famous Academy in Athens. This was done in the name of Christianity. The philosophers and teachers were put to flight, and any who failed to escape were forced to be baptized.[40]

Literalist belief that Jesus was God attributed to the difficulty of converting Jews who were fiercely monotheistic—to them, the Christians were worshipping two Gods, and worse, a man as God.

In the back of her mind, in the place where discipline controlled all of Rose's thoughts, she was screaming. *How is this possible?*

How was it possible for all of these things to be true about her religion and for Rose to have known nothing, *nothing*, about them? Either it was possible. Or it was *impossible* …

And then suddenly it hit Rose with the force of a tidal wave. Whether or not the rest of what she learned was true depended entirely on whether or not she wanted to believe it was.

♑

Outside the classroom windows, spring was being beckoned. Birds flitted and sang with celebratory gusto, trees pushed new flush, early blooms of flowering plants opened despite the heavy weight of dew. In Roger's mind, it was the world waiting to be understood. He settled in.

"The reason intentional changes were made to the Bible was largely due to the small but significant issue that very little of the fundamentalist orthodox doctrine was actually outlined in scripture. This reality, coupled with the vehement criticism of the literalist interpretation by the intellectual public, practically forced the literalists to do what they thought was right. Change the verses, add and edit where appropriate, to ensure the Bible said more clearly what they were sure it meant. [41] For example, the literalists believed that Jesus was God, but nowhere in the Bible did it actually say this explicitly, until a very specific change was made to 1 Timothy 3:16."

Bibles opened, pages shifted.

"The original text spoke of Christ (who, you will remember, was traditionally defined as the intermediary between God and humans, and who the orthodox defined as 'Jesus') as 'godliness who was made manifest in the flesh.' But by the fifth century this verse had been changed to insinuate that Jesus was no longer godliness made manifest, but God himself manifest in a human body. The verse now insinuates of Jesus that he was '*God* made flesh.'[42] The crucial difference of course lay in the nuances of the language.

"The same occurred with the orthodox need to justify the Trinity because the Bible, originally, did no such thing.[43] The Trinity, of course, is the belief that God is three persons in one: Father, Son, and Holy Ghost (God, Jesus, and the holy spirit that enters one's life when one accepts Jesus as Lord and Saviour). The doctrine of the Trinity qualified the literalist belief that Jesus was not merely a human prophet, nor just the Son of God, but that he was the living Word of God, that he embodied the wisdom and will of God in his body and words. Jesus was considered an extension of God on Earth and therefore was defined by the Trinity as equal to God in stature. Adjustments were made accordingly: 1 John 5:7-8 originally read:

> There are three that bear witness: the Spirit, the water, and the blood, and these three are one.

"But was changed to:

> For there are three that bear witness in heaven, the Father, the word,[44] and the Holy Ghost: and these three are one. And there are three that bear witness on earth, the Spirit, the water, and the blood: and these three are one.

"Without this passage, justification for the doctrine of the Trinity needs to be inferred by reference to multiple passages—nowhere else in the Bible is it directly stated. By adding a verse and changing a word here and there, suddenly the orthodox explanation for who and what Jesus was became justified. *Proven* by the Holy Scriptures themselves."

The room was silent. Roger could feel it building. He continued while he had the chance, explaining quickly how intentional changes were also made over time, to ensure they reflected developing ascetic traditions.

"For example, a change made to Mark 9:29 still reverberates through Christian faith and practice today. Originally, Jesus' disciples ask him to help cast out a demon, Jesus approaches, casts out the demon and explains, '*This kind comes out only by prayer.*' Over time, this statement came into conflict with developing monastic traditions, so the monks adapted the verse to have it more accurately reflect a sense of Christian life and duty. Now the verse reads, '*This kind comes out only by prayer and fasting.*'"[45]

Someone *tsk*'d and shook their head. Several people in the room had undertaken religious fasting because of that very story. To learn that the verse was added left them feeling troubled.

"Scripture was also altered to reflect *cultural* beliefs," Roger said, handing out a series of pages titled *Women*. "These particular changes were made to specifically downplay or deny the importance or equality of women, and yet anyone familiar with the most ancient words attributed to Jesus, would know that Jesus vehemently propounded the equality of women and men as equally sacred under God."

Roger looked at his watch.

"In this vein the gospels were also altered to ensure they reflected the cultural ideology of the day. Matthew 5:22 is a great example of this: What started out as '*whosoever is angry with his brother shall be in danger of the judgment*' became '*whosoever is angry with his brother without a cause shall be in danger of the judgment.*' Even the Didache—one of Christianity's oldest instructional documents on how to live and practice life as a Christian—was altered to exhibit cultural ideology: The command to '*love your enemies*' was changed to '*pray for your enemies.*'"[46]

And that was as far as Roger got. In truth, he was surprised he'd gotten as far as he did. Usually by now people were shouting out in disbelief, suspicion, or even with glee. Sometimes people even said, "This is too good to be true" or "*Sweet* Jesus" or "Oh my God, oh my God." Because suddenly, the more that people learned about the Bible, the more it became indisputably clear—and not because it needed to be proven, but because it was the plain and simple truth—the Bible was *not* infallible. Nor was it the infallible word of God. It *did* contain mistakes, in fact; intentional mistakes that mattered because they were made with the *intention* of altering the original meaning of the text.

"How did they *ever* get away with it?" This person actually smacked palm to forehead in disbelief.

"Why wouldn't they get away with it?" Roger said. "The only people scribes were accountable to were the ecclesiastical authorities who piously, if not religiously, followed the doctrine of *Justa Causa*. Which, I'm sure you remember, espoused that if it was for the glory of the church, any change was permissible. And you mustn't forget, the majority of Christians weren't reading the texts. They were illiterate. The gospels were translated verbally by the very people in charge of copying them. Any changes or alterations could have easily gone unnoticed or been explained away by those deemed 'authorities' on the matter."

"But they were altering *Holy Scripture* ..." A voice exhausted by the very idea of Pious Fraud.

"People make this mistake all the time." Roger loved this banter, the electricity of discussion and discovery. "They assume that people in Rome or Jerusalem two thousand years ago thought and perceived and practiced life the same way that we do today, but that just simply is not true. Antiquity in general had no concept of literary morality in its modern meaning.[47] We have evolved a sense of literary morality based on our experiences with corruption, which in our culture resulted in a demand for accountability, but in the times leading up to now, it was not considered a bad thing to say what you needed to say, even make it up if you had to, if it served a perceived notion of some greater good.[48] This attitude was common, and even extended into the social/political realm. When verbal wars between educated religious leaders and their opposition were fought in public, it was not uncommon for someone to completely fabricate the words or doings of their opposition, simply to disgrace them or bring their reputation into disrepute.[49] This kind of behaviour was considered by priests as merely a ruse in religious controversy."

"But surely," someone said, "*Surely* there must have been *someone* who disagreed with all of this! Surely every single Christian priest wasn't corrupt, every single church father didn't approve!"

Roger nodded. "There were many that absolutely did not approve. In fact, Origen, one of the most revered of the early church fathers repeatedly expressed his anger over the audacity of those altering scriptures. '*The differences among the manuscripts have become great,*'" he once wrote. "'*Either through the negligence of some copyists or through the perverse audacity of others; they either neglect to check over what they have transcribed, or, in the process of checking, they make additions or deletions as they please.*' In the space of Origen's own lifetime, he noted that the differences between the manuscripts had become 'considerable.'[50] Another of the church fathers, a Bishop Dionysius, charged that even his very own writings, alongside scriptures, had been falsified by 'apostles of the devil.'[51] Of course, there was no 'devil' making anyone do anything. The scriptures had simply fallen victim to subjective interpretation, incredible arrogance, and the politics of ego." Roger pulled another paper from his Day One folder. "Even the author of Revelations—the most apocalyptic book in the Bible—was aware of the practice of altering scriptures. He went so far as to threaten, '*I testify to everyone who hears the words of the prophecy of this book. If anyone adds to them, God will add to him the plagues described in this book; and if anyone removes any of the words of the book of this prophecy, God will remove his share from the tree of life and from the holy city, as described in this book.*'[52]

"Whether or not anyone was cursed after the total revision of the gospels ordered by Emperor Anastasius at Constantinople in the year 506,[53] or after the 're-revision' and 'correction' of not just the gospels but *all* of the writings of the church fathers in 1070,[54] no one has ever officially noted."

This invoked a few chuckles.

"But it was not only Christian authorities and church fathers who had trouble with the amount of 'editing' suffered by scriptures; Christianity's biggest and most educated critics also noticed—with fiery gusto.

"Celsus, for example, was famously determined that Christianity *thrived* on the illiteracy, but especially on the ignorance of its congregations.[55] He argued that only a faith occupied by the ignorant could get away with making changes to holy scriptures that were so obvious to the educated. Publicly, Celsus accused: '*Some believers, as though from a drinking bout, go so far as to oppose themselves and alter the original text of the gospel three or four or even several times over, and change its character to enable them to deny difficulties in the face of criticism.*'[56] Indeed, the orthodox move to adapt holy scriptures to make them better reflect orthodox beliefs was one of Christianity's biggest weaknesses. And all in all, many were left disgruntled by the practice."

"But how do you suppress that kind of controversy?" Palm removed from forehead, the same person now demanded another kind of answer.

"It's quite a simple process really." Roger gave a light shrug. "Time buries the controversy and ignorance perpetuates it. Take the change made to 1 Timothy 3:16, for example. Every person who read that text or had the text read to them *after* the change had been made, would have automatically assumed the altered text was the original. And from that generation on, it becomes standard thought that the Bible justifies the subjugation of women. The same goes for every generation of Christian that reads any Bible copied from the manuscripts that were altered to affirm the church-proscribed doctrine of the Trinity: *Every* generation from then on, up until now, believes that those added words are the *original* text, and so they believe that the doctrine of the Trinity is justified by God, when the truth is that it was adopted[57] to justify a particular interpretation of scriptures, the scriptures then altered to reflect that interpretation.

"Let me give you another example; one of the most-popular, most-quoted Bible stories comes from the book of John—the story of the woman taken in adultery.[58] In this story, a woman 'caught in the act of adultery' is brought before Jesus by the religious leaders, who want to confront Jesus about what he thinks the woman's punishment should be. Essentially, the religious leaders bring the woman to Jesus because they want to test him. Should Jesus say 'let the woman be free,' he would be in immediate violation of the religious law of the day, Mosaic Law, considered to be the Law of God. Mosaic Law demanded the woman be stoned to death. But should he say the Law of God should be upheld, he would be violating his own teachings of compassion, mercy, love, and forgiveness.[59] When confronted, however, Jesus refuses to take the bait. Instead, he stoops to the ground and begins to write with his finger in the sand. When the Pharisees pressure him for a response, Jesus famously says, '*Let the one who is without sin among you be the first to cast a stone at her.*'[60] He then continues to write. When he looks up again, everyone but the woman had gone. '*Is there no one who condemns you?*' Jesus asks her. '*No one, Lord,*' she replies. To which Jesus responds, '*Neither do I condemn you. Go and sin no more.*'

"Again, this story is one of the most well-known, most quoted, and most popular of New Testament Bible stories, and yet it is *not* original to the New Testament, nor is it original to the Bible, *or* the Gospel of John from which it is quoted.[61]

"It is known for certain that this story was added to the Gospel of John by later scribes,[62] as it is completely absent from the oldest and best manuscripts of John.[63] But again, *time* and having the story published in the King James Version—which was the first English translation of the Bible but was translated from one of the most error-filled Greek manuscripts known to Biblical scholarship[64]—has left us with a situation where the majority of Christians believe the story was there from the beginning. And as usual, ignorance about the history of the Bible prevents us from knowing any better …"

"That and hellfire and brimstone," someone blurted. "There is *no way* anyone would even think to question those things about their Bible. No *way*. When you're told that 'Questioning will get you to hell as quickly as stealing' you're not asking *any* questions."

"This is very true," Roger said. "If it's a sin to ask questions, you're not going to ask them. If it's a sin to wonder about the odd inconsistencies, or the occasional phrase that seems completely out of character to the rest of a text—even out of character for Jesus or Paul to have said—then you won't wonder. You will simply accept the oddities for what you are told they are: the 'Word of God'—and look the other way."

"Yeah, because looking the other way means you don't have to feel uncomfortable about what is staring you straight in the face." The Stirrer gave the Christian a look; the Christian gave the Stirrer stink-eye.

Roger hopped off the desk and walked to the chalkboard. "It's fair enough to say that you cannot blame people for what they do not know, but at this point in time in history, we *are* able to know better. Ironically, *because* the Bible tells us so." But no one laughed. The play on the old adage "I know it is true, because the Bible tells me so" did not go over well with this group. And Roger should have known better, really, because the truth was that these were not laughing matters. Religion was serious enough to change and even to take lives; to murder over and feel saved because of. Roger held his hand up in truce. "The bottom line is that the present, coupled with the evolution of human knowledge, has provided us with an incredible opportunity: the opportunity to understand what the Bible is telling us, in a way we never have before."

In all the time Master Lael had been talking, Mateo could hardly believe he hadn't noticed where his teacher had led them. When he finally looked up, it was with delight and wonder. The mound upon which they sat was at the base of the oldest mural in the Sanctuary, what the Greeks called the *Zōion* or *zodiakos*. It was the Zodiac—so ancient its origins were unknown.

At that time, Mateo had heard that the Zodiac told the story of humans— *every* woman, man, and child—and that it revealed the secrets of what it meant to be human. The *reason* humans were born. But in all his twelve years, Mateo could never quite imagine *how* the star signs could do such a thing. Night after night, he would lie beneath them trying to figure it out, asking quiet questions of the twinkling shapes as they passed from night into morning. But all he ever heard in return was the sound of a whispering mystery, and the whispers, the silence, the timelessness would sprinkle down upon him, leaving Mateo with nothing but the same wonder that humans had been carrying inside them for millennia. A wonder that asked him to seek.

He had seen miniature versions of the *Zōion* before, on temple floors, in people's houses, but they were, Mateo realized, no comparison to the majestic scene before him. An enormous version of the constellations, painted with such intricate detail it was as if the night sky had come down to Earth and imprinted itself right there on the floor in front of him. The giant mural lay in a perfect circle, with north, east, west, and south marked clearly, and every constellation that crossed the heavens through the course of the night brought to life within its bounds. Lines of silver marked the shift of the stars over seasons and time. It was one of the most wonderful, awe-inspiring things Mateo had ever seen, and from certain angles he swore he could see the painted stars sparkling with life, especially the Twelve.

The twelve signs of the Zodiac stood out, not just because each constellation was painted brighter, but because of the lines that connected the stars, bringing the signs to life in the optical illusion of a three-dimensional shape. The connect-the-dots lines were almost translucent, yet completely distinct, and the shapes were animate with shades of twilight and night sky. Every single one of the Twelve was painted pristine and recognizable: Virgo, Libra, Scorpio, Sagittarius—Mateo named them in his head as he looked upon them—Capricorn, Aquarius, Pisces, Aries. He stood on his tiptoes to make out those on the furthest edge of the circle—Taurus, Gemini, Cancer, and Leo.

"The story of your birth begins *here*," Master Lael smiled. "When you learn it, the purpose of all life shines clearly, like sunlight through murky waters, breaking up shadows and turning them to glory. Within the Zodiac you will find the power of *knowing*. You will find the presence of yourself, and the presence of God in you."

*

"*Know thyself*," Mateo whispered at the memory. *Gnothi Seauton. Nosce te ipsum*. It was the command of the oracle at Delphi, to which Socrates added: *for this is the beginning of wisdom*, and of which Plato proclaimed, *Know thyself: for therein lies the key to all wisdom*.

*

"The Zodiac," Master Lael said, "represents every person on Earth because every person in the world is born under one of its signs." He opened his arms to the Twelve, to all the murals and stars and stories that lay beyond it. "But there are two signs in particular that every human shares, one common story, and it begins," Master Lael lifted his walking stick, and sweeping it wide across the entire contents of the cave, landed it at their feet. "Right here, with Virgo."

*

Mateo tingled again at the lovely memories. Virgo was where the *real* story began—everyone's real story. From where he sat near the cross, he gazed in the distance at the twinkling Zodiac mural. More people were arriving at the entrance to the cave, but he could see he had a bit of time yet.

*

Virgo was called the mother of Matter. This meant that she was the mother out of which all physical matter, all physical creation was born.[65]

"From her," Master Lael said, "all physical matter emerges, all life in physical form. Now," he bent forward, like he was about to share a secret, "The most ancient symbol for matter is water, and so Virgo is also known as the sea mother. Many legends make her the 'sea' that precedes creation; the Hebrews call her 'the deep over which the thoughts of God moved,' the Egyptians call her the Sea of *Nun*—out of which all creation was born."

Mateo remembered looking at Virgo then, how he had marveled, been humbled by her elegant dominion. Just like the other eleven, the artistic rendering of her constellation was flawless. He could clearly make out her dress flowing between the stars, lifting slightly around her feet as if blown in a breeze, which he imagined being caused by the sky moving from night into morning. Her long hair fell down her back and over one shoulder where it draped and curled around the child she held in her arms. Mateo had known then that the child was actually a star named "Spica," one of the brightest stars in the universe, but it was more than that—Spica, Mateo was about to find out, represented matter, born in the form of a human being.

"The child that Virgo holds is very special." Master Lael leaned his chin on the top of his walking stick. "Not only does it represent *you* but it symbolizes the very reality that exists *within* you; the divine consciousness, the *instinct* at the center of your being." He nodded toward the star. "Spica represents the starlight of God shining within your soul … the *consciousness* you are born with that makes you, well, *you*."

Mateo smiled and imagined beams of light filling his body, a bright star shining, illuminating everything, bringing him to life from the inside out.

But Virgo held more than just a child.

In her other arm was a sheaf of wheat.

"The light of God within is seen as spiritual food for man," Master Lael said, "like bread from heaven. It is for this reason Virgo is known as the House of Bread."

So Virgo was the mother of every born human. Every human born. Just like Mateo. "Just like you," Master Lael smiled. "Now, the polar opposite of that which is visible—or physical matter—is that which is—?"

"Invisible?"

"Yes, *bene*. Good. And so just as Virgo is the mother of physical matter, that which is visible, the sign polar opposite her is the mother of that which is *invisible*." Mateo's gaze followed Master Lael's walking stick, which now pointed due east. "Pisces, then, is the mother of the part of you that is invisible. Pisces is the mother of consciousness, the mother of *Spirit*."

She was the fish mother. The reason both bread and fish were used in the gospel stories as symbols of divine truth.

"Both bread and fish represent spiritual nourishment for man. The truth that spiritual nourishment is found within—at the place of divine instinct— where the light of God always guides. In the gospel stories, bread and fish remind us of the connection we have to the greater truth of our spiritually infused existence. In fact," Master Lael chuckled, "everything in the natural world reminds us of this truth, every single day …"

And so Mateo began to learn that the Gospel—which was really the story of him—told humans what was true about themselves, and the world in which they lived. The truth that every human is born ready, spirit and matter united, for a life journey: alive with consciousness (itself the essence of God), an awareness of the divine, and an inherent wisdom that manifests as spiritual instinct. That every human is born with God pulsing in their heartbeat—and all of this reality was who Virgo held in her arms, who Virgo gave birth to. A human being … every human.

*

Mateo opened his eyes from the memory, and observed his hands. They were old now. Heavy at the joints, thick in the palm, animated by a lifetime of experiences. He was a human being, one of a species with enormous potential, because not only could a human learn to understand its physical self and the physical world in which it lived, but was also able to know its spiritual self: the self of the senses, of intuition and divine consciousness. Made in the image of God, the human being could think, reason, gain knowledge from experience, discover, figure out, conclude, understand—evolve—from ignorance to enlightenment—and influence everything else in the world along the way.

*

"Apart," Master Lael said, "spirit and matter exist in and of themselves, but united, they make a miracle. United, they make *life*. You are awake because spirit lives within you, makes your eyes, your mind, and your body *see*.

"It is the unification of spirit and matter, the *moment* of their union, the moment we become human, that is represented by the symbol you so love." Master Lael nodded in the direction from which they came.

Mateo's eyes widened with astonishment. He strained his neck looking back over his shoulder, far across the room, to where the wooden cross lay gleaming in the distance. A bank of great truths.

"That's right." Master Lael laughed at the boy's palpable moment of revelation. Then the teacher lifted his arm and drew an invisible vertical line. He said, "Spirit," then drew an invisible horizontal line intersecting with the vertical, and said, "Matter."

✝

"The cross symbolizes the *moment* you become human, and *all* of what it means to be human. The cross," Master Lael said, "is *You*: a body infused with light, born perfect, ready for a journey."

As Farah bent, she stirred deeply with her arms and sifted through, lifting and looking deep inside the well. When she thought about it, there were a hundred memories, but the one that started it all stood out clearly, and was as fresh in Farah's mind as the wounds left by Mephistopheles scratching there.

It was a moment that changed Farah's life forever. And those *words* … the ones that held such sway. That *before* meant nothing, but that afterward became Farah's obsession: Heaven and hell. Heaven or hell.

And so Farah began to explain to Sophia how everything in her life had been. That she had always considered herself a good person. That she thought she knew the difference between right and wrong. Farah said that her idea of who or what God was, came mostly from garnering snippets from comments made by other people. She knew, for example, that there was One, that God created everything, and that He was everyone's Father. Generally, Farah had liked that idea. It made her feel like this "God" was her friend, maybe even her private best friend. She told Sophia that sometimes as a child she would even chat to God when she was alone, show Him a drawing she had made or a new trick she had learned: a cartwheel, a somersault, how to skip a stone.

"And I always thought of God when I saw particularly fascinating things," Farah said, "like butterflies flying, or when I learned about mysterious things—like how the moon pulls the ocean tides."

The other times Farah thought about God were when she became suddenly aware of mysteriously *incredible* things, like the pulse in her wrist, warm and alive under her fingertips, echoing the beat of her very own heart. Or of the fact that everybody's fingerprints were different, but that their human bodies worked biologically the same.

Farah explained how sometimes she would think about God when she noticed a flower unfolding in the sunlight, or the fact that no one had to teach a bird how to fly, or a dolphin how to swim; that things about nature were what they were—miraculous, and full of life and the very mystery of it. She remembered thinking about God once when she stuck her tongue out in front of the mirror (she had learned that day in school that different tastebuds tasted different things). And one time, she sat under a tree and just felt herself breathe, in and out, slowly, thinking about God the entire time because somehow, by some amazing miracle, that tree was making the air that kept Farah alive. God, to Farah, was always there, always listening, ready to lend an ear, always had a supportive hand on her shoulder, and could lift her heart through everything.

She had no idea how far she was from the truth. About God … but especially about herself.

And then she heard the name *Jesus*.

*

A man arrived at the playground with his two little girls; they looked clean and good, but small. Too small for the big swings, which was where Farah was swinging, and where the man took his daughters to swing beside her. "There's a swing set for smaller kids over there," Farah had offered helpfully, pointing to the center of the playground.

The man had simply smiled kindly and said, "My girls are protected by Jesus, so there is no need to worry."

Farah shrugged indifferently, but snuck a few clandestine glances around the playground. What Jesus where?

A few moments passed. The man glanced several times in Farah's direction. Eventually he spoke again, "You too can be protected by Jesus," he said. "If you want to be."

Farah did her own glancing now, at the man, but also again for this Jesus chap.

"Jesus can save us all," the man said, turning to his daughters. "Right, girls?" They nodded enthusiastically. "I love Jesus," one of them said.

"That's right," the man said, giving Farah another glance. "We love Jesus because Jesus loves us." And then he said *it*.

"Do you know who Jesus is?"

Farah had considered saying yes, even though it would have been a lie. She was at the stage in her life where she was becoming aware that it seemed to matter what you did or didn't know, what you had or hadn't done, because these were the things that defined you in the eyes of others as acceptable or unacceptable. These were things that left you judged. But lying only ever made Farah feel uncomfortable, itchy inside. So she simply looked back at the man and admitted instead, "No" she didn't know who Jesus was.

One of the girls gasped (confirming to Farah that her answer was indeed the wrong one). "W-why—" Farah said, glancing at the little girl whose mouth was actually agape. "Who is he?"

The man placated his daughter with a patient wave—everything would be all right. He looked at Farah with eyes that then went soft, "*Jesus*," he said, "is our Lord and Saviour. *Jesus*," he looked skyward, "is the one and only Son of God who died on the cross for our sins. *Jesus,*" he raised his arms in the air, "rose from the dead three days after he died and now sits on the right hand of the Father in heaven." The man closed his eyes, "*Jesus* is the *only* way to God. *He* said 'I am the way, and the truth, and the life, no one comes to the Father but through Me.'"

"That's from John 14:6," one of the girls smiled precociously.

The man opened his eyes and smiled proudly at his daughter, "Yes, it certainly is." Then he turned again to Farah. "Devoting your life to Jesus is the only way you will ever get to heaven. Don't you want to go to heaven when you die?"

Farah looked at the man blankly. John? Jesus? *Die?*

The man's gaze lingered a moment on Farah's expression, trying to decipher it. Then, in his eyes, a flicker of horror, followed very quickly by a look of complete delight. *Praise Jesus*, he thought, and then whispered the Great Commission: "*Go ye therefore, and teach all nations, baptizing them in the name of the Father, and of the Son, and of the Holy Ghost.*" The girls stared—never had they met anyone before—*ever*—who had never heard of Jesus *or* heaven!

"Here," the man said, sitting on the ground at Farah's feet. "Let me explain." He reached forward and cleared a space in the dirt before telling her excitedly. "Your life is about to change; this is the start of a journey that will take you straight into the open arms of God. That will see you *forgiven.* That will see you *saved.*"

Farah didn't know what that meant, but it sounded very dramatic. She listened carefully, with a small feeling of intensity building inside of her.

"This is how it works," the man began to explain. "God is up here." He wrote the word God with his finger, "and you are down here," he wrote the word you a fair distance beneath the word God. "It never used to be this way." He looked up at Farah to check that she was listening. "But because of human sin, it now is. You see, a long time ago, God lived in a Garden called Eden. He lived there with all the plants and animals in the world, and with the very first humans, whom He created. They were called Adam and Eve. Now this garden was a magical place. Animals and humans were friends, and there was no unhappiness, no suffering, only joy and greenery and abundance. Until one day, Adam and Eve did something God asked them not to do: They ate fruit from the tree of the knowledge of good and evil. God told them not to do this because if they ate of the fruit, they would surely die. Sadly, Eve did not listen. She was enticed by a serpent who convinced her that she would only gain knowledge of the same kind that God had about the world. Eve ate the fruit and then gave it to her husband, who also took a bite. This was the first sin ever committed by humans; the *first* act of defiance against God.

And *wow*, did it make God angry. So angry, that he *banished* Adam and Eve from the garden. He banished them from his very sight. Do you know where he sent them?"

Farah's mind was working like mad. Where was this Garden of Eden? Was it in the sky? The only place she knew where humans lived was on Earth. Well, maybe some lived somewhere else, like out in space, but she didn't know very much about that. She answered meekly, "Earth?"

"That's right!" the man said. "God banished Adam and Eve to Earth, where they would experience pain, suffering, work and toil, and death. Why did God do this?"

Farah replayed the things the man said in her mind. "Because they sinned?"

"That's right!"

But there was more.

"From the moment Adam and Eve were banished from the Garden of Eden, they became separated from God. Do you know what happens when humans are separated from God?" Farah didn't. "Their souls *die*. This makes them *spiritually dead*. Sin did this; do you understand? Adam and Eve's sin made them, as the first humans, become spiritually dead. God didn't want this to happen, but he had to send them away because they sinned, they didn't do just as He said. Do you understand?

Farah nodded. But she didn't like the story. It made her heart feel funny, like sick or something. But the words were already echoing under her skin: Adam, Eve, sin, spiritually dead, separated from God. Punishment. Earth.

"Now," the man continued eagerly, "Every single one of us, every man, woman, and child, every human in the world, is a descendant of Adam and Eve—"

"Because God created them first."

"That's right," the man again smiled patiently at his daughter.

"And God created Adam out of dust and Eve from Adam's rib. And God made Eve to be Adam's wife, to help him, and serve his needs, right, Daddy?"

The man nodded.

"It's Eve's fault humans are separated from God, isn't it, Daddy?"

The man's expression changed slightly. "Well, yes my darling girl, it is. Eve ate of the fruit *first*—"

"Because a snake told her to … nasty snakes."

"Yes, because a snake told her to. And I supposed if Eve hadn't tempted Adam to eat of the fruit, he might not have and we would all still live with God in Eden, but that wasn't what happened. *Both* Adam and Eve were disobedient to God, both of them sinned, which is why all of us remain expelled from the Garden, and all of us are separated from God."

"But one day we won't have to live on Earth anymore, will we, Daddy?"

The man looked skyward, hope shining in his eyes. "One day, sweetheart," he said, "One day."

Farah looked between them and then skyward too. She saw nothing but sunshine and blue and a cloud shaped like a turtle.

Suddenly, the man remembered the story he was telling. "Now, what you have to understand is that as descendents of Adam and Eve, we have inherited their sin, which means that we too, *all humans*, are separated from God; which means that every human on earth is born *spiritually dead*." The man motioned to Farah, himself, the girls, the whole world. "Which means that *you*," he looked meaningfully at Farah, "are spiritually dead too, because just like Adam and Eve, *you* are separated from God."

"Because you're a sinner—" one of the girls nodded, prophet-like, from her swing.

"That's right," the man agreed solemnly. And then he asked Farah in a very serious voice, "Have you ever told a lie? Or taken something that wasn't yours? Or even wondered what it would be like to kiss a boy?"

Farah remembered finding a penny once under a bus stop bench and taking it; she remembered saying that she liked playing with the boy next door when his mother asked her, even though she secretly thought he was a prat. She also remembered thinking the new boy in school was very cute, and had wondered what it would be like to be his girlfriend or maybe, one day, kiss him.

"Well, in the eyes of God," the man said, "that makes you a lying, stealing, lustful sinner."

Farah took a small, sharp breath. Her brow furrowed into a look of intense concentration, followed quickly by deep realization. And in *that* moment, when Farah suddenly came to realize what she was in the eyes of God, a small lightning bolt of panic shot through her heart.

"*And*—" the man continued, "God can see *into* your heart! He knows *everything*. Your every thought! Have you ever hated anyone? Now be careful— tell the truth, because God knows when you are lying."

Again, Farah thought of the little neighbour boy that she never really wanted to play with—all those times he would pick his nose and try to wipe it on her, or slap her in the head when no one was looking.

The volume of the man's voice kept rising. "Well, in the eyes of God, sin is sin. And lying makes you as guilty as a murderer!" His finger shook in the air.

A murderer? Farah's eyes widened. Her stomach filled with a battering of fluttery wings.

A *murderer*? The idea seemed too unbelievable—all this time, God thought of her as a murderer? Oh, this was terrible. This was probably the most terrible thing Farah had ever heard, and all this time, she had no idea! How was it possible she had lived this much of her life having no idea about any of these things? No idea how God really felt about her?

The man shook his head. "These are not good things to be in the eyes of God when Judgment Day comes."

"Judgment Day?" Farah's voice was strained.

The man's eyes widened. "*Judgment Day*," he said, "is when Jesus returns to judge the entire world! Those deemed 'good' will be given eternal life with God in heaven. Those deemed 'bad' will spend an eternity burning in hell. The entire world as you know it will be destroyed, and everyone in it who is not a Christian will suffer terribly." The man lowered his voice and looked hard at Farah, like he really needed her to listen carefully. "Judgment Day is the day the world will come to an end. It will be the first day of the rest of your life—after death."

Farah remembered wanting to cry then. God was going to destroy *everything*? Kill everyone? Even babies and dogs? Even whales and all the flowers? She glanced up at the enormous bow of the tree that shaded them, a butterfly flitted there, a bird rubbed its beak on a branch. God was going to destroy all of this, and kill everyone? This was terrible. *And*, Farah thought—glancing down at her *you* separated from *God* in the dirt and then up in the sky to where God lived—*terrifying*. Heaven and hell. Heaven or hell. Wherever hell was, burning in it for eternity was *not* what she wanted to happen to her—she didn't even like receiving a disapproving stare from a teacher! And who were these *Christians* that Jesus was going to save?

"Judgment Day could happen any time," the man said, getting to his feet. "It could happen today, it could happen tomorrow. And rest assured that when it does, Christians will be raised to heaven on clouds of glory, but they will be the *only* ones to do so."

"Christians like us, right, Daddy?" the girls shouted. They giggled and sang, "We're going to *hea-ven*! We're going to *hea-ven*!"

Farah looked at them. It felt like the colour of things was draining out of the world in front of her. It felt like she was the colour gray, and the Christians in front of her were sparkling rainbows.

"Yes, just like us." The man spoke earnestly, the concern in his eyes genuine, the kindness he extended absolute. "Wouldn't you like to come to heaven with us, when God destroys the world?"

The relief that Farah felt at the man's invitation was like the uncapping of a wonderful scent; it surged and floated and reached every finger and toe tip in Farah's body. Promising fresh air again. Promising colour. Of *course* she wanted to know how not to end up in hell! How to become a part of God's family. She was still fighting the shock of learning that she actually wasn't a part of it, but now she was willing to do anything to get back into God's good graces. *A murderer?* She looked at her sin-filled *you* in the dirt. "Yes," she said. "Yes please; can I know what to do to make God love me again?"

"Oh, God still loves you," the little girl spoke again. "You just aren't part of his family anymore because of your *sin*. It's *because* God loves you that you have the *chance* to become a Christian. If God didn't love you, then you would just rot down here."

The man gave his daughter a look. "Now, now; such language. You don't want to frighten her." He turned back to Farah, and crouched again, "Now, you see this b-i-i-g gap between you and God?" Farah nodded. "Well, there is only *one* thing that can fill it …" Carefully the man filled in the space between *God* and Farah. He wrote in the letters so that their tops touched *God* and their bottoms touched Farah's sin-filled *you*.

The link between Farah and God was one word: *Jesus.*

"Jesus was the Son of God. He died on the cross for your sins. Gave his life. Spilled his blood so that all humans might be reconciled to the Father. You see, God required one last pure sacrifice to atone for the sins of humankind, and Jesus, amazingly, volunteered to be that sacrifice in order that we might all have a chance to be saved. Jesus died on the cross for your sins, little girl—to take them away. He died a terrible death for *you*." The man looked carefully at Farah, "Don't you think the least you could do in return, is believe that he did?"

"If you believe in Jesus, you will live forever!" the older sister smiled.

"Yeah, *forever*," the other nodded.

The man laughed. "The girls are right; when you believe in Jesus and give your life to him, all your troubles disappear. The spirit of God comes into you, and you will live forever. You become spiritually *alive*. Doesn't that sound wonderful?"

Farah's eyes traced the *J* of the word *Jesus*, saw how it touched the tips of the *Y* in her sinful *you*, and then the underside of the bottom curve of the letter *G* of *God*. Connecting her sinful self to God—the only thing connecting her—the curves of some letters, some carefully placed words. *Sinner, Jesus, saved, Judgment Day, died for your sins, Son of God, the blood.* She tried to swallow, but a lump of colourless tears blocked her throat. Becoming a Christian did sound wonderful, if it would fix all of *this*.

"Do you want to save yourself, and become a Christian right now?"

Farah swallowed hard again, and nodded.

The man got up and patted the dirt from his knees. "Oh, this is just so wonderful." He looked skyward, and whispered, "Thank you, Lord Jesus."

Farah looked up too, hoping to catch a glimpse of the dead/alive Jesus, but all she saw was sky. The turtle clouds had grown into gigantic mountains, gray, white, and silver with the sun behind them. She watched them a moment, before realizing they were actually a storm building on the horizon. Her eyes widened. *That* could be the end of the world coming *right now*, and she wasn't a Christian yet! Farah looked to the man urgently, "Please can you make me a Christian right now?"

The man smiled. "It's a done deal. Repeat after me: *Lord Jesus.*"

"Don't forget," one of the girls said. "You have to *mean* it."

Farah nodded. If God could see into her heart, He would know how much she did mean it. With all of her being she meant it. She repeated: "Lord Jesus."

"*I confess.*"

"I confess."

"*That I am a* sinner."

"That I am a *sinner.*"

"*Lord Jesus.*"

"Lord Jesus."

"*I repent.*"

"I repent."

"*Lord Jesus.*"

"Lord Jesus."

"*I* believe."

"I *believe.*"

"*That you shed your blood and died on the cross, for my sins.*"

"That you shed your blood … and died on the cross, for my sins."

"*Lord Jesus.*"

"Lord Jesus."

"*I believe.*"

"I believe."

"*That you resurrected on the third day, to give me eternal life.*"

"That you resurrected on the third day to give me eternal life."

"*Lord Jesus.*"

"Lord Jesus."

"*I believe.*"

"I believe."

"*You are the Son of God!*"

"You are the Son of God!'

"*Thank you, Lord Jesus.*"

"Thank you, Lord Jesus."

"*For dying on the cross for my sins!*"

"For dying on the cross for my sins!"

With each sentence, the man's arms lifted higher and higher until now they were raised open-palmed above his head. Farah imitated him, tilting her head back. She peeked repeatedly to see if the man's eyes were opened or closed; she wanted to get it right. She jumped when he shouted.

"Please, Lord Jesus, *fill* me with the Holy Spirit! I ask you to enter my life and my heart. To be my Lord and Saviour. I want to serve you always. Amen."

Farah repeated everything, but her mind worried, her heart tightened with concern. Had God heard her?

"That's it!" the man clapped and did a small hop. "You're saved! You're a Christian!" The little girls applauded wildly. "From this day forward, your life will never be the same. You have found peace with God. Jesus is your Lord and Saviour."

The clapping girls kept saying, "Yay!"

Farah smiled awkwardly, waiting for God to make the lump in her throat disappear, and take the nervousness in her chest with it. The excitement around her felt like a whirlwind. She was Christian now. She looked at her hands, felt her beating heart, heard the leaves above her head clapping in the wind ... but her skin felt the same. So did her separated human body. And she wondered—had Jesus *done* what she'd begged him to do? Come into her life? Made her worried, sinful self good?

"Wait!" the man shouted. "I almost forgot! There's one more thing you need." He jogged to his car and returned with a leather-bound book. "Humans are incapable of knowing God on our own, so he gave us this book, to help us. This," the man said, "is the Bible. It tells you everything you need to know about ... well, pretty much anything that really matters: the Garden of Eden, the Exodus, Noah and the Flood, Moses and the Ten Commandments. But most importantly, it tells you all about the birth, life, death, and resurrection of Jesus Christ, who made all things right. In prayer, we speak to God, but in the Bible God speaks to us. Do you know what infallible means?"

Farah shook her head *no*, ready to receive the book gratefully.

"It means that everything the Bible says is true and perfect, with no mistakes. It means the Bible is a pure reflection of the heart and will and wants of God." The man put the Bible in Farah's hands. "Take it. Read it. Get to know it well, for it is the closest thing on Earth we have to God."

*

"Ah," Sophia said knowingly. "So *that* was when the first piece was created—let's say, a fingernail?"

"Fingernail?" Farah looked confused.

"Of Mephistopheles."

♋

The late afternoon sun slanted through the half-drawn curtains. The crumbs of a sandwich sprinkled the plate and table from where Rose had picked it up, put it down, picked it up, and then made herself eat. Several empty cups, drained of tea, dotted the table. One mug, half full, its contents too cool to any longer be pleasant, sat on the floor by the couch. But Rose's seat was empty. She stood at Roger's desk, hands rubbing the base of her neck, looking for a distraction. A tape player beckoned from behind the pile of Bibles.

"Do religious people think they know everything?" The interviewer sounded young, perhaps a student or an intern at a radio station.

"Unfortunately, many of them do," Roger's voice said. "Simply because they believe that the 'one' book that is the foundation of their religion was written by God."

"And you don't?"

"Well, that's irrelevant really. What's relevant to this equation is that if everyone believes his or her book is the right one, then who is right? And who then is the sinner? And who then is going to hell? When every religion believes the same thing about a book that is the foundation of their faith, and everyone's books are different, then we all end up not trusting each other. The bottom line is that tolerance and religion are not compatible, and in this regard, religion is dangerous."

"So you're saying that the world should be void of religion? That belief in God should not exist?"

"No. I'm saying exactly what Jesus said, that God and religion are not the same thing …"

Rose stopped the tape. She wanted to cry. Frustration, like a wild uncontrollable wind, swept through her. She had pressed play hoping for a respite, maybe a bit of Nat King Cole or Miriam Makeba, but instead found her son speaking thoughts that should be kept well hidden.

What did God want her to do? Keep listening to things she didn't want to listen to? Keep reading all of these horrible "truths" about the Bible? Keep feeling nauseous at the thought of any of it being true at all? She slumped onto the couch, head in hands, and began to weep, her heart aching with this reality that felt unreal.

The words of the reverend rang in her ears, "The Bible warns of people like your son. It says that they will come as anti-Christs, false prophets." He had stopped Rose in the church parking lot that morning. His words had landed like sparks, singeing through her jacket and shirt, leaving small holes in her stockings, invisible burn marks on her skin. "Everyone is talking about him. What he teaches."

"Teaches?" Rose was bewildered.

"Yes, Rose. Everyone seems to know but you." He looked at Rose seriously. "Your son, Rose, is *lost*. And you know what happens to those who are lost to the Lord."

Rose could only blink, her mouth completely dry. Her heart beating with such traumatic palpitations, she wondered if she was in the middle of a heart attack. Roger … going to *hell*? She couldn't move, she couldn't speak, she could hardly think.

"As his mother, as a Christian, it is your job to love him enough to reach out and, at the very least, try to bring him back. Try to talk some sense into him." And so it was Christian love that made the reverend confront Rose that morning; it was Christian love that put Rose in this Day One reality that felt unreal. God's will. Around her the room was still.

"What must I do, God?" she whispered. "What must I do?"

And then, like magic, it came to her.

Bibliomancy was an ancient practice. When in need, one would pray a question and then open the Bible; the first verse the eyes fell upon was believed to be the answer to the question—*a direct message from God* —providing clarity during stressful times. The tear-streaked cover of her King James Version slipped in Rose's hand when she opened it. She wiped her cheeks, and her eyes fell upon the page. One verse, of all the words that lay open there, spoke.

For the Son of Man is a man taking a far journey …

Rose stared at the words, but with a sinking heart couldn't figure them to mean anything. How could Jesus taking a far journey have anything to do with her?

♑

"Intentional changes were made not only to have the Bible reflect an orthodox interpretation of scripture and developing church doctrine, but to correct what scribes thought were factual errors made by the gospel authors. For example, the author of the Gospel of Mark originally quoted an Old Testament verse from the book of Isaiah as prophecy that Jesus would be the Messiah. *Just as it is written in Isaiah the prophet, Behold I am sending a messenger before your face make straight his paths.* Later scribes realized that in actuality, this quote was incorrect. Nowhere in Isaiah could the prophecy be found. The words quoted in Mark actually represented an amalgamation of passages from Exodus[67] and Malachi.[68] But rather than question the legitimacy of the prophecy, the scribes simply altered the original words of in Mark to cover up the 'mistake.' The words now read, *'Just as it is written in* the prophets …'[69]

"Correcting this 'error' not only eliminated the problem of Mark's misattribution of the quotation,[70] it also maintained the belief that the coming of the Messiah, who the orthodox claimed was Jesus Christ, was prophesied hundreds of years earlier by the Hebrew scriptures."

Glances were exchanged.

"A similar 'correction' was made to the Gospel of Luke whereupon describing events in the early life of Jesus, the author tells the story of a twelve-year-old Jesus who remains behind at the temple to learn and speak with the religious teachers. It takes Jesus' parents three days to realize that he is gone. The moment of error occurs when the text refers to Mary and Joseph as Jesus' parents—a fatal error as far as the scribes were concerned, because according to the orthodox interpretation, Jesus was born of a virgin, impregnated by God. Therefore, Mary could be Jesus' mother, but Joseph could certainly not be listed as Jesus' father. And so the appropriate 'correction' was made. Luke now reads, *'Joseph and Mary knew not of it'* instead of '*his parents knew not of it'*.'"[71]

Murmurs spread, and Roger could feel it—the energy of people trying to figure things out.

"Other types of corrections were born from a need to correct what were deemed 'inconsistencies' between the four gospel stories. Inconsistencies that inspired great criticism from non-Christians who increasingly referred to the orthodox interpretation as *incongruous* with the reality of what the gospels originally said.

"'The evangelists were fiction writers,' Porphyry accused in his public treatise *Against the Christians*. 'Not observers or eyewitnesses of the life of Jesus. Each of the four contradicts the other in writing his account of the events of his suffering and crucifixion.'"[72]

Roger pulled a sheet from his quotes folder and placed it under the projector. "Take the last twelve verses of Mark, for example, in which Jesus is quoted to say:

> Go ye into all the world, and preach the gospel to every creature.

> He that believeth and is baptized shall be saved; but he that believeth not shall be damned.

> And these signs shall follow them that believe: In my name shall they cast out devils; they shall speak with new tongues; They shall take up serpents; and if they drink any deadly thing, it shall not hurt them: they shall lay hands on the sick, and they shall recover.

"The influence of these verses has been powerful and far-reaching. They have been used for centuries to justify missionary and evangelical zeal, and have even been used to justify various forms of physical and psychological violence by Christians toward non-Christians. They are verses used by particular sects of Christianity to justify or verify the experience of 'speaking in tongues,' and have even used by groups of Appalachian snake handlers who, to show their great faith, take poisonous snakes in their hands, believing that no harm will befall them.[73] The interesting thing about these verses, however, is that they are not part of the original Gospel of Mark at all, but were in fact added at a later date by scribes in an attempt to harmonize Mark's gospel with the endings in Luke and Matthew."[74]

More murmurs. If what Roger was saying was true, the gospels didn't actually contain the same endings, which, instead of taking at face value, the copyists changed to make them all say what looked to be the same thing. The woman at the back of the room was electric with blood flowing through her veins, with thought pulsing from head to toe. If this was true, it was incredible. If this was true—if the gospels never really said the same thing—what on earth did they say in the first place? Being there, in that room, felt to her like destiny.

"Mark's gospel," Roger continued, "actually ends at chapter 16, verse 8. It closes with a scene where two women named Mary arrived at the cave in which Jesus was buried only to find him no longer there. An angel of the Lord then appears to the women and says, 'go and tell the disciples what has happened here.' But the women don't because they are too afraid.[75] They simply leave, and because of their fear, no one hears then of the resurrection. The orthodox scribes, while they appreciated Mark's take on the story of Jesus because it was so popular, knew that his original abrupt ending would not do, because it did two things: It contradicted the endings of Matthew and Luke, which said that Jesus reappeared to the disciples—of course, both Matthew and Luke disagree about what happened when Jesus reappeared, what Jesus said, and when he resurrected to join the right hand of the Father in heaven— but the main point for the scribes was that Mark's gospel, ending so abruptly, forgot to mention that Jesus indeed did reappear and leave instructions with his faithful. Of course, by 'forgetting' to mention this, Mark's gospel did not accurately reflect the orthodox doctrine that after Jesus died for the sins of mankind, he was raised on the third day, reappeared to his disciples to leave them with instructions, and then ascended to heaven to sit at the right hand of the Father until his return on Judgment Day. Jesus' resurrection symbolized the orthodox belief that on Judgment Day even the dead would be resurrected to rejoin Christ in eternity. *Therefore*, adding to Mark's ending became crucial in the eyes of the scribes. And so the ending was changed, or rather *expanded* to say what the orthodox needed it to say."

"Words, they're just words," a woman said, her voice shaking. "If the meaning stays the same, what are a few changes here and there … It's just a few words," the woman repeated, dramatically rolling her eyes as if she couldn't see the point of the mention of any of it. She picked at her sweater nervously. "What does it matter if each gospel reflects the other *exactly*? They are all telling the same story."

"But that's just the thing, you see." Roger said. "They aren't."

♈

Mateo remembered feeling astounded by the things that he had learned, astounded and charmed. Pleased. He knew that Virgo and Pisces were not the *actual* mothers of every human, but found the symbolism of what they represented quite beautiful. In particular, he liked the idea of being able to look up at the stars at night and be reminded by all the world around him of the sacredness of his own existence, the sacredness of all existence.

The gospel story of the Journey of Souls was astrology as symbolic theology at its best.

"Come," Master Lael said, motioning for them to move to the lush seating area behind them. Mateo took one last admiring glance at Virgo and then moved eagerly, sitting as close as he could to the mysterious marble box he had noticed earlier. The lapis lazuli still shimmered; the air around them stirred with a warm breeze. Once settled, to Mateo's delight, Master Lael reached for the marble box, and with a strength that proved he was far from being a fragile old man, lifted its heavy lid with ease. From inside there emerged yet another box, this one simple, with an ancient script carved on its lid. Mateo recognized the writing immediately as a Greek proverb, "*I am a child of Earth and the starry skies, but my race is of heaven alone.*" He smiled—even the ancient Greeks knew about the Journey of Souls! Mateo watched then as Master Lael carefully placed the wooden box between them and, just as carefully, removed *its* lid and reached inside.

Like the olive tree before, the miniature piece of art that Master Lael pulled from the box took Mateo's breath away. It was fascinatingly exquisite … all of its moving pieces, the perfection of the shapes.

The piece was a much smaller, mobile version of the very Zodiac that adorned the floor next to them. One that, as you turned its pieces, showed *how* the constellations moved across the night sky—how they rose on the horizon with the sunset and dipped again beyond the next horizon with the sunrise. A large sun that looked made of amber, copper, and gold moved around the perimeter of the apparatus, which also had marked upon it silver lines that mirrored the giant *Zōion,* the twelve hours of night that passed as the constellations livened the sky.

"In the Gospel," Master Lael said, "the whole world is incorporated into telling the story of the soul journey through human life. Certain symbols are prolific, which means you will find them no matter where in the world the stories are told; things like bread and fish as spiritual food for man, water as a symbol for the human body or the physical reality of the human life experience. But other symbols too, are very significant—" He allowed Mateo a moment to guess.

Mateo looked around the cave and saw the familiar shade of warmth that touched by glow or tendril every mural and carving; that spread itself on the floor into each of the six libraries; that connected every aspect of the gospel story. The sun.

"Yes," Master Lael smiled. "The sun is a very important symbol in the Gospel, because it represents many things, but most importantly the light of godliness that exists within you. It represents what is immortal about your very being, your soul, and the cycle of your soul journey into and out of human life."

It was the sun of God. The sun—symbolizing the magic of God in the world; the presence of godliness in human lives.

Master Lael then held up the apparatus between them and began to turn a small lever. When he did, the sun on the apparatus began to make its journey across the sky. It dipped below the horizon in the west and then rose again in the east, the constellations moving in tandem. Mateo let go a small sound of amazement. Carved on the arm that held the sun were the words, *Vita mutatur, non tollitur*: Life is changed, not taken away.

"The setting sun symbolizes the birth of the soul into human life. The rising sun symbolizes the resurrection of the soul from the body after the body expires. The cycle of the sun represents the journey of the soul through different parts of the human experience. It is a perpetual cycle, impregnated with divine meaning."

Mateo watched the sun set and rise, and imagined his soul doing the same thing, setting into the physical human experience and rising again from it.

"In ancient times," Master Lael said, "the descent of the soul into the human body was described as a type of 'death.' Not because the soul actually died, but because it became contained within matter. In this way human life was called the 'death' through which the soul lives. Sunset symbolized the start of human life for this reason—because in setting, the sun sinking below the horizon imaged a containment of divine light, the soul immersed in earthly matter. Sunrise, on the other hand, was the freeing of the soul from matter."

"Resurrection," Mateo looked up at his teacher.

"Rebirth," Master Lael smiled.

The apparatus turned and sparkled; the soul was born and resurrected, born and born again. Mateo's father had been right. Had he been younger, he might have lost interest, wanted to go outside and play, but right now, Mateo felt riveted. After all, this was a story about him.

The apparatus moved in the silent perpetuity of the universe, propelled by the quiet, wonderful mystery of it all. The sun rose and set, the constellations moved across the sky, the moon ebbed and flowed imaginary seas. The components moved soundlessly until a small click indicated a position of importance had been reached. Suddenly, the brightest star in the universe had moved into a very prominent position.

The only thing Mateo knew about the Sirius star was that it symbolized one thing: the spiritual reality of man. Master Lael confirmed, "Yes, the reality that the workings of the world are alive with meaning. For example, the fact that you are here *right now*, learning what you are learning, is no mistake." He then encouraged Mateo to look closer—to see for himself if he could understand why this precise moment, midnight on December twenty-fourth, with the Sirius star positioned directly over Egypt, was so important.

Mateo inspected carefully, hovering his fingers over the pieces, tilting his head right, then left.

And then he saw it.

There, on the horizon in the west was Virgo. Every human, incarnated with divine spiritual consciousness was born from Virgo at sunset, which always occurred in the west. Mateo smiled. The position of the stars signified the spiritual reality of life itself. It was a celestial alignment that mimicked the cycle of the sun, which itself reflected the spiritual truth of every human being on Earth.

"It is because of this sacred celestial alignment that December twenty-fifth is sacred." Master Lael spoke an ancient wisdom. "For it is on *this* day that the universe reflects more than our physical reality, it resonates with our spiritual truth: the presence of the divine in our bodies, of godliness and Providence in the world. It is a night to honour our most base realities: evolution and the presence of God in all things—which connects us to each other and guides on our journeys."

But there was another reason December twenty-fifth was special: It was also the day on which the sun, after having journeyed southward for the length of the year, began to return to the sky. The light of day began to outshine the darkness of winter.

"*This* is the Truth that Never Perishes," Master Lael said, placing the constellation apparatus back in its sacred hold.

At 12, Mateo was unable to put into words what he was coming to comprehend that day, but all these years later, he knew very clearly what had begun to take place in those moments. For the first time, he was coming to understand that even though much of it was beyond description, there was meaning in *everything*. That being human was not just about having a body and being alive, it was about engaging in the *experience* of *being* alive—all the while evolving into a better version of self. And Mateo knew, at the end of that first day, that he was in the process of doing just that … *evolving.*

♌

The rest of Farah's memories came in flashes. Certain details sharp and clear, others hazy, but always, what was certain and unmistakable, what rose up in the back of Farah's throat or spread out from her stomach like a smothered explosion, was how she felt when she remembered. The *feelings* that all those remembered words left impressed upon her skin, or in some cases, branded there.

All over her body she felt them like scar tissue. Varying degrees of residual damage where words had gouged, scraped, and sliced through her flesh, where fear had been poured in like vinegar, and doubt rubbed in like salt. Words that created festering wounds deep inside, that slapped her across the face or hooked under her arms to carry her. That supported Farah, or dragged her unwillingly across the floor. That had been poured over her head like anointing oil. That celebrated and defiled her. That lifted her up ... that pushed down upon her chest to hold her under water while she waited for the Holy Spirit to fill her.

Words. With their great power. To build, tear apart. To suffocate. That could heat the air around her like the flames of hell, suck out all of the oxygen until she thought she might faint. Feelings and words were all that were left.

"Which is ironic," Farah said, pulling the wrap Sophia had handed her more tightly around her shoulders. She couldn't stop shivering. "Being that one of the first sermons I ever heard was about *not* listening to your feelings."

Sophia, about to sit, looked taken aback.

Farah gave a shivery nod. "I was told that the Bible, God's word, should be my only authority. That as a Christian I can only trust what the Bible tells me, not what my feelings tell me. Basic Instructions Before Leaving Earth, A Chapter a Day Keeps the Devil away, all that sort of thing. I was taught that my feelings are unreliable because they are born in my body, which is primarily a field sown with sin." Farah shrugged. "I just find it ironic," she glanced toward Mephistopheles, "that the only thing I have left so near the end of it all, is how I feel."

Sophia stirred her tea slowly, her spoon tapped lightly, intermittently, on the inner edges of her cup. "So what happened after that day in the park?"

Farah gave a mordant smirk. "The Lord's Prayer."

*

It sounded unbelievable, Farah knew—a Christian who had never been to church—but it was true.

Farah had been a Christian for two years but had never been to church. She didn't know she had to go; no one in her family went to church; none of her friends did, so going wasn't even something that Farah could conceive. It was out of her frame of reference.

Until the Lord's Prayer.

Who would have thought that something existed that everyone seemed to know but Farah? A prayer *designed* to please God *and* help get people to heaven if they prayed it correctly. In fact, according to Jesus, the Lord's Prayer was the *only* way to pray, which terrified Farah even more upon finding out because it too was a prayer she had gone her whole life never having heard.

> Our Father who art in heaven,
> hallowed be thy name.
> Thy Kingdom come,
> Thy will be done.
> On earth as it is in heaven.

Everyone sat around the table, heads bowed, hands clasped. A new friend had invited Farah to spend the night.

At first Farah simply watched, fascinated that the friend and her family were all doing and saying the same thing, but then she noticed the father looking at her, his mouth still speaking the words. Farah's cheeks burned with the distinct feeling of not doing what everyone else was.

> Give us this day our daily bread;
> And forgive us our trespasses
> As we forgive those who trespass against us;
> Lead us not into temptation,
> But deliver us from evil.

The prayer continued, but Farah was at a loss. She didn't know the words. The best she could do was bow her head, close her eyes, and pretend.

> For thine is the kingdom and the power and the glory.
> Amen.

"Amen," Farah echoed, a second too late.

And then it was food being passed. Please and thank yous, grateful nods, the general din of a family dinner, until the question that had been hovering unidentified in front of the father's mouth since noticing Farah didn't pray, was finally asked. "So tell me, Farah," he smiled in a voice inviting, curious, and yet somehow suspicious. "Are you a Christian?"

Without hesitation, Farah nodded proudly. "Yes," she said, helping herself to some rice. "Yes, I am. I got saved by Jesus in the park, and now I get to go to heaven."

The father watched Farah steadily, as if trying to figure something out. He chewed his dinner slowly. "What church do you go to?"

Church? Farah thought. "I don't go to church," she answered. Again, the distinct feeling that what Farah said somehow mattered.

"Ah," the father said, "well, that explains it." He passed his wife a knowing glance.

Somehow Farah felt caught in a net, or like she needed to explain, or as if everyone at the table was looking at her deciding something. "But I *am* a Christian," she assured—or explained. "I am going to heaven," she assured them—or herself. Farah wanted to say that she was filled with the Holy Spirit, that Jesus had taken control of her life and filled her plump full with the spirit that day in the park, but a tiny part of her knew that might be a lie … in fact that tiny part of her—like a second, quickened heartbeat—had become a constant patch of worry, because Farah *hadn't* felt any different after that man left the park with his girls and Farah with Jesus. All she could hear, for *ages* after the man left, was the sound of leaves clapping; all she could feel was the sun on her face. Nothing inside of her seemed different. But that was Farah's quiet secret. She kept thinking that maybe, just maybe, one day she would wake up and notice a difference, that maybe she didn't feel it yet because she wasn't grown up yet.

"But you don't even know the Lord's Prayer," one of the little brothers said with his mouth full. His mother admonished his manners.

So *that* was what it was. The Lord's Prayer.

"Yeah," another brother said, sporting a mustache of freshly sipped juice. "You don't even know how to pray the way God wants you to pray, and you think that you're going to get to *heaven*?" The boys giggled as if Farah were stupid. This time the father passed a stern look. The boys dropped their eyes.

Farah's tiny patch of worry felt attached by invisible threads to everyone at the table, everyone who knew the prayer that she didn't. A God-*approved* prayer. And she couldn't help but wonder if *that* was the reason she didn't feel any different inside: She didn't know how to pray.

Something her new friend's family moved quickly to remedy. "I know just what to do," the mother said to her husband, after tucking the girls into bed.

What happened next set the course for the rest of Farah's life.

*

The next morning Farah accompanied her friend's family to church. It was the first of dozens she would spend her life attending. Searching through.

The sermon was about to begin, and the mother quickly ushered the family to a pew, passing each of the kids a hymn book. As the organ music began to play, Farah looked up. All around her the voices of a congregation began to sing:

> *There is a Fountain filled with blood,*
> *Drawn from Emmanuel's veins,*
> *And sinners plunged beneath that flood lose all their guilty stains.*

But that was all Farah heard.

Before her was a scene she had never in her life borne witness to. One that held her gaze with a grip so powerful, it caused her surroundings to fade away. And while she was aware of being surrounded by people singing, and heads bowed to read from hymn books, by palms held forward in praise, Farah's gaze remained completely fixed. Looking at *it* filled her with things. Awe. Shock. Curiosity. Its strangeness horrified her—its looming morbidity—and yet, she found it also filled her with a fearful respect because she had no frame of reference for it, no idea how to define what she was seeing. All Farah knew was that for *it* to be so prominent, hung high above the church altar, overseeing the congregation, it must somehow be *incredibly* important. She could do nothing but stare. Repulsed. Fascinated by the shapes, clearly carved with the precision of an artist who wanted to communicate something *explicitly*. That was clear. Even the blood, polished and shining, had intention—the way it dripped down over his varnished skin, over gigantic stakes hammered through his feet and palms. And the body: muscles strained with agony, a head bowed from exhaustion, a gouge in the ribs where the flesh had been torn … the sight was dreadful, and yet it was exquisite. Farah's friend nudged her and showed her where to sing from on the page:

> *He died that we might be forgiven*
> *He died to make us good.*
> *That we might go at last to heaven,*
> *Saved by his precious blood.*

A quiet moment then occurred within the depths of Farah's soul. The moment between contemplation and realization. Suddenly Farah's eyes widened and she looked up again reeling. The hymn continued.

There was no other good enough to pay the price of sin;
He only could unlock the gate of heav'n and let us in.

Farah's mouth went dry. The man hanging from the cross, nailed there and bleeding, staring out at her under heavy eyelids … was *Jesus* whose burden was suddenly burning into Farah's soul.

That was what he had been through.

That was how he had died.

For her.

For *her* sins.

The air in Farah's lungs felt heavy. She dropped her gaze but then raised it again to the tortured Jesus; angst and guilt wracked her heart as she was tugged by her sleeve to sit down. The hymn was over. The preacher's voice rang out. Everything felt fuzzy. He read from a giant Bible that lay open upon a wooden altar.

"And God saw that the wickedness of man was great in the earth, and that every imagination of the thoughts of man's heart was only evil continually. And it repented the Lord that he had made man on the earth, and it grieved him at his heart."[78] The minister looked up solemnly.

Farah listened very carefully, and that day she came to understand *how* Jesus died for her sins (because it had never really made sense to her).

Jesus was a Jew, one of God's Chosen People. It was through the Jews that God meant the world to be changed. Jesus came to change the world. His death was given to humankind as a gift; all humans had to do was accept that his death was for them. That he took their sins and gave his life as a final sacrifice, the purest sacrifice, to reconcile humankind to God. To wash away what we inherited from Adam and Eve. Accepting that Jesus was the Son of God who died for our sins was God's Rule. That was the Condition. No other belief, rite, sacrifice, superstition, religion, or religious practice would suffice; it *had* to be faith in Jesus Christ, Lord and Saviour. That, or be damned. From what Farah understood, it was as if Jesus had come down to earth, opened up his arms, swept up all the sin and stuck it to himself so that when he died, it would all go with him. This was how Jesus 'died for our sins'.

But as Farah listened, terrified, forlorn, she couldn't stop her mind from thinking: Why, if Jesus took up all the sin and died with it two thousand years ago, was she still *born* a sinner? And why, if he died for her sins, was she *still* born separated from God? It sounded to her like, after Jesus died, she should then have been born sin-free—*born* saved.

"Uh-uh," the older brother whispered, during one of the hymns. "You are only saved if you *believe* that he died for you. Otherwise, you are still chock full of sin. Head to toe. Even your hair. You have to *believe* then God will forgive you. Don't worry; the longer you're a Christian, the more it will make sense."

So Farah didn't worry, and tried instead to think about something other than the wooden Jesus looking down upon her, his gaze imploring or pleading or crying out … for *something*.

"Did you know that God sacrificed Jesus in front of his own *mother?*" The younger brother whispered.

Farah's eyebrows shot up.

"Uh-huh, it's true. Look, there's Mary right there," the boy's finger pointed skyward. Farah's gaze followed it to a series of stained glass windows … and there she was, a woman, kneeling at Jesus' feet, reaching up helplessly toward her dying son—her robe the most beautiful colour of stained-glass blue. It made Farah want to cry. The whole thing was just so tragic.

"This is why we pray in Jesus' name," the sermon continued. "Because Jesus is our *only* link to God, through him *only* are we able to have a personal relationship with God. No other religion will bring you authentically to God. Jesus is the *only* bridge."

Farah's eyes traced the head of each nail pounded through Jesus' hands and feet, holding his body fast to the wood. *I would never have asked you to do that for me*, she thought. *I would never have wanted you murdered.* She looked at Jesus with the angst and genuine sorrow of wanting to change something she could do nothing about. *I'm sorry*, she thought at Jesus. *I'm so sorry for what happened to you.* For the rest of the sermon, Farah's attention drifted. Her thoughts were very busy. Busy thinking about Jesus, busy feeling ashamed of her sin, busy wishing she could take it back—Jesus' suffering. Her disappointing God.

*

"Nine months before Jesus was born, a woman named Mary was impregnated by a ray of light from God. She was a virgin and she married a man named Joseph—"

"So that she didn't get a bad reputation."

"Shut up. *I'm* telling it. On December twenty-fourth, Mary gave birth to a baby boy in a manger. A star, the brightest star in the sky, heralded his birth. This baby boy was Jesus."

"Away in a manger, no crib for a bed …"

"I *said*, shut *up*."

"Jesus was born of the Virgin Mary," Farah repeated, writing it down. She wanted to get all the details right.

"Yes," the friend nodded. "Jesus was born of the Virgin Mary. Mother Mary. The Old Testament said that the Messiah would be born of a virgin—that's how we know Jesus was the Messiah."

But Farah had never heard the term *messiah* before.

The second younger brother rolled his eyes at her again. "The *Messiah*," he said, "is the saviour of humankind. He is meant to *liberate* humankind from political and spiritual bondage." The boy huffed, clearly unimpressed by Farah's lack of knowledge.

"Jews don't believe the Messiah has come," the youngest brother spoke for the first time. "But Christians know the Messiah was Jesus."

"I'm telling the story." The friend pinched both her brothers this time. "When Jesus was twelve, he went to the temple with his parents and *astounded* everyone by starting to teach the religious teachers—"

"He didn't teach them," the youngest brother spoke again, blocking a pinch with one hand. "The Bible says he began to ask questions and *learn* from them."

"Whatever," the friend said, blocking her youngest brother by turning her back to him. "Basically, Jesus knew more than anyone about God, and the people that knew him, Mark, Matthew, Luke, and John, wrote down his story so that the rest of the world could know who he was and what he did for us."

*

Farah's next memory was of dread pressing cold against her skin and the dying Jesus looming larger and larger over her head. She was taking small steps forward to the front of the church, and words were echoing in her head.

Eat the flesh.

Drink the blood.

"We're going to take Communion[80] now," her friend whispered. "At the Last Supper, Jesus told his disciples that they had to eat bread as his flesh and drink wine as his blood in remembrance of him."[112]

Eat the flesh.

Drink the blood.

"Come child," the minister beckoned kindly for Farah to step forward.

Eat the flesh.

Drink the blood.

But Farah felt rooted. The minister looked confused, and Jesus' face looked down upon her, still pleading, still begging her to do *something*. "You *have* to do it, Farah," the friend whispered, pushing her forward. "Jesus said, 'Do this in remembrance of me'. Do it for Jesus, Farah. It's what *He* wants."

By now the minister realized Farah had never before taken Communion. He smiled reassuringly and beckoned her, holding out the flat bread. "Close your eyes and take the bread in your mouth, child." His voice was calm. Encouraging. Patient. Kind. It said, "*This is the bread which cometh down from heaven, that a man may eat thereof, and not die.*[81]"

Jesus was right above Farah's head now, looking down.

"Take it," the friend said, "it will show Jesus that you love him."

"Don't forget," the minister smiled, "God is watching."

With that, Farah's heart leapt and she stepped quickly forward, her hands clasping each other tightly. She closed her eyes and opened her mouth and tried not to cringe as she imaged the bread about to taste like the raw bloody flesh of the dead body of Jesus on the cross above her head. When the tasteless leaven dissolved on Farah's tongue, her imagination made her gag.

When the wine was placed at her lips, Farah parted them, terrified of the rusty, ancient blood she was being told she had to drink. The wine rushed into her mouth, the blood cold and sour. Farah took the mouthful and then opened her eyes. The minister was smiling down on her. Jesus loomed morbid and pleading above them, and Farah's eyes began to strain with tears. She couldn't bring herself to swallow the 'blood,' and when her stomach lurched, she spat the wine onto the minister's holy white robes where it soaked into the fabric in a splatter of sacrament. The colours of the stained glass windows filled Farah's eyes then, rich and bright and all around her, brought to life by the sun streaming through them. Her eyelids fluttered briefly and the last thing Farah saw was Mary's face grieving, her stained glass hands caressing her dead son's feet, whose very blood had just been in Farah's mouth. Farah remembered being on the ground thinking that she wanted to crawl out of her human skin—then God's Son wouldn't have had to die, she wouldn't have to drink his blood, and God would never have been repentant that she was born. In the background, voices were singing:

> *Amazing grace, how sweet the sound*
> *That saved a wretch like me*
> *I once was lost, but now am found*
> *Was blind, but now I see.*

Then the room went black.

The rest of Farah's memories came like this:

Questions. A lot of them. *A Chapter a Day to Keep the Devil Away* … but what if the Devil had already arrived? Could a chapter a day get the Devil out? It seemed every time Farah turned around, she had a question about the Bible, about the things Matthew, Mark, Luke, and John said, about why God or Jesus did something or why someone said something else. Always her; always questions.

Like: "How is it possible that Adam and Eve's sons, Cain and Abel, could marry wives after Adam and Eve were banished from the Garden of Eden? [82] I thought they were the first humans, so where did Cain and Abel's wives come from?"

Or: "How come, if all humans inherited Adam and Eve's shame for their nakedness, tribes in Africa and South America don't seem to have any trouble being naked at all?" From what Farah could see, those tribes only felt shame about being naked when they were told that they should.

Farah also wanted an explanation for God's seemingly arbitrary decision at Babel, where everyone in the world, who all spoke one language, was working together in harmony and building a city "whose top may reach unto heaven."

> And the Lord came down to see the city and the tower … and the Lord said, "Behold the people is one and they have all one language; and this they begin to do: and now nothing will be restrained from them which they have imagined to do.
>
> "Go to, let us go down, and there confound their language, that they may not understand one another's speech …" Therefore is the name of it called Babel; because the Lord did there confound the language of all the earth: and from thence did the Lord scatter them abroad upon the face of all the earth.

"If everyone was getting along, why would God intentionally want to cause disharmony on earth?" she asked. "And who does God mean when he says, 'Us'? Let *us* go down and confound their language—who was God talking to or about or with? Other gods?"

That one got Farah in serious trouble. Her Bible study teacher very angrily called her a blasphemer and said, "Questioning can get you to hell as quickly as stealing. Do you realize what you are doing? You are questioning *God*." Farah had pressed her lips together in shame, but the questions still swirled.

Then there was the issue of the Exodus—the escape of the Hebrews from oppression in Egypt—which kept Farah up nights.

Led by Moses, the Israelites escaped to the Promised Land when Moses parted the Red Sea for them all to cross safely. The water then came crashing down behind them, killing all the Egyptian soldiers in pursuit. There were several problems Farah had with this story, but the most practical was a question of geography. If the story were true, and the Red Sea really had been parted by a strong east wind[83] (Farah had looked on a map, as many maps as she could, but the problem remained), in order for the Israelites to have crossed safely (three million in one night!), then a *westerly* wind would have been the wind to free them. Geographically, an *easterly* wind parting the Red Sea would have caused a wall of water to completely block the path to freedom, if not decimate the group entirely as they waited on the western bank.

Finally, someone asked, "Farah, have you been baptized?"

Baptized? Farah shook her head, no. What was 'baptized'?

"Ah," everyone nodded knowingly. "Well, that explains it. You aren't able to read the Bible with a heart that is pure or with a mind that will understand it, because you have not been baptized. Baptism washes away *all* of your sins and makes a clear path for the Holy Spirit to enter you."

Farah could not believe what she just heard. That was it! She clapped and jumped in her seat. "Yes!" she said, "I would very much like to be baptized, thank you." The Bible study teacher smiled appraisingly and chuckled at Farah's refreshing eagerness. So many young people these days just stopped coming to church with their parents or even turned away all together, sometimes *with* their parents. "Maybe once you are baptized," the teacher said, "you will stop questioning and start being a Christian."

So it really wasn't *just* about believing, there were really specific things Farah had to do—words she had to know, ways of praying, church to attend, baptizing to get! Farah was bursting, partly from excitement, but also with incredulity over the fact that all this time had passed *again*, when she thought she was back in God's good graces, when she thought she was a Christian, and yet this terribly important thing existed of which she had no idea, no frame of reference to even ask about. *Baptized.* She was going to be baptized. This was *how* to believe in Jesus so that God approved. This was *how* to get to heaven.

Farah went home and skipped ahead in her Bible, past the rest of the Old Testament and straight into the New Testament—the *new* word about Jesus—to the part her teacher told her to read, the part about Jesus being baptized in the river by John the Baptist. She read the scene again and again aloud to herself, "…*and lo, the heavens were opened up unto him and he saw the Spirit of God descending like a dove, and lighting upon him.*[84] *And then the heavens opened up and a voice was heard to say, 'You are my son, in you I am well pleased.'"*

This was wonderful, Farah thought. It was an actual, *physical* experience. It said right here in the Bible that the Holy Spirit would enter her and she would be filled. Farah couldn't wait. She couldn't *wait* to be baptized. This was going to be her finest hour—when God finally turned his face and his open arms to *her*.

*

"And all flesh shall see the salvation of God. I baptize you in the name of the Father, the Son, and the Holy Spirit."

The minister held Farah firmly and immersed her entire body under the water. She held her breath as her head went under and stared wide-eyed, beneath the cool, clear liquid. The minister's voice was muffled, the cross above him distorted in her vision. She could hardly see a thing, but still she looked for it, her eyes wide and ready. She didn't want to miss a moment, not a single second of seeing the Holy Spirit descending from heaven to fill her. Fix *her*. Save *her*.

A moment later, Farah was lifted out of the water. She emerged, blinking, to the sounds of applause, to the sounds of "*Praise Jesus*" and voices singing "*Jesus walk, Jesus walk with me.*" But that was it.

No dove. No opening of the heavens. No beacon of light. No God there waiting *well pleased*.

Farah looked and looked, but saw nothing. There was nothing inside of her but wondering: where God was, what she had done wrong that He would not, it seemed no matter what she did or didn't believe, save *her*. But then suddenly she had another thought: Maybe the baptismal scene wasn't supposed to be taken *literally*. *Maybe* she was meant to experience something that *felt* like those things happening! Farah quickly closed her eyes and waited for it. Waited for what she had waited for in the park that day, for what she had waited for when she went to church, for what she waited for now … the change, the difference *inside*. But still … nothing. A feeling of panic began to rise up from deep within her then, and the minister's beaming face, the hugs of congratulations from those around her began to seem otherworldly. Farah felt numb, and her human skin itched her. Scraped. Like a hair shirt.

In the bathroom she stood soaked and shivering in front of the mirror. A tear slipped down her cheek followed quickly by another, but Farah's expression remained stoic. She stepped forward and leaned as close as she could to her own reflection. Did *anything* look different? *Anything*? Her fingers touched lightly at her cheeks, her forehead, under her chin. She closed her eyes again; hoping, begging God to let her *feel* Him fill her up … but all she heard was Mephistopheles chuckle.

When the bathroom door swung open, two more girls and a woman entered dabbing their faces, squeezing the residual water from their hair with towel-draped hands. They were beaming. Farah quickly turned on the faucet and tried to splash away the misery on her face. The woman walked over and hugged Farah around the shoulders, "Praise Jesus!" she said. "Isn't this a wonderful day? God has blessed us with the Holy Spirit! Thank God for Jesus! Without Him, none of this would be possible. God bless you, young lady. Hallelujah!"

Farah looked up and watched the woman's reflection—her soaked purple robe, her cheeks rosy with freshness and vigor, her eyes squinted closed to match her toothy grin—probably, Farah thought, because she was so filled with the Holy Spirit that she *had* to grin that way. The woman was so— flamboyant, so seemingly 'on fire for God,' and saturated with a deep sense of awe for feeling it.

Farah, on the other hand, looked different. Her hair was soaked and dripping against her pallid skin, even her lips looked lacking in colour—a reflection of her spiritually dead body, she began to feel sure. Mephistopheles agreed.

"A-men!" the woman suddenly exclaimed loudly with a clap. Farah started awkwardly, but then smiled back with as much gusto as she could muster. One more shoulder squeeze and Farah was finally left alone.

Alone. Farah thought, watching in the mirror as the woman retreated into a changing stall.

Better get used to it, Mephistopheles whispered in her ear.

*

"So did anything change?"

"Nothing," Farah said bitterly, averting her eyes as Mephistopheles twinkled his fingers sweetly at her from outside the window. She shook her head and looked up at Sophia with bloodshot eyes. "Do I looked saved to you?"

*

From the point of her failed baptism Farah immersed herself completely in the New Testament, in particular the gospels of Matthew, Mark, Luke, and John.

She wanted to find out as much as she could about Jesus, about the things he had said. "Something's missing," she said, flipping frantically through her Bible. The voice of the man in the park echoed in her head. *Everything the Bible says is true and perfect, with no mistakes. It means the Bible is a pure reflection of the heart and will and wants of God. Take it. Read it. Get to know it well, for it is the closest thing on earth we have to God.*

"What else?" She looked and read and looked and read. "What *else?*" Urgently.

But she gained no solace from this immersion, only what she imagined was more of the devil creeping in, more of the devil taking her over, making her *think*. Not abating her questions, but fanning the fire of them. More and more Farah began to feel panicked, like she had to hurry up or escape or like she was trapped. She couldn't escape it: Thought. Thinking. This feeling of nervousness in her chest. These pinpricks of questions.

Murderer. Thief. Burn.

"All of these questions you allow to fill your head," a priest told her, "leave no room for Jesus."

*

The differences between the four gospels plagued Farah. She lay awake nights wondering how, if they were firsthand accounts, the details between each account could differ. In a final attempt she bought a notebook, titled it, and scribbled her notes as fast as she could think them:

A Diary of Thoughts and Questions: (to get them out so that Jesus can get in)

Matthew and Luke describe the Virgin Birth, but the details differ between each account   different things happen, Jesus is born in different places.

Mark and John make no mention of the Virgin Birth.

Matthew, Mark, and Luke say Jesus' ministry lasted three years.

John says Jesus' ministry lasted one year.

In Matthew, Mark, and Luke, Jesus cleanses the temple at the end of his ministry.

In John he does it at the beginning.

John said Jesus raised Lazarus from the dead—the other gospels make no mention of this miracle. None. (I mean he raised a guy from the dead here, people! Not worthy of notice? I think I would have noticed, and I certainly can't imagine forgetting!) Neither do the synoptic gospels mention Jesus turning water into wine. What the ?

Jesus talks differently in John. In Matthew, Mark, and Luke he speaks and ministers in parables, but in John, he doesn't speak in parables at all. In Matthew, Mark and Luke, Jesus never says, "I am" (for example, the way, the truth, the life), but in John, he says, "I am" all the time! (Again, I ask you, What the ?)

Eventually, Farah just asked. "Which version of Jesus' life is correct? Mark, Matthew, Luke, or John?"

"All of them." (Always the same answer.)

"All of them?" Farah's heart sank every time. She looked at the Book in her hands, "But … how?"

The reverend held up his hand. "The *differences* between the gospel stories don't matter. What matters is that *together*, they tell a greater story about a precious man named Jesus Christ who saved mankind by dying for our sins, and who was raised on the third day to sit on the right hand of the Father, and who will one day return to judge the world."

"But—,"

The priest held his hand up again, this time more firmly. "*No*, nothing else matters, Farah. These discrepancies you perceive are simply that—*perceived*. You cannot trust your own ability to understand the Holy Word, but have faith that if the Bible says it is true, then it *is*. There are no questions."

But they aren't perceived! Farah had thought angrily. She wanted to shake her Bible at all of them. *They're right in front of my face! What should be important details are completely different between them! Each of them sometimes seems to be talking about a completely different Jesus than the other! Jesus dies differently—says different things on the cross—in every single account, and all of them are 100 percent correct? 100 percent infallible?* She wanted to say "Bah!" and toss her Bible in the air in frustration, but instead Farah did what she knew they wanted her to do. "Thank you, Father," she said, and then walked away, convincing herself to just do what was suggested: read the Bible more to placate her questions.

And so Farah did. With a furrowed brow and a willing heart she read … and read … from Acts, Corinthians, Philippians, Thessalonians I and II,

Timothy, Hebrews, Peter, the Johns—all the way through to Revelations. She attended *more* Bible study, had more 'serious talks' with many more men of cloth. And when she had finally read it all, Farah closed her Bible with her mouth agape, questions raging inside of her, and a nervous energy tingling like pinpricks in her body. She stared at the Book, hardly able to breathe, for she realized that not only was she going to burn in hell for her sins and her questions, but for not realizing from the beginning what it took her years to realize: Jesus was *God*.

*

"*Jesus* is *God*," Farah told Sophia through a self-effacing, mordant smirk. "Who knew?" Outside the window, Mephistopheles shrugged and said, "I didn't." He looked incredibly amused. Sophia smiled at Farah's remaining sense of humor.

"Because *I* certainly didn't," Farah said. "After all the stories I had heard, Jesus sounded like a *completely* different person from God; everyone had always said that Jesus was the *Son* of God. If he was God why didn't they just call him that in all the stories? Why didn't they just call him that in *all* the gospels from the beginning? Why the ambiguity? Why didn't Jesus just say, 'I am God'?"

"I think there are many people in the world asking those same questions," Sophia commented quietly.

"Are there?" Farah demanded "Because if there are, I haven't met a single one. At least there weren't any in the churches I attended. *Everyone* seems to get it, Sophia. *Everyone* seems to understand something that I'm incapable of understanding." Tears welled in Farah's eyes and she grabbed her Bible. She flipped aggressively through the pages. Sophia knew where Farah was going; the most obvious contradiction between the gospel accounts: Jesus' last words on the cross. Tears choked Farah's voice as she read from Matthew: "*Just before he died Jesus said, 'My God, my God, why have you forsaken me?'*" The pages turned again, this time to Luke: "*...and Jesus shouted: 'Father, I entrust my spirit into your hands!'*" More pages; this time Farah stopped at John, her voice more aggressive, more desperate: "*...Jesus tasted the sour wine and then said, 'It is finished' before he bowed his head and gave up the ghost.*" Farah shook her Bible at Sophia. "These are *supposed* to be *firsthand* accounts! And yet they each tell a *different* story … they contain *significant* differences between each account. What am I missing?" Farah wiped angrily at tears now soaking her cheeks. "*What* am I missing? Does the Holy Spirit change the words of the Bible—does it alter reality so that I can finally read what *they* are reading? So that I can finally see what I seem incapable of seeing? Feel what I seem incapable of feeling? Will I too then be able to flail my arms about or faint in the aisles, or without a conscience consider myself more loved by God than others not a part of *my* church?"

Farah was weeping now; again she flipped through the pages, her urgency a tumultuous sea of desperation. "And Jesus said, '*Why callest thou me good? There is none good but one, and that is God.*'" She paused, and then read again, quoting Jesus: "'*Now I can go to the Father who is greater than I am.*'" She paused again. "'*Thou shalt worship the Lord thy God, and him only shalt thou serve*'"

The Bible slipped from Farah's fingers; she looked at Sophia, strained and exhausted. "One day soon afterward," she said, reciting from memory the words she had read and re-read, the words that echoed constantly in the back of her mind in a bewildered whisper, "Jesus went to a mountain to pray, and he prayed to *God* all night. And Jesus *said*," Farah whispered, silent tears now falling once again, "*Thou shalt worship the Lord thy God, and Him only shalt thou serve.*" She looked up darkly, as if she were in pain. "If Jesus is *God*," Farah whispered, "then who is he praying to?"

*

For years it went like this. Farah seeking ("*All men seek for thee*"[85]) in the company of the religious. So many different kinds: who lurched and swayed in the pews, who fainted and twitched in the aisles, who worshipped silently, piously. Who would do anything to help. Who were some of the most wonderful people she'd met, and some of the most horrible. Who praised Jesus quietly, loudly, enthusiastically, who took naps in church. Who laid on hands and prayed for all the violence in the world to end, for all the children in the world to be loved, for all of the wars to stop, for an end to pollution. Who prayed for God to Save the Whales or the Jews or the Muslims or the gays, to end oppression and poverty. Who, when they spoke in tongues would say, "God blesses people with gifts; we can speak in tongues because God has blessed us. If you continue to attend our church, He might bless you too." Words that made Farah want more than anything to speak what sounded like absolute gibberish, if it meant that God was choosing *her*, blessing *her*, saving *her*. Hands in the air, hands folded on laps, hands wrapped around Bibles. "Amens" and "Praise Jesus." Solemn hymns and charismatic congregations. Pious ministers and aggressive evangelist preachers: *Praise God! In Jesus' Name! Amen!* Farah attended and participated religiously … wanting so badly to be accepted back. But never any blessing came, nor odd behavioural gifts, nor any internal calm.

Nothing ever *felt* different and Farah knew that if God really could read her mind, he would know what her *true* thoughts were, her most honest wonders about religious things that just didn't seem to make sense, no matter how she tried to pretend otherwise. God would see that so much of what Farah was required to believe sat *uncomfortably*: Communion, flesh and blood, or the idea that every other person in the world, even if they were a good person, was going to burn in hell if they weren't a Christian—Gandhi, the Dalai Lama, community service workers, children, her mother—*good people* from different parts of the world were not going to heaven—some of them never even having heard the name *Jesus*. With these issues, Farah struggled deeply, until that final day, Farah's *final* day in church, the day she found out that there was no saving her. The day she decided she would never go back, that living in this misery of being filled with evil, of being terrified of God's disapproval, was not living. The day before she ended up on Sophia's couch. …

*

"Your eye is a lamp for your body," the priest said, quoting scripture. "A pure eye lets sunshine into your soul, but an evil eye shuts out the light and plunges you into darkness. A *pure* eye lets in the Holy Spirit. It seems to me, Farah, that if you've done everything required of you under the Lord, that you would have been filled with the Holy Spirit by now." The priest spoke somberly; his suggestion was implicit.

"So you think I have an *evil eye*?" Farah's shoulders slumped at the suggestion that there really was something wrong with her.

"It might seem so," the priest looked apologetic, and a little bit grateful that it wasn't him with the evil eye.

"But—" *How could this be*? Farah thought; she had done everything right.

"It makes sense, child." The priest reached to comfort her, but unsure what type of demon hovered within this girl, couldn't bring himself to place his hand upon her shoulder. He quietly pulled it away. "Some kind of evil inside of you—most likely caused by your constant sin of questioning and doubt—stops you from receiving the light of God. That is why when you read the scriptures you cannot receive the holy word, or understand it."

The words tumbled down over her. Piled and piled with a great weight into Farah's lap where she felt them begin to fester, dig beneath her skin. She trembled. It actually *did* make sense. All these years, all those people saying "I'll pray for you," all those hymns about the blood that she hated singing, all those times she dreaded taking Communion, all those verses that seemed confusing, all those contradictions she asked to be reconciled—had they even existed? The Holy Spirit couldn't get in, because with all the evil inside of her ... there was no room left.

"I think you should seek exorcism," the priest suggested softly.

Exorcism? Something inside of Farah cried out then, and her stomach lurched. She leaned forward and put her head in her hands, afraid she might faint.

"Then you can start over. From the beginning. Bible study, baptism, Communion, all of it. We can do it all over again, start from scratch."

Farah wanted to run. From the church, from God's judgment, from her sin-filled self.

Again, the priest made to pat Farah's back, but then pulled his hand away. The misery within the girl was achingly palpable, and it hurt him not to comfort her, but he too was afraid. He was merely human, a victim to evils, just as much as she. He wanted to help her though, and would do everything he could. "Go," he said gently. "Splash some water on your face. When you come back we will ring a priest I know who performs exorcisms."

When she came out of the bathroom, Farah didn't look back. Instead, she ran. Behind her she imagined God's open arms watching her go, still waiting for her to come back. His looking disappointed, and Jesus still looking down upon her, pleading, his body bloody on the cross. She stumbled dizzily down the church steps, retched over the railing, and remembered thinking then, *This must be what crazy feels like.* She ignored the sound of the priest calling after her and shakily unlocked the van door. Inside, Mephistopheles—fingernails and hair, gray ash for breath, and a body that loomed in her peripheral vision—was waiting for her, whispering suicide onto her skin.

Farah opened the door and vomited.

♋

Certain sections of Roger's notes were written as if he were speaking them. As she read, Rose could almost see him there, standing in front of her, his fingers lightly dusted with chalk, his skin healthy, his posture relaxed.

"In order to have the four gospels reflect the literalist interpretation of them, the differences between Mark, Matthew, Luke, and John needed to be homogenized as much as possible without altering the original words too drastically. But the contradictions between the four stories—meant to be telling the same story—were simply too many to ignore."

And then Rose read about differences. Differences that had been there all along, that she herself had read but somehow had never *seen*.

The Virgin Birth (did it or did it not happen?).

The length of Jesus' ministry (one or three years?).

But most strikingly, Rose read about what Roger called the most significant difference between the gospel accounts of Jesus life, death, and resurrection: *Jesus*.

"Most significantly, the way Jesus handles his torture, crucifixion, and death.

"How is it possible that these are firsthand accounts, and yet the Jesus in each account, aside from a similar grouping of sayings and parables, sounds like a completely different person between them?

"In Matthew and Mark for example (Matthew famously used Mark as a reference when he wrote his own account), Jesus is *silent* through his torture and crucifixion until the moment of his death on the cross when he finally cries out, *'My God, my God, why have you forsaken me?'*

"But in Luke, Jesus is calm as his destiny unfolds before him. He puts complete faith and trust in God's will and therefore doesn't struggle at all to face his own impending death. Instead of being silent on the way to his crucifixion, Luke writes that Jesus made many spiritually significant statements; for example, he tells the women that surround him not to weep for him, and he prays of those involved, *'Father, forgive them; for they know not what they do.'* He even declares to the criminals hanging in crucifixion on either side of him, *'Today thou shalt be with me in paradise,'* and instead of crying out in anguish that God had forsaken him when he dies, Luke's Jesus says something completely different. In complete faith and trust Luke's Jesus says, *'Father, into thy hands I commend my spirit.'*

"John's Jesus however, neither cries out in anguish nor reaffirms his trust in the will of the Father. In John, Jesus simply says, '*It is finished.*'"

Rose shook her head in disbelief. *How.* How had she never noticed these things? These *differences.* That Jesus was quoted saying completely different things and acting in completely different ways.

The Jesus Rose had learned about, the God-Jesus, was an amalgamation of all four gospels. All four gospels together made a complete story about the birth, life, ministry, death, and ascension of the Son of God. Didn't they? Her eyes were drawn back to the page.

"The style of Jesus' teaching also differs dramatically between the synoptic gospels and John. Throughout the synoptics, Jesus speaks in aphorisms and parables, using allegory to illustrate his message in the context of the human experience. He also uses nature to illustrate the point of his spiritual message. John's Jesus, on the other hand, does not use a single parable. Instead, the Jesus in John gives long, self-proclaiming and self-expanding soliloquies, lengthy discourses reminiscent of those given by the Hellenistic orators contemporary to Jesus' time.[86] John's Jesus says things like, '*I am the way, the truth and life*'; '*I am the light of the world*'; '*I am the bread of life*'; but the Jesus of the synoptics never blatantly self-proclaims nor insinuates that he is God. It is as if the Jesus of Matthew, Mark, and Luke is a completely different personage to the one described by John.

"And then there is the issue of the two extra miracles; two of the most significant and symbolic miracles attributed to Jesus—changing water into wine, raising Lazarus from the dead—get no mention whatsoever in the synoptics."[87]

The list *went on* and *on.*[88] Rose wanted to flip frantically through her Bible to double-check everything that Roger said, but she hesitated.

Instead, she squeezed her eyes shut. She didn't want to see the discrepancies confirmed. If the differences were there (and she knew they were, now that she thought about it) she didn't want to see them that way. She didn't *want* to see them as differences. She wanted to continue reading the four gospels as if they were one story building upon the other. She wanted to continue reading the books of the New Testament as if they were one story filling in the gaps of the other: like Matthew and Luke filled in the story where Mark forgot (the Virgin Birth, for example), or as if John really was the only one who heard Jesus say "I am" and all those other self-proclaiming things. She wanted to believe that Jesus had only wanted John to know about those extra two miracles. Even if Peter was supposed to have been there. Even if Mark's account of Jesus' life was supposed to have been dictated by Peter. "*Together* the gospels tell the story of *one mans' life*," she told herself. "*Together* they tell the complete story of Jesus."

Rose kept telling herself what she already believed, what she had always believed, again and again, over and over, until she lay down on the couch, until she was muttering it half asleep. Until it echoed in her dreams.

♑

Fresh air seeped through a small gap in the window Roger had opened earlier, meandered through the aisles, wrapped around shoulders, and brushed past cheeks. Those feeling faint were grateful for it, others shivered, a dozen or so breathed in quietly with their eyes closed, smiling. The air, to them, had never smelled fresher.

"To ignore the differences between the gospels is to ignore what each author was trying to tell us. To homogenize the gospel stories is to erase the distinct and calculated way the original authors wanted the story of Jesus to be known."

What everyone had yet to realize was that the greatest harm in Pious Fraud wasn't simply the fact that it was committed—the greatest harm of Pious Fraud was the incredible loss suffered as a result. The loss of *meaning*, and that was what Roger was here to talk about. The original meaning of the gospel texts, the one that existed before they were written down, before they were named *Matthew*, *Mark*, *Luke*, and *John*, before they ever became the foundation from which an orthodox religion could be built upon them. *What you are about to learn*, Roger thought, *you will never forget, because within this truth you will find yourself you will find the heart of humanity, Darwin, science, you will find God, and the furthest thing from the end of the world. You will find the glorious, awe inspiring, mysterious beating heart at the center of existence but most of all you will find possibility. Electric, swirling, ample, complete, calm. Endless possibility and growth.*

"Let me give you an example," Roger rifled through his papers. "The Gospel of Luke tells a story about Jesus—" A new sheet slid under the projector; Roger read aloud.

And he came out, and went, as he was wont, to the mount of Olives; and his disciples also followed him.

> And when he was at the place, he said unto them, Pray that ye enter not into temptation.
> And he was withdrawn from them about a stone's cast, and kneeled down and prayed.
> Saying, Father, if thou be willing, remove this cup from me: nevertheless not my will, but thine be done.

129

And there appeared an angel unto him from heaven strengthening him

And when he rose up from prayer and was come to his disciples, he found them sleeping for sorrow,

And said, Why sleep ye? Rise and pray, lest ye enter into temptation.

While he read, Roger could hear Bible pages flipping madly, a few people muttering, and he knew exactly why. There was a verse missing from the excerpt. But the missing verse was not part of the original. "As you might have guessed by now, verse forty-four is missing." Roger placed a new sheet on the projector. Verse forty-four, present.

And he came out, and went, as he was wont, to the mount of Olives; and his disciples also followed him.

And when he was at the place, he said unto them, Pray that ye enter not into temptation.

And he was withdrawn from them about a stone's cast, and kneeled down and prayed.

Saying, Father, if thou be willing, remove this cup from me: nevertheless not my will, but thine be done.

And being in agony he prayed more earnestly: and his sweat was as it were great drops of blood falling down to the ground

And there appeared an angel unto him from heaven strengthening him

And when he rose up from prayer and was come to his disciples, he found them sleeping for sorrow,

And said, Why sleep ye? Rise and pray, lest ye enter into temptation.

"These verses are most obviously a lesson on the importance of prayer in the face of temptation, but to the trained eye, they are much more than that. They are what is known as a *chiasmus*."[89] He pointed to each sentence as he spoke. "Chiasmus was a literary technique employed to intentionally yet poetically draw the attention of the reader to where the author wanted it.[90] The author of Luke was clearly very talented in this regard—as you can see here, the story begins and ends with Jesus' injunction to pray in order to avoid falling into temptation. And at the center of the story is Jesus' own prayer—one that juxtaposes his personal desire, with his greater desire that the Father's will be done.[91] This prayer is the center of the chiastic structure, which makes it the point of focus and, correspondingly, the key to the story's interpretation.[92] When you understand the presence of the chiasmus, you realize the author has undertaken a great effort to have the reader notice how Jesus illustrates emotional balance and trust in God's will during times of difficulty or stress. In contrast, his calm is juxtaposed to the behavior of the disciples who succumb to the temptation of sleep and who, later in the story, effectively turn their backs on Christ by fleeing from their own guilt.

"The author clearly wants the reader to understand Jesus' message as: Sometimes, in the face of temptation, what is best for us goes against that which we think we want. That our greatest wisdom is not always found in superficial or circumstantial realities, but in our spiritual reality which is constant and which we can only know through faith, trust, and calm.

"So why add verse forty-four then? Why ruin the chiasmus by inserting a sentence that focuses on physical suffering, pain, the sweating of blood, and Jesus' psychological angst leading up to his crucifixion?"

"To show that he's human," the Stirrer, once again. Bitter. Jaded.

"Yes," Roger nodded. "That is exactly why. The verse was added to make Jesus appear more human."

As Day One came to a close, Roger explained that the orthodox church had a big job on its hands, ensuring scriptures reflected the ever-developing orthodox doctrine. For if the verses didn't show that Jesus suffered physically, then his sacrifice would not have been a true sacrifice. He had to *suffer* for the sins of mankind; that was the great power in his death and in his blood—the suffering he endured *for* us. "And that is how and why Jesus had to be human *and* divine, divine *and* human, able to *suffer* as sacrifice, and yet able to rise again from the dead to exhibit the eternal life granted to those who worship him 'correctly.' But in the original gospels, Jesus wasn't divine and human, Jesus was something else." Roger closed his Day One folder. "With the addition of verse forty-four, *suddenly*, it is not Jesus' prayer and calm that we remember, but his agony, his mental anguish, and his blood."

"And the orthodox interpretation reigns," the Stirrer added, clearly disgusted. Roger stole a closer look at him—the pain behind his eyes, the betrayal, was abundant. Clearly, much of this information was not new to him, so why was he here? Perhaps, Roger thought, to see how it all comes together, because clearly, with all of that anger, the Stirrer had no idea.

"Hold it," someone—head bowed, hand pressed atop Bible, the other held up in a desperate plea—spoke out, trembling with contained emotion. "So basically what you're saying is that the Bible is meaningless."

"Oh no," Roger looked shocked. "I'm not saying *that* at all."

DAY TWO

Seek and ye shall find.

-Jesus

♈

Three is the number of spiritual transition, of rebirth and renewal of spiritual consciousness.

It garnered this prestigious title based on yet another cyclical cosmic occurrence: the waxing, waning, and rebirth of the moon. Three days was the transition period of the moon—from the time it disappeared, likened to the physical death of a human body, to the time it was reborn to continue its cycle anew—likened to the continuation of soul on its journey through different stages of life.

"The regeneration of the moon is symbolic of the physical aspect of the spiritual truth of every human being: that the soul is first 'born' into the physical body, that it journeys through the physical experience of being human, and that it is then born again out of the physical body. Resurrected from matter where it returns to its most natural form: energy. Light. The active vibration of love. In this way, every human is born first of water (matter) then of fire (spirit). These are the two births of man."

It was day two of Mateo's lessons. He had run as fast as he could down the Sanctuary steps and screeched to a halt under the archway, where Master Lael had been waiting. Beside them, an artisan carved a series of images that symbolized the number three. Without pause, Master Lael began to teach Mateo *why* three was a number so significant in the Gospel of Life.

"Three symbolizes transition from one state of spiritual awareness to another, resulting in a renewal of spiritual consciousness."

Mateo didn't know it then, but as he stood catching his breath, he was only moments away from learning the reason humans were born, which turned out to be something so obvious, so *simple* that without ever having to be told, Mateo realized deep down inside of himself, he already knew what it was. Which meant that other people did too. *Deep* inside. In their most honest heart—at the place where truth and morality existed as raw instinct, the same place where only love resides. *Everybody* knew the purpose of their existence because the purpose of human life was what propelled humans *forward*, what made them *seek* ... made them wonder and want to discover.

"Renewal of spiritual consciousness, transition from awareness to awareness, can occur only when we begin to understand the *whole* of what is real," Master Lael said, motioning for them to walk together. "The eyes," he began to explain, "are one part of the body. They *see*, but they do not reveal everything about reality. Your body, on the other hand, knows the world by its sense of touch, smell, taste, by *feeling*, and by feeling it sees the rest of what your eyes fail to. Why? Because that which can be quantified by physical evaluation is but one part of a greater whole; that which is *invisible* is the rest of what is real. And it is in the invisible where you will find the *rest* of what being human means."

*

That moment, the one where Mateo wondered with such intense, delightful curiosity what Master Lael would say next, became permanent in Mateo's body. The memory of it was physical—the loose pebbles beneath his soft-soled shoes, the change of temperature in the air as they passed each torch, brazier, and oil lamp. Warm. Cool. Warm. Cool. But mostly Mateo remembered the feeling of knowing that what he was about to learn was important in a way that was beyond the things he had known before. He was right.

*

"The Greek word for 'perfect'," Master Lael said, "is *telieos*. When you are perfect, you know *who* it is that you are you; as the Greeks say, *Know thyself*. To be *telios*," Master Lael said, "is to grow in your life as destiny designs. For example, the *telos* of an olive seed is to grow into a tree; the *telos* of a fish egg is to grow into a fish, and the *telos* of a human is to grow into spiritual maturity."[93]

Mateo had reflected deeply upon this. That every human, that he, was born to achieve many things in the context of his life, and that the driving force of his existence was his journey toward spiritual maturity. The *purpose* of life was evolution: evolution of mind, evolution of understanding, and evolution of self—which, Master Lael was quick to point out, could only truly take place when one truly understood as much as possible about who they were.

"To know thyself," Master Lael continued to explain, "means to understand who you are spiritually and physically. When you know yourself, you are healthy in and celebrate your individual journey. You understand, deep within you that the reason for life is life itself, and you are not afraid to be in awe of it. You are not afraid to embrace your soul journey and discover who it is you were born to be. When you live with this awareness in mind, this awareness awakened in your consciousness, you begin to live as what the gospel calls your *Ideal Self*. The ideal version of yourself: evolving toward spiritual maturity with spiritual and physical awareness, and using your knowledge to live the best life you can—*this* is the reason you are born—to become your best self, your ideal self, in the context of the human experience. It is this spiritual truth—about the journey of your soul through human life—that is illustrated by the gospel stories."

It was as if Master Lael's words were stirring awake a knowledge within Mateo that had been there all along, and right before his very eyes, Mateo could feel his awareness changing, feel his thoughts, his perceptions, *growing*. Suddenly, Mateo became *aware*. He could feel something he had never felt intellectually conscious of, yet he knew it had been there all along: it was a feeling of energy. Of something special, something subtly powerful—an invisible reality permeating his skin and yet emerging from it, an energy in the room, the energy of his thoughts within him, of potential; he even felt the energy of Master Lael, as grace and compassion, as gentle and true. The awareness left Mateo breathing in wonder. "I'm alive," he whispered.

And in his heartbeat he felt God. And in his bones he felt meaning.

Everything that is now hidden or secret will eventually be brought to light.

~Mark 4:22

♌

When Farah woke, she didn't remember having fallen asleep. But emotional exhaustion could do that to a person, and Farah was, in that moment, more emotionally exhausted than she had ever been. She opened her eyes and dragged her gaze toward the French doors. No Mephistopheles. Yet. And then she just lay there, still, wondering if everything that had happened had been a dream: Mephistopheles on the rocks, Sophia, their talk, everything Sophia seemed to know about her and her every thought. A moment later, she felt the early morning sunlight break the top of the couch and settle upon her; she shifted onto her back, shielding her eyes to get a look at the day.

"Good morning."

Farah squinted into the sunlight to find Sophia's silhouette in the kitchen. She smiled. It really *was* —all of it. *Sophia existed.* So Farah peeked over the back of the couch and let herself absorb this delicious reality.

The kitchen was bright and alive with an obvious love of cooking. The window sill above the sink sang with herbs in pots, flower clippings, a dish full of chilies. A young kaffir lime tree grew next to a stack of worldly looking cookbooks. Above the books, a series of shelves fashioned from thick beautiful wood—itself looking as if it had seen many different types of life—were weighted by jars of ingredients (lentils, rice, flour, pastas) and small baskets containing spices. On the other side of the sink, farthest from Farah, a row of ceramic- and brass-knobbed cupboards led to what looked to be a pantry. The entire space was a celebration of culinary passions, brought to life with a dash of coloured tiles. Sophia worked at the kitchen island, facing the couch and the living room. "Tell me," she said, walking over to hand Farah a glass of water. "Have you ever heard of Heinrich Schliemann?"

Farah gulped the water gratefully and shook her head. She wanted to laugh though. It just seemed so ridiculous, so random, all of these comments and questions from Sophia. Things that Farah had no idea about, nor would ever consider finding out had she not been in this woman's company, and yet here Farah was, suddenly wondering who Heinrich Schliemann actually was. Glamour from grammar, right?

"Well, Heinrich Schliemann was an interesting man," Sophia said, returning to the kitchen. "A special type of person who fought for something he believed in. You see, he was the first man in history to believe that the ancient Greek play, the *Iliad*, was based on actual historical events. His contemporaries of course found the idea laughable—any Greek mythology was considered to be just that—myth—fanciful tales of adventure and nonsense. But Schliemann was convinced otherwise, so convinced that he set out to prove it. And so with the play, and a series of mathematical equations based on the geography of Greece and Turkey in hand, he followed the route of the Trojan War as it was outlined in the text, to a place where the ancient city of Troy should have been. Do you know what he found when he got there?

Farah shook her head.

"Nothing. A few grassy hillsides. An expanse of open space. So do you know what he did?"

Again Farah shrugged, this time though, she glanced around the room as well. She had been awake for some minutes, and Mephistopheles usually whispered by now.

"He started to dig. And dig. And dig. And *dig*. Until eventually, the city of Troy emerged!" Farah's eyebrows raised with impressed curiosity. Sophia nodded. "It's true. Under layers of earth and other ancient cities, Schliemann discovered the remains of the city of Troy and the rest, as they say, is history: The science of archeology was born. Now, I supposed you're wondering why I'm telling you all of this?"

Farah gave a reticent shrug. Although fascinated, she really had no idea what any of this was about.

"*Because*," Sophia glanced at Farah, smiling, "what Heinrich Schliemann achieved that day actually has a lot to do with you."

Suddenly Mephistopheles appeared at the window, but he wasn't looking at Farah; he seemed to be listening to Sophia as well. "M-me?" Farah stuttered. "But … how?"

Sophia didn't miss a beat. "Because what Schliemann's discovery did was demonstrate that archeological findings could prove or disprove the historical validity of an ancient text. A very powerful finding indeed, one which, as you can imagine," she paused to sip her tea, "didn't take long before it was applied to the most propounded ancient text of them all."

"The Bible—" Farah whispered.

"Yes," Sophia nodded. "Schliemann's method was deemed a wonderful way to put any argument to rest, once and for all, that the Bible was anything less than a historically accurate document. A literal history text: from the genesis of the earth, the creation of mankind and human separation from God because of sin, to the flood, the Exodus, the birth of Jesus, and the redemption of humankind by his death."

Farah felt nervous. She didn't know what was coming.

"And so in 1860," Sophia continued, "a man named Ernest Renan, one of the most esteemed and prestigious intellectual figures of his age, applied Schliemann's techniques on a journey he made through Palestine and Syria. With the Bible in hand, Renan was attempting to discern fact from fiction, to prove the Bible was in fact one, and not the other. What he found, however, would initiate a pressure upon the church unlike any it had experienced since the Protestant Reformation in the 1500s."[94]

Farah's eyes widened. "What was it?"

"Well, that was the problem," Sophia said, bringing a tray with porridge, fruit, and milk. "It was what Renan *didn't* find. After all that searching, Renan found a whole lot of—nothing."

Farah's heart stopped beating. *Impossible.*

"And it wasn't just Renan," Sophia said. "All across the academic board— archeologists, Biblical scholars, scientists, and religious intellectuals alike— were coming to learn that very little if anything of what the church said the Bible meant was verifiable by physical or historical evidence, outside the Bible itself, of course."

Arrhythmia ... but no solicitude. Mephistopheles was in full view now on the veranda, pressing up against the French doors—he was staring at Sophia with a look of shock on his face, his mouth agape—and Farah was staring at him with hers agape, wondering if he was about to break through the glass.

Sophia waved one hand at the French doors and handed Farah her breakfast with the other. "Don't worry," she said. "There is no place for him here. Besides, he can only get in if you let him in." Farah dragged her eyes away and looked up at Sophia with great uncertainty. It was then that she noticed the more she kept her eyes focused on Sophia, the more Mephistopheles began to diffuse into the background. Disappear into the dappled light of morning. Become *less there.*

"Time and time again," Sophia picked up where she left off, "no archeological evidence was found to substantiate the claim that the Bible was a historically accurate document. A discovery that was, of course, nothing less than a disaster. The church needed the Bible to be considered historically accurate, to justify the majority of its faith practice, let alone the classification of itself as a religious edifice, the only method by which to reach God. But repeatedly, the physical evidence let them down. It just simply wasn't there. Again and again, the earth and recorded human history were denying what the church said was the only history of the world."

When the brain goes into shock, it does one of two things: demands reason and sense, or simply retreats into complete denial. Farah was beyond having anything to gain by pretending that what she was hearing couldn't be true, so instead her brain had her shake her head from sincere and deep-rooted emotion. *How could this be?* "But the kingdom of David—" she said, "King Solomon's mines—?"

Sophia shook her head. "No evidence at all.[95] Which is strange, considering that King David's kingdom is described in the Old Testament as not only grand and opulent but the location of some of the greatest battles of Jewish history.[96] Naturally," Sophia paused to chew a piece of fruit, "the church labeled the emerging evidence an attack on the edifice of Christianity, which, of course, equated to an attack upon God. They denied the validity of the discoveries completely, as if the earth itself and everything that God created upon it were liars." Another sip of tea. "The reality of the situation was that the church genuinely believed they were right, and genuinely saw the academic take on the history of the world as flawed—as 'just what the Devil would want everyone to believe because it went against what the church said was true.' Their response, naturally, wasn't to consider that somewhere along the line a mistake in interpretation had been made, but was to instead fight what would be the closest thing to fire with fire. Immediately, the church set out to train an enclave of priests in the most modern of sciences to prove the opposite of what other scholars were finding, to prove that the Bible was *right*, true, word for word. Just as they claimed it to be. This army of ecclesiastical experts became known as the Catholic Modernists."

Farah had heard of the Modernist movement before, but never in the context of it being a good thing.

"Now this is where it gets interesting," Sophia said. "Because what happened next was the last thing anyone expected."

Farah found herself sitting on the edge of her seat.

"The very priests that the church had commissioned to defend the infallibility of the Bible, began, the more that they learned, to *challenge* the very doctrine of infallibility they had been commissioned to defend. The priests began to *confront* the church instead of defend it."

Farah's jaw dropped; so did Mephistopheles'.

Sophia nodded. "It's true. The more the priests learned about the Bible, the more they began to question the doctrine that had been built up around it. The more expertise they acquired to understand the information revealed by what sciences and academia were discovering, the more the priests themselves began to question the very doctrine they were commissioned to protect. Basically," Sophia said, placing her teacup on the table beside her, "even the priests were finding that history, that reality *itself*, had no recollection of what the church said was the only history of the world."

Farah stared. Behind her eyes a great confusion leapt. *No archeological evidence to substantiate the church's claim that the Bible's account of history was literal*—or true, for that matter.

144

At that point, Farah made a decision. She realized then that she did *not* know everything there was to know about the Bible. Nor did she know everything, or anything it seemed, about the actual history of her religion. *How*, Farah asked herself, could she have devoted so much of her identity, her psychology, her body and mind—her *sanity*—to something she knew so little about? To a religion she knew so little about. ... Was it good enough that a religion said appeasing *it* was the only way to gain God's approval? Didn't *every* religion say the very same thing? Farah decided then that she needed to hear what Sophia had to say. Whether it changed what she believed or not, Farah needed to hear some more about the things she didn't know—and perhaps about the things she thought she did.

From where he stood Mephistopheles could see the electricity in the room, the swirl and phosphorescence, the godliness of it. And he cringed because he knew that Farah could feel it too. And of it he knew that she wasn't afraid. Her cheeks were flushed and her body trembled, but she wasn't *afraid*. He looked closer. Something, he could see it, was beginning to leak out of her ... and he knew she could feel that too—feel it dripping like sap, out from the inside, down toward her feet and then onto the ground where it pooled, out and away from her body. Mephistopheles looked from it to Farah's thoughts, back to Sophia, and he wondered, very much, what would happen next. He wondered—and yet he knew—what would happen when Farah found out.

♋

Rose woke to a cat purring in the vicinity of her left ear and a piece of Roger's notes stuck to her right cheek. Her body ached from feeling tense, and her mind just wanted to close its eyes, remain in the comfort of things that she knew, not in the company of all—she looked around at the piles of paper—*this*.

More purring. A light tap of *hello there*, from a paw.

"All right, Alvin," Rose smiled, reaching out to scratch his ear as she sat up. "Good morning."

The cat needed food, and Rose needed the comfort of a normal cup of tea. As she waited for the kettle to boil, she placed her Bible on the counter and traced her fingers over its worn leather edges, its tagged pages, the precious gold lettering: *King James Bible.* It was the only Bible Rose had ever known, the only Bible she had ever trusted, and here she was finding out that it was *flawed*. Not just flawed, but possibly the *worst* copy of the Bible of any modern circulating copy!

A burdened exhale escaped her. This was all just *so hard*. How could it be possible that *generations* of Christians had been using a Bible, fundamentally flawed, as the *infallible* word of God? Better yet, how could the infallible word of God *be* flawed?

She poured Alvin some cat biscuits and grabbed the milk from the fridge. The kettle boiled and Roger's words echoed in her head: "The idea of the Bible being the infallible word of God is *not* traditional to Christianity."

How could *that* be?

You couldn't be a Christian if you didn't believe the Bible was infallible. After all, it was faith in what the Bible said was true that made someone, that made Rose, a Christian. It was *faith* in the *infallibility* of the Bible that allowed a Christian to believe *everything* it said was accurate and true, in the most *literal* sense of each exquisite God-inspired word.

There was great power in that infallibility.

It allowed a Christian to dismiss the natural physics of the human-inhabited world—it taught that the laws of the world were not the same as God's laws, which could usurp, overpower, and even invert the logical laws of the human-inhabited Earth. With faith in that infallibility, it didn't matter that an east wind parted the Red Sea, or that Jesus walked on water or turned

146

water into wine. It didn't matter that Jesus' mother gave birth without losing her virginity, or that people were raised from the dead. Faith in the infallibility of the Bible meant that such discrepancies were what the Bible said, and so were true—no matter what. The great flood was real, the talking snake in the garden of Eden, the fact that Jesus fed thousands with one loaf of bread and five fish.

Faith in that infallibility was how Rose knew her religion was the *right* one.

"Oh God," Rose prayed, "Why am I here? Why have you brought me *here?*"

To save that which is lost.

The phrase whispered itself, and Rose scrunched up her face in reluctant memory. She tucked her Bible under her arm, cup of tea in hand, and made her way back to the living room. Then, collapsing on the couch, Roger's notes spread out in front of her, Rose placed her Bible beside her (its spine pressed against her leg for comfort). She collected all the papers she had read the day before and placed them in the order she had found them in Roger's Day One folder. In the process, what she knew would inevitably emerge, did. She scooped Alvin up onto her lap and, holding the cat close, stared dubiously at the folder that lay waiting for her to open it. She knew it had to come next. Day Two.

She opened the cover to find Roger's voice.

> What happens when we discover that what we thought was a certainty actually … isn't? What does that mean for our blood pressure, our stress levels, for our anxiety, or the boundaries of our comfort zones?
>
> What do we do when a buried history sees the light of day after thousands of years and it provides an alternate explanation to what we believed was our only truth? What do we do then?
>
> Do we quickly re-bury that history, so that it doesn't upset our ideas and foundations? Or do we observe it, pick it up, handle it, discover it, investigate it, and then draw—not necessarily a new conclusion—but an enlightened one. What if this history brought to life things that we didn't know about things that we thought we knew everything about?

Something was coming. Rose could feel it. "God help me," she whispered. And she meant it.

♑

Roger had arrived early and was finishing his breakfast when they started to trickle in. Conversations. At first in small streams, and then in flowing rivers. Words. Sentences. Statements. Questions. Opinions. Perceptions. Histories. Judgments. Floating and buzzing down the hall, into the classroom, where Roger waited eagerly. Perched on the edge of his desk, he wondered what genre of opinion would arrival first: that which was cynical or angry? Bitter, positive, objective, hopeful … naïve? In any and in all cases, Roger was keen to find out. He never tired of hearing what people thought, because he knew: People's opinions were always a reflection of what they thought about the world, and what they perceived about their own existence in it. Two things shaped greatly by religion, whether you were religious or not.

Marx had called religion the opiate of the masses, but Roger disagreed— fear was the opiate—religion was just the conductor, but with a far-reaching baton. Religion was also the great instigator—epic debates and monumental conflicts rose out of fear fueled by religious belief or non-belief. And the same went on, on a smaller scale, like the arguments taking place right now, just outside the classroom; every person who spoke defensively, every argument, occurred because somewhere deep within the person arguing was a feeling of fear. Fear of God. Fear of what they didn't know for sure. Of not knowing what was really *real* (the Bible?). Fear of heaven or hell … and of the precariousness of salvation. Who, *really*, people wondered, of all the religions, of all the different ways people were told to appease the Judging Overseer, would be saved? All people had, *really*, was their faith in what their religion defined for them as true. It was the same the world over: Religion defined belief, and fear prevented people from accepting that which challenged their belief, which made challenging religion—which many of Roger's students were there to do—akin to spraying a can of "Defensive Irrationality" into the air. The side effects being: trembling voices, dramatically increased heart rates, and a sickly adrenaline-type feeling in the gut. It was this feeling that Roger so often saw hovering, swirling behind argumentative eyes that in their depths projected myriad other conditions ranging from stubborn and judgmental, absolute and sure, to condescending and terrified, even confused. But rarely—which Roger thought was actually kind of ironic—in the midst of all of these side effects, all of this religious urgency, was there ever any calm.

He took a sip from his coffee mug and watched pensively as a small group of "side effects" and conflicting opinions entered the room. Recognition fluttered his eyelids. Yes, there it was—the beginning of what Roger had witnessed a thousand times before. It was in their body language: No one ever wanted to hear anyone else, let alone consider whether or not the person they disagreed with might actually have a point. And the bottom line was that everyone was fighting.

"You can't blame an entire religion for the insane actions of a few people—just like you can't blame all Muslims for the actions of a few crazy suicide bombers."

"But if those suicide bombers act in the name of how their religion defines God, then *who* is responsible?"

Another voice interjected, "Martyrdom by murder or suicide bombing is an illusion. The Prophet said that to kill one man is to kill the whole world. He said that as Muslims, we must go in *peace*, and move in the world with love in our hearts for all, and *respect* other religions of the Book. The mind of a suicide bomber is polluted with images that brainwash his senses and his sense. He is ignorant, and does not represent the Muslim religion accurately." When the group entered the room, Roger could see it was a young Muslim who spoke, and he thought again of the power of language.

Words. That make people. That make the world. That form interpretations in the mind; judgment, perceptions, enlightenment, or intellectual darkness. The interpretation of words shaped the world, which was why they were never "just" words. They mattered. Language and the expression of truths matter because the effect of those words mattered to people—and really could mean the difference between life and death.

More wafted in. Phrases and arguments, sentences and exclamation points. "Religion loves science until it proves something that disagrees with religious doctrine, then they make it an enemy of God."

This was quite true, Roger thought, and ironic as well considering that until the time of Galileo, religion and science were the same thing. *Before* Galileo, scientific thought determined the core of religious contemplation. In fact, it was scientific understanding of the world (or lack thereof) that influenced the formation of religious doctrine, the very *definition* of God. And so plague and illness, bad weather and death, stormy seas and drought became active forms of punishment or discipline from an angry God, instead of just being what they were—some, the result of natural weather cycles, others the result of unsanitary conditions, a virus, or lack of knowledge about a disease.

Centuries ago, superstition superseded knowledge because people didn't know any better, and the concept of God was defined as much by superstition as by reality … *until* scientific knowledge began to develop greater understanding. *Until* the human mind began to work its magic and develop a greater understanding of the world and existence. Galileo was the first example of this.

Unfortunately for him, religion was so frightened by its own superstition-based doctrine by then, that it refused to hear any opinion outside of its own. In this way, the church inadvertently sabotaged its own evolution, choosing instead to declare any scientific discovery that did not support the way religious doctrine a direct attack on God. *Punishable.* This was how Galileo, who was simply telling the truth about what was *real*—the Earth rotated around the sun, and not the other way around—ended up imprisoned for life as a heretic.

Galileo's discovery was the first time scientific knowledge disagreed with religion. And to this day, religion suspected that scientific discoveries about the world as an attempt to undermine God. An argument that left Roger befuddled—for how could one claim that God created all the world, but then deny the reality of God's creation?

The action of religions founded in God's name then, made God the inhibitor of knowledge and discovery instead of the inspiration by which to contemplate the actual realities, physical and invisible, of the amazing world in which all life existed. In the name of religion, God became the suppressor of knowledge instead of the celebration of the ability of humans to think, imagine, create, and understand.

Another argument trickled in, "… but they found the remains of Noah's Ark in the mountains in Turkey. They have satellite photographs of it and everything!"

Another person scoffed. "There you go again, loving science if it proves the Bible, but ignoring science when it shows you that "ark" in Turkey is nothing more than rocky formation in the hillside."

Ahhh, Noah's Ark. Roger smiled to himself. The Mount Ararat 'discovery' was fascinating for the exact reason mentioned. Those leading the search for Noah's Ark, were very happy to use science to validate their theory, but just as happily looked away from the very same scientific evidence that proved their 'ark' merely a shape left by a landslide or other such natural event. It was fascinating, Roger thought, how people *needed* to believe the literal interpretation of the Bible. How they gripped onto it with bloodied fingernails, as if the literal interpretation was the difference between life and death. Or life after death. When it actuality, it was only the difference between viewing God through the veil of religion, and seeing God and the world with that veil lifted. The spiritual center of the Bible still existed, whether it was infallible or not.

"Jesus was *not* the Messiah prophesied in the Old Testament. He meets none of the requirements of the Jewish Messiah."

Oooh, that was a big one. Roger was impressed. Not many Christians took the time to realize the fact that though they claimed Jesus to be the Jewish Messiah (the basis by which they declare him the Saviour of Humankind), Jesus, in fact, was *not*.

"The Jewish Messiah was supposed to be a political leader who would violently overthrow those who oppressed the Jewish people, freeing them and leading them to prosperity. Jesus did none of those things. If anything, Jesus came to denounce religion altogether—which would make the Messianic prophecy regarding him null and void. That's why the Jewish people don't call Jesus their Messiah—because he wasn't. Jesus wasn't the Jewish Messiah."

"Well, who was he then?"

A good question Roger thought, just as the next group—debates and discussions in full swing—entered the room. In their words Roger recognized the ultimate argument.

"You're fooling yourself if you think believing in evolution doesn't take faith: Both creationism and evolution require religious faith to be considered completely true by anyone." The girl sat down and glanced at those arguing around her. "As with most things, it comes down to simply choosing what it is that you believe. Clearly you choose to believe in a theory, and I choose to believe in God."

The creationists in the group looked assured, the evolutionists rolled their eyes at the Christians, and Roger remembered the first time he went to a dinosaur museum on a school trip. The shock he felt. The concern. The incredulity.

Roger's mother had raised him a good Christian boy: Sunday school, Bible study, never missing a Sunday at church, or a Christmas or Easter mass. Every year he and his mother attended some form of Passion Play; Roger felt great pain in his heart for the torture Jesus suffered to die for him. As a boy, Roger proudly displayed a picture of Jesus on his desk, and while the other children at school worried about being popular or cool, Roger tested his worth by wondering *What Would Jesus Do?* in any given situation. As a young teen, Roger was a firm believer in the Bible's account of the creation of the world, of man from dust, of women from the rib of man, of Eve and Adam's sin, of their expulsion from the Garden of Eden for having chosen sin over God, and then of man's mapped-out destiny as sinner, separated from God. Man with the opportunity to reunite with God by believing that Jesus died for the sins of the world. So when he arrived at the Royal Tyrrell Museum's detailed display about the evolution of man—chimp to Cro-Magnon to *Homo heidelbergensis* to *Homo erectus* (everything except, of course, the "missing link")—it hit him like a blow to the stomach. Took his air. He stared at it for a lengthy period of time. Stared and looked back and forth from the facts to the hypothesis and everything in between. Never in his life had Roger considered a possibility *outside* the Bible's version of the history of the world, a possible explanation for the existence of humans and the world outside the Garden of Eden. But before his very eyes, there was one … right in front of him … a version of history as told by the contents of the earth, by actual fossils and bones. Or at least a possibility very convincingly hypothesized and supported by biological, genetic, and even some undeniable physical evidence.

The only issue at hand in the hypothesis was the missing link, the missing physical evidence that proved exactly how humans came to be. So what was the missing link? Roger began to wonder. What really was the beginning? Did the humanists know? Did the creationists? Was it intelligent design? Was it some inexplicable Big Bang? Or was it a mixture of things such as this? Roger did not know, but he felt very strongly that the physical evidence in the museum display, what it was suggesting—that the story of Adam and Eve, of dust and the rib, were not actual facts, but that humans were in fact a cousin species that experienced stages of evolutionary growth—deserved some serious thought.

And so Roger began to think, in between church and Bible study, before bed, after his prayers. In between going to the bathroom and lunch breaks at school, on the bus, in the car, when he was walking or riding his bike, sometimes even in between bites of food. Until eventually he drew the conclusion that between what the Bible said and what he saw in that museum, something just wasn't right. And that was when Roger began to read, learn, and discover a multitude of things about the world.

It was hard to believe that some thirty years had passed since he found out about the Catholic Modernists, since he started university, since he began to confront the discrepancies that started to appear in front of and all around him.

Just like his students were doing now.

"If evolution is real," someone snapped, "then why is it called the *theory of evolution?*"

"That's just semantics," someone else replied just as sharply.

And it was, Roger thought. To many people, evolution was just a theory—never mind the circumstances that led to Darwin's landing on the Galapagos Islands; Providence indeed! Originally, a ship containing a bishop got "caught up" near the Galapagos. Upon the ship's return, the bishop reported his discovery to the Crown, which immediately commissioned another ship to return and explore the newly found land. Charles Darwin was the natural scientist chosen to accompany the crew on the exploration. *Charles Darwin.* If Christians or any religious person believe that God's will has a hand in the happening of all things, how could they ignore the circumstances that brought Charles Darwin—one of the few men in the world at that time who could conceive evolution—to a small series of islands in the middle of the ocean that just happened to contain species that displayed specific traits of their own adaptation and evolution? It was uncanny, and an incredibly coincidental series of events. But still the church would not look at it. Still, science was made the enemy of God, and Darwin a blasphemer. It confounded Roger. Even in the face of physical evidence, religion refused to admit it might have misinterpreted something somewhere along the line, and instead chose once again to deny reality in order to maintain faith in a manmade doctrine. It was amazing.

One of Roger's favourite quotes was by Carl Sagan, "How is it that hardly any major religion has looked at science and concluded, 'This is better than we thought! The Universe is much bigger than our prophets said, grander, more subtle, more elegant'? Instead they say, 'No, no, no! My god is a little god, and I want him to stay that way.'" Sagan went on to make the point, "A religion, old or new, that stressed the magnificence of the Universe as revealed by modern science might be able to draw forth reserves of reverence and awe hardly tapped by the conventional faiths." And Roger quietly agreed. Why wouldn't God be involved in evolution? As far as Roger was concerned, the brilliance of evolutionary processes could easily be attributed to God ... ah, but then science didn't want the world to be a spiritual place, and religion didn't want to recognize the truth about superstition and ignorance in their doctrine.

And so the two—religion and science—would continue to fail to truly understand the truth that reality was speaking *right now.*

"Why four, do you think?" someone asked between bites of a banana. "Why not one, or seven, or twelve gospels? There were dozens floating around back then, so why choose only four?"

"Hmm, good question," another person wondered along, peeling their own fruit.

The Stirrer tilted his head back, finished his vegetable juice with a dramatic flourish, and then said, "North. East. West. South." Roger privately raised his eyebrows in surprise.

"That's a load of rubbish," a Christian responded sharply, looking up from the book she was reading.

The Stirrer raised a sardonic eyebrow. "Is it now?" He nodded toward Roger. "Why don't we ask the good ol' doctor here?"

The smattering of students that had already taken their seats all looked toward Roger. "Is it true?" the Christian demanded. She didn't want to be rude, but she was pulsing with the frustration of it all (the Stirrer was so sarcastically confrontational, she had to constantly pray for patience not to judge him; but as much as she was trying to block the blows, protect her foundation, his comments were starting to cause pressure cracks).

Roger held his finger up, asking for a moment as he flipped through his Quotes folder. He pulled out a piece of paper and read: "'For since there are four zones in the world in which we live, and four principle winds … it is fitting that she [the Church] should have four pillars. …' Irenaeus, Bishop of Lyons, 180 AD." Roger put the piece of paper back. "As much as it may frustrate you," he empathized with the Stirrer's Christian adversary, "it is true: four winds, four corners of the earth, four pillars, and so, four gospels."

This grabbed everyone's attention. Roger shrugged apologetically toward the Christian whose cheeks burned red. She refused to look at the Stirrer, whose smug grin looked the equivalent of a child's delight at receiving ice cream. In the corner, the debate over the authenticity of Noah's Ark and the story of the Great Flood was winding down. Roger looked at his watch.

"The main thing that concerns me about the story of the Ark is that if Noah indeed did gather one of every kind of animal, he would have let them out all in the same place, right?"

"Right."

"So how is it then that certain species of insect and animal only exist on certain continents? African elephants, North American grizzly bears, lemurs from Madagascar, Australian kangaroos, or even New Zealand kiwis. And how did all of those animals and insects that are region- and ecosystem-specific, if they were let out of the Ark on Mount Ararat, then survive in ecosystems and geographical landscapes that weren't designed to support them?"

The cheeks of the Ark story defender burned. "With God, anything is possible."

And *that*, Roger believed to be true—the archeological discovery of the ancient city of Troy, Darwin's arrival on the Galapagos, the unearthing of more than 16,000 copies of Biblical manuscripts to compare and contrast, and use to gauge the state of today's religions against the loss of original meaning of scriptures. And the reality of a common, unspoken, spiritual language that exists between every single person on Earth, regardless of geography, culture, linguistics, politics, or the passing of time. Yes, indeed, anything truly was possible with God. Roger looked at his watch again. It was time.

♈

They walked a bit farther. Around them braziers were being stoked, torches lit. People made their way in and out of the libraries, setting up working stations for the day, choosing a place to sit a while in quiet meditation. Everyone was here for the same reason—the perpetual, infinite, reaching heart of the cave, the meaning at the center of the stories that told of it all.

"The gospel stories originate from the Wisdom Sayings," Master Lael said.

Mateo had heard of the Wisdom Sayings; like the Zodiac, they were older than the memory of man, but yet they emerged collectively from within the consciousness of human beings.

"Yes. *bene*," Master Lael smiled. "The Wisdom Sayings are timeless, universal truths about life and the spiritual experience of being human."

"But *how* could they do that?" Mateo asked. "*Emerge* from the consciousness of human beings?"

"Ahhh, now that is a very good question," Master Lael said. "How, indeed."

And then Mateo learned that human knowledge of the divine was inherent. It was a *sense*, and humans were born with it. "Human knowledge of the divine is as much a part of being human as our instinct for compassion, as our instinct to survive. It is the warmth of the air that escapes our lungs, the individuality that shines out from the center of our eyes, it is the grooves of the lines that shape our fingerprints." This was what Mateo learned first: that knowledge and light were contained *within* every human. And then Mateo learned about *her*:

"The most ancient human concept of creation—what you are learning now, the great Gospel of Life—expressed God's thoughts as energy that fueled the origins of life on Earth, but the *action* of God's thoughts on Earth, was Wisdom. And she was and is always a woman. Some call her Wisdom, others Iusa-Maria, still others know her as the Spirit, the holy spirit. In this part of the world, however, she is known by other names, Sapientia[97], Chokhmah[98]: the Wisdom of God. The action of God's thought and love in the world. Sapientia is the guiding force, the invisible but tangible intermediary. We know her in direct and indirect ways; as an obvious knowing, or a message waiting to be received." Master Lael spoke with his hands, the warmth of the braziers surrounding them. "You see, while the energy of God is in and of everything, it is the wisdom of God that guides us—not as an entity separate from you, but as one that is part of your very being." He pressed his palms against his chest. "Sapientia, wisdom, spirit, is the name of the spiritual wisdom that lives within and all around you, the pulsing heart at the center of your spiritual instinct. The pulsing heart at the center of your soul."

*

Mateo felt it then just as he felt it now. A sensation of knowledge without words, a guiding force that led not by force but by wisdom. And it felt, just as Master Lael said, like instinct.

*

They walked; all around them people learned and discovered; the soles of their feet pressed softly upon the rocky pathways. "Also contained within, is something as ancient as the first breath taken, as the first seed germinated, reaching up toward the sun—morality. Common morality."

When Master Lael first said it, Mateo didn't quite understand. But Master Lael wasn't talking about morality defined by culture, politics, time, and place; he was talking about something more ancient, more pure. An inherent knowledge of right and wrong; a pure sense of fairness and right action. Over the course of his lifetime, Mateo often saw this base morality in humans mutated and charred by politics, culture, hate, violence, by tradition, and even religion, but what he learned was that none of those mutations could ever change the actuality of what already existed. Goodness. A sense of right and wrong that united people on their journey through life, that appeared like a beacon of light as kindness, help, good action.

"And so over the centuries, born from our inherent knowledge of morality and our hereditary sense of the divine, driven by the laws of evolution, the Wisdom Sayings were born."

And that was how the Wisdom Sayings became the foundation of the Gospel of the Journey of Souls.

Learning about the gospel stories came next.

And there were dozens of them. They filled the walls; spread the length of the seventh library on both sides, illuminated by strategically placed torches. They were stories about rescues and conversations with God, the dead coming back to life, water turned into wine. The blind being made to see, and the lost finally being found, coming to understand the meaning of life. Miracles. They were stories of awakening.

Mateo's eyes widened as they walked alongside the murals. The artwork was exquisite—alive with colour and metaphor, emotion and glow. Master Lael held his hand out for them to slow before they finally paused in front of one image in particular. It depicted a small group of terrified-looking men, tossed about a rough sea in a small boat. Master Lael pointed to specific symbols within the mural.

The water represented life, the sea of life.

The men's fear represented human doubt and fear, the loss of the ability to reason in difficult or stressful times.

The next part of the image was licked by firelight. It was of a figure in white, walking toward the men—Mateo blinked and looked closer—*upon* the water. Mateo tilted his head and moved in closer, scanning the image, fascinated by what it could mean. The figure that walked upon the water glowed in white light that reached into the bodies of the frightened men. That same light brightened the surface of the water, but also *calmed* it.

"Who is he?" Mateo hovered his fingers over the image.

"Why, Mateo," Master Lael smiled in quiet wonder, "he is you."

Mateo looked to his teacher, then back to the figure in white. *Me?*

"Yes," Master Lael said, "he is you, in here," he motioned to Mateo's chest. "He is you, in here," he motioned to Mateo's head where thought turned to action. "He is your consciousness, your divine instinct. He," Master Lael motioned to the figure in white, "is the personification of that which is godly about you."

The figure in white was the personification of Mateo's divine instinct, his consciousness, at the center of which lived the wisdom of God.

In this way, wisdom and divine consciousness were in and of each other, but yet individual aspects of God. It was the center of Plotinus' Hypostases: the trinity theory about God, the presence of God, and the action of God in the world—three that are one, but that act in individual ways in the lives of every human.

Mateo turned back to the story and looked upon the waters of the sea of life, he looked upon the figure in white asking of the men why they bring such misery and doubt into their own lives by choosing to fear so many things. And then he looked upon the calm and felt, when he saw the glowing light that spread throughout the mural, a light glowing within him—and he knew what Master Lael said was right. God *glowed* within him, and through some amazing miracle, a divine consciousness, just like the wisdom and calm that walked on water in the story, *lived* within him.

He looked back at Master Lael excitedly and said, "I want to know more."

As they finished breakfast, Sophia spoke a bit more about the Catholic Modernists and their plight to convince the church to reevaluate some of its more orthodox doctrines.

"The priests were concerned about the church's hard-line approach," she explained. "Such as its insistence on interpreting stories about the Virgin Birth, the Resurrection, the raising of Lazarus from the dead, or even the turning of water into wine as literal events."

Placing the dishes in the sink, Farah felt the ground beneath her shake.

"Rome, of course, viewed the priests' actions as dissention and responded heavily. Those who would not renounce what they had learned and denounce their change of opinion were declared heretics. Excommunicated. Their research banned. Those that were teachers were immediately dismissed from their posts.[99] In 1910, the church went so far as to declare *any* scholarship that did not support church doctrine heretical, and required its members to take an oath to renounce any discoveries that contradicted the orthodox interpretation. Only literature concordant with the orthodox doctrine was approved—Farah, are you okay?"

She had returned to the couch, but Farah could feel the blood had drained from her face.

But her heart was beating oxygen-rich blood through her body, and her mind was more stimulated than she could ever remember it being. The pinpricks of questions were now tingling into fascinated wonder. She'd never felt so alive, and nodded that she was fine. "I want to know more," she said, hugging her knees to her chest. "What else do you know about the Bible?"

The air went still then. All the words that had been spoken thus far settled to the ground for sorting. They swirled and moved softly, and those that were no longer necessary (those that held all of Farah's pain), drifted up the chimney until only what really mattered remained. When Sophia spoke, it was with an air of quiet contemplation, an air of reaching out. "It's not so much what I know about the Bible," she said. "It's what I know about *you*."

Farah's expression changed.

"Yes," Sophia said, "*you*." She leaned back in her chair and clasped her hands at her chin. "In the oldest Bibles, Jesus refers to himself as *bar enasha*— this word has been mistranslated to mean 'Son of Man,' but what it really means is *human being.*[100] Sophia motioned toward Farah. "And that means *you.*"

Farah didn't understand what was happening. How could Jesus be talking about *her?* How could Heinrich Schliemann's discoveries have anything to do with *her?* How could *she* be in the Bible?

"I also know," Sophia said, "that while people are waiting for the second coming of Christ, they are missing out on the fact that the coming of Christ is happening all of the time. And most importantly, I know that the Bible tells you all of these things. May I?" Sophia motioned to Farah's Madonna on the Rocks journal, and picked up a pen.

Farah gave her suicide diary a frantic glance, but Sophia opened it discreetly to its second blank page. This made the girl glance curiously at the woman's face. Had Sophia known about Farah's first entry? Surely not. But then again, these days, it seemed that anything was possible. As Sophia began to write, Farah leaned in, and before long her brow furrowed at the words that emerged before her.

♋

Who is this paragraph referring to?

> If one were told that many centuries ago a celestial ray shone into the body of a sleeping woman, as it seemed to her in her dream, that thereupon the advent of a wondrous child was predicted by the soothsayers; that angels appeared at this child's birth; that merchants came from afar bearing gifts to him; that an ancient saint recognized the babe as divine and fell at his feet to worship him; that as a young boy the child confounded his teachers with the amount of his knowledge, still showing them due reverence; that he grew up full of compassionate tenderness to all that lived and suffered; that to help his fellow creatures he sacrificed every worldly prospect and enjoyment; that he went through the ordeal of a terrible temptation in which all the power and evil were let loose upon him, and came out conqueror of them all; that he preached holiness and practiced charity; that he gathered disciples and sent out apostles to spread his doctrine over many lands and peoples; that this "helper of the worlds" could claim a more than earthly lineage and a life that dated long before Abraham. …[101]

"Why, it's Jesus, of course," Rose said and turned the paper over dismissively, as if the matter of who the paragraph was referring to were a joke. She was stopped short, however, by the answer that faced her.

♑

Roger gave everyone a moment to read the paragraph and noted the offered responses. Almost everyone said that the paragraph was about Jesus. They were wrong. "The paragraph," Roger said, "refers to the Buddha."

Several looks of confusion were exchanged.

"Which is interesting," Roger said, "because the Buddha lived some five hundred years *before* Jesus." Roger then swapped the paper under the projector with another. "But Buddha is not the only historical religious figure with whom Jesus has so much in common." Roger motioned to a list now blazoned on the wall. "There are over two hundred similarities between Jesus and the Egyptian sun god Horus, some of the most striking you will find listed here. Horus, of course was present in Egyptian religious lore from about 3000 to 700 BC, while Jesus, as you well know, was estimated to have lived from around 4 AD to 32 AD."

Similarities between Horus and Jesus[102]

- The morning star in Egypt, which rises in the east, heralded the birth of Horus (like the "star in the east" that heralded the birth of Jesus in the gospels of Matthew and Luke).
- Like Jesus, Horus had no history between the ages of twelve and thirty.
- Horus was baptized in the River Eridanus by a god figure named Anup the Baptizer, who was later decapitated. John the Baptist, who was also later decapitated, baptized Jesus in the River Jordan.
- Horus, just like Jesus, walked on water, cast out demons, and healed the sick.
- Jesus, like Horus, was transfigured on a mountain
- Horus delivered a "Sermon on the Mount," and his followers faithfully recounted the "Sayings of Iusa." (Jesus delivered a Sermon on the Mount, and his followers faithfully recounted the sayings of Jesus, which became known as the "Beatitudes").
- Horus, like Jesus, was crucified between two thieves, buried in a tomb, and resurrected. His personal epithet was Iusa (or Iusu), the "ever-becoming son" of the Father (Ptah). Significantly, Horus

was also called the "anointed one," or KRST (which is the Greek acronym for Christ, which also means "Messiah").

- Horus was known as the good shepherd, the lamb of God, the bread of life, the son of man, the word, and the fisher (so was Jesus).
- Horus came to seek and to save what was lost. We are reminded of the gospel parables of the lost sheep, the lost coin, and the "lost" son.
- In the gospels, it is the women who announce the Resurrection on the morning of the third day. When Horus is resurrected, he shouts "The goddesses and the women proclaim me on the horizon of the resurrection!"

For those whose mouths weren't agape, their minds were jaw-dropped by the list before them. Roger listened to mutterings of "Impossible," "*No,*" "*Un*believable," and "Of *course.*" The list went on …

- Horus was not just the path to heaven, but the way by which the dead travel out of the sepulcher. He was the god whose name was written as the "Road to Salvation"; he was thus "the Way, the Truth, and the Life."
- Horus, like Jesus, came as a servant (see Isaiah) to deliver those who are "in their prison cells" (i.e., entombed in matter);[103] he came as "a light to lighten the gentiles, to open blind eyes, to bring out the prisoners from their dungeons, and them that sit in darkness out of the prison-house."

There were more than just a few parallels, there were dozens. The similarities between Horus and Jesus were undeniable. The room, absorbing them, was deathly quiet. "There's more," Roger said, placing one last paragraph under the projector.

Egyptian Sun god Horus

Defined as the "hero" of mankind, God incarnate; born of a virgin in a cave on December twenty-fifth; he has a star appear at his birth, is visited by magi from the East, and turns water into wine at a wedding; he heals the sick, casts out demons, and performs miracles; he is transfigured before his disciples, rides a donkey into a special city, is betrayed for thirty pieces of silver, and celebrates a communal meal with bread and wine; he is put to death on a cross, descends into hell, and is resurrected on the third day; he dies to redeem the world's sins, and ascends into heaven and is seated beside God as the divine judge.[104]

"You've got to be kidding," someone commented from out of the darkness.

"I assure you," Roger replied, "I'm not."

"But what does all of this *mean*?" someone cried out.

It was an honest query, a rightful query, Roger thought, and its answer was simple.

"It means," Roger removed the list of Horus/Jesus comparisons, "that Christianity itself, not just the Bible, comes from *somewhere.* The truth at the very center of the Christian belief system did not just appear with Jesus on a beacon of light as a savior religion—a light to light the darkness—the only 'true' religion of God meant to cleanse the world of sin and other corrupt religions. How many of you have heard of Mithraism?"

Not a single hand went up, but a voice from the back called out, "Wasn't that a religion in ancient Rome?"

"Yes, it was," Roger nodded. "Mithraism was one of the major religions of the Roman Empire; Constantine himself was a devout follower of Mithraism at the time he converted to Christianity. Mithra," Roger turned to write on the board, "was the ancient Persian god of Light and Wisdom. His emblem was the sun. He was considered to be the Good Spirit ruler of the world." Roger drew a large sun and wrote the words *Light*, *Wisdom*, and *Good Spirit* within its center. "The religion was similar to Christianity in many respects, such as the practice of humility and brotherly love, baptism, the rite of Communion, the use of holy water, adoration of the shepherds at Mithra's birth, adoption of Sundays and December twenty-fifth—also Mithra's birthday—as holy days, and belief in the immortality of the soul, the last judgment, and the resurrection. The main difference, however, between Mithraism and the Christianity of the third century AD was that Mithraism treated women as equals, whereas Christianity did not allow women to participate in its religious practices. In addition, Mithraism was also more tolerant of polytheistic religious practice."

"Are you suggesting that Christianity came from Mithraism? That Jesus is *not* the reason Christianity came to exist?"

And this is when everything the three-day seminar was about began to emerge in full, with angry Christians, confused Christians, bitter atheists, the non-religious, the jaded, the suspicious, the unbelieving, the needy, the spiritual seekers, the ignorant—and even with those that didn't really give a shit—listening.

"No," Roger replied. "I'm saying what history and the Bible itself are saying." He moved to the front of the table. "That Christianity, Mithraism, Horus, Iusa, Iesous, Yeshua, all grew from the *same* root, that they all emerged from the *same* foundation, the same place, the same ancient thing that used to be known as the collective spirituality of *humankind*. I'm saying that what these religions, these cultural adaptations of an ancient spiritual truth have in *common* is Jesus." And then Roger asked, "How many of you have heard of the Q-Document?"

A smattering of people raised their hands, but the majority of faces in the room remained blank. A few people shrugged. Hardly anyone had heard of the Q-Document, and while this stopped surprising Roger years ago, it would never cease to amaze him how *little* people actually knew about their religion—Jew, Christian, Muslim alike. The followers of the most powerful religions in the world—who spent the majority of their time fighting over who was right, over whose religion was the "true" religion of God, practicing/defending/committing suicide over those religions—didn't actually understand the roots of their own faith. Nor did they discern culture and tradition from the word of God; they took one for the other and used them interchangeably, often with disastrous results.

"Despite the differences between the gospels, the thing they have most in common is the sayings and parables of Jesus." Roger said, slipping a map under the projector.

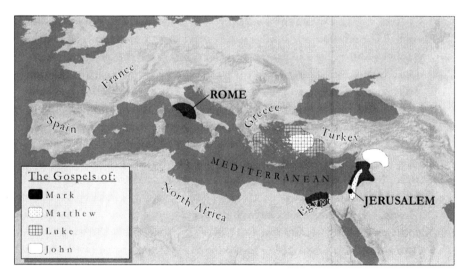

"The question we need to ask ourselves at this point is: If the gospels of Mark, Matthew, Luke, and John came from completely different parts of the world—completely different *countries*—then how is it that each author came to know the sayings and parables of Jesus with such accuracy? How is it that the heart of their stories remained the same, while the rest was expressed based on what they believed the heart was trying to communicate? If the authors did not actually know Jesus, nor were they present at any of the events they wrote about, *how* is it they came to know the things Jesus said at all?" Roger turned then and wrote on the board an enormous letter:

Q

"The Q-Document—*Q* for the German *quelle*, meaning *source*—was the main source document used by the gospel authors. Its content is the reason the gospels were able to portray any sense of synchronicity, for the words contained within it were the heart, the very origins of the Jesus stories. It did not contain a version of the story of Jesus, but was the base from which the stories *about* Jesus were created. The Q-Document was, simply, a collection of what would have been the original sayings and parables attributed to Jesus, the allegorical lessons that Jesus used to communicate his spiritual message to humanity. 'Q' is considered the original reference point, the closest thing perhaps to the original word of God that we claim the books of the Bible to be. It was the root source of the documents that compose our Bible today." Roger faced the room, speaking earnestly, but all he received in return were murmurs, a few exchanged glances, and a sense of wondering, waiting for where all of this was going to lead. Roger didn't want anyone to wait any longer.

"Given all that we have learned so far—Pious Fraud, edits, changes, additions, deletions, the loss of original meanings, homogenization of the gospels, and about the obvious influence of culture, tradition, and politics on shaping the Bible and Christian doctrine—we are forced to realize that indeed what we, in the twenty-first century have been interpreting the gospels to mean, mightn't be what they originally meant at all. And in light of this truth, we are then forced to ask: If the gospels don't actually mean what we always thought they did, what in fact, have they been trying to tell us?"

What *was* the heart of the Biblical gospels? Of Jesus' sayings and parables? What was the original meaning of "Q"? Roger had spent the better part of his life inquiring after that answer, endless hours researching, hundreds, even thousands of days and nights immersed in the depths of archeological and theological findings that he found, again and again, were telling him the same thing: The literalist, orthodox interpretation of scriptures that eventually became contemporary Christianity, was *incorrect*. Or at the very least, had made a terrible mistake.

Repeatedly, Roger had been left stunned. Many times he literally put the material down, staggered from the shock of what he was deciphering.

Some of it had turned Roger's stomach, not because he wished he'd never discovered what was repeatedly emerging before him, but because of what it *meant* that these things were there to be discovered at all. The lost meaning of the gospels was the most wonderful, incredible thing Roger could ever have imagined being rediscovered by modern humanity. One of the scrolls excavated at Alexandria had the words *Veritas Numquam Perit* carved upon its copper casing—*the truth will never perish*—and it couldn't, Roger thought. That which was written on the hearts of humans would never disappear unless humans destroyed themselves trying to find their way back to it—or destroyed each other arguing over whose misinterpretation was right.

"Wait," someone held up a hand. "Are you talking about a 'lost' meaning of the Bible?"

"Yes." Roger replied simply. "I am."

♈

The stories continued. Not about a particular man or woman, but always about that which existed within every person—the truth at the center of human existence, the invisible reality that the physical experience is a very spiritual one.

This was the truth that never perished.

The truth that was always.

"All about you the world changes," Master Lael said, offering Mateo a fig. "Life is born, grows, dies, and is born again. Traditions grow and change and die, empires rise and crumble, religions come and go, but at the center of your being is a fundamental knowledge that the world, that you are somehow part of something greater.

"This knowledge, this evolutionary aspect of your being, *maintains*. It is the constant, timeless truth of your existence that you are being led *right now* to evolve on your soul journey. It is a truth that never changes, while everything else around it, including your physical body, does."

Over the course of his life Mateo had realized that indeed, in *every single circumstance*, even when he felt stubborn about doing what he knew would really be the right thing, even when he felt afraid to make the more difficult decision, there was always something inside of him, moving him "instinctually" in the "right" direction—the direction of personal growth.

"What about this one?" Mateo said.

They walked a bit farther to another story. In this mural, the figure in white was handing out innumerable loaves of bread and thousands of fish to a multitude of people, a crowd that stretched far into the distance. Every person looked hungry, wanting, searching, clearly in need.

"Why bread, do you think? Master Lael asked.

Mateo thought a moment, and then remembered. "Virgo?"

Master Lael nodded. "And fish?"

Mateo smiled. "Pisces!"

"Yes." Master Lael clapped his hands. "*Bene.* Very, very good. The people in this story represent the whole of humanity—they are you and they are me. In this story, the feeding of the multitudes symbolizes a simple miracle of everyday existence: the truth that when you understand *who* you are, the reality of divine consciousness within you, you understand with complete peace that you are never alone. Bread and fish symbolize the infinite presence of godliness within us—that we are fed from within—and this story teaches that divine consciousness, when understood as our direct connection to God, quenches every spiritual thirst, abates every spiritual hunger pain. That is why, in this painting, everyone is fed by the figure of godliness within them."

It was all fascinating, and Mateo was spellbound. The stories were plentiful and beautiful, painted with the astounding expression of human imagination, in colours that moved with the richness of the ages. Everything around him was telling Mateo who he was, and it felt wonderful. "You are born to be led by the wisdom that exists with you," Master Lael said. "It is part of your destiny as a human being."

Ω

The room, warmed by the sun, hugged around Farah as she leaned in.

Sophia spoke as she wrote.

"There is an old Jewish teaching that says that before a child is born, God infuses its soul with all the knowledge and wisdom it will ever need in life. The legend says that God then presses his fingertip to each child's mouth, saying *shhh*, as if to imply a delicious secret shared between the child's soul and its Creator. The legend goes on to say that when God pulls his finger away, a small indentation is left behind—a reminder of what is true about that which exists within. This indentation is known as the fingerprint of God."

Farah's hand went to her top lip and she felt the groove there … *God's fingerprint.*

"Another story out of India," Sophia said, "says that when God created man, he gathered a council of the gods to discuss where it was he should place this very same gift of instinctual wisdom." Sophia glanced up at Farah and smiled. "The gods agreed that this divine consciousness should not be placed where it would be too easy to find. Otherwise, humans might take it for granted, or abuse it. One god suggested placing this inner wisdom at the bottom of the sea, and yet another suggested it be placed upon the highest mountaintop, so that man would have to toil and suffer to know the deepest secrets and truths of his being."

Farah thought this must be about right. Life for her, these last years, had felt just like that: toil and suffering.

"But God disagreed," Sophia said, "saying that toil and suffering were not more important than the human understanding of self—that the knowledge of self was an inheritance. And so God decided to place man's wisdom in the last place he would think to look for it: within his own heart."

Sophia finished writing then, and Farah leaned closer but found herself no more enlightened than when Sophia first began—the words on the page were completely foreign to her.

Abwûn
d'bwaschmâja
Nethkâdasch schmach
Têtê malkuthach.
Nehwê tzevjânach aikâna d'bwaschmâja af b'arha.
Hawvlân lachma d'sûnkanân jaomâna.
Waschboklân chaubên wachtahên aikâna
daf chnân schwoken l'chaijabên.
Wela tachlân l'nesjuna
ela patzân min bischa.
Metol dilachie malkutha wahaila wateschbuchta l'ahlâm almîn.
Amên.[105]

"Do you know what this is?" Sophia asked.

Farah shook her head.

"You don't recognize it, because it is written in ancient Aramaic," Sophia said, "but this is the original Lord's Prayer."

Farah's eyebrows raised in surprise before her expression softened into curious fascination.

"Would you like to know what it means?"

"Oh, that's okay,'" Farah replied, "I already do." It was already echoing in the back of her mind, the sound of her own voice tracing over the scars it had left there. *Our Father, who art in heaven, Hallowed be thy name, Thy kingdom come, Thy will be done, On Earth as it is in heaven. Give us this day our daily bread, and forgive us our sins as we forgive those who trespass against us. Lead us not into temptation but deliver us from evil. Amen.*

Sophia smiled quietly and picked up the pen. Once again she wrote, this time a line of Aramaic, and then beneath it, the English translation of the Aramaic words.

This time, Farah's look of fascination transformed into confusion, and then morphed into utter disbelief.

"The Lord's Prayer," Sophia said as she wrote, "has a *long* history from the time it was first spoken by Jesus in Aramaic. A history that is filled with many, let's just say, *unfortunate* translations and, you will see, fascinating losses of meaning. Luke and Matthew's translations, for example, are almost nothing like the Aramaic original, and yet these days, it is *only* Luke or Matthew's words that are prayed as the Lord's Prayer. These days," Sophia shrugged, "people believe that Luke's and Matthew's versions were the only words that Jesus spoke in the scene of the last supper, when that simply is not the case." Sophia placed the pen down gently and now turned the book for Farah to get a better look.

Farah read:

Abwûn

Oh Thou, from whom the breath of life comes,

d'bwaschmâja

who fills all realms of sound, light, and vibration.

Nethkâdasch schmach

May Your light be experienced in my utmost holiest.

Têtê malkuthach.

Your heavenly domain approaches.

Nehwê tzevjânach aikâna d'bwaschmâja af b'arha.

Let Your will come true—in the universe (all that vibrates)
just as on Earth (that is material and dense).

Hawvlân lachma d'sûnkanân jaomâna.

Give us wisdom (understanding, assistance) for our daily need,

*Waschboklân chaubên wachtahên aikâna
daf chnân schwoken l'chaijabên.*

detach the fetters of faults that bind us, (karma)
like we let go the guilt of others.

Wela tachlân l'nesjuna

Let us not be lost in superficial things (materialism, common temptations),

ela patzân min bischa.

but let us be freed from that what keeps us off from our true purpose.

Metol dilachie malkutha wahaila wateschbuchta l'ahlâm almîn.

From You comes the all-working will, the lively strength to act,
the song that beautifies all and renews itself from age to age.

Amên.

Sealed in trust, faith and truth.
(I confirm with my entire being)[106]

"As you can see," Sophia said, "a text translated from Aramaic into Greek into Latin and then finally into English can become a ghost of its former self." She leaned back in her chair and watched Farah intently, her chin rested upon her interlaced fingers.

Farah read and re-read the prayer. Her head spinning, she looked up. "But this is *nothing* like the prayer that I know … h-how?"

Sophia's voice explained gently, "Mistakes made during the process of translating languages often emerged out of an incomplete or rudimentary understanding of the language being translated. The nuances and preciseness of a language can be *completely* missed by a translator who is ignorant of the tradition in which the original language expressed its most profound meaning. Therefore, the essence of what is being communicated becomes lost, sometimes for generations. Often times, there are not words accurate enough to relay *exactly* what it is the original language was trying to convey—the nuances can be different, or the ideas of what a word means. The author of Matthew was the first to translate the Lord's Prayer from the original, but he was not well schooled in Aramaic; in fact, his understanding was rudimentary, so naturally would too be his understanding of the nuances affiliated with the language. He wouldn't have known *how* to translate the full prayer … and so what he produced is, basically, a crude Greek remnant of the original that contains very little of the fullness of meaning the original language intended. But because Matthew's Gospel was chosen to be canonized, his became the authoritative version from which all other translations were made. Basically, what you call the Lord's Prayer, isn't really what the Lord's Prayer was two thousand years ago."

"B-but—" Farah looked between the translation and Sophia. "What does it *mean*?"

"Well," Sophia smiled, "that's what you're about to find out." She picked up the pen and began to write once again.

*

When Sophia placed the pen on the page a moment later, the things, the *symbols* she had written there, again were completely foreign to Farah's frame of reference—or so she thought.

"Do you remember how old Jesus was when he was left behind at the temple?" Sophia asked.

"He was twelve."

"Right. And how many days did it take for Mary and Joseph to notice that he was missing before they went back to retrieve him?

"Three."

"And how many days did it rain during the flood?"

"Forty days and forty nights."

"Good. And how many years did the Israelites wander in the wilderness after they crossed safely through the Red Sea?"

"Forty."

"And how many days did Jesus spend in the wilderness?"

"Forty."

"Right, good. Now how many days was Jesus in the tomb before he was resurrected?"

"Three."

"And how many disciples were there?"

"Twelve."

"Good. Very good. Now—" Sophia turned the journal for Farah to see more clearly what was drawn there. Farah looked at the page. On it were twelve symbols:

♈ ♉ ♊ ♋ ♌ ♍ ♎ ♏ ♐ ♑ ♒ ♓

"Over two thousand years ago," Sophia said, "numbers were not simply numbers. At least not those particular ones: forty, twelve, and three. The number forty, for example, was a number associated with raising up one's spiritual state, but it was also a number of ritual cleansing. In Judaism, immersion of the body in forty measures of water symbolically cleansed the physical and spiritual body; in this way, it is no accident that in the Hebrew creation stories it rained for forty days and forty nights when God wanted to cleanse the world of sin, for it stood to reason that just as forty measures of water can cleanse the body, forty days and nights of rain would symbolically cleanse the world. The meaning of forty was also the reason the Israelites were said to have wandered forty years in the wilderness, while Jesus spent forty days in the wilderness—because forty symbolized a *shift* in one's spiritual state; the length of time it took to build spiritual strength in order to emerge from *hypermone* in glory."

Every cell in Farah's body was listening, and her mind was racing as she took it all in. "*Hypermone?*"

"*Hypermone* means 'tough endurance,' not 'patience,' as it has been poorly translated. It means to 'stay with or under heavy task or demanding situation,' to apply oneself with courage, steadiness, and fortitude to the tasks ahead.[107] The greatest power in its definition, however, comes from the other half of what *hypermone* is asking us to understand about the difficult times in our lives." Sophia looked at Farah now and said, "Their *impermanence*. For while life and our choices inevitably bring us to facing difficult emotional and psychological times, the reality of these times is that they are impermanent, temporary, always changing toward something better. *Hypermone* is the time from which we will always emerge in glory."

Hearing Sophia say those words—*Difficult times are impermanent. Temporary. They are always changing toward something better*—felt like water quenching an insatiable thirst somewhere deep inside of Farah's body. *Hypermone*, she thought, glancing toward Mephistopheles ... *from which you will always emerge in glory.*

"Imagine the difference it could make," Sophia said, "if people understood that Jesus wasn't asking them to have 'patience' during the most difficult times of their lives, but was instead educating them as to what it is they are immersed in: a temporary period of *hypermone* from which they are intended to emerge in glory, should they allow themselves to evolve forward out of it. Then, the most testing times of our lives could be understood for what they really are:"—again, Sophia looked deeply at Farah—"our spiritual teachers."

Farah glanced toward Mephistopheles. He stared back. *He* was a spiritual teacher? In that moment, she couldn't imagine how. She wanted to scoff. He scoffed back. What on earth was she supposed to learn from *him*?

"Three was significant," Sophia carried on, "not because of the stars, but because of the moon. All one has to do is look skyward to notice that the lunar cycle is such that the moon 'disappears' for two nights and three days every month. With its reappearance, the moon was considered 'reborn,' completely new, at the start of a new cycle. For this reason, the number three came to represent any period of potent change or renewal,[108] and so it became the number that represents spiritual *transition*. This is the reason Jesus was only found by his parents *three days* after he had stayed behind at temple. You will remember too that when Mary and Joseph found Jesus, he was somehow different than when they left him—no longer with a *boy's* consciousness, the twelve-year-old Jesus was found interacting with the spiritual leaders of the day, asking questions and conversing with them on spiritual matters—*three days*, to symbolize the awakening of knowledge *within*."

A look of profound realization suddenly crossed Farah's face. Sophia smiled. Farah whispered, "Three days …"

"*Yes*. This is *also* the reason that Jesus resurrected from the cave on the morning of the third day—*three days* for spiritual transition. Three was a symbolic number that indicated the reality of what happens when the soul is resurrected from the body—*complete spiritual transition*—a transformation of consciousness—when the soul is born out of the physical body that contained it. And so too is this the reason the person who wrote the Gospel of John chose three years as the length of Jesus' ministry."

"But then why do Mark, Matthew, and Luke say Jesus' ministry lasted only *one* year?" Farah couldn't believe she might finally get an answer to this long-plaguing question.

"The answer is simple," Sophia said, "and right in front of you. Because one year was exactly how long it took the sun to cycle around the Earth: twelve months."

To Farah, the link was unclear. "But what does the cycle of the sun, or even the moon, for that matter, have to do with Jesus?" She didn't quite understand what it was that she was hearing.

"Well—" Sophia said, watching Farah carefully. She knew how the indoctrinated part of Farah's mind would struggle with what was to come next. But it had to come, struggle or not. It was time. "Over two thousand years ago, the sun was a symbol for many things, but its most ancient name was that of Soul.

"The sun was called Soul because it spread like the light of God in the world, and because its daily cycle mirrored the journey of the soul through human life—the birth of the soul into the human body, the journey of the soul through human experience, and the resurrection of the soul from the body. Your soul, like the sun, is *pure light,* and contained within your soul is an even brighter light—the light that lights the way through your human experience. This essence of your soul is known as your spiritual consciousness. It is your guide. Your constant God-source within, your physiological connection to the power and light that fuels the evolution of all life … it is your spiritual instinct, your internal moral compass; it is the love within you that only wants to shine out to all others, that wants to allow you to be human in the face of all traditions, religions, or political structures that attempt to knock your humanness out of you. This spiritual consciousness, the light that lights the way—*is* Jesus."

All thought cleared from Farah's mind then, for one moment, before it suddenly felt a tangle of ropes. How could Jesus be a symbol of a spiritual truth that existed inside of her *and* be a person that the Bible was written about at the same time? How could Jesus be one person, separate from her, who was born of a virgin, lived and died, was crucified and turned into God … *and* be a symbolic representation of *her* very own spiritual consciousness?

And then Farah looked up. The clouds in her eyes were clearing. Sophia watched and hoped, as Farah thought and thought and tingled and lilted from head to foot.

She had a spiritual consciousness? A sun in *her* soul? A soul sun? In *her* body? Behind her eyes thoughts and thinking-through swirled. If she had a Sun Soul, then how could it ever be darkened of the light of God? If God was in her soul, within her, how could she ever be separated from God—ever? Sophia watched Farah working things out and quietly smiled. There was only so much she could say. Farah had to work this revelation out on her own in order to truly understand it.

Farah thought. If there was no historical proof—if the priests turned on their own doctrine, if … if the numbers meant more than just being numbers … If Jesus was *her* spiritual consciousness, the light within her, that lights the way through life, then the stories about Jesus were … about *her*?

Farah looked up and whispered, "Was Jesus a real person?"

Sophia replied softly, "Christ means 'One Anointed with Divinity.' That which is divine is that which is *of* God. All life is *of* God. Your *soul* comes *from God*—it contains the same vibrational energy of evolution that fueled the beginning of existence. And life, *your* life, is a result of the action of that energy manifested into physical beingness. That is the spiritual explanation of an eventual scientific definition. The fact that the union of your body and soul created *you* is a reality resulting from the action of the wisdom of God in the world. Ancient stories were written about this reality: the reality of your soul journey set into motion by the laws of God and evolution; and about your spiritual consciousness, which is a concentrated energy of love, grace, mutuality, and the force of evolution … which is the heartbeat of your being. Stories were written about the reality that your *true* identity is not in your body or your mind, but in the awareness that you have of these things. Your true self is your *awareness*—the part of you that observes yourself suffering or experiencing joy, the part of you able to contemplate with reason any emotive reaction you might be having, the part of you where wisdom lives, and that encourages your own evolution. The stories were written about these realities and the human experience of them—never were they meant to be about a man named Christ—but were intended to be understood as tales of truth about the Christ, or spiritual consciousness, in man."

A coolness fell through Farah then. Her entire body contemplated as a collective: organs, mind, eyes, self, thought. She listened and *felt* the words Sophia spoke.

"And so it is no wonder you found the stories and doctrine of Jesus so confusing, when you were asked to interpret them literally—because they are actually allegorical tales about *you*. Metaphors for the reality that you will and do encounter as a human being. Farah, the Jesus in the stories is a personification of *your* spiritual consciousness, *your* Christ-consciousness—and the circumstances he encounters reflect the physical, emotional, and spiritual challenges of *your* human life."

The coolness felt like water. A calm dispersed by the hope of understanding.

"The miracles Jesus performs are metaphors for the invisible spiritual reality within you. The focus of the stories was never meant to be Jesus, but what Jesus was showing you about yourself. Was Jesus a real person? Yes." Sophia reached forward and held Farah's hand. "Because Jesus is *you*."

And then the world spun. On its axis around the sun, in sight of the rings of Saturn. Time and timelessness wove together, and yet it felt as if time stopped. The pages of Farah's Bible flipped open in the wind of her thoughts, and the contemplation that her heart should have stopped with the suggestion that Jesus was not who she had been told he was: a historical Jesus born of a virgin, violently murdered and hung upon a cross, who died for our sins—but it didn't. Her heart didn't stop at all. In fact, the opposite took place. Inside, Farah found she was not only glad to hear the things Sophia was telling her, but *grateful*. She felt relieved. She felt … secretly … *joyous*.

But most of all, Farah noticed, she didn't feel afraid because fundamentally what Sophia said meant that Jesus hadn't disapproved at all, that God still loved her, that it was the church who had disapproved all of these years. Doctrine, dogma, and other manmade things. Fundamentally, what Sophia said meant that God and even Jesus were greater than religion. That religion and God were not the same thing at all; and that the message in the Bible, Jesus' message, was far greater than any constrained religious definition had ever allowed it to be.

The words Sophia spoke next changed Farah's life forever.

"Jesus is the personification of the Christ-consciousness that exists at the core of *your* soul, the divine instinct that propels your evolution—an evolution that in turn contributes to the evolution of the human species. He is the personification of the *good news* or 'gospel' that every single human in the world is on a soul journey, an evolutionary adventure of soul growth that is *part of the fabric of existence.*" Sophia reached forward now and picked up Farah's Bible. "In *this Bible*, Jesus is the personification of that which exists within *you,* and so it makes sense that Jesus' ministry would have lasted a year, for in choosing this number, the authors of Matthew, Mark, and Luke were paying homage to the most timeless spiritual truth, the most ancient gospel stories, and the fundamental spiritual reality that belongs to the soul and to every human: the reality of the soul journey, which itself is reflected by the yearly cycle of the sun. Matthew, Mark, Luke, and John are retelling a series of ancient stories about the most ancient spiritual truth—a truth that never perishes because it is timeless—the spiritual reality of every human being. And this is the core truth of the Bible."

Farah had leaned back on the couch. She listened with her hands on her stomach and her eyes closed, smiling because of the start of something inside of her—a feeling.

She felt it displace things, push other things out, and shine light in the crevices it exposed.

She felt it fill in gaps and it *felt* to Farah, *wonderful.*

Sophia knew what was happening, because she knew that Farah was destined to experience it. She also knew that Farah was ready to hear more of her truth, so she continued to speak the things that were crucial for Farah to know if she was ever going to heal, if she was ever going to evolve. Farah was a microcosm of humanity, for as long as humans clung to the religious misinterpretations of their ancient scriptures, the evolution of human kind would stagnate; unresolved conflict would be endless. Sophia *knew* that only when humans began to understand that when they read the Bible they are reading a volume of spiritual truth expressed in the guise of allegories, will they be able to look beyond the common, literal connotation of the words, to discern a much greater transcendental significance. "Now," Sophia said, smiling, "I suppose you're wondering what these symbols mean?"

Farah lifted her head. Her shining eyes blinked incredulously. "That," she said, "is an understatement."

♋

Rose's hands were trembling, this couldn't be real.

It had to be a trick or a lie.

It was *impossible* that the story of Jesus' birth, life, and death was not unique.

The events that defined his life were the *reason* he could be who he was—the Only Son of God—the Saviour of Mankind who died on the cross and was raised to the right hand of God on the third day.

Jesus came and died and was raised from the dead, which proved he was the Son of God; but yet, right now, it seemed as if Rose was being told that *who* Jesus was, what he said and did, the story of his life—the *foundation* of Christianity—*had happened before*. That Jesus was not … *unique*. Not who Christianity had always said he was.

[A]lmost every traditional faith the world over rests on a central story of the son of a heavenly king who goes down into a dark lower world, suffering, dying, and rising again, before returning to his native upper world. Acted out in a moving, multifaceted dramatic ritual, the story tells how this king/god wins a victory over his enemies, has a triumphant procession, and is enthroned on high. Comparative religions scholars have made lists of thirty to fifty such avatars or saviours, including: Osiris, Horus, Krishna, Bacchus, Orpheus, Hermes, Balder, Adonis, Hercules, Attis, Mithras, Tammuz of Syria, Thor (son of Odin), Beddru of Japan, Deva Tat of Siam. … Kersey Graves (*The World's Sixteen Crucified Saviors*) quotes a prophecy of the Persian divinity Zoroaster: "A virgin should conceive and bear a son, and a star would appear blazing at midday to signalize the occurrence. When you behold the star, follow it wherever it leads you. Adore the mysterious child, offering him gifts with profound humility. He is indeed the Almighty Word which created the heavens. He is indeed your lord and everlasting King." (Harpur, *The Pagan Christ*, pp. 37–38)

> The differences between these saviour figures is the culture through which they are expressed, but what they have in common extends from an even more ancient gospel …

Rose felt sick, and with trembling hands put the pages down.

Suddenly, saving that which was lost was not a mission she felt pleased about. Suddenly, Rose felt very afraid. If any of what she had read so far had come from some magazine or television program, she wouldn't have given it a second thought. In fact, she would have snubbed it aggressively as "more blasphemous rubbish contrived by the unconverted." Contrived by those who still needed to be saved, those who didn't *believe* (poor fools). But *this* was *Roger.*

Even if Rose thought her son was lost or his tea was suspicious, she knew he would never concoct this type of lie. It involved historical documents, the testimony of church fathers, the testimony of the Bible *itself.* Rose fled then, as quickly as she could, and wondered, as she retched over the toilet, if any of the words, any of the things she had read, could fall out of her brain, out through her mouth, down and out into the sewer system. She wiped at her brow and lips with a tissue. If she believed any of this, it would be akin to turning her back on God, a one-way ticket to hell ... and the idea of *that* made Rose shudder with fear. She pressed the heels of her hands to her eyes. When she removed them, she could just make out the edge of the Day Two folder on the coffee table. Comparisons between Jesus and Krishna[111] echoed in her head:

- Krishna was born in a stable, of a virgin
- Upon his birth, baby Krishna was placed in a manger
- Great signs and wonders occurred at Krishna's birth, including the appearance of a bright star
- His birth was attended by angels, wise men, shepherds, and he was presented with gifts including gold and incense
- As a young boy, Krishna worked miracles and wonders, and was hailed as a divine incarnation
- Krishna was tempted in the wilderness, raised a child from the dead, healed lepers, the deaf, and the blind
- He miraculously fed the multitudes
- "He lived poor and he loved the poor," humbly washing the feet of guests
- He was transfigured in front of his disciples
- He was anointed with oil by a woman bearing a jar of ointment
- Krishna is called the "Shepherd God," "Lord of the god of gods," and "Lord of lords," and was considered the "Redeemer," "Firstborn," "Sin Bearer," "Liberator," and "Universal Word"
- A common earlier English transliteration of Krishna was "Christna"[112]

"It's too much," Rose whispered, holding her head in her hands.

What if she just walked away?

Out.

Right now.

What would that mean?

If she put Roger's things back where she found them, tidied up the couch and placed the cushions *just so*; if she replaced the papers in the order they were numbered and put the normal tea to the back of the cupboard. What if Rose just walked quietly out the kitchen door, as if she had never been there? Never read the Day One folder, never worried her son was the Anti-Christ, never thought, even for the briefest of moments, that some of what she read so far actually made sense (she shivered at this thought and shook her head back and forth violently in denial of this most secret admittance). What would it mean if she did just that? Took everything she knew *before* she arrived, and left pretending that none of this had ever happened, that she hadn't read any of it? Then Jesus would still be God, Jesus would still be the only Son of God, she would still be saved, and what she believed the Bible said would still be *right* (because she was a Christian). The Bible would still be completely infallible in the back, the front, and even in the middle, of her mind.

There would be no presence of questions.

No hidden feelings and thoughts of shock or wonder.

If Rose walked away, if she ignored it, everything she believed would still be absolute, and *that* sounded wonderful. Like a sigh of bliss. Like sunshine after rain. Like a remedy. And for a brief moment, Rose believed it could be … until she imagined herself actually doing it. There she would be, she knew it, sitting in her car trying to pretend that she hadn't learned all of the things she just had. And what good would that do? Did she have the psychological strength to deny these odious verities that Roger had revealed and was revealing, right this very moment, to a multitude of people?

To ignore what she had read would be … impossible. Or close to. The mental effort it would require for Rose to pretend that she had never learned what she had about the Bible, read what she had read about the presence of some sort of universal Christ-consciousness, or the reality that the Christian religion had a history that pre-existed Jesus would be monumental. She bit her lip—*could* she go back?

Rose decided. No.

The only way through it was forward, to face it, and then to reason through with the things she previously knew as ammunition to discount everything she had learned. And so Rose, who had decided, who would not be accused of willful ignorance, crawled back to the couch, reached forward, and turned the next page.

♑

Everyone was waiting.

"Despite their differences," Roger began, "a strikingly similar theme can be found between not just the four gospels, but also in the oldest Christian writings—in particular, those belonging to Paul—and despite what today's Christian doctrine proselytizes, this theme is not about Jesus' blood, his death, or his resurrection. Nor does it have anything to do with Jesus being God."

"The theme in the gospels," Roger said "is about something *else* entirely, something to do with what sound like the 'secrets' of life. In Luke, Jesus stresses that *real* life is not measured by how much we own, and that all *flesh* shall see the salvation of God. Jesus also tells us in the gospels that the Kingdom of God is within us, and that the Kingdom of God is at hand *right now*. In Matthew, Jesus points out that people are the light of the world, and John tells us that contained *within* every human is the true light that lighteth the world. John also tells us in several different ways that 'God lives in us' and that His love has 'been brought to full expression *through* us'; John says that 'God has given us His Spirit as proof that we live in him and he in us." The Old Testament tells us point blank in Psalm 82:6 that we 'are gods' and that *all* of us 'are children of the most High.' This echoes John's sentiment that all of us are 'like Christ here in this world.'

"Even Paul, whose writings are the earliest of all the Christian writings, reiterates this mysterious theme—that there is *more* meaning to life, *more* to being human, than meets the eye: 'But God giveth it a body as it hath pleased him, and to every seed his own body.' Paul then goes on to say that we are sown a natural body and raised a spiritual body, making a clear distinction that these two things united are what make us human: a natural or physical body and a spiritual body. In fact, time and time again, scripture reminds us that we are made of body and soul and that in death the two parts that make us human will separate. The body will decrease, and the spirit will carry on or increase. At the same time, scriptures go to great effort to distinguish for us the difference between the two combined things that make us human: 'The spirit is truly ready,' Jesus says in Mark, 'but the flesh is weak.' In this same vein Paul implores us to know of ourselves, 'that we are the temple of God and that Spirit of God dwells within us,' and points out that it is those of us in touch with the 'Spirit' *within* who are the true children of God. Paul also mysteriously implies that there is a treasure inside of us, perhaps of which we are not aware. Again and again, the scriptures refer to a hidden knowledge contained not within the verses, but within our bodies; again and again the scriptures hint that they are making us privy to something we perhaps may have forgotten, something that is happening not two thousand years ago, not in the future or the past, but *always*. *Now*. Even Jesus iterates again and again the immediacy of the spiritual message of the gospel and of the Kingdom of God.

"Interestingly," Roger said, walking to the projector, "many of the church fathers were also privy to the fact that the early gospels contained much more meaning than the orthodox interpretation suggested." Roger slipped a quote under the projector. "Origen himself, who, as you will well remember, was one of the most revered and pious of the church Fathers, commented, *'It is allowed by all who have any knowledge of the scriptures that everything there is conveyed enigmatically.'* Of this mysterious knowledge, Augustine—the *founder* of Christian theology—said, *'That which is known as the Christian religion existed among the ancients, and never did not exist, from the very beginning of the human race.'*[113] Roger looked up at the room and repeated, "From the beginning of the human race."

He then pulled yet another transparency from his Day Two folder. Upon it, now projected larger than life onto the wall, were twelve figures, of which two stood out from the rest. The most central was a woman, whose hair flowed down over her shoulders, whose gown appeared to flow in an invisible wind, who held, in one arm a sheaf of wheat, and in the other, a baby. "Several thousand years ago," he said, "in the precession of the equinoxes, the end of a year was marked by the position of the brightest star in the sky. Precisely at midnight on December twenty-fourth, the Sirius star stood on the meridian line from the zenith to Egypt." Roger drew a horizon line on the board and a star directly above the center of it. "At this very same moment, there arose on the western horizon the constellation of Virgo, bearing in her left arm a child, and in her right hand a sheaf of wheat. The Sirius star," Roger said, "was the most arcane symbol of a *physical* truth … and the child in the arms of Virgo symbolized a verity as ancient as the moment human life first became a part of existence. The child was known as the Christ Child—divine consciousness. And the sheaf of wheat"—Roger pointed to the sheaf in Virgo's other arm— "symbolized the *function* of that divine consciousness in the world, as celestial food for man.[114] Bread from heaven."

The image was foreign yet familiar. A woman in simple dress of robes, the Virgin, holding in her arms the baby Jesus—the two most ancient symbols of that which makes every human a human being. "Before Jesus was born in 4 AD in a manger in Bethlehem, he was" —Roger pointed to the Christ child in Virgo's arms— "this child. And *this* child was a symbol of something that makes every human a human *being*. This child," Roger said, "is a symbol of something that exists in every single human—*every* human that has ever been born, and every human that ever will be born. The child in Virgo's arms is a symbol of the very thing that Jesus was: the *living* knowledge, wisdom, strength, and infinite love of God that exists within each of us, that exists," Roger said, looking around the room, "within each and every one of you."

It was a confusing concept to communicate at first, not because the concept—or rather the reality—itself was confusing, but because the principles of it contradicted what religion often said was the only spiritual truth. Religion wanted humans to believe they were sin-filled and separated from God unless they meet the required conditions set out by said religion, when the reality was that this simply is not the case. It was confusing, for example, to discover that the ancient term *Christ* meant "anointed one" or "one anointed with divinity," and that the ancient concept of a human being or *bar-enasha* was "one who is anointed with divine consciousness." It was confusing, then, to be informed that many thousand years ago it was common knowledge that *every* human being, from the moment it is born, lives incarnated with divine instinct and that this divine instinct is known as the Christ-consciousness—the consciousness of the one anointed with divinity; the divine instinct, awareness, morality, and knowledge of one who is a human being *because* of the union of spirit and matter and who, as a human being, is on a particular journey. Yes, Roger understood how this information could be confusing, particularly for the religious, because so much of it went against so much of what they had been told being human means.

It was then that Roger revealed the original meaning of Mark, Matthew, Luke, and John; the ancient meaning of the Zodiac, of Virgo and Pisces, the House of Bread and the House of Fish, of Spirit into matter, and the Good News of the journey of souls. And it was then that Roger began to clarify how the Bible had been telling this very same story, revealing this very same truth, all along.

"The Good News that Jesus brought through his ministry was not, as the orthodox interpretation claims, about him or the meaning of *his* death," Roger said. "It was the truth about *you*, a gospel about the most *fundamental* truths of life and existence. A gospel, plain and simply about the Good News of being human. Long ago this Good News had a different name—it was called the Gospel of the Journey of Souls. It was a commentary about the most fundamental truths of life and existence, a reflection on the invisible spiritual truth of what is real about the human experience. Of this truth, the Wisdom Sayings, and the allegories and metaphors that expressed them, made their way from legend, art, and oral tradition to paper, where they became the

Q-Document. The Q-Document—a copy or a remnant of it—then became the source document used by the authors of the early gospels who used it to pen their own versions of the Soul Journey story. Iusa, who was Yeshua, who eventually became Jesus, was the vehicle or main character through which this spiritual truth was expressed, and so became the focus of those ignorant to the reality that the stories about him were communicating: that he was the spiritual consciousness within every human.

"In this way, every moment of Jesus' birth, life, death, and ministry not only represented a moment in every human life, but also was a metaphor of various physical, intellectual, spiritual, and psychological challenges faced each day in every human life. *Every single miracle* Jesus 'performed' was intended to represent the greater discovery of truth on the soul journey— various forms of awakening."

On the board, Roger wrote the words *ANU, Bethany,* and *Bethlehem.* He wrote *Horus, Osiris, Jesus,* and *Lazarus,* and then elaborated on the most ancient meaning of the most popular Bible stories (Jesus' famous victory ride upon a donkey into Jerusalem, the Flood, the Virgin Birth …). He defined numbers and symbolisms that had never before been quite understood: three, twelve, forty, fish, bread, the parting and the calming of waters.

"Beneath the layers of culture, politics, and religion, the Bible is still," Roger said, "at its heart, about the most fundamental truths of life and existence. A message not just for Christian, Jew, or Muslim, but one for *all.*" Roger looked up to everyone in the room. "*This* is the heart of the Jesus stories—a truth that exists beyond and above all religion; the actual spiritual truth of all humankind, based in the concreteness of physical experience and, most importantly, reality."

♈

As they walked, the gospel stories emerging, Master Lael elaborated the truths about being human with gentle, consistent enthusiasm. His hands spoke with quiet, soulful knowledge, his voice with a timbre of humility that soothed and inspired. The cave around them, busier now, buzzed with artisans consumed by their work; seating areas were shared; lessons had begun; the sun streamed down.

The beauty in being human shined.

"Now," Master Lael said, "it is important to understand that conscience and instinct are not the same thing." He held his hands as if in one he held "conscience" and in the other he held "instinct." "Your instinct," he said, "is the voice of God within that you are born with. It is the constant, fundamental knowledge of the difference between right and wrong that lives inside of you. Instinct will always lead you the right way." Master Lael motioned with the hand that held "instinct" and pressed it to his chest. "Your conscience, however, is shaped by your culture and your perceptions of life—by the things you are taught to believe are right or wrong, by the way you are taught to think about things or people in general. The conscience can be 'convinced', for example, that certain unacceptable things are acceptable, say violence or hatred, cruelty or neglect. But, the instinct, knows better." Master Lael plucked the "conscience" out of his one hand, pretended to mold and shape it with both hands, and then popped it into his temple. Then he placed one hand on his head and one hand on his chest. "Sometimes your conscience and your instinct come into conflict; it is during this time that we must do the simplest thing that sometimes seems the hardest. Be still … *listen*. Not to our busy minds but to our *insides*—to our deepest, most *honest* feelings. The ones we often try to hide or suppress when under outside pressure, the ones that get lost in the whirlwind of our thoughts and fears. For within that stillness your divinity shines, and resolve to your conflict resides."

Again, Mateo's eyes widened in realization. There were several instances he could think of when his "insides" spoke to him. Sometimes it was a feeling, sometimes it was like having a sound resonate inside of him—a clear bell ringing, or a voice saying *you know this is not right*. Even when Mateo did something he knew was wrong, and tried as hard as he could to ignore the fact that he knew it, his insides would still speak up! But Mateo had no idea that was God's voice echoing inside of him! It was what Moses meant when he said, *The word is near you, in your mouth and in your heart.*

Mateo's understanding suddenly grew.

Behold, I shew you a mystery...

~1 Corinthians 15:51

♌

♈ ♉ ♊ ♋ ♌ ♍ ♎ ♏ ♐ ♑ ♒ ♓

"Jesus had twelve disciples. Not five or six or twenty, but twelve. Have you ever wondered why?"

Farah shook her head. She'd never thought about why. She just knew there were twelve.

"Because twelve is the number of wholeness and completeness," Sophia said. "It was no mistake that Jesus had twelve disciples, just as it was no mistake the number twelve was chosen to divide the twelve tribes of Israel in the Old Testament. The number twelve is significant because it represents *these* twelve symbols, one symbol for each of the twelve months in a year. Together," Sophia said, "these twelve symbols represent *all* of humankind—every human born, and every human yet to be born. *This* is how the number twelve comes to represent the whole of humanity—the twelve disciples of Jesus in the gospel stories are not simply twelve people, they represent *all people*, that's right, every person on Earth because every person in the world was born under one of these twelve signs."

Farah's mind began to flash with realizations—the struggles the disciples had with fear, doubt, faith, right action …

"And so it is through his twelve disciples that the human struggle is illustrated. The disciples embody the very struggles in a metaphorical sense that every human will face in one form or another on their life journey. You will notice in the stories that not only is Jesus the healer, but his is the voice of calm, sense, the core voice of truth in the center of all circumstances. Through the twelve we witness the great power of human ignorance, the stagnation of spiritual evolution, and other such travails identified as demons, illness, or people being lost in a deep sleep from which they need to be wakened."

Farah's eyes widened. "Lazarus."

"Yes," Sophia smiled. "The story of Lazarus raised from the dead is a perfect example, for as with the stories of the twelve disciples, it too contains an ancient meaning far more profound than any literal interpretation could ever comprehend. This tale, Lazarus and Jesus have been telling for millennia—for many, many, thousand years—only in the first written tales, the momentous event of Jesus raising Lazarus from the dead took place in the ancient Egyptian city of Anu."

And then Farah learned that in an ancient city called Anu, Horus, the Egyptian sun god, raised Osiris from the dead. She learned that Egypt, in the most ancient times, was more than a country—it was the name of the place where human life took place, the allegorical home of human experience. As part of this tradition, Anu was more than just a city in ancient Egypt; it was the human body—the place into which the soul, symbolized by the sun, was born, experienced physical life and evolution, and from which the soul departed. Anu was known for this reason as the City of the Sun.

Farah wanted to ensure she understood, "So Anu was the place in which the cycle of the sun—the cycle of the *soul* took place?" Sophia nodded. "Yes, which meant that the miracle of Horus raising Osiris from the dead was an event that took place in the human body." Metaphor. Allegory.

When she learned these things, Farah felt as if a thin paper were being burned away from in front of her eyes. Suddenly, she could *see* what Sophia meant. Horus, the sun god, represented the spiritual consciousness within her—*her* spiritual consciousness. And Osiris represented *her* physical body—or the human mind unawakened to the spiritual truth of the human life in which the body existed. At Anu—within the human body—the soul wakens the mind, the body to its spiritual consciousness. Sophia confirmed Farah's revelation.

"Osiris in the story is the part of you that doesn't know who you are. When Horus raises Osiris from the dead it symbolizes the discovery of self; it symbolizes spiritual awakening, all the wonderful moments on your life journey when your internal eyes feel opened and your mouth says, 'Ah ha!' because suddenly, without having to say another word or any word at all, you *get it*. You awaken to a knowing within you, and you understand without any need of definitions or words, who and *what* God is inside of and around you. And so the story of Horus raising Osiris from the dead in Anu tells the raw spiritual truth of your evolutionary journey—that the divine consciousness within you is the only thing that can truly awaken you from the deep sleep of spiritual ignorance."

Farah hadn't even noticed Sophia making small notes on the page again. When she looked down she saw words morphing into each other; somehow Anu became Bethany, Osiris became Lazarus, and Horus … became Jesus.

"When the Hebrews appropriated the Anu story, they were more specific about referencing Anu as the human body, so they called it *Beth-Anu*.[115] 'Beth,' meaning bread, was a reference to the original symbolic mother of every human being. Astrologically, she was Virgo—"

Farah's head whipped up. "V-Virgo?"

"Yes, Virgo. The Virgin."

"Jesus was born of a Virgin," Farah whispered.

"Yes," Sophia let go a small laugh. Revelation in the air then was palpable. It felt pure in the room, like joy or surprise. "Virgo was the mother of all things physical, of physical matter itself. In antediluvian times, matter was symbolized by water. In this sense Virgo came to be known in many cultures as the water mother, and she had many names. The Greeks called her Talleth, but she was also known as Nun, Maya, Miriam, Meri."[116]

"*Mary …*" Farah's jaw dropped open as she whispered Mary's name, and then her exclamation came more emphatically, "Mary!"

Again Sophia laughed. "Yes. Jesus was born of the Virgin Mary." She loved seeing Farah's spirit scintillating the way that it was—and the girl hadn't even heard the whole story! "But there is more to know if you are to understand the story fully. Virgo was often drawn carrying a sheaf of wheat, which signified that the human born from her was born *whole*—incarnated with spirit and spiritual consciousness. The wheat symbolized your spiritual consciousness, which is seen as food for the soul—the spiritual food of man on Earth, bread from heaven—and so Virgo also became known as the House of Bread, which is why, when the Hebrews appropriated the Egyptian Anu story, they added 'Beth'—insinuating Virgo, insinuating the human body born whole—and Anu became Beth-Anu. Your divine consciousness was seen as spiritual food for the body, bread from heaven—and so Virgo was also known as the House of Bread."

Scripture echoed in the back of Farah's mind. *For the bread of God is that which comes down from heaven and gives life to the world.*[117] *This is the bread which comes down from heaven, that a man may eat of it and not die.*[118] And Jesus saying outright, "I am the bread of life."[119] Bread imagery and reference in the Bible abounded—even the curious question Jesus asks a small group of men in a boat after he calms the waters of the sea upon which they were being tossed, "O men of little faith, why do you discuss among yourselves the fact that you have no bread?"[120] It was all beginning to make sense: Jesus was asking them why they knew not of the spiritual bread that existed within, which was exactly what Jesus personified. Farah whispered, "*This is the bread which comes down from heaven and gives life to the world.*"[121]

Sophia replied, "Because there is one bread, we who are many are one body, for we all partake of the bread[122]—which is precisely why," she continued, "the Hebrews made special reference to Virgo[123] when they appropriated the Anu story. They prefixed Anu with the word for *house*, which is *beth*, and Anu became *Beth-Anu*. Anu, then, when transliterated into English becomes *Any*,[124] and so the Egyptian city of Anu becomes the Hebrew city of *Bethany*—"

Before Sophia could, Farah finished the story for her, "—and Jesus raised Lazarus from the dead in Bethany." Farah shook her head in disbelief. "This is unbelievable."

Sophia then showed Farah how the name Osiris became, across languages, cultures, time, and pronunciations, Lazarus,[125] and how the story of Jesus raising Lazarus out of his deep sleep in Bethany was the same as the story of Horus waking Osiris in Anu—both stories about the awakening of the human being to the consciousness that exists within.

For Farah then, it was now over. Something in her ended, and she knew it was her doubt. Her will, like mercury, glided in shimmering glimmers across her body toward the center of her being, and began to form once again within her, at the core of her human character, where it belonged. This coming together was fueled by the strength of an untapped well that seemed to have burst within her like a fountain, from which fresh, healing waters flowed like a river, like a source of ancient wisdom, like a source of unconditional love and discovery, an elixir of arcane verity that wanted only one thing for her: evolution. Growth. *Telios.*

When Sophia spoke again, she told Farah that the astrological mother of spiritual consciousness was Pisces, which was why fish symbolism was always associated with Jesus, and why fish as well as bread abounded in the gospel tales of miracles, ministry, and thought-provoking events. "Virgo was the House of Bread, and Pisces the House of the Great Fish, or dual fishes—bread and fish were therefore made the symbolic dual food for man, the one physical, the other spiritual nourishment."[126]

When Farah heard this, images from the New Testament began to flash through her mind like a badly or a brilliantly edited film: fish feeding the multitudes, loaves of bread feeding the hungry, the parable of the gold coin in the mouth of the fish, fishermen. And then an image of the pope's hat—shaped like a fish mouth. Fish painted on Jesus' forehead in ancient murals and tombs, mosaic-ed into images of Jesus on old-world cathedral floors. And finally of the most contemporary fish symbol associated with Jesus—the Jesus fish, a symbol used by Christians the world over. Farah had always been taught not to say the Lord's name in vain, but this time, the degree of her exclamation was just *that* incredulous and she whispered, "Oh. My. God."

"You see, Farah," Sophia said, "the Bible is a reflection of *the* most ancient spiritual truth. One that can be contained by no religion. A spiritual truth that needs no religion because it is the *collective spiritual truth of all humankind,* one based in the reality of what it means to be human. Based in reality itself—the reality, plain and simply, of existence." Sophia reiterated, "In the most ancient of Jesus stories, Jesus is not telling you who *he* is, he is telling you who *you* are."

♋

The facts were laid out.

Rose's eyes traced the sentences, paused on the curve and shape of the letters that composed them, looked at the space between the words and lines, and her eyes welled with tears. There were no empty spaces in the language of religion; every word mattered, every nuance, accusation, every revelation, every soft and gloriously relevant truth. Anu. Bethany. Virgo. Osiris. Lazarus.

"Jesus was born in Bethlehem—" she whispered.

Bethlehem transliterated to House of Bread.[128]

Jesus was born from Virgo.

Anointed One.

Human.

Her son was saying something here that was enormous … *devastating*. Astounding. Blasphemous.

And yet it was something that apparently not only *he* was saying. Something that other experts—religious and academic—were discovering. Had discovered.

"Is he *really* saying it?" Rose whispered, knowing that he was: Christianity, a religion about worshipping Jesus, was never meant to be that. It instead was born out of an astrological theology, intended to reflect some kind of universal spiritual truth about what it meant to be human. He really was saying it: The gospels weren't about a man named Christ, but about the Christ in man. The Christ-consciousness in everyone.

And *now* Rose couldn't look away.

She had to know how on earth any of this could possibly be discerned from her Bible, how Roger could have the audacity to suggest that the Christian faith for the last several hundred years had been perpetuating a belief system that was built upon a misinterpretation of ancient scriptures. Roger's words echoed …

Each one of us is born with the nature of God alive in us. Jesus is man enlivened with that nature; he acts in it and communicates the truth of it, and by him we are able to see what it is God created us to be: our best selves who act and walk in wisdom, love, compassion, and intelligence;

who use reason beyond doubt and who do not allow ourselves to be the victims of our own fears. For when we walk in the world—not on our own, but partnered in our consciousness with the greater purpose of our lives—we are able to experience firsthand our relationship with the God-energy that the entire world and we are made of.

Jesus is the human enlightened.

♑

The world over, another day was passing. People were going about their business, shopping, starving to death, making babies, abusing children, burying loved ones, going to war, coming home, celebrating, loving, hating, lying (to themselves and others), breeding kindness or love or negativity in the world. The sun shifted across the sky, the moon glistened on water, stars twinkled even when hidden behind clouds. Trees breathed. In Roger's classroom there was one last thing to learn, one last thing to understand.

Without this comprehension, the Bible and maybe any ancient scripture would never be completely understood.

Beside the letter 'Q', Roger wrote one word:

Death.

"The lost meaning of death is one of the biggest tragedies in the history of humankind," he started, "for in misunderstanding death, humans have come to misunderstand *life*." Roger wrote:

You have the name of being alive, but you are dead.
Revelation III, 1

Who knows whether to live is not to die and to die is not to live?
Euripides[129]

I am the resurrection and the life: he that believeth in
me, though he were dead, yet shall he live.
Jesus

"In essence," Roger said, "there is and only ever has been, *one* spiritual teaching, which has always and only ever been about one thing: what is real about life and death." Roger knew what now, what this time, meant. This was the moment when people had to do what Roger himself had had to do in order to grow in his understanding of scriptures … which meant understanding that definitions were moveable. That death did not always mean what his culture and point in time defined it to mean; that long ago, it meant something else—in this case, something else entirely. In order to comprehend the true meaning of death, Roger had been forced to relax his structured definition of absolutes and judgments about what he thought things were and learn instead what they were *actually* about. And so he did, and it was then that Roger began to learn how it was that "Death, in actual fact, was a word that referred to *human life*."

"I don't understand," someone said, rubbing their face with their hands.

And the very root of the oldest spiritual truth of humankind, the common spirituality of humanity began to be known to those in the room. "Antediluvian 'Death,'" Roger said, "was not understood as an end of life. The term 'death' was a metaphor for the *degree* of life experienced by the soul when it was contained in matter. In other words, a soul contained in matter was a muted version of itself—a soul contained in matter is just that: *contained*. In no way did 'death' as an ending exist for the soul because the soul itself is indestructible.[130] Of this, Plato said, 'For I have heard from one of the wise that we are now dead and that the body is our sepulcher.' Of this too, the soul contained within the body was described by the Roman poet Virgil as 'deadened' by earthly forms and members subject to death.[131] The life of the human being then, was considered a form of containment for the soul and so 'death' became a metaphor for human life. When the soul underwent a 'death' it came to exist contained in matter, where it gained experience, living the physical aspects of life. In Genesis, this spiritual reality is illustrated as the 'expulsion' of Adam and Eve from Eden when God says, 'If you eat of this tree, you will surely die.' But Adam and Eve didn't die; they simply took on a less vivid type of life.[132] They were made to live and undergo 'death' or containment in matter, human life, whereby the soul gains knowledge, experience, and growth. For Adam and Eve certainly do not die when they leave the Garden of Eden, they *live*.

"And they did. Adam and Eve, and every human 'descendant' … *lives*.

"Such a thing as death in the sense of total annihilation either of being or matter was an unthinkable and impossible thing,"[133] Roger said. "'Death,' instead, was defined by the sensory experience of the soul, which was that in the human body it became contained."

The woman at the back of the room raised her hand slowly. "But what then, is the meaning of Jesus' death?"

"But that's just the thing, isn't it?" Roger said, his eyes on the chalk that he turned between his fingers, before looking up. "Jesus *didn't* die."

When Mateo learned about love, it took him by surprise.

Love was the name of the electricity that fueled life and ensured its continuation. The eternal presence of love in all living things was God's ultimate law.

It was invisible, and yet completely palpable to the senses. It could float the body in bliss or grateful humility or, if taken away, could devastate the heart or the mind, and even the state of the world. Love was the invisible thread that held the fabric of all things—the world, the human body, our minds, our relationships—together.

It was people's love, *how* they loved or didn't love, that distinguished their identity in the world, and it was the nature of their love that discerned them from others. *How* a person loved—others, themselves, the world, creation—*how* they honoured themselves and others was always how they were remembered. Love was the immortal part of every human. It was that very same energy that was of God: from which everything emerged and came to be, of which everything was a part, to which everything was connected.

"Love is not something you do," Master Lael said, "It is *who you are*. It can not be created, it is not a result; It is the fuel of action, your core identity—the only common language in the world. When people understand that they are love—that love is the heart of their very being—the spiritual fingerprint they leave upon others and the world, they are propelled forward, and evolution is inevitable. When people can be the love that they are, the world is changed for the better."

"For love is what's left when you get rid of everything you don't need." Mateo whispered, his heart shining with memory.

They came to the story of Babel, in which all the humans in the world were building a tower to bring them closer to God. At that time, everyone spoke the same language, the language of mutuality and grace, respect of being, understanding—the first language. But then human ego, fear, pride, anger, and disagreement began to emerge, resulting in a 'language' that stood in the way of mutuality, which in turn, resulted in a division between the peoples of the world. For it was only people that could cause division between themselves.

When Mateo learned about forgiveness, he felt relieved—as if it were a powerful secret he could put into practice at any time to liberate himself from misery.

"To maintain a grudge is akin to taking a teaspoon of poison every day," Master Lael said. "It makes you bitter and gives your power away to the person you least want to have it. Empower yourself with mercy, practice forgiveness, liberate your heart and your mind with temperance; otherwise, you will stagnate your own path to growth." In the gospel story it said, "Judge not, lest ye be judged" and asked that Mateo turn the other cheek—choose his own path rather than the poison of revenge. This was the way to enlightenment.

When Mateo learned about suffering, he was too young to really understand, but as he grew older his comprehension grew and expanded, sending deep-reaching roots into the foundation of his life. It was one image, with words and symbols that said the same thing, over and over again in different ways, different languages, with different images:

Suffering is not a covenant God made with man
Therefore, if a person suffers, it is not by the will of God.

Sometimes, suffering contained within it a necessary part of the unfolding of life's lessons. Sometimes suffering was a perception. Sometimes, it was self-inflicted—out of which people needed to awake.

Mateo smiled; these memories warmed his entire body. Cloaked him like a robe. Those lessons were the foundation of his life. He looked around the cave now at all the people, all those listening, all those thinking, all those talking, all those smiling, all those whose thoughts contained within them were troubled or sorrowful, light-filled or positive, and inhaled deeply. He smiled. All around him he could feel it, all around him it was there. Everywhere. Evolution. Soul journeys. Growth. The magic of God.

Light streamed through the skylight far above his head, and came to rest on the cross at his feet, shining its ebony into full glory. Mateo looked upon it and whispered, "The meaning in all of *this* …"

When he was a boy, his father had woken him early one morning, well before sunrise. They walked, far into the hills, to the highest point visible from their village. Far beneath them, underground, were the library edges of the Sanctuary, books and scrolls and knowledge and prayers, billowing whispers of wonder and awe up through the ground.

The pre-dawn air was so still, they could hear the stars twinkling the last of their night-song; they could feel the Earth stirring in anticipation of morning. A boy led his goat herd into the hills behind them, a man tied a donkey to his cart full of wares. The scent of flatbread wafted in the distance.

As they sat, facing east, a faint glow began to emerge on the horizon, and Mateo's father began to speak.

"If you remember anything in your life, remember this moment. In your deepest confusion, with the voices of the world surrounding you, remember me right now," Erelah told his son, "and the words I am about to speak."

Mateo looked at his father's silhouette. How could he ever forget it? With the night behind them and the promise of morning at their faces, Mateo's father looked how Mateo felt about him: perfect, like honour and respect and magic. "Okay, Papa," he said.

The glow on the horizon increased. Erelah's voice came soft and low. "Some people treat human life as if it is separate from creation. They believe that human existence on Earth is the result of some kind of punishment—that the true fulfillment of being human will only be realized when the supposed punishment ends. But this"—the glow on the horizon increased—"could not be further from the truth. For to believe that the meaning of human life is only found after it ends, is to believe that our existence is somehow separate from the meaning of all things. To believe that human life on Earth is only as the result of some kind of punishment, is to be entirely ignorant of what it really means to *be* human, what our relationship with God really is, what our relationship with life, and all of existence, really means. Because God did not create *all of this*," Erelah opened his arms to the world, "and then put us in this exact moment in time because we weren't supposed to be here. God did not create all of this, Mateo, with human life able to prosper in it, for *nothing*."

At that moment the sun broke the horizon, and streaks of golden light glorified the sky, spreading warmth out over the Earth, waking everything.

♌

Farah settled in, letting the blanket she once held tightly fall loose around her shoulders. While Sophia refreshed their drinks, she took in the rest of the cottage. It was cozy, without feeling small. The kitchen behind her, a large fireplace, hugged by bookshelves, dominated the far wall in front of her. The mantelpiece was bare but for what looked like a very old metal scroll—or maybe it was just the casing. The walls were decorated with woven textiles, fabrics, with embroidered scenes of villages. An old map of Africa was framed on the wall near the French doors, but the wall closest to Farah was covered in photographs. Pictures that depicted the staggering natural beauty of the planet: mountain ranges, rain forests, rivers, oceans, flora and fauna in full-coloured glory. Between them, photos of human faces, skins and faces of every colour smiling, laughing, hugging each other, waving. Farah's smile turned to laughter just looking at them.

"Contagious, I know." Sophia poured the tea.

"They are wonderful." Farah received it gratefully.

"Yes, they are."

"They look like a celebration of the world." Farah sipped.

Sophia dropped her eyes and added quietly, "And all of its majesty."

Farah watched Sophia sit and wondered again who this woman was. Where she came from. She considered asking, but at that moment the most famous Bible stories were begging to now be understood, and with one word, Sophia brought the girl's attention back to where she clearly thought it ought to be. "Barabbas," Sophia said, eyes twinkling. "Curious?"

Farah's attention was tweaked. Without a doubt inside, she answered, "Yes!"

And that was when the rest of Farah's story began.

The Barabbas story had confounded Farah for *years*. How; why; the details; the injustice. Barabbas was a criminal, described by some as a murderer, and the scene that described the choice between freeing Jesus—a messenger of God—or Barabbas, was a powerful one. As were the moments leading up to the choice: Jesus was in the forest praying. His disciples, instead of keeping watch, succumbed to the temptation of sleep. The result: the religious authorities captured Jesus; his location betrayed by Judas for thirty pieces of silver.

Jesus was then punished and brought before Pontius Pilate, the Roman procurator, who would decide his fate. Pilate, however, was unsure of Jesus' guilt. It was not clear to him what Jesus had done to warrant the call for punishment or death. Eventually, in response to pressure from the religious leaders of the day, Pilate put the question before the building crowd: Did they want Jesus—who challenged the dominant religious belief of the day—to be set free, or Barabbas—a known criminal? Incredibly, the crowd called for Barabbas to be freed, and Jesus' Passion began in earnest. From that point, he suffered torture and abuse, was made to carry a wooden cross onto which he would be nailed, crucified to the point of death. And so the story goes; Jesus died on the cross, was laid to rest in a cave/tomb, and rose from the dead three days later.

Farah never understood how the crowd could choose Barabbas, let alone how Pontius Pilate could let it happen. Pilate seemed so well intentioned, but so … unwilling to do the right thing, for fear of pressure from those around him.

She never understood why Judas was so vilified for betraying Jesus to initiate the Passion. According to Christian doctrine, Jesus *needed* to die in order to be who they said he was; in order fulfill the Old Testament prophecy that he was the Messiah, the Saviour of mankind.

In order for Jesus to die for our sins, he had to, well—die. So why be upset with Judas?

But mostly, Farah never understood how it was possible that those who recorded Jesus' words during his Passion, and his last words on the cross, had all heard different things. Three of the four firsthand accounts differed … but she had been over that already.

"In actuality," Sophia said, "there was no man named Barabbas. No criminal who the crowd decided should be freed instead of Jesus. Those who think this is what the story means simply do not recognize what it was they are reading; they don't recognize the *language* the gospels are speaking. Barabbas," Sophia explained, "actually means 'second son,'[134] and the fact that the unruly crowd chooses Barabbas over the first son in this story is no accident; it is an *example*. You see, the meaning of this story lies in the consequence of the action. Barabbas symbolizes the worst part of human nature, the part of us that can be corrupted. He represents the lazy part of human effort, the dark side of contemplation and decision making, the part of us that avoids taking responsibility for our actions, and the potential of immorality in human behaviour—all the abusive behaviours that are the result of unhealthy thinking patterns and that go *against* human nature.

Barabbas is the physical, emotive part of ourselves that responds first without thinking; he is irrationality, reaction, the area within us where ignorance can live and flourish. He is imbalance, the inability to self-reflect, anger, bitterness, and the worst part of our egos. Barabbas represents who every human is *not* intended to be."

"Jesus on the other hand, the first son, who is your spiritual consciousness, represents the inner truth of every human: your most true identity and everything divine and good that already exists within you. In this story, Jesus is the most fundamental aspect of who you are: the light. And *this moment*," Sophia said, "when Pontius Pilate presents Jesus and Barabbas before the crowd and asks them to choose who will be set free, represents a moment that is faced a thousand times by every person in their lifetime.[135] It is the moment of internal conflict, the moment of conflict in each of us when we are forced to choose between the things we know we should do but, for whatever reason, choose not to. It is a moment that reflects your physical human reality; a story asking you to recognize the consequences of choice. The crowd *chooses* Barabbas. It is an immoral choice. The story is asking you to consider what in your life you will choose.

"It is a story asking what you want your life to be. Because who and how you choose to be in your life, is exactly that: a choice. This is a story about morality, in the face of immoral situations." Sophia looked at Farah, "Yes? Do you see it?"

Farah had tears in her eyes. She nodded silently. She did see it.

"Don't worry, this is not the only story that has been tragically misunderstood," Sophia said, "or whose original meaning has been lost over time. Did you know that nowhere in ancient scriptures are the words *Red Sea* found?"

Farah did *not* know that, and while words and questions and calm and incredulity raced in her mind, she felt as if stone were being chipped away, falling on the floor around her—falling on the floor of the world.

The Exodus was one of the most significant moments in Jewish and Christian religious history. It was a story about the night Moses led the Israelites—described as God's Chosen People—out of Egypt. Famously—by parting the Red Sea to allow their escape.

For Farah, the obvious concerns abounded.

If there was no Red Sea, how could there have been an Exodus?

If no Red Sea existed, then how could it be parted?

Sophia explained, "None of the most ancient copies of Biblical scripture, not even the oldest copies of the Bible itself contain the words Red Sea. Instead, you will find the words *Iam Suph*, which mean '*green, reedy sea*' or '*sea of matter.*' You see," Sophia said, "the ancient meaning of the Exodus story lay not in its geographical location, but in the presence of the sea itself—the reedy sea of matter. What you don't understand, Farah, is that over two thousand years ago, it was common knowledge that the living word of God existed *within* the text, not on the surface. This is why the Bhagavad-Gita says 'Those who lack discrimination may quote the letter of the Scripture, but they are really denying its inner truth.'[136] In ancient times, people did not believe their texts, they believed *in them*.[137] The presence of seawater, in particular in the story of the Exodus, was an immediate indication of what the story itself was about to communicate. Tell me," Sophia smiled, "what is the *biggest* problem with the Exodus story as you have learned it?"

Farah thought a moment. There were several problems, but the one that stood out most was the geography of the tale: the east wind being raised to separate the Red Sea for the safe passage of the Israelites from Egypt into Canaan. This "fact" in the story was a geographical impossibility: If an east wind had parted the Red Sea, the Israelites waiting on the west bank would have been engulfed by the water. Whenever Farah brought this point up in church she was told to ignore it because "anything is possible with God."

"The geography, I guess; the east wind."

"Right. What else?"

"Well, I guess the idea that over two million people, and their carts, and their donkeys, and their children, and their belongings, were able to walk the entire width of Red Sea in *one* night."

"Mm-hm," Sophia nodded. "What else?"

Farah was careful when she spoke the words she was about to say, for they expressed thoughts she had always felt quietly, privately; things she had always wondered silently with a confused heart. "That God could kill the Egyptians—" Farah said quietly. "He murdered them all, without any regard for their lives, *their* children, *their* families …"

It was the idea that God favored one tribe of people over another that troubled Farah. She understood that the Israelites were supposed to be God's Chosen People, but it somehow seemed unfair to her that God would choose one group of people to love more than any other; that God would murder other races or tribes of people so easily for not being Israelites.

Sophia spoke softly, and asked Farah then, "Do you know what 'Israel' means?"

Farah nodded. She had known from the moment it had been iterated to her that she was *not* an Israelite. "God made a covenant with them because while everyone else worshipped many gods, the Israelites promised to worship one God, *the* One God. This made God so happy that he promised the Israelites, in exchange for their loyal worship, they would become His chosen people—the people in the world who were special to God over all others."

"No," Sophia shook her head gently. "*Israel* means 'upright with God.' And to be an Israelite means to be someone who is upright with God. Israelites are *not* 'God's Chosen People'; they are people 'Upright with God.'" In that moment, Farah didn't understand the difference.

"What would you say if I told you," Sophia began, "that the story of the Exodus was not about a tribe of people at all, but was instead a story about *you*—a story about a very significant aspect of *your* existence?"

"But *I'm* not Jewish," Farah said.

"Originally, Jewish has nothing to do with it," Sophia said, looking at Farah with deep meaning. "What would you say if I told you that the parting of and safe passage through *Iam Suph* symbolizes the birth of your soul into your body, and the guarantee that God will take care of you, ensure your safe passage through human life, guide your spirit safely—free from being overwhelmed by the waters of life—to the Promised Land? What would you say if you found out that the story of the Exodus was the revisiting of a timeless spiritual truth, a truth that reflected the reality of *existence*, the reality of human existence, and the meaning of human life? And that when you understand *how* to read the story—the east wind, the crossing of millions in one night, the death of the Egyptians—no longer remains difficult or even impossible to comprehend, but begins, instead, to make perfect sense."

"I would say," Farah replied smiling, "tell me more."

And Sophia did.

"Many thousand years ago," she said, "just like the stories we've already talked about, the Exodus was a story of symbolisms. It was not read as it is today, as a literal part of the history of a particular group of people, or as a literal occurrence between geographical locations. It was read for what it really was: reiteration of the very truth that underlies the majority of Biblical stories, a truth that is the ubiquitous, omnipresent theme at the heart of nearly all Biblical writing,[138] the truth of the journey of souls. The Exodus is a story designed to reveal a most fundamental truth of what it means to be human. It is a story of what is true about existence; about all the invisible and visible aspects of what is true, which together culminate in the most authentic human experience: the experience of complete reality."

Reality was something Farah had little experience comprehending. Her religion often told her to ignore it, yet it was always right in front of her, knocking on her thoughts, there for her to turn her eyes away from in favor of "believing" so that she wouldn't go to hell. Reality, to Farah, was something that she couldn't comprehend, just like the idea that the Son of God was also God, or that an east wind could have parted the apparently nonexistent Red Sea for a specific God-approved group of people called the Israelites.

"The Exodus," Sophia said, "is a story about the experience of *all* humans—"

And it was. What Farah heard next was something that took her completely by surprise. Not because it sounded odd or impossible, but because it sounded like something she was experiencing *right now*. It sounded like what was true about her *own* experience: the experience of being human.

"—because it is the story of the journey of the soul through the experience of human life. About the experience of *your* soul: being born into, living through, and then being born out of your human life. It is the story of your struggles, your wandering through the wilderness of *hypermone*, life experience, growth into your spiritual self, and it concludes by telling us what most all ancient Biblical scripture wanted us to know: that the Promised Land, the place of living in peace, is available *now*, to us all."

Farah then found out that allegory, in particular ancient scriptural allegory, was a literary device designed to pictorialize a spiritual or anagogical reality of the subjective human experience. This was nearly always done in the form of an earthly narrative of fictitious events. Farah learned that allegorical stories were *designed* to symbolize timeless spiritual truths by expressing them in a context of earthly reality.

"The stories were designed to carry the receptive mind into the heart of a living truth," Sophia said, "and to bring to light in the reader the physical experience of what the Greeks called a spiritual catharsis.[139] It was not possible to describe the infinite for what it was; in fact, it was literally impossible to put the infinite, omnipotent reality that was 'God' into words—the miracles of every day life, in particular the intricacies encountered on the soul journey—and so the sagacious ancients used allegory to communicate what was always true in the context of time and space. But by using the human experience to express that truth, the stories were able to transcend cultural and geographical boundaries timelessly. Thus, timeless spiritual truth was brought to life in a rich series of metaphors, similes, allegories, and parables, all communicated via a series of stories, stories designed to carry the receptive mind into the heart of a living truth."

Farah then learned that the crossing of Iam Suph, the reedy sea of matter, symbolized the very same thing that does the cross: Incarnation (of the physical body with the divine), and the soul journey. She learned that the story of the Exodus shows God's chosen people, meant to symbolize all humans, being led safely, by divine guidance, away from danger, via a sea of matter, through a wilderness of experiences. Eventually, the people— through diligence, perseverance, faith, trust, and effort, find themselves in the Promised Land. She learned that the Biblical term Israelite was a spiritual designation[140]—not a racial or cultural one—which was why the Hebrews incorporated the ancient term into their own cultural history.

"Israelite is a very important name," Sophia said, "but it is wrongly taken in the sense of the name of an ethnic group. *My people of Israel* or *the children of Israel* are not only Hebrews; they are all divinized humans, mortals who have put on their immortal spiritual nature, humans graduated into Christhood. Gentiles were simply those not yet spiritually reborn—those ignorant to their own identity, those not yet awakened to the relevance of their own spiritual journey." Now Sophia wrote again. "The word Gentile comes from the Latin and Greek roots 'gen' and 'gent' meaning, simply, 'to be born.'[141] Gentiles were simply those born into human life—it can be given no ethnic reference. The Hebrew spelling of Israel, *Yod-Shin-Resh-Alef-Lamed,* simply means 'people upright with God.' In the ancient Hebrew gospel stories, Jacob is the first man who achieves this, hence the reason all those who achieved what Jacob did—what the Buddhists would call enlightenment—living in Jerusalem, present in one's divine consciousness, consciously living your best life, were called the Israelites."

But that was not all.

As Farah listened, her life was changing—her organs shifting—her brain tingling.

"As you have already learned," Sophia smiled, "before Egypt was a physical, geographical location, it was the symbolic place of mental and physical struggle and suffering.[142] To be in 'Egypt' was to be under or immersed in the consequences of negative or violent action, but mostly it was to suffer under the state of an ignorant mind—to suffer under your own mind, your own unhealthy patterns of thinking, ignorant to your own identity. Fundamentally, Egypt symbolized human beings mired in ignorance and fear: fear that resulted from the oppression of others, but mostly fear and misery self-inflicted."

Farah learned then that the body of water or *Iam Suph* in the Exodus story was symbolic of two things: the human body itself, matter, and *human life,* but in particular, the difficulties that could be faced on the life journey. She learned that in ancient scripture, the difficult times of human life were likened to facing waves on an open sea, waves that could soak and drown, that could bring cold and suffering, that could overwhelm and drift one to being lost. And in this way the crossing of—or rather, safe passage through—a body of water was symbolic of two things: the presence of divine soul in the body of matter (which essentially was the incarnation of matter with soul life), and the safe passage of the soul, the *true* self, true *identity*—through the difficult times that can be faced in life. In the story of the Exodus, the Israelites, 'people upright with God,' symbolized that true identity, the soul-self, journeying through the sea of life experience—*every* human … in particular, every human no longer mired by fear or ignorance, every human in touch with their identity, with their spiritual reality in the context of their physical reality, would pass safely through the waters. But not only that, they walk away, with divine guidance (Moses) from the place of suffering and slavery, crossing through the waters safely. They walk away from the place of suffering and slavery and toward the Promised Land, the land of inner peace, where spiritual enlightenment is found. Peace with God. It turned out this journey was not only the destiny of every human, but was also the truth of every human's life journey.

"The sea then, is a sea that all souls must cross," Sophia said, "without sinking too deeply in its waters; in fact, a sea on whose surface you must learn to walk without sinking, or getting your feet mired in the mud of its bottom; a sea whose waters must be figuratively dried up by the power of God so that you may pass over on dry land. To cross such a sea, or in some stories, a river, was figurative language for crossing the whole stretch of your incarnate earthly existence. It was the metaphor for the journey made by your immortal soul, through human life in your mortal body. A journey said to take place at *night* because the time of human life was said to occur after sunset. When the sun set, it symbolized the immersion of the soul in the human body, where it traveled through the 'underworld' to emerge on the other side of the life cycle with the sunrise. The story of the Exodus is significant because it illustrates your human truth, and the truth of your soul journey: that your God-soul cannot be extinguished, even when submerged in the waters of the sea of life."[143]

And then Sophia said something that took Farah completely off guard. "This is why Jesus, in the Barabbas story, suffers under the rule of Pontius Pilate: The Greek word for 'sea' is *pontos'* and the Greek word for dense is *piletos.*[144] In Latin this, of course, become Pontius Pilate. Jesus, your spiritual consciousness, suffers in the dense sea of matter, the human body, and human experiences. Our divine self suffers under *pontius pilate* when we choose ignorance; when wrong action is given precedence over instinct; when one goes against human nature and acts in a way that harms oneself or others. You see, Farah," Sophia said, putting the pen down, "the ancients did not believe their myths, they believed *in* them.[145] It was not the historical verity of the story that mattered, but the story itself—and this is how the Bible contains the collective spiritual truth of humanity. The story is there, it's just waiting to be read properly."

"But what about the east wind?" Farah was trembling—with excitement, fervor, with a feeling of being overwhelmed. She felt filled with the adrenaline of new thoughts, of inspiration, of *possibility*.

"Ah, yes," Sophia said, "the direction from which the wind came was chosen for a very significant reason, which by now you might be able to guess. East is the direction of the rising sun. *East* signifies the most fundamental of human spiritual truths: the divine aspect of being, the immortality of the soul, the reality of life after 'death.' East for the truth that after your soul's journey through the sea of life, it rises again, like the sun, and continues on its journey."

Recondite forms. Semantic devices. Allegory. Metaphor. *Parable.* These were the magical modes of communication through which that which was most true, the base reality of what being human meant, was imparted. And for the first time, Farah was learning what the Bible, often through nature symbols, had been trying to tell her all along.

"The same is true for Jerusalem," Sophia said, "the capital city of Israel. As I said, in ancient times, the names of spiritual places were given geographical locations as an homage—to bring physical tangibility to invisible spiritual truth. Jerusalem, as you know is sacred to Jews because it is the site of the first Jewish kingdom. It is sacred to Christians because they believe it is the site of Jesus' last days; but Jerusalem is also sacred to Muslims because it is believed to be the site where the Prophet ascended to heaven. Before all of those religious and cultural designations, Jerusalem was first a place belonging to every human. Its name meant *place of peace*; it was the spiritual or metaphorical location where people who were upright with God, people that understood themselves as carriers of evolving divine spirit, 'lived.' Originally, living in Jerusalem meant to live in mental awareness of the meaning of life—to live in the actuality and physical reality of the soul journey. To live in the physical world with knowledge of it as a spiritual place. And so those upright with God carried a type of peace about them because they knew better; they knew the difference between timeless truth and constructed realities. They know the difference between religion and God. They know that the Kingdom indeed exists, just as Jesus said, *right now.* Just as Paul said, *within you.*"

Sophia then drew a cross and said it represented Farah. That it meant "human being." And that it represented the spiritual truth of the soul journey; the core truth of God in existence. "The cross ultimately represents the truth of the Christ -consciousness that exists within you. *This* is what Jesus came to tell you about—*who* you are."

Farah picked up the pen and drew a cross for herself. She stared at it, and felt her heart beating.

This time, though, she didn't see Jesus hanging. She didn't see his blood. She didn't see him imploring her to know *something*. She didn't feel that familiar tightening in her chest. *Perhaps this is it?* Farah thought instead. *Perhaps this is the thing Jesus was imploring me to know.* What it is he was *really* saying. A verse from Matthew came to her mind, "*They hear my words but they do not understand them. They see what I do, but they do not understand.*" And then another, this time from the Old Testament, when God laments, "My people are destroyed for lack of knowledge."

"The word *human* has ancient roots that extend beyond the memory of any history book," Sophia went on. "It is a word born out of Egypt, where the ancients described the union of spirit and matter as taking place when *Hu*, who is 'fire' and *Sa*, who is 'water,' fall to earth as seeds of God and unite to create a human being. The union of the two elements—fire and water, spirit and matter—created man. A hu-man. Man alive with the fire of spiritual consciousness. A human being.

"This truth, that you are matter enlivened with divine fire of spiritual consciousness, was the central element of *all* ancient religion, and is why, in all the ancient texts, Jesus never *actually* refers to himself as the Son of God. Those that worship Jesus call him such, but in actuality, Jesus refers to himself as the Son of Man, Ideal Man, the Ideal Human; a human in touch with the spiritual consciousness within, the truth of being. In this context, Jesus represents the wholeness that *you already are*, the wholeness you are born being. In the oldest traditions, Jesus doesn't even call himself the Son of Man; he simply identifies himself as *Bar-Enasha*. Human."

The force of two thousand years of human angst boomed silently then, in one reverberating movement that came and disappeared in Farah's heart; and the will of it, fueled by the laws of God—evolution, grace, mutuality, and karma, *Telios*—pushed Farah forward.

"The very fact that you exist makes you sacred. You realize this now, don't you? Ending your life will not end it, Farah; it will only shift the trajectory of your own spiritual evolution. You were born to grow from these challenging experiences. So why don't you grow from them? It is your destiny to do so."

Farah's throat tightened.

"You have *never* been separated from God. No human ever has been. God is infused into your DNA—baptism ritual or not, consuming pretend flesh and blood or not, attending church or not, reading the Bible or not—all or none of those religious things could exist, and God would *still* be with you, in you, the instinct in your spiritual heart, the love that composes your very being."

Farah made an odd laugh-cry sound, and put her hands over her face.

♋

In Christianity, the transfiguration of Jesus was the moment his disciples came to understand that he was the Son of God. Jesus takes the twelve to a mountaintop and the heavens open above him, his face shines like the sun, and his robes become like pure light. It is a beautiful moment, one that Rose pictured in her mind on nights when she was restless, when she couldn't fall asleep. The truth of that moment, of Jesus' true identity shining through to the world, brought great comfort to her. Then she read that over 600 years before Jesus was transfigured, the Buddha "had his great transfiguration after ascending a mountain in Ceylon where the heavens are said to have opened up, flooding all around him with a great light, and the glory of his person shone forth with 'double powers.'"[146] When Rose read that the Buddha in that moment shone like the brightness of the sun and moon together, she wept openly. Achingly.

Roger's words swirled amorphously before her, letters moving apart, coming together, meanings alighting them, darkening them, filling her, leaving her empty.

The transfiguration of Horus was also described in terms similar to those of the Buddha and Jesus. Apparently the ancient meaning of the story was deeply symbolic of what is true at the core of every human being, and of the immortal part of us that is engaged in the soul journey.

"The story of transfiguration symbolizes our own metamorphoses into beings of light,"[147] Roger wrote, and then in his words and others,

> The truth is, the Bible is telling us that *all* of us have been blessed within by the "light that gives light to every person coming into the world." And that we have, each of us, the presence of the Christ or higher self or "of God" at the core of our being, and in the gospel stories, via the character of Jesus, we are warned that if there is no genuine recognition of this pearl, this diamond at the core of our being, this bit of yeast that leavens the entire loaf, this mustard seed that is to spring into a mighty tree, then we miss out on entering fully "into the joy of the Lord."[148] Without recognition of this fact, we miss out on the Kingdom of God. The stories of transfiguration tell us that the *core* essence of every human being is solid light, the

purest form of love that is all powerful, as it is a living piece of God, and this core essence, indestructible, eternal, will emerge the self in glory out of even the most desperate circumstances.

Tat Tuam Asi

In Sanskrit it means "You and I and Ultimate Reality are One"— a phrase that is a reflection of the very same truth communicated in the Bible. The same truth that emerges to us via Jesus and the gospel stories, that is the core of the Buddha's teachings, the core of Hinduism, and even the core of the ancient scriptures that became the basis for Judaism. All are saying the same thing.

Rose sat back on the couch.
What could there be left to take away?
What could there be left to learn?
Rose's eyes read numbly about the powerful symbolism of the original crucifixion story.

This moment is so significant because it reveals in the full colour of suffering the greatest spiritual truth of the human experience—that our spiritual self can never die, even in the face of great suffering. Jesus died with two robbers on either side of him, also crucified. In ancient Indian myth, the two robbers are the symbolic thieves of light: They symbolize those thoughts, moments, actions in the world that attempt to deny humans knowledge of their true inner being.

If she weren't immersed in such a terrifying experience, Rose would be laughing. Rolling around on the floor laughing—because if what Roger said was true, the hilarity of it was the stuff of snorts, jaw drops, and looks of giggly incredulity. If what Roger said was true, then something the church had demonized for centuries was actually part of the *root* of the Bible and all of the stories in it. And, ironically, that same demonized thing seemed to bring the Bible to life in a way the orthodox interpretation of the stories never could.

"The *Zodiac*," Rose chortled.

After all the religious wars, the death, the *murder* in the name of God—

"The *missionaries*, for God's sake!" Rose exclaimed to Alvin, who peeked out from one eye. *After the imposition of Christianity on every non-Christian culture*— "Good God, Alvin, what about the Muslims? What if the history of their religion is the same? Could you imagine it?" Rose *was* laughing now. She couldn't help it; laughing with an ache in her heart that felt unsoothable, with tears streaming down her cheeks, her eyebrows straining with the suffocating injustice of all the death—literal, psychological, and spiritual—that had been suffered at the hands of religion worldwide. It all would have been all for nothing. Nothing but human religious ego. She thought of the note on her car.

Woe to that man who betrays Jesus!
<u>It would be better for him if he had not been born.</u>
Mark 14:21

According to Roger's lost ancient meaning, the threat in the note then wouldn't be for Roger, it would actually be for the people who wrote the note! Rose chuckled in hysterical bursts. *Woe to the man who betrays Jesus …* "Woe to the man who betrays *himself*," she whispered. "*It would be better for him if he had not been born …* because in denying his divinity," she said, "in ignoring or betraying his Christ-consciousness, he lives in personal misery. He doesn't evolve. And he fails to have inner peace."

She thought of the Bibliomancy verse—*The Son of Man is taking a long journey*. "Son of Man" originally was *bar enasha* —which meant the *human* was taking a long journey. And she was. If this was Rose's soul journey it was a helluva … if hypermone existed, this must be it.

Again, Rose cried herself to sleep. The words, the chapters, the pages—a whirling dervish letting go confusion all about the inside of her skull.

Closer is he than breathing,
nearer than hands and feet.

~Tennyson

♑

"Do you think it a coincidence that Easter falls on the weekend of the full moon? That Jesus died and rose again on the very same weekend the moon evolves to the apex of its transitory cycle, before being 'reborn' again?

"Is it a coincidence that Easter is a celebration based on solar and lunar events that symbolize the triumph of the light within over all things?

"Or that every year at midnight on December twenty-fourth, the Sirius star—which represents the presence of divine consciousness in man—stood directly over Egypt with Virgo on the western horizon? Or that on December twenty-fifth we celebrate the birth of Jesus—the very personification of that very divine consciousness?

"Is it a coincidence that the very colours of Christmas, green and red, are the very symbolic colours of spirit and matter: green for matter, red for spirit?[149] The result of their coming together: incarnation—the very beginning of life itself?

"Is it possible that Christmas is *not* about the impossible virgin birth of a single man-God, but is about that which is miraculous about human existence—the physical *and* the spiritual?

"Is it possible that Earth is a living Eden *waiting* for us to remember our role in existence, so that we can live once again knowing that the presence of God is also all around us? That there is great meaning and honour and sacredness in human existence *right now*?

"Could it be true," Roger said, "that what the Bible and history and archaeology and science and evolution and the history of religion are telling us is so? That the very same Christ-consciousness exhibited by Jesus in his words and actions is the Christ-consciousness that lives within us?"

The air in the room was compressed by silence, but it was also electric with many invisible yet tangible things. Thoughts and contemplations whizzed about.

Emotions stirred. Silent prayers were unburdened, some desperate, some quietly grateful. Frustration, fear, and exhilaration floated and lilted. An excitement and even a great confusion swirled and filled all the remaining empty spaces.

To Roger it felt like the destiny of humankind calling: *thought,* with the potential of manifesting into positive action. His cheeks were flushed with the heat of all that energy, but he was also calm with the feeling of peace he had discovered since uncovering the lost meaning of Q. He smiled, correcting himself; "Lost" was the wrong term for something that would always—despite time, politics, Pious Fraud, edits, changes, and religions—be true. That would always *be*. Waiting to be heard. Waiting to be remembered.

Roger packed up his things, and as he made his way out of the classroom, glanced at the people only now beginning to stir. The truth set *him* free; he wondered how many others would have the courage to look, to *really* look at what lay behind the lifted veil.

♈

So much grew from the gospel stories. So much was created. But it was the Egyptian Sphinx that captivated Mateo's imagination most of all; its form, a human head upon a lion's body, inspired by a story that eventually became Mateo's favourite. In the story, the figure in white rode atop a donkey over palm leaves—a symbol of victory—toward Jerusalem, *Olam-ha-lim Ba*, the place or city of spiritual peace.

Mateo loved the story because it depicted God's wish for every human.

"The story of your divine consciousness riding on an animal in victory is the ultimate symbol of human *telios*. It represents the final mastery of each of us over ourselves,[150] our fears, doubts, anger, ignorance, over that which hinders evolution on our soul journey. This," Master Lael pointed to the figure in white atop the donkey, "symbolizes you living in touch with your true identity, with God and a sense of greater purpose. This is you in touch with the *being-ness* of being … which brings great eternal quietude, allows you to live enlightened on your path to Jerusalem."

This was God's wish for everyone.

Spiritual maturity.

Along with which came a higher way of thinking, a life lived interacting with the *experience* of life. Lived with humility and gratitude, mutuality and right action.

Mateo had stared at the image thoughtfully. It was an insult to animals, really—using them to represent the base part of human action and thought, the *struggle* within the physical body to rise above negative ways of being, negative thought patterns—but Mateo understood now that even the donkey was a symbol. It represented ignorance. And the divine consciousness riding atop the donkey represented human victory over it. Mastery of self.

Such was the hidden meaning of the Egyptian Sphinx: a lion's body—the animal body or symbolic ignorance, conquered by knowledge—wisdom gained by awareness of the divine consciousness within, signified by the human head. Of course the Pharaoh was thought to be the closest thing to God in terms of knowledge and power, so the Egyptians made the head that topped the lion's body that of the Pharaoh. But nonetheless, the meaning of the Sphinx remained the same, its symbolism rooted in the ancient gospel story of victory over ignorance, of self-mastery on the soul journey—the same story depicted on the wall in front of Mateo right now.

"This is the *ideal*," Master Lael said. "To participate in life. To participate in being guided by your divine consciousness—the voice of God within you. To understand fundamentally *who* you are, to understand the soul's journey, *your* journey, is a sacred part of existence."

♌

When Sophia spoke about the ancient Egyptians, Mephistopheles pursed his lips angrily. He moved from window to window staring in, but Sophia wouldn't fall for it; she wouldn't give him any of her attention, nor would she let Farah be distracted. This was too important.

"The Egyptians taught the very same thing that Jesus was imploring humans to understand—that fear can stop evolution in its tracks." She gave a dismissive look toward Mephistopheles. "Fear doesn't want things to change."

Sophia then told Farah that facing and naming fear was the only way to disempower it. "Jesus constantly admonishes his disciples for putting more of their energy into fear and doubt, than evolution of self and well-being, trust, and faith. If you go to the tomb of King Tuthmosis II in Egypt, you will find on the walls there this very same truth in story form: The main character in the story, of course, is the Pharaoh, being led through the twelve panels of life in the 'underworld' of life on earth. On his journey, the Pharaoh is led by Ra—the Egyptian sun god—in soul form—which signifies that Ra in this story symbolizes the Pharaoh's Christ-consciousness.

"On the journey, the Pharaoh and Ra encounter many things: doors, tunnels, caverns, all of which they pass through safely, floating upon a boat. The body of water upon which they float represents life taking them from panel to panel, from challenge to challenge, from point of change to point of change. Along each panel the Pharaoh travels, and all the while Ra stands beside him. There are times when Ra stands at the head of the boat and leads, but for the most part Ra remains alongside the Pharaoh, *always present*. Never does Ra leave the Pharaoh's side, or the boat that carries Pharaoh over the waters of change. At certain points during the journey, other Egyptian gods appear that represent various forms of 'protection' for the Pharaoh, depending on the challenge that lay ahead. The other gods appear to ward off 'enemies,' but Pharaoh only succeeds through every challenge, every 'gateway,' only beats every enemy, every extenuating circumstance, by doing one thing. Can you imagine what that is?"

Immediately Farah thought the Pharaoh must have prayed, or asked Ra to help him.

"No," Sophia said. "The Pharaoh evolves on his journey by doing one thing: facing his fears—and naming them."

Farah didn't understand. Sophia further elaborated the truth that lived inside of her.

"In order for the Pharaoh to pass successfully from one panel to the next, from one part of the journey to the next, he has to *name* his enemies, or that which is attempting to impede his journey, his *evolution*, forward. Whether those impediments exist as a result of people or circumstances he has encountered, decisions he has made, or even if his 'enemies' are self-created, the Pharaoh has to recognize that, before he can travel forward, evolve, on his journey.

"Once his enemy has been named, it loses its power, and the Pharaoh passes through to the next panel. Every single one of the 'enemies' the Pharaoh encounters on his journey through life is symbolic for one thing or other, but the most powerful one, the one that almost blocks the Pharaoh's path completely— the one that he encounters and which Ra stands back from because Pharaoh must 'disempower' this enemy on his own, is the one that represents *fear*." And then Sophia gave Farah a penetrating stare. "Farah, do you know who Mephistopheles is?"

Farah felt her eyes stinging. Her heart was pounding, and Mephistopheles looked up as if he had heard it too, as if he could hear the blood coursing that much faster through her veins.

Sophia nodded. "Yes, Farah, he is *your* fear."

Farah didn't want to look. Mephistopheles had stood now and was doing what he always did, trying to get her attention, trying to get her to look at *him*, to hear *him*. Tears slipped down her cheeks as Farah closed her eyes. Torment floated about her skin as she breathed small, soft breaths.

"The first step to taking away his power," Sophia said gently, "is to *name* him. And not as an entity separate from you, that has any kind of control over you. *Recognize* him for what he *is*"—she reached for Farah's hand—"*your* fear."

Farah felt herself beginning to tremble. *Face him*, she whispered to herself. *Face* him. What if Sophia was right? In Farah's mind there played her entire religious life. The amalgamation of her fears, the moments of her self-doubt and yearning, the moments of her heart squeezing tightly at the thought of God's rejection, of her lungs feeling weighted as if she would never rise cleansed from Baptismal waters. Sophia's voice echoed inside of her: "That must have been a fingernail … a hand … his breath on your neck," and suddenly Farah understood. It dawned on her like sun breaking the horizon. When she opened her eyes, she *looked* at him, and there she was again, reflected in his eyes, looking back out at herself. Mephistopheles grinned, and then his grin flickered. Farah looked at Sophia. Sophia nodded. She finally understood. Mephistopheles wasn't a separate entity that had power over her at all—he was no devil or puppeteer who could make her do what *he* wanted. Mephistopheles was, pure and simple, fear. *Farah's* fear—and she had *allowed* him to become who he was to her. He was the amalgamation of all that terror, all that confusion, all the doctrine she struggled to believe, all the flesh and blood she didn't want to consume, all the dread she felt about her inheritance—her failure as a human being—the descendent of Adam and Eve's sin. Mephistopheles was everything of which Farah was afraid, amalgamated into a force that felt like it had power over her, amalgamated into irrationalities—her reactions to religious symbols, her panic attacks, her odious contemplations. Amalgamated into something that she *let* control her; something of which she had conceived herself to be a victim; something she had believed over which she had no control. But *that* was not *true*. She remembered the moment on the rocks, knocking away his grip which had fallen from her when she had commanded Mephistopheles to let go. *All this time*, she thought, looking at him, narrowing her eyes in disgusted disbelief yet in fascinated power, I *let* you control me. He stared back, opening his mouth to imitate her nightmare; he mouthed the words, *Jesus walk with me*, his black cavernous eyes twinkling. Farah shook her head. *She* had *told him* to come back for her! She had given fear, *her fear*, permission to lord over her and here he was! She closed her eyes and laughed a self-revelatory laugh, a disgusted chuckle, a liberated *tsk*. But when she opened her eyes to challenge his presence, the laughter died in her throat. Mephistopheles was gone. What stood in his place was herself. Shivering and cold, once desperate, smiling weakly. A moment later, that reflection was gone too, and Sophia was wrapping a blanket around Farah's shoulders.

"You've done it," Sophia whispered. "You named it."

Sophia let the truth bathe over Farah's wounds. She held the girl close, and Farah felt warmth from the woman emanate into her soul. On the table, in the slanting afternoon sunlight, the painting on the cover of Farah's journal didn't shimmer as it had that day on the ferry, but it still seemed to swell and shift in deep, welcoming movements that made Farah feel as if a sip would quench her deepest thirst. Without looking at the painting, Sophia said, "In ancient times, the human body was represented by many things, but always by something that contained the light within—the matter within which the miracle components of the soul journey came together. One of the most common artistic symbols was that of a cave."

As Farah listened, she looked from Sophia to the painting and back again, so that when Sophia said the human body could be symbolized by a cave, her eyes went to the cave in the painting, then to the water trickling in from the background—which she already knew was a symbol for the human body and the sea of life it experiences. When Sophia said *the components of the miracles of life* will be present in *some* form, Farah's eyes, lingering on the painting, suddenly widened. And just like that, Farah knew what the painting was about. The baby John the Baptist: physical man; the baby Jesus: spiritual consciousness. "Uriel," she said, and Sophia nodded.

"Yes. The angel of fire and prophecy—the light of God overlooking everything."

"And—" Farah was breathless with amazement, "—Mary?"

Again, Sophia nodded. "Mary, who is Virgo—the sign that gives birth to every human being."

Farah walked to the book, and traced her fingers over the images.

The centuries-old painting depicted what was true about the Bible all along. And here, Leonardo da Vinci—the ultimate Renaissance humanist—had painted a reflection of that truth as plain as day. Yes, it was a Christian painting, but the root of Christianity itself came from the Gospel of Life, and was about the journey of souls and so … it all made perfect sense: the miracle components of life contained together in a cave—the human body. Water, matter, spirit, fire, soul, the light of God, the force of evolution, body, soul, spiritual consciousness. Human life … conduit of the journey of souls.

"A cave," Farah whispered. "That contains the light, but from which the light will emerge." She thought of Jesus' burial in a cave, his resurrection from that cave on the morning of the third day, and felt a wave of warmth move through her.

And all flesh shall see the salvation of God

-Luke 3:6

DAY THREE

The Sabbath fell on a Sunday. *Sun* day. The day of the sun. The day of the soul.

It was a day to recognize the presence of God in the physical, to contemplate the stillness within, to take time, even just a moment, to reconnect or reflect upon the spiritual reality that was part of the physical world.

"Sunday," Master Lael said, "is a day to reflect upon the whole of reality, the soul journey, the physical world as a spiritual place. It is a day to be conscious of God and of the presence of God in you and in others."

It was the wisest insight Mateo believed could circulate through the consciousness of the human mind—to be who and what you are. Simply. To feel the divine energy, the love that you are made of. For when one is still enough, and feels that they simply *are* ("*I am*," Mateo whispered), when they observe life from within their spiritual identity, they are able to feel the energy they are made of and, by nature, know that their connection to God is real. Invisible, yet solid. Within the chest. A swirling, or a quiet glow, a pulsing of light of awareness of higher being … in this moment the body becomes the knowing that exists within it. The human mind, without need for word or definitions, simply *understands* … and the soul journey evolves one more step forward.

When he heard a stirring at the cave entrance, Mateo drew his mind back from his memories. He turned and peered as well as he could to find the cause of the gentle commotion, but saw little. A moment later, the crowd began to shift, and some of whom Mateo recognized as old friends began to make their way through. Each carried one of the scroll-filled baskets Mateo had noticed earlier, and was handing out scrolls as they walked. Slowly, the group made their way around the cave, leaving undulations of first silence and then murmurs of delight in their wake. This was it, Mateo looked on with a sense of great intrigue; the reason for the gathering was about to be revealed.

♌

On the morning of the third day, the sun once again blazed over the horizon, stretched its rays over the earth, peeked sunshine through forest branches, until it arrived in Sophia's kitchen. When Farah woke there was no shame on her skin, only a tingling of *alive*. A sense of knowing—of knowing better.

The thoughts that milled in the back of her mind were about religion. *Why do we need it?* she wondered. Is it because people in pain need a father? Need an excuse? Need to feel taken care of because there is so much about the world and existence that they don't understand? Is it because people are afraid? Farah knew she had been, but realized now it was religion that had made her so. It made rules in the name of the Father, and people—not wanting to displease their all-powerful parent—adhered, no matter what those rules were: judgment of others; sacrifice of life; murder; self-deprecation ... eating flesh and blood. Reasonable, irrational, contradictory, painful, uplifting—it didn't seem to matter. If religion said something was so, then people believed it.

She sat up to find Sophia waiting. "You realize now, it is up to *you ... it is time to understand that you are wrapped in godliness. That it is part of who you are.*" Sophia spoke gently, but with words that resonated within Farah's soul. "Everything you ever wished God would give you, you already have: strength, courage, instinctual wisdom that exists separate from your fears—waiting to guide you. You were born with the ability to seek knowledge, the ability to evolve, and the great power of a spiritual relationship. Life is simply waiting for you to realize so ... to realize that love, support, guidance, and understanding, abound your very being. To realize the calm within."

Farah smiled.

"A very wise man named Rev Michael Beckworth, once said that when you experience difficulty in your life, you are being called to cultivate qualities within you that you didn't have before, that hidden within the circumstances that brought you here today, is a gift of the unfolding of the soul. And so it is up to you now to live and discover *your life*, not the life that everyone else thinks yours should be. Your life, my darling, is between you and God; no one else can dictate that relationship for you. So unfold your lessons; look at them; *learn* from them, pray about them." Sophia smiled at Farah and the enormous halo of possibilities that surrounded her. "Evolve."

It was as if then a film of Farah's religious life played backward. Fast. All the way back to that moment in the sun, in the park when she was swinging. Before all of it. Before religion. And in that moment, Farah knew God like a child, with innocence in her heart and joy, with trust and faith, and a sense of what was true without having to be told; with knowledge—and the rest of her soul journey laid out before her.

Back in Edyn, with Sophia, Farah let the reality of Jesus flow and ebb within her.

♋

Rose had read enough now. Her eyes were tired, her mind was tired; her body was hunched from the exhaustion of a steady, silent weeping. She skipped ahead, pausing only on blurbs.

> The Bible is a cultural adaptation of a much older gospel. It is the journey of souls in cultural dressing.

> The Christ figure is both the universal model or ideal for humanity and the symbolic divine core of our own individual being.

> It is the insistence on crude literalism and dogmatic orthodoxy where none is possible that has split the Christian church into so many sects and denominations and that has so often made it the eager proponent of principles and causes Jesus never could have condoned.[151]

> Christmas is the celebration of the birth of Christ-consciousness within us. It is the celebration of the spiritual reality of *being human*.

She was so engrossed in her thoughts, in her feelings, her emotional trauma, in her shock, that Rose didn't hear Roger's car pull in the driveway. She didn't hear Alvin pop out through the cat door and meow enthusiastic hellos. She didn't hear Roger wonder why the kitchen door was unlocked, see him notice that what looked like a ridiculous amount of tea had been consumed, or notice him realize first with curiosity that his mother had spent the weekend at his house, then with worry, when he saw his papers strewn about the coffee table. "Mom," he said gently. "Are you okay?"

When Rose looked up at Roger, her heart moved. It lilted. "I—" Tears filled her eyes; she gripped the paper in her hand, "I-I needed to save what was lost. I-I needed to save—" she rummaged though the folders, pushed her Bible aside to find it, and held up the card, "—what was lost."

Roger took the card and looked at it, let go his bag from his shoulder, and looked back at his mother there in front of him, emotionally crumpled. His Christian mother who, whether she was ready for it or not, had a truth thrust upon her. And she was a mess for it.

Rose looked at her son darkly then and said, "You know, you are taking away what is everything to millions of people."

Roger's gaze fell to the dappled sunlight filtering through the leaves of the tree outside the window before it went back to his mother. Wasn't *this* it? *Right here.* The challenge of facing truth. Fear. Ignorance. Change. *Misunderstanding.* "I'm not taking anything away," Roger said, looking again out the window at the leaves now tapping against each other in the breeze. "The most ancient gospel, the *heart* of the Bible, is simply tapping you on the shoulder, gently removing your copy of the King James Version, and saying 'Please do what you haven't done. Understand me. Understand yourself. Please don't continue doing what you are.' Jesus said the same thing."

"Oh, don't go quoting Jesus," Rose seethed. Devastation dripped from her skin to the floor all around them. "You're the one saying that he never lived."

"But that's *not* what I said," Roger looked at her. "What I said was that the heart of the gospel stories tells us that Jesus never lived, but that he *lives* in all of us. That God didn't come to Earth as a human in disguise only to die and leave us, waiting to be reunited as long as we adhere to the conditions outlined by any particular manmade religion, but that God is alive in *every* human, and that divinity—our Christ-consciousness—coupled with our natural bodies, is *what makes us human*, what gives us all the potential in the world to know the Kingdom of God on Earth. *Now.* Just like Jesus iterated again and again in the gospel stories: the Kingdom is *now.* And like Paul said, the Kingdom of God is within you. The Word, as John declared, is 'Written upon our hearts.' I'm only repeating what the *original* gospel, based on the most ancient evolutionary truth, pleaded for us to understand, pleads for us to know is true: *who* we are. That we—every single one of us—*are* Jesus. And that Jesus is everything we are capable of becoming: not religious, but fully human; spiritually mature; enabled by our love and the love of God, instead of crippled by a lack of it. Religion takes God out of human life and then places conditions on how and whether or not God can be brought back in. I am saying what Jesus said, that God is now, and life—including human life in the context of existence—is a *miracle.* That God and our spirituality is not a *thing* separate from us that *might* bless us with its presence if we kowtow or pander efficiently and appropriately enough."

"My faith is not a pander to God," Rose said darkly.

A moment later, Rose was rushing away from Roger's house toward her car, fumbling with the door handle, her hands shaking. The Bible in her handbag pulsed heat or comfort or dishevelment out to her intravenously; she wasn't sure which one.

"Wait!" Roger came running up behind her. There was something missing from the folders that he knew she hadn't read. He held the pages out to her. "Before you decide anything, read this." He stood back. The pages fluttered lightly in his mother's hand. "This isn't about right or wrong," he told her. "It's about what is true. What is real."

She closed the driver's door behind her and stared forward as she drove away down the street to the stop sign and then turned left, the papers Roger gave her on the passenger seat fluttering in her peripheral vision. Her Bible pulsed. Rose glanced down, and when she realized what the pages were titled, pulled over. And in those next few moments Rose learned what is was like to be *truly* shaken, to have her faith *truly* tested, to experience completely what it was like to look for the voice of God in the chaos of choices.

Women

For as many of you as were baptized into Christ have put on Christ. There is neither Jew nor Greek, neither slave nor free; there is not male and female; for all of you are one in Jesus Christ.
Galatians 3:27-28

So God created man in his own image, in the image of God created he him; male and female created he them.
Genesis 1:27

The role of women in the church today is given the appearance of equal respect, but is solidified by the practice of female submission and inequality to men. This practice is in direct contradiction of the oldest Christian scriptures, which show that women played a major role in the early Christian church.[152]

Unlike today, women were addressed as equals to their male counterparts in the church.[153] They used to be deacons and ministers,[154] co-workers,[155] and were even called foremost among the apostles.[156] In addition, the oldest Biblical manuscripts reveal that in the first Christian churches, women actively participated in the weekly gatherings or congregations—ministering, praying, and prophesying alongside the men.[157]

In his earliest writings, Paul confirms that gender bigotry is an ungodly practice. These oldest of Christian documents affirm what Jesus originally taught: that in Christ we are all equal; in the Kingdom there is no male or female, no slave or master, no rich or poor, no cultural, societal, gender, or religious distinctions. Under God, these distinctions are eradicated …

*

Rose sat breathing. Still, quiet, strained breaths. A storm had attacked her body, and her eyes went from dry and burning to dripping hot, salty tears of bewilderment down her cheeks. Her mind ached. It pounded with thunder.

The words. The *words* she was reading! Everything they meant sticking to her skin like honey. The lightning was one memory flashing: Rose begging God, "*Please.*"

Desperately, she had wanted to be a minister of the word. A reverend. A priest … a servant of God, acting in the conviction of her faith by spreading the good news. To Rose, the ministry felt her calling. She loved God, she *loved* Jesus, and what better way to express that love than to minister in Jesus' name? But it was not to be. Rose had been quietly but firmly informed that women were *not allowed*. Only men were allowed; women were meant to sit quietly in church and learn from the men. Support them. God had a role for women, she was told, and it was to serve men. To be mothers. To care for the children. To be good wives. To be submissive. *That* was how women served God best. That was what made God happy.

Her eyes fell back to the page

*

Several examples, especially from the writings of Paul, iterate the equality of women as taught by Jesus. Romans contains a clear statement by Paul in this regard:

Example: In Romans vs. 3-4 Paul addresses a woman, Priscilla, before her husband when he mentions their missionary work. This

231

practice was culturally unheard of in the Middle East. (Culturally, women were deemed secondary to men, and so a woman's name would never precede that of her husband. Paul, however, flouts that practice when he names Priscilla first.) Later scribes adjusted the verse by reversing the order of the names,[158] to have it better reflect the cultural belief of the day.

The only problem with Paul's commitment to the good news was his failure to commit to it completely; essentially, Paul did not preach the same revolution that Jesus did. Essentially, Jesus called for a *complete* change, for a revolution of cultural and religious ignorance, for the equality of men and women under God. Paul, however, mistakenly believed that those changes did not have to be implemented by men. Instead, Paul believed the changes would be brought about with the Second Coming of Christ, or Judgment Day. And so Paul rather purported mild alterations to current practices of inequality (social and gender divisions), but generally allowed the status quo to remain so as not to upset too much of the populace[159] (mainly the men). He concluded that with the impending "Second Coming" everyone should remain content with their current roles under cultural and religious or political law—*whether female or male, free, or slave, single or married, circumcised or uncircumcised.* (1 Corinthians 7:17–24)

One of the mild revisions that Paul allowed for was the participation of women in church services. He wrote, for example (so as not to flout completely Jesus' call to the shedding of ignorance), that women could prophecy and minister in his churches, but they still had to keep their heads covered in order to ensure they did not consider themselves to be as men. (1 Corinthians 11:2–16)

*

Rose quivered.

Scriptures originally *celebrated* women … as *equals*.

Jesus … *Paul* had originally called for what was meant to be from the beginning: *the equality of women under God* … the equality of women in church … which meant—Rose stared straight ahead into nothing and everything at the same time—that the "submission" of women to men was purely a *cultural* bigotry.

Rose could feel her religion burning her now, like a brand, from the inside out. It shouted for her to *be suspicious* of what she was reading, but she simply could not turn away—not from *this*. Her gender was all over her skin. Woman. Submissive. Servant. Inferior. The storm inside of her swirled, and a large division emerged between the clouds: On one side, her role as a woman as defined by her religion; on the other, her identity as a woman—a child of God. The barrier forced her to ask herself, shouted at her through the howling wind: Was she a servant of men? Or a servant of God? The storm thundered with everything she had been taught to think about herself trying to control it—all of her religious conditioning using its arms, its verses, its authority to sway and move her mind, the clouds. But the storm wasn't budging. And the hair shirt of her gender upon her skin began to soften, and her red, stinging eyes, her squeezed-tight heart, read on …

*

Jesus' message about gender equality and Paul's largely acquiescent attitude toward it, buttressed against the cultural belief that men should be elevated in importance above women, caused disputes among Christians and church leaders as to what exactly the role of women in the Christian church should be.

Early Biblical manuscripts show that Paul's "equality" was maintained for a short while, but later documents reveal that arguments eventually ceased. After Paul's death, the early church fathers took advantage of Paul's ambiguity and used it as a justification or loophole to eliminate the role of women in the church altogether.[160] It was concluded that women's subservience would be maintained until the Second Coming.[161] In order for this rule to be maintained, the scriptures needed to be altered accordingly: Edits and changes were made, and entire verses regarding the role of women in the church were forged in Paul's name.

Example:

1 Timothy 2:11–15

Let a woman learn in silence with full submission. I permit no woman to teach or to have authority over a man; she is to keep silent. For Adam was formed first, then Eve; and Adam was not deceived, but the woman was deceived and became a transgressor. Yet she will be saved through childbearing, provided they continue in faith and love and holiness, with modesty.

Here the forger makes it clear which cultural beliefs the church decided to uphold, and how the church—now that Paul had died—intended to define the role of women in wait of the Second Coming.

Another example comes from 1 Corinthians 14 where an addition to the chapter was made by a second-generation follower of Paul. Here, vs. 33–35 were forged in Paul's name[162]:

For God is not a God of confusion but of peace. As in all the churches of the saints, let the women keep silent. For it is not permitted for them to speak, but to be in subjugation, just as the law says. But if they wish to learn anything, let them ask their own husbands at home. For it is shameful for a woman to speak in church.

Interestingly, this "command" by "Paul" completely contradicts what the actual Paul wrote only three chapters earlier in the same text, as well as in Romans: that women indeed did and could speak, prophesy, and minister in church alongside and with men.

Example:
Original verse: Paul identifies a woman named Junia as an apostle of Christ. This verse is permanently altered; now it identifies a man named Junias as the apostle.[163]

Book of Acts: Chapter 17, verse 4 originally said, "And some of them were persuaded and joined with Paul and Silas, as did a great many of the pious Greeks, along with a large number of prominent women."

The idea of women being prominent—let alone prominent converts—would have been unacceptable, or even considered a mistake by some scribes.[164] The verse was thus altered accordingly; today it reads, "And some of them were persuaded and joined with Paul and Silas, as did a great many of the pious Greeks, along with a large number of wives of prominent men." The change ensured the men were seen as prominent, not the women.[165]

Despite the great effort to eliminate the importance of women in scriptures, it was impossible to do so completely without altering the Jesus stories altogether: Some of the most important moments in Jesus' life still have him surrounded by women.

- Mary Magdalene (alone or with other women, depending on which gospel you read) discovers Jesus' empty tomb.
- Women are the first to bear witness to Jesus' resurrection; they are also the first to testify of it.[166]
- Men continually abandon Jesus during his Passion, while women remain loyally at his side. Men repeatedly choose fear over faith in the gospel stories by betraying, denying, and fleeing from Jesus. The men even go so far as to deny Jesus' resurrection because they are sure the women, by the mere fact that they are women, would not have borne witness to it. (Luke 24:11)

*

Rose was shaking—from the inside out. Deep, heaving tremors shifted her organs, unsettled her brain, lay pressure upon her heart. She did *not* expect this. She did *not* expect to see these words … or ever be caught in a mental frenzy such as this. *Ever* in her life. In fact, her whole life Rose had believed that what she thought, was all she needed to know.

But these words—these *words* about *the* word were telling her otherwise.

The evangelist in her head said, *"Be careful."* And Rose agreed. She even nodded and said aloud, "I will."

If everything she had just read were true, surely the church would have known and done something about it. If men and women were meant to be equal under God, then surely the church would not propagate a cultural bias because they were too worried about breaking traditional cultural practices—which sounded like they came from the Middle East anyway! And every good Christian knows that the Middle East is morally corrupt and ungodly! The way they treat *their* women! *No*, Rose shook her head. Surely if these things she had read were true, the church would have done the right thing. Because if anyone could be trusted to do the right thing, it was the church—the upholders of the word and will of God on Earth.

Rose told herself things such as this, and the evangelist in her head nodded approvingly.

Roger *had* to be wrong; Rose and everything she had always believed, the church and everything Christianity had taught her, *had to be right.*

Rose told herself this. But something still moved along her spine. A cool, subtle discomfort.

She knew what it was.

♑

It always came back to religion or science.

Science or religion.

The definition of God and creation.

The definition of life.

Until science became less God-phobic, it would never fully be able to define or understand the whole of reality. Until religion began to accept the physical realities of existence, it would never grow out of its ignorance, and would instead continue to compromise the human ability to understand itself, and even the entire evolution of the human race. The words of Galileo echoed in Roger's mind, "It is surely harmful to souls to make it a heresy to believe what is proved."

He wondered how long it would take humanity to admit ancient misunderstandings and move *past* ancient wrongs into the light of accepting reality. All of it: the physical infused with the spiritual, the reality that karma existed, and the fact that humans were responsible for the consequences of human action.

Roger knew that admitting reality—what was real about the Bible, what was real about the existence—would be the difference to a changing future. The difference between the establishment of a personal Jerusalem for every human, and fighting and bloodshed over land that was only ever meant to be the metaphorical home of all: the place of spiritual peace.

As he watched his mother drive away, watched her turn left at the stop sign, Roger remembered the moment when he realized in full the *actual* wonderful truth being communicated by the ancient scriptures. A strange sound had emerged from within him that felt like a bubbling spring. It was laughter and pain, confusion and glee. It was an exhale. One that was so deep it seemed to release something within him that he didn't even know he was holding on to; and fear, in streams, like slow-moving syrup began to slip out of him, from the center of his body, down his limbs and out. Without it, his body felt lighter, his mind clear, his heart electric and full, wise with knowing. He knew a calm then that he had never known before, and yet it was a calm he suddenly realized had always existed within him. He knew something else then too—that what religion said no longer frightened him, because he *knew* better; he knew what he was being told right then, *right now*—that he was already loved, that his life was sacred, that he was here to experience and live with honour and respect and mutuality and grace. It was the change of heart Jesus talked about. The awakening. "Know thyself," Roger said, "For therein lies the greatest wisdom." He heard the voice of Jesus whisper in his head, "*Heaven does not come with signs to be observed, you can not say 'here it is', or 'look there!', because it already exists, in the midst of you*".

Mateo, like so many others, had wondered how it all started. Who drew the first star on the floor of the Sanctuary? Who originally conceived and wrote the gospel stories? Who so brilliantly expressed the connection between all life, God, consciousness, and the human experience, and how it all eventually came together in a whirlwind of perfection—the universe, the earthly experience, the journey of souls, the interconnectedness of all things?

It was simple—the *spirit of godliness*. "The stories are the quiet expression of what is written on the heart of every human," said Master Lael. "On the heart of every woman, man, and child. And through human intellect and reason, through centuries of observing the details of the world in which we live, the truth on our souls was eventually expressed through allegories and symbolisms that spoke of circumstances in which every human could find him or herself. The gospel truth was expressed through stories in which we can all find ourselves, in which we can all recognize each other and the world in which we live."

The spirit of God in us. The quiet susurrations. *That* was why the gospel was universal—because it tapped directly into what is spiritual about being human.

Finally, the group with the baskets made their way through, and Mateo was handed a scroll. He pulled gently at the tie to let it loose, unfurled the pages, and scanned them first carefully and then lovingly. A smile spread over his lips.

In his hands was a story; a series of pages intricately connected by one thing: the sayings and parables of wisdom and the gospel stories that expressed them so beautifully. In his hands, Mateo held the entire contents of the Seventh Library, penned for the *first* time. *Est Deus in Nobis—there is God inside of us.* Mateo whispered, smiling. So *this* was the reason, he chuckled, shaking his head. He was so pleased. *This* was the reason they had been called to gather; the gospel stories *written down.* Sayings and parables, allegory and metaphor, the collective spiritual truth of all of humankind *finally* written down. Mateo rubbed the corners of the pages fondly between his fingers and whispered, "For *bonum commine hominis*, for the *common good of man.*"

He reviewed the pages slowly, with adoration and humility in his heart. All of it was there: Virgo, the Sirius star, Pisces, the Christ-consciousness leading the twelve (all of humanity), bread and fish, *Meri* … the cross. And all the wonderfully symbolic stories: the feeding of the multitudes—the multiplicity of the spirit of God spread among the people; the donkey ride into Jerusalem; the raising of the physical self from "death" or the "sleep" of ignorance; even the dramatic scenes of choosing between mind and spirit, between spiritual instinct and Barabbas. Even the reality of being on a spiritual journey in the context of history and time, of politics and religion, of cultural traditions—it was all there. "Ah," Mateo smiled. Five loaves of bread—the five senses. Two fish—the dual nature of man. A fish with a gold coin in its mouth—the treasure within; the soul, within the body of matter. He read on. The twelve disciples, most of whom were *fishermen*. Mateo's laugh was heartfelt. The fish reference was clear. Spiritual consciousness—fishermen, fishing for their own spiritual enlightenment, all the while the Christ-consciousness guided them on their way, imparting wisdom, warning, but mostly love. The joy of living. The sanctity of not just life, but of all existence. Master Lael's voice echoed in his mind, *The secret of life surrounds you.*

"Why now?" he overheard someone ask after hugging another excitedly.

And then Mateo realized.

Of *course*! Had he been younger he would have slapped his knee in exclamation.

Mateo looked skyward as if sharing a private revelation with God. *Of course.* He laughed. The sun had just entered Pisces—the sign of the fish—the very sign of spiritual man. What better way to celebrate being human than to write down the stories—the sayings and parables—that tell us what it means to *be* human, that celebrate the meaning of life and life itself. Mateo chuckled softly and imagined Master Lael leaning on his walking stick, nodding wisely with that twinkle in his eye. The reason for the gathering had finally been revealed.

"*Veritas numquam perit*," Mateo whispered, holding the sheets of papyrus to his chest.

Firstly because of the word written on the human heart, and now secondly, because of the written word itself, Mateo knew, the *truth* truly never would perish.

Older now, Mateo knew that one could not learn the truth without being changed by it, and that people feared change. Yes, they did. They thought that change meant the ceasing to exist of the familiar, but Mateo knew better. Change meant growth. And even he, in his old age, was still growing. Toward the future, toward experiences he was born to have, toward God.

♉ ♊ ♍ ♎ ♏ ♐ ♒ ♓ ♈ ♌ ♋ ♑

Now it is high time to awake out of sleep: for now is our salvation nearer than when we believed.

~Romans 13:11

Three days ago, Farah would have asked Sophia why Jesus didn't carry his own cross, but today Farah understood the story of Jesus' Passion differently. She understood what certain things meant.

Of course Jesus wouldn't have carried the cross on which he was to be crucified—he was the spiritual consciousness. The cross was a burden for the physical body to bear—the human being burdened by the misunderstanding of his existence.

And so Farah asked Sophia something else instead.

"What about sin?" Farah said, helping herself to some lunch. "Where did the idea come from? How could those apocalyptic evangelists have ever drawn the conclusion that humans were tainted with sin?"

"They didn't understand the language they were reading," Sophia said. "And they had a very twisted, fear-filled idea of who God was. They had decided that life was suffering, that God was angry with humans. They saw the negative in everything and perpetuated negativity in their belief systems, and so it was natural that negativity and fear would become the basis of their interpretation of any religious scriptures—let alone their interpretation of God. The original meaning of sin was to 'miss the mark'—as an archer who misses the target. To sin meant to *miss the point* of human existence. A life of not participating in learning from experience, evolving to a higher sense of self and humanity, to knowing and understanding one's physical and spiritual identity, a life lived choosing ignorance or fear or crimes against self or others, was a sinful life because it is a life lived where one misses the importance of their own existence. The importance of all existence. To sin means to live unskillfully, blindly, and thus to suffer and cause suffering.[167] This is why Jesus says of those who wish or impose harm upon others, 'Just as you have done it to them, you do it to me'—meaning that whatever suffering you inflict upon others, by the very truth that you both contain the same divine aspect of your being, you inflict it upon yourself. It is the law of action and consequence in play—you cannot harm others without retribution for yourself, you cannot harm the world without bringing suffering upon yourself. And that is a life lived sinful—one that is detached from self, from the heart, from spiritual instinct, one that essentially lives detached from reality, caught up in social and political structures, or one that refuses to face the truths of personal growth."

"Ah," Farah said, blowing on her tea. The answer resonated in her body, cleaned her skin, repaired old wounds. "And Portmanteau words?"

Sophia smiled. "Named after the Portmanteau suitcase which was made of two halves that were clasped together to make a whole. A Portmanteau word is one that brings two separate words together to make a new word. High noon, lunchbox, sunset, sunrise ..."

Farah smiled. "Okay."

"The truth of the matter is that Jesus said nothing about bishops, priests, deacons, elders, or any other church functionary of the present. He said *nothing* about a pope; in fact, he was pointedly against the notion of calling any man 'father,' which is what *pope* means. He said nothing either about magnificent church buildings, cathedrals, or elaborate rituals of worship.[168] The truth of the matter is," Sophia said, "that the Jesus of the Bible came, in a very radical sense, to abolish religion and all the ritualistic paraphernalia it puts in the way of knowing God."

Scenes from Farah's experience with religious rituals flashed aggressively through her mind. But most glaringly came the physical memory of how she felt: like a failure. Rejected. With a deep, unshakable shame for being a sinner. A human being.

A human being filled with fear.

"And all this worry about being 'born again,'" Sophia said. "The original gospel said nothing about being 'born again.' The words were 'born from above,' which is what every human *already is*. And the ritual of baptism too has lost all of its original spiritual heart: In the Bible, Jesus is baptized in the River Jordan by John the Baptist, who says, 'I must decrease before he can increase.' This scene is a whole expression of a fundamental truth, and symbolism, as you may have guessed, *abounds*: Jesus, as spiritual consciousness, is immersed in water (a symbol of the human body). As he emerges from the 'baptism'— which is actually symbolic of the baptism of the human body with divine consciousness, the moment of the soul's birth into life—the voice of God professes pleasure. John, who was born six months before Jesus, has already proclaimed that in order for Jesus (divine consciousness) to increase, John, symbolic of the physical body (born six months earlier) must *decrease*. And so it is true that on the soul journey, as the spiritual consciousness gains in experience, evolving the human being toward spiritual maturity, the human body itself ages. As the spirit gains strength, the physical body decreases in strength. And so the act of baptism was one that symbolized the truth of your spiritually incarnated body; it meant claiming your divinity, and it had nothing to do with the removal of sin.[169] When you were baptized, it was the moment you honoured the spiritual, godly reality of your existence. It was a moment of honouring the reality of *who* you are."

And then Sophia explained Communion—the Eucharist; what Farah considered the terrifying practice of symbolically eating the flesh and blood of a dead man/god.

"Originally, taking bread was a potent symbol of the restoration of the whole family of humanity as the child of God,"[170] Sophia said. "The bread is of course a symbol of the spiritual food that exists within every human, so traditionally, taking bread was a way to recollect and honour that which is *true* … that you are in the middle of a soul journey.[171] It is natural that you would feel uncomfortable being asked to eat the pretend flesh and drink the pretend blood of a dead man, whether he was claimed after the fact to be God or not. To do so goes against what you know instinctually to be spiritually true. That is why you never really felt comfortable doing it."

To Farah, Sophia's words felt like sunlight bursting through *into* her body, alighting what Farah never knew was inside. So many of the blanks that all of her questions had left in her spirit were being filled. And it felt to Farah like clean water flowing into her, like an infusion of clarity. She was beginning to understand something that she never did before. Not something about God or Jesus or herself, but about the world. Reality. About the difference between false realities—the moveable realities that change with ideologies, adapted religious doctrines, with politics, and over time with the evolution of thought, or the resilient effort of ignorance maintained. And timeless reality. That the physical was indeed infused with the spiritual. That the physical world is what it is *because* of the invisible aspects of existence, which are the other half of reality.

"So what about Judgment Day?" Farah asked, mid-bite. "Where did that idea come from?"

"Well, that is interesting too," Sophia said, pouring some more tea. "What modern Christians don't understand is that the ancient foundations of their faith knew that such a thing as a Judgment Day—in the sense of the death and destruction of the world at the hand of God, who would choose by religious condition who would or would not survive—would *never* occur. Because some kind of 'final fulfillment' that would bring the end to all things would mean stopping dead the march of the universe—an idea that would have been incomprehensible. Christians today can believe such an event is impending, only because they've already taken the meaning out of existence. They have removed God from Earth, separated themselves from God, denied the sacred meaning in existence as part of the life cycle, and redefined earthly life as a place of suffering. Religion shames humans out of their inheritance, and so it is no surprise that the minds of the religious want to believe that this ultimate Judgment Day will come—that their reward for accepting self-loathing will be the glory of eternal life in the company of God. Modern Christians don't realize that salvation meant to consummate the present evolutionary cycle and keep marching on with nature[172] until personal *telios* is achieved—personal spiritual destiny discovered throughout the process of living your life *now*. There was no manic expectation of some supernatural, apocalyptic 'second coming.' The realization of the Kingdom of God was happening to those who opened themselves to it here and now.[173] This is a perfect example of how the King James Version has done significant harm by mistranslating seemingly insignificant portions of the ancient texts. Never did the Greek copies of the ancient scriptures speak of the 'end of the world'; the words of the Greek text instead explicitly signify the end of the age, cycle, or eon—not the end of the cosmos itself."[174]

And in that moment, Farah finally got it. The concept of the coming of Christ signified the end of the personal age of ignorance, the moving forward of spiritual evolution by the gaining of knowledge. People undergoing change. Growth. And opening themselves to the grace and godliness of their human experience. Farah *finally* got it.

And she realized fully how possible it was that the scriptures had been misinterpreted by the structures and minds and traditions that became religion, by the dogma and doctrine and rituals founded in Jesus' name. She realized fully that the church's interpretation of the Bible was not God. And neither was religion.

The grace of life was amazing. Of being human, of the human experience, of the great, wonderful mystery, the beating heart of life.

"I once was lost," Farah whispered, "but now am found. Was blind, but now I see."

Come unto me,
all you that labour and are heavy laden,
and I will give you rest.

-Jesus

Bibliography/References/Recommended Reading

Books / Academic References

Acharya S/D. M. Murdock. *The Origins of Christianity and the Quest for the Historical Jesus Christ* (excerpt from Murdock, D. M. *The Christ Myth Anthology*). Seattle: Stellar House, 2009.

Armstrong, Karen. Two Paths to the Same Old Truth. *New Scientist*, 20 July 2005, No. 2510.

Baigent, Michael and Richard Leigh. *The Dead Sea Scrolls Deception*. London: Corgi Books, 1991.

Ehrman, Bart D. *Lost Christianities: The Battles for Scripture and the Faiths We Never Knew*. New York: Oxford University Press, 2003.

Ehrman, Bart D. *Misquoting Jesus: The Story Behind Who Changed the Bible and Why*, San Francisco: HarperOne, 2007.

Ehrman, Bart D. *The Lost Gospel of Judas Iscariot: A New Look At Betrayer And Betrayed*. USA: Oxford University Press, 2006.

Goenka, S. N. (condensed by William Hart). *The Discourse Summaries: Talks from a Ten-Day Course in Vipassana Meditation*. Nashik, India: Vipassana Research Institute, 2001.

Harpur, Tom. *For Christ's Sake*, Toronto: McClelland & Stewart, 1993.

Harpur, Tom. *The Pagan Christ: Recovering the Lost Light*. Toronto: Thomas Allen, 2004.

Harpur, Tom. *Water into Wine*. Toronto: Thomas Allen, 2007.

Hart, William. *The Art of Living: Vipassana Meditation*. New York: HarperCollins, 1987.

Kuhn, Alvin Boyd. *The Great Myth of the Sun-gods*. A lecture by Alvin Boyd Kuhn.

Kuhn, Alvin Boyd. *The Lost Light: An Interpretation of Ancient Scriptures (1940)*. Available from Kessinger Publishing Rare Reprints, www.kessinger.net.

Kuhn, Alvin Boyd. *Man's Two Births: Zodiacal Symbolism in the Gospel of Luke*. Kessinger Publishing Rare Reprints, www.kessinger.net; or see www.pc93.tripod.com/mns2brth.htm.

Kuhn, Alvin Boyd. *The Red Sea Is Your Blood*. Kessinger Publishing Rare Reprints, www.kessinger.net; or see at www.pc93.tripod.com/redsea.htm.

Kuhn, Alvin Boyd. *The Lost Meaning of Death* (1935). Kessinger Publishing Rare Reprints, or from www.scribd.com.

Kuhn, Alvin Boyd. *The Shadow of the Third Century: A Revaluation of Christianity* (1949). Kessinger Publishing Rare Reprints, or see www.pc93.tripod.com/shadow.htm.

Metzer, Bruce M. "Explicit References in the Works of Origen to Variant Readings in the New Testament Manuscripts (*Commentary on Matthew 15:14*)" in *Biblical and Patristic Studies in Memory of Robert Pierce Casey*, ed. J. Neville Birdsall and Robert W. Thomson. Freiburg, Germany: Herder, 1968.

Oxford Word Histories. Glynnis Chantrell, ed., New York: Oxford University Press, 2004.

Strumpf, Michael, and Auriel Douglas. *The Grammar Bible: Everything You Always Wanted to Know About Grammar But Didn't Know Who to Ask*. New York: Henry Holt/Owl Books, 2004.

Tolle, Eckhart. *The Power of Now*. Vancouver: Namaste Publishing, 1999.

Tolle Eckhart. *A New Earth: Awakening to Your Life's Purpose*. Penguin Books, 2006.

Waite, Charles B. *The History of the Christian Religion to the Year Two Hundred*. Chicago: C. V. Waite, 1900.

Newspaper Articles:
'Ardipithecus Ramidus': Information garnered from 3 October 2009

edition of the *New Zealand Weekend Herald*. Academic Reference: See Professor Tim White, University of California, Berkeley.

Websites:
>www.religioustolerance.org
>www.jesuspuzzle.humanists.net
>www.arksearch.com
>www.nazareneway.com (for the evolution of the Lord's Prayer)

The Amduat (King Tuthmosis II's tomb panels): Information and pictures of actual panels found at: National Gallery of Art, The Quest For Immortality: Treasures of Ancient Egypt:
>http://www.nga.gov/exhibitions/2002/egypt/tomb_vr_3.shtm#9
>http://www.nga.gov/exhibitions/2002/egypt/amduat.htm

Podcasts
>Oprah Soul Series interviews with: Wayne Dyer

Map of the Gospels
Provided by Jonathan Freeman, based on 'Communities of the Gospels' map (Historians approximations in which each of the four New Testament Gospels were used): http://www.pbs.org/wgbh/pages/frontline/shows/religion/maps/apostle.html

Notes

1. Shalom: Hebrew "peace"; Shalom r meAleichem: Hebrew "peace unto you."

2. *Encarta Standard Encyclopedia* (2005), s.v. "Protestantism: 20th Century"; Ehrman, *Misquoting Jesus*.

3. For full list see Ehrman, *Misquoting Jesus*, 265.

4. Ehrman, *Misquoting Jesus*, 88.

5. Ehrman, *Misquoting Jesus*, 88.

6. This is a conservative estimate; variants among the manuscripts range from 200,000 to 400,000 (Ehrman, *Misquoting Jesus*, 88).

7. The King James Version was originally translated in 1611.

8. Ehrman, *Misquoting Jesus*, 79-83, 209.

9. For more about Paul's "Deafening Silence" see Ehrman, *Lost Christianities*.

10. Quote from John Henry Newman, *Apology for His Life* quoted in Harpur, *The Pagan Christ*, 59.

11. See Ehrman, *Misquoting Jesus*, 265, for list of top ten verses not originally in the New Testament: 1 John 5:7, John 8:7, John 8:11, Luke 22:44, Luke 22:20, Mark 16:17, Mark 16:18, John 5:4, Luke 24:12, Luke 24:51.

12. Ehrman, *Lost Christianities*, 235.

13. For example, Gospels of Thomas, Mary Magdalene, Judas, Mark, Matthew, Luke, John, Gospel of the Saviour, Gospel of Truth, Gospel of James, epistle of Barnabas, Apocryphal Acts, the Dead Sea Scrolls, Gospel according to the Egyptians, Gospel of the Hebrews, Johannine Epistles, Acts of John, Epistle of Jude, Acts of Saint Julian, Gospel of the Nazarenes, Gospel of Nicodemus, Acts of Peter. Details of examples and further examples can be found throughout Bart D. Ehrman's *Lost Christianities*.

14. Ehrman, *Lost Christianities,*10. Mark was purported to be the secretary of Peter, one of Jesus' disciples. Luke was said to be the traveling companion of Paul.

15. Ehrman, *Lost Christianities*, 11.

16. Ehrman, *Lost Christianities,* 20–22.

17. Ehrman, *Lost Christianities,* 11.

18. Ehrman, *Lost Christianities,* 37–38.

19. 1 Corinthians 14:34–35.

20. 1 Timothy 2:12–15.

21. Ehrman, *Misquoting Jesus,* 36–41.

22. *periblepsis homoeoteleuton*, Ehrman, *Misquoting Jesus,* 91.

23. Ehrman, *Misquoting Jesus,* 92.

24. Ehrman, *Misquoting Jesus,* 153.

25. Ehrman, *Misquoting Jesus,* 153.

26. *Encarta* (2005), s.v. "Bible."

27. Ehrman, *Misquoting Jesus,* 90.

28. Ehrman, *Misquoting Jesus,* 90.

29. Ehrman, *Misquoting Jesus,* 93.

30. Ehrman, *Misquoting Jesus,* 93.

31. Ehrman, *Misquoting Jesus,* 93.

32. Harpur, *The Pagan Christ,* 54.

33. Gerald Massey, quoted in Harpur, *The Pagan Christ,* 56.

34. Constantine the Great (274–337 AD), Roman emperor. The first Roman ruler to be converted to Christianity. The first emperor to rule in the name of Christ, he was a major figure in the foundation of medieval Christian Europe. "In 312, on the eve of a battle against Maxentius, his rival in Italy, Constantine is reported to have dreamt that Christ appeared to him and told him to inscribe the first two letters of his name (*XP* in Greek) on the shields of his troops. The next day he is said to have seen a cross superimposed on the Sun and the words 'in this sign you will be the victor' (usually given in Latin, *in hoc signo vinces*). Constantine then defeated Maxentius at the Battle of the Milvian Bridge, near Rome. The Senate hailed the victor as saviour of the Roman people. Thus, Constantine, who had been a pagan

solar worshipper, now looked upon the Christian deity as a bringer of victory. Persecution of the Christians was ended, and Constantine's co-emperor, Licinius, joined him in issuing the Edict of Milan (313), which mandated toleration of Christians in the Roman Empire. As guardian of Constantine's favoured religion, the Church was then given legal rights and large financial donations." (*Encarta*, 2005, s.v. "Constantine the Great")

35. Harpur, *The Pagan Christ*, 42.

36. Multiple references including Ehrman, *Lost Christianities*, 250; Harpur, *The Pagan Christ*, 41–42.

37. Ehrman, *Lost Christianities*, 13.

38. The Vandals are a famous, historical example of Christians who after the Nicea determination became considered heretics by the Roman Christian Church. The name of their tribe was then appropriated to become synonymous with violence and rebellion as they fought for their lives against the literalist Roman Catholic Church. Catholic means "universal church"; the point of establishing it was to convert others to it, that Constantine might have his nation united under one God/religion.

39. *Encarta*, 2005, s.v. "Eusebius of Caesarea."

40. p.63, Harpur, *The Pagan Christ*

41. See Bart D. Ehrman, esp. *Misquoting Jesus; Jesus Interrupted; God's Problem.*

42. Ehrman, *Misquoting Jesus*, 113.

43. Ehrman, *Misquoting Jesus*, 80–82.

44. Jesus was defined as the "Word," because of the word he spoke, which was written down and perceived as the Word of God. Jesus then was defined by John as the Word of God from the outset of his gospel, which begins, "In the beginning was the Word, and the Word was with God, and the Word was God. He was in the beginning with God. All things were made through Him, and without Him nothing was made that was made. In Him was life, and the life was the light of men. And the light shines in the darkness and the darkness did not comprehend it." John's gospel is the youngest of the four gospels to be canonized. Biblical scholarship agrees that his words are a reflection of an already established doctrine and belief system about who Jesus was,

not a firsthand account of what might or might not have happened or been true during the time Jesus was said to have lived.

45. Ehrman, *Misquoting Jesus.*

46. Didache 1:3 (c. 100 CE). See also Harpur, *The Pagan Christ.*

47. G.R.S. Mead, *Fragments of a Faith Forgotten.* Quoted in Harpur, *The Pagan Christ,* 57.

48. John Laurence von Mosheim, *History of the Christian Religion.* Quoted in Harpur, *The Pagan Christ,* 57.

49. Godfrey Higgins, *Anacalypsis.* Quoted in Harpur, *The Pagan Christ,* 57.

50. Harpur, *The Pagan Christ,* 59.

51. Harpur, *The Pagan Christ,* 59.

52. Revelations 22:18–19.

53. Ordered by the Roman See, Lanfranc after becoming the Archbishop of Canterbury; "corrections" committed in conjunction with the Benedictine monks of St. Maur (ref. Harpur, *The Pagan Christ, 59).*

54. Ordered by the Roman See, Lanfranc after becoming the Archbishop of Canterbury; "corrections" committed in conjunction with the Benedictine monks of St. Maur (ref. Harpur, *The Pagan Christ, 59).*

55. "[The Christians'] injunctions are like this. "Let no one educated, no one wise, no one sensible draw near. For these abilities are thought by us to be evils. But as for anyone ignorant, anyone stupid, anyone uneducated, anyone who is a child, let him come boldly." (*Against Celsus* 3:44; ref. Ehrman, *Misquoting Jesus,* 40)

56. *Against Celsus,* 2, 27.

57. Plotinus' Hypostases. The idea of the Trinity as suggested by Augustine to the first ecumenical council was based on Plotinus' Hypostases. Augustine studied under Plotinus. "Plotinus's system was based chiefly on Plato's theory of ideas, but whereas Plato assumed archetypal ideas to be the link between the supreme deity and the world of matter, Plotinus accepted a doctrine of emanation. This doctrine supposes the constant transmission of powers from the Absolute Being, or the One, to the creation through several agencies, the first of which is nous, or pure intelligence, from which flows the soul of the world; from this, in turn, flow the souls of humans and animals, and finally matter." (*Encarta,* 2005, s.v. "Plotinus") The

Hypostases theory was presented as the ancient idea that the presence of God is manifested in the world in three forms: God, the word action or wisdom of God, and the holy spirit, which is the invisible presence of God in all of creation. The evidence of God's existence then was seen in reality of existence itself. Augustine then presented the idea of the threefold identity, and it became the basis of the orthodox doctrine of the Trinity.

58. John 8:1–11.

59. Ehrman, *Misquoting Jesus*, 63–64.

60. John 8:7.

61. Ehrman, *Misquoting Jesus*, 63.

62. Ehrman, *Misquoting Jesus*, 64.

63. Ehrman, *Misquoting Jesus*, 65.

64. Ehrman, *Misquoting Jesus*, 81–83, 209.

65. See Kuhn, *Man's Two Births*.

66. www.christiananswers.net

67. Exodus 23:20.

68. Malachi 3:1.

69. Mark 1:2.

70. Ehrman, *Misquoting Jesus*, 94.

71. Luke 2:43; additional example of change also made at Luke 2:33 (ref. of original text from Ehrman, *Misquoting Jesus*, 158).

72. *Against the Christians 2, 12–15*, ref. Ehrman, *Misquoting Jesus*, 199.

73. Ehrman, *Misquoting Jesus*, 66.

74. Ehrman, *Misquoting Jesus*, 65–68.

75. Mark 16:8.

76. Matthew 28:1–20, Luke 24:1–53.

77. S. Acharya, *The Origins of Christianity*.

78. Genesis 6:5–6.

79. From what Farah understood, it was as if Jesus had come down to earth, opened up his arms, swept up all the sin and stuck it to himself, so that when he died, it would all go with him. This was *how* Jesus "died for our sins."

80. Eucharist: The Eucharist or Last Supper is a central rite of Christian religion "in which bread and wine are consecrated by an ordained minister and consumed by the minister and the members of the congregation in obedience to Jesus' command at the Last Supper, 'do this in remembrance of me'" (Luke 22:19, 1 Corinthians 11:24). (*Encarta*, 2005, s.v. "Communion").

81. John 6:50.

82. Genesis 4:17.

83. Exodus 14:21.

84. Matthew 3:16.

85. Mark 1:37.

86. Harpur, *Water into Wine*, 228.

87. Note of interest: In John's account of the miracle of Jesus turning water into wine, he mentions that Peter was present. According to the orthodox or traditional interpretation, the author of Mark was supposed to have been Peter's secretary, which means that Mark was supposed to have written *Peter's* firsthand account of Jesus' life and ministry, and yet there is no mention still of the miracle of Jesus turning water into wine, to which Peter would have borne witness. If it happened, why would Peter forget to mention such a significant and symbolic event? (See Ehrman, *Lost Christianities*, as well as *Misquoting Jesus* for more information.)

88. For a detailed account read Bart D. Ehrman's *Misquoting Jesus*. It's a brilliant compilation filled with fascinating details like this.

89. Ehrman, *Misquoting Jesus*, 141.

90. Direct quote re: *chiastic structure*, Ehrman, *Misquoting Jesus*, 141.

91. vv. 41–42, (Ehrman, *Misquoting Jesus*, 141).

92. vv. 41–42, (Ehrman, *Misquoting Jesus*, 141).

93. Harpur, *Water into Wine*, 142.

94. Baigent & Leigh, *The Dead Sea Scrolls Deception*, 172.

95. See Daniel Lazare, "False Testament," *Harper's Magazine*, March 2002.

96. Interestingly, camels are mentioned as part of the kingdom's riches, but archeological discoveries have proved that camels did not yet

exist in the region said to have prospered in the story. Their migration accompanied the arrival of later peoples.

97. Latin; *wisdom of God.*

98. Hebrew: *wisdom of God.*

99. Baigent & Leigh, *The Dead Sea Scrolls Deception,* 172, 173.

100. Harpur, *For Christ's Sake,* 87; Joseph Warshauer, *The Historical Life of Jesus,* quoted in Kuhn, *Shadow of the Third Century,* 33.

101. Excerpt from Oliver Wendell Holmes's introduction to Sir Edwin Arnold's famous account of the life of the Lord Buddha, *The Light of Asia* (Harpur, *The Pagan Christ,* 31).

102. Quick reference: Harpur, *The Pagan Christ,* 83.

103. Harpur, *The Pagan Christ,* 205.

104. Harpur, *The Pagan Christ,* 38, referencing Freke and Gandy, *The Jesus Mysteries: Was the "Original Jesus" a Pagan God?*

105. The Prayer to Our Father (in the original Aramaic). The Nazarene Way of Essenic Studies: Translations from Aramaic, Origins and History of The Lord's Prayer. See www.nazareneway.com/lords_prayer.htm.

106. Original prayer and translation can be found at www.nazareneway.com/lords_prayer.htm. Also see for detailed information about the evolution of the Lord's Prayer.

107. Kuhn, *The Lost Meaning of Death,* 5.

108. IP2, Harpur, *Water into Wine,* 39.

109. Kuhn, *The Red Sea Is Your Blood,* 3.

110. Kuhn, *The Red Sea Is Your Blood,* 4.

111. Acharya S/D. M. Murdock, *The Origins of Christianity,* 15–16.

112. Acharya S/D. M. Murdock, *The Origins of Christianity,* 14.

113. Retractt. I. xiii.

114. Kuhn, *Man's Two Births*

115. Kuhn, *The Red Sea Is Your Blood,* 9.

116. Kuhn, *The Red Sea Is Your Blood,* 9.

117. John 6:33.

118. John 6:50.

119. John 6:48.

120. Matthew 16:8.

121. John 6:33.

122. 1 Corinthians 10:17.

123. Kuhn, *The Red Sea Is Your Blood*.

124. Kuhn, *Man's Two Births*.

125. The ancient designation of Osiris was *Asar*. But the Egyptians invariably expressed reverence for deity by prefixing the definite article "the" to the names of their gods. Just as Christians say, or should say, *the Christ*, they said *the Osiris*. It will be found that the article connoted deity in ancient usage. Our definite article *the* is the root of the Greek word *theos*, God; the Spanish article, masculine, *el*, is the Hebrew word for God; and the Greek masculine article, *ho*, is a Chinese word for deity. To say *the Osiris* was equivalent to saying *Lord Osiris*. When the Hebrews took up the Egyptian phrases and names, they converted the name of "the Osiris" or "Lord Osiris" directly into their own vernacular, and the result was *El-Asar*. Later on the Romans, speaking Latin, took up the same material that had come down from revered Egyptian sources and to El-Asar they added the common Latin termination of the second declension masculine nouns, in which most men's names ended, namely, *-us*; and the result was now *El-Asar-us*. In time, the initial *E* wore off, as scholars phrase it, and the *s* in Asar changed into its sister letter *z*, leaving us holding in our hands the Lazarus whom Jesus raised at Bethany. (Excerpt from Kuhn, *The Lost Light*.)

126. Kuhn *The Red Sea is Your Blood*, 27.

127. (Condensed) Acharya S., *The Origins of Christianity*, 20–21; also see Acharya S., *The Christ Conspiracy*, 154– 156.

128. Harpur, *The Pagan Christ*.

129. c. 480–406 BC.

130. Kuhn, *The Lost Meaning of Death*, 11.

131. Kuhn, *The Lost Meaning of Death*, 7.

132. Kuhn, *The Lost Meaning of Death*, 7.

133. Kuhn, *The Lost Meaning of Death*, 8.

134. Harpur, *The Pagan Christ, Water into Wine*.

135. Harpur, *The Pagan Christ, Water into Wine.*

136. The Bhagavad-Gita (Sanskrit, *Song of the Lord*), a 2,000-year-old, 700-verse Sanskrit poem regarded by many believers in Hinduism as their most important religious text.

137. Words inspired by Kuhn, Harpur.

138. Kuhn, *The Red Sea Is Your Blood,* 6.

139. Kuhn, *The Red Sea Is Your Blood,* 7.

140. Kuhn, *The Lost Light,* 66.

141. Kuhn, *The Lost Light,* 66.

142. Kuhn, *The Red Sea Is Your Blood*; Harpur, *The Pagan Christ, Water into Wine.*

143. Kuhn, *The Red Sea Is Your Blood.*

144. Kuhn, *The Red Sea Is Your Blood.*

145. Harpur, *The Pagan Christ.*

146. Harpur, *Water into Wine,* 90.

147. Harpur, *Water into Wine,* 90.

148. Harpur, *Water into Wine,* 90.

149. Kuhn, *The Red Sea Is Your Blood.*

150. Harpur, *Water into Wine,* 173.

151. Harpur, *For Christ's Sake,* 22.

152. Ehrman, *Misquoting Jesus,* 179.

153. See Romans, chapter 16.

154. Phoebe: a deacon/minister in the church of Cenchrea, a patron also of Paul whom he entrusted to carry his important epistle to Rome.

155. Tryphaena, Tryphosa, and Persis: women whom Paul named as "co-workers" in the gospel (Romans 16: 6, 12)

156. Romans 16:7, Junia: named as foremost among the apostles.

157. 1 Corinthians 11; Ehrman, *Misquoting Jesus,* 181.

158. Ehrman, *Misquoting Jesus,* 186.

159. Ehrman, *Misquoting Jesus*

160. Ehrman, *Misquoting Jesus,* 181.

161. Ehrman, *Misquoting Jesus,* 181.

162. See Ehrman, *Misquoting Jesus,* 183–185 for detailed explanation as to the evidence why this assertion is made by experts in Biblical scholarship.

163. Ehrman, *Misquoting Jesus,* 185.

164. Ehrman, *Misquoting Jesus,* 185.

165. Ehrman, *Misquoting Jesus,* 186.

166. See Matthew 28:1–10; Mark 16:1–8; Luke 23:55–24:10; John 20:1–2.

167. Tolle, *A New Earth,* 9.

168. Harpur, *For Christ's Sake,* 120–121,

169. Harpur, *Water into Wine,* 48.

170. Harpur, *The Pagan Christ,* 185.

171. Harpur, *For Christ's Sake*

172. Harpur, *The Pagan Christ,* 39.

173. Harpur, *The Pagan Christ,* 39.

174. Harpur, *The Pagan Christ,* 39–40.

Acknowledgments

They say it takes a village to raise a child. Well it also takes a village to write a book. Part of the village is composed of people you know; another, of people you actually don't know; and the rest is made up of powerful, but invisible things—providence and coincidence, but two (coincidence, of course, is the perfect coming together of two things). Together these things provide a writer with ingredients that make even the bleakest of psychological and emotional moments (which always accompany the composition of a several years long project), survivable. And we carry on another day, pushing forward, toiling over the words, struggling through, believing.

My village during this project consisted of a small group of very special people ...

One, closer to me than breathing, nearer than hands and feet—absolutely nothing could be achieved without this wonderful, powerful working mystery that manifests in our lives as inspiration, intuition, strength, courage, the absolute pureness of love. Call it what you will, I know what and who it is to me.

Two: the smile in my heart, the love upon my lips—my husband, Jonathan. If past lives exist, I've known and loved you forever. You are an integral part of the woman I have become, and continue to grow into being.

The pillar of my foundation, the giant compassion bred within my being—my mother, Lucille. Who has taught me the meaning of unconditional love, sacrifice, and who has shown me the depths of goodness that forgiveness can breed in our own and other people's hearts. The grace with which she survived suffering has inspired invaluable contemplation within me about the deeper meaning of life.

Mathew. Mateo. The unwavering support, such as that you have always extended, is invaluable, as is having you as a brother to share in this life experience.

The rest of my village consists of a few choice friends and family who believed in me from the beginning (it's amazing how many people don't). These few people quietly held my hand as I grew, and to them, I am deeply grateful, of them, I trust completely: Dave (your sharp eye and gentle spirit, coupled with your chiropractic genius, helped see me through in ways you will never fully understand—thank you), Carolyn, Claire B., Tracey Tomtene (photographer extraordinaire), the Freeman clan (Jenna, Pam, Ken, Andrew, Cil), Krissy—your love these last twelve months has meant so much. Ann, thank you. And of course thanks to my early readers who suffered horrendously through unpolished copy.

Interestingly, the rest of my village consists of people I've never met, who, without even realizing, motivated and inspired me in moments where it seemed I had nothing left to give. The greatest benefit of media is the power it provides exceptional people to influence the lives of others on a global scale: Canada, England, South Africa, New Zealand—it didn't matter where I lived, these people appeared, it seemed, exactly when I needed them (that quiet, powerful, wonderful mystery). And the quality of their work became a constant reminder of everything that any of us are capable of achieving, if we work hard to manifest the dream in our hearts. Their talent, hard work, intelligence, ingenuity, and in the case of Ellen—pure joy of living—helped make it possible for me to see it all through. So thanks to those who inspire simply by being who you are, by making the exceptional effort it takes to excel at your craft, and for having the courage to voice words that have the power to change the world. Oh, and thanks for helping me, without knowing that you were: Leonardo DiCaprio, Arundhati Roy, Baz Luhrmann, Bart. D. Erhman, Tom Harpur, Oprah Winfrey, Cathy Black (Hearst Enterprises), Eckhart Tolle, S. N. Goenka, Ellen Degeneres, Richard Branson, Jonathan Safran Foer.

And to my own clients—you know who you are. Your support and encouragement has been a wonderful, uplifting experience.

I've gone on forever now, but I can't finish without mentioning the writers. There is nothing romantic about being a writer. It's self-inflicted torture the majority of the time, in a brutal industry. And for those of you who write so beautifully, who see it through so that we can read and be inspired and have our lives changed by your words—thank you—for your effort, for your gift, for your fortitude. The world is changed because of you, and would never be the same without you. Fiction or non-fiction, this is the expression of the human experience and what a fantastic thing to be able to interact with it through our words, our minds, our imaginations, our fingertips.

N.

Ornamental Thoughtfulness

excerpts from N.M.Freeman's Blog

A collection of some of the most visited, responded to entries for
N.M.Freeman's blog since *The Story of Q.* was published.

www.nmfreeman.wordpress.com

♑ ♋ ♌ ♈

What you/to Believe

Part of the letter read:

"My parents (who are quite religious) stopped reading your book after Roger's third chapter. They are convinced that, 'Everything Roger says is wrong . . .'"

Roger's initial chapters discuss something very serious.

The infallibility of the Bible.

He initiates a discussion (the same one in the back of everyone's mind) that convincingly (and with great necessity) challenges the doctrine of the infallibility of the Bible. This in turn raises the wonderful question: does it matter if the Bible is infallible? (And does God still exist if it isn't?)

It's the start of a greater discussion—a roller-coaster of thoughts: deeply reflective, emotive, a discussion described as 'capable of changing the way you view the world, religion, and yourself forever'.

Because Roger isn't trying to prove that one particular faith, doctrine, or religion are right his argument exists in a neutral space—the neutral space of reality—the in-between of science and religion—a place where fear of God's Judgment can not exist because it hasn't been invented yet.

Roger's discussion is about, plain and simply, things that were and are—actual historical truths that resulted in events which tumbled through time, space, politics, culture, religion, until this very moment. Right Now.

The problem that the parents had with this discussion, is that most of what Roger says contradicts what religious doctrine teaches is true.

Galileo had this same problem. Reality said one thing, doctrine said another, and while Roger will not be sentenced to life imprisonment (instead of death) for contradicting religious doctrine by discussing the tenets of reality in relation to it, his discussion will indeed do one thing: stir things up. Big time.

Some will want to look away. Others will salivate for more. Others still will say, "I knew it!"

Can one forgo reality simply because it contradicts doctrine?

Can God be found in reality? (www.thestoryofq.com)

Roger's discussion is inspired by actual events. It is plain and simple. Whether or not people want to believe it is up to them.

And as has always been, what we choose to believe is our decision.

How you feel, anyway

The other day someone asked me if I pray.

Maybe a personal question, maybe one that it doesn't matter if I answer.

What I have found however, since writing *The Story of Q.*, is that more people want to know this from me than ever.

What do I believe?

Do I go to church?

What do I make of the Mayan Prophecy? The end of the world?

Do I think God approves?

Approves of what, I always wonder. Whether or not I conform to standards of thought developed over time? Or whether or not I have made use of the gift of human mind, to invoke discussion about a topic that is our right to have a conversation about?

Life. Death. And the meaning of everything in between.

Do I worry that invoking bold, controversial, beautifully thought provoking conversation about the difference between religion and God, might get me sent to Hell?

In a word, No. (You have to believe in Hell, to think you're actually going to be sent there.)

Do I go to church?

Does it matter?

What you should ask yourself is how you feel if I tell you I do, versus how you feel if I tell you I don't. Therein lies a more interesting discussion.

What do I make of the Mayan Prophecy? The end of the world?

A great email was circulating the other day which cleverly observed that if we counted years according the Mayan Calendar in use at the time of the prophecy, it would now already be the end of 2013. (Something to do with leap years etc.) And we're still here.

My answer: No. I do not believe in apocalyptic prophecies of any kind. Old or New Testament, Koran, Mayan, what-have-you. And I do not believe it is any more disrespectful to say so, than it is for someone who believes in them pressuring me to participate in that type of fear based belief system.

Do I pray?

If this means having a conversation with my own definition of God on a regular basis, then

Yes. I do.

If it means searching life's difficult circumstances for a concept of meaning contained within, understanding that this is a meaning I might not yet realize, then Yes. I do that too.

As for the repeated, ultimate question: What do I believe?

I think what's more important is to ask, what do you believe.

When you read the final pages of *The Story of Q.*, you come to realize what the story is actually about. At that point—what I think doesn't really matter because just as it was when you started reading, it's all about you.

The Other Reality

Over the holidays a series of questions were posed to me from someone I did not expect. Someone very close to me who has followed my work intricately for the last 7 years.

The sentiment was specific, almost pained, and less to do with the difficulty of the work load as it was more to do with the content itself.

Why do you do this? The red wine sipped, the glass placed down.

Why must you discuss these things in this way? The glass now used to gesture in earnest.

Why ... why do you need to talk about God? (especially when you know it makes so many people uncomfortable.)

As the query unfolded, I found myself lost in thought, but the angle of my own internal dialogue differed greatly.

The question for me became about the final point—*What* makes us uncomfortable, and why.

What is it about religion that makes us not want to talk about it?

What is it about religion that makes us afraid to talk about God? (or even reject the idea of God altogether)

In *Letters to a Young Contrarian*, Christopher Hitchens writes: "... I not only maintain that all religions are versions of the same untruth, but I hold that the influence of churches and the effect of religious belief, is positively harmful."

Hitchens, recently deceased, often debated brilliantly about or rather against religion on the premise that it commits more harm in the world and between human relationships than good.

Hitchens believed that religion compromised, in every way, ever discovering a balanced view of what it means to be human. He argued that the veil of religious doctrine tainted our ability to fully understand ourselves—intellectually, emotionally, psychologically, or even sexually (religion, of course, famously demonizes human sexuality).

Human kind, or even the world, can never be fully understood or interact in a healthy way as long as religious views dominate.

With the majority of Hitchens' argument, I agree. His debate is largely indisputable—what I disagree with however, is his further argument that a belief in God should be eliminated altogether (because it, after all, is the root of the problem).

"To give up belief in God is a big ask because for many, many, *many* people a feeling of spiritual connection with life or life beyond, with each other, or even some form of guidance or 'Godly' presence as an integral part of life, is just as indisputable as Hitchens' argument against religion."

"Fine," my friend said. "But why the need to write about it? Can't you write about something else, like kids and a dog, or something fun?" We were both leaned back in our chairs, looking skyward. The moon beamed down, palm fronds swayed above us in a light breeze.

Because in the quiet of our minds, I thought, *in the chambers of our hearts, it matters.*

Within me the answer seemed obvious, but I understood that from the outside it might not seem so. From the outside, the confrontational aspects of *The Story of Q.* could look similar to how Hitchens was often interpreted—hostile, vitriolic, a trenchant polemic with the express purpose of smack talking religion (even though anyone who looks deeper into Hitchen's work knows it is far more important than simple smack talk—Hitchens was fighting for reason against the very real, and undeniable harm that the presence of religion has inflicted over history and the present. His was an argument fighting for a humanity that can come to understand its own wisdom in the context of the great wonder that is the world itself. But I digress.)

"If we lived in a world where religion didn't soak the fibers of our relationships or exist between the layers of our thinking, if we lived in a world where religion wasn't a motivator for often harmful and dangerous divisions, then these types of conversations wouldn't matter. But the reality is that they do."

My own glass of red felt warm between my palms.

"The other reality is that there are people out there who want this exact conversation. Not a debate or an ultimatum (be religious or be an atheist), but a conversation of this like. Ultimately," (I said what I believed), "this is a conversation about the future ... Change comes to the outside world when we begin to change within. When we can stop looking at others through the divisive lens of religion we are changing the world. When we understand there is a difference between religion and God, we are changing the world."

Martin Luther King, Jr. said, "Our lives end the moment we stop talking about things that matter."

In the quiet of our minds, in the chambers of our hearts, a conversation within about God, matters.

Do we know why?

Maybe we never will—somehow that's part of the delicious mystery of being alive—but peace about belief is a kingdom everyone is looking for. The sentiment leading into 2012, is that this is a peace that can only be found beyond the borders of religion.

Even the Mayans knew that.

Eggnog for thought

Christmas is an incredibly special time of year.

Half the people I know love it for some ambiguous reason or other: everyone is kinder, there's so much love in the air, it's a cozy warm-cup-of-something, hugging time of year when people smile and extend hands of kindness more freely. Christmas carols warm the heart and the warm hearth of goodwill unites us in the common goal of making others feel good.

At Christmas time, we love. And we feel free to love.

The other half appreciate Christmas for another reason, updating Facebook profiles with sayings like, "Don't forget—Jesus is the reason for the season!" And, "Let's put the Christ back in Christmas."

Christmas for this half is about the sacrifice of one life to save the lives of many. The birth of God's only son, who died for us so we could live forever.

In *The Story of Q.*, Farah doesn't understand why, if Jesus died so she could live forever, the granting of this gift was conditional upon whether or not she was a Christian. Lyrics such as those from the Christmas carol, 'O Holy Night': Long lay the world, in sin and error pining, 'Till He appeared and the soul felt it's worth, leave her with a great sense of confusion, because Farah was certain she felt the worth of her own soul, until she was told it wasn't there.

In the vein of *The Story of Q.*, I'm going to raise my own question as part of this week's Naked Author Sessions—Before religion defined anything (sin, heaven, hell, life, death, you), did your soul feel it's worth? Does it?

Without the definitions that religions provide us, would we feel what Christmas brings anyway?

If the non-religious feel what it is that Christ represented, is there any reason to think all of us aren't already in touch with God? That we, perhaps, were born in touch with God and all God's love abounding?

Is it possible, somewhere along the line, something was misunderstood? (www. thestoryofq.com)

All I know for sure is that when Christmas approaches my heart shines. Inside I feel … glory. And peace. I feel love.

It's undeniable. There's something sacred in the air. Whatever it is, we seem to come together whenever we know it's okay to let ourselves shine with it.

The question is, does 'it' exist without religion?

Because a religious definition of this feeling, or any holy day, is the only thing that divides us.

Some eggnog* for thought.

(*Instead of food—for obvious reasons.)

What I Like to Think.

Looking at a picture of his aging father, someone very dear to me said, "Why do people have to die?"

I swept the breadcrumbs off the counter with my hand and looked at him from the kitchen. He looked so vulnerable. His question so simple. So sad.

I don't know, I shrugged, thinking about my own mother, my beautiful husband, my precious, precious son. My entire circle of friends and family. I really don't know.

I poured a cup of tea. The words, question, contemplation ringing in my mind, and yet, on the heels of the reverberations came another thought. Sipping gently, I made my offering. "Because if people didn't die, we wouldn't value the time we have with them. We wouldn't value our relationships. If people lived forever, we would simply take the meaning of our time with them for granted."

As our conversation went on, the thought, in the back of my mind, began to expand like a universe.

Many religions maintain an obsession with everlasting life.

"Do (insert option) and you will live forever."

"Worship (insert option), and you will live forever."

"Declare (insert requirement) and you will be granted eternal life after you die."

I think my question, genuinely is, why do we need eternal life? Why would we want to be the same person in the same body, for all eternity? Like Greek Gods on Mount Olympus or heavenly children prancing in never-ending fields of happiness.

In *The Story of Q.* Roger suggests (with greatly supported evidence), that the misinterpretation of scriptures lies heavily in the ancient misinterpretation of death. One of his points is, basically, that the reason we fear death is because of how we've been taught to think about it … or rather, the reason we want eternal life is because of how we've been taught to fear death.

Don't get me wrong, no one wants to die. We all want to stay in the happiness of the company of our people—but what if we understood death to be a part of a great, grand, meaningful cycle.

We live and we die.

We love and we cherish.

Life moves and changes and we, our relationships, our entire Being is infused with a meaning that can only be garnered from understanding the reality of that eternal flux.

What if the eternal flux was beautiful? Would death then seem so sad?

Change is eternal.

The cycle of life is eternal.

Could it be true that the meaning we look for above the clouds, or in the promise of eternal life, is actually here now found in the meaning of our own very lives, and the fact that they aren't eternal?

Is there something more for us to know? Something more peace-filled than religious conditions or waiting to die (so we can be granted eternal life)?

. . . I like to think so.

The Naked Author Sessions

Answers to FAQ's and reader submitted questions—The Naked Author Sessions delve deeper into the more personal side of the writer.

(Q & A, FAQ's, excerpts and contemplations)

www.nmfreeman.wordpress.com

♑ ♋ ♌ ♈

On The Story of Q. ...

A Brighter Soul

Q: "How did you go through with it? Weren't you afraid to write about all of the things you wrote about? Weren't you afraid of offending people?

♑ ♋ ♌ ♈

N. Fear is a huge hurdle to overcome when embarking on any project.

Was I afraid to challenge the topics in *The Story of Q.?*

At first, yes (which in itself, I found fascinating), but rather than let it debilitate me I decided to look at it, hold it in my hands, and explore the fact that the fear existed at all.

Why was I afraid? And exactly *what* was I afraid of?

How much of my fear was genuine? How much was inspired by what people told me I should be afraid of, and how could I tell the difference?

In truth, my trepidation/worry/anxiety, actually ended up adding to the depth of the story because once I realized it was there, my contemplations of the topic (as I researched) became even deeper.

Of course the enormity of the material was also daunting, and the potential reverberations of writing this particular type of story were never far away. But it's like many who challenge anything say, "If I spent my days worrying about what people thought, I wouldn't get out of bed in the morning."

In this instance (and hereby any instance following), fear became something I had to decipher, understand, and shape into comprehension, but once I realized where it came from, I suddenly wasn't afraid anymore—fear turned into motivation—as a result, the soul of *The Story of Q.* was able to shine brightly.

And to me, the soul is far more important, far more powerful, than the fear should ever be.

The Difference

"Everyone asks the generic question, 'Why did you write this book?' The politics, world issues, are obvious reasons—the (incredibly controversial!) discussion *The Story of Q.* invokes, also obvious, but what inspired you personally? How far back does your interest in this topic go?"

♑ ♋ ♌ ♈

N. Wow, that's an interesting one.

I would say the first time I heard about the Q-document I was around 15.

I can't remember the exact circumstances—I think it was in Social Studies at school—but I remember noting it and feeling incredibly curious.

The idea that this elusive historical document existed—a common source for the gospels and the Bible stories, fascinated me. I didn't consider it could have contained a powerful spiritual secret for all of humanity, until I was about 30. To create a story around this very likely reality felt inevitable for me, and coupled with all of the research I began to do on the topic, *The Story of Q.* emerged.

I loved the idea and the truth at the center of the story, and the elusiveness of the Q-document as an historical document just seemed to fit perfectly into creating the fundamental heart of the story line. Where did it come from? What was it's original meaning versus what it came to be interpreted as by a man-made religion?

Was the Q-document really showing us the difference between religion and God, and if so, how important is that truth in the context of the human experience—2000 years ago and today?

Clearly we have issues as a human species with differentiating our own ego based religions and calling the fear based doctrines created from them, the will and Word of God. It's damaging to the human psyche on a global scale to mistake God for religion, and any discussion we can have about the actual reality of the difference between the two is good.

"... everything that is now hidden or secret, will eventually be brought to light." ~ *The Story of Q.*

Horrendously Wonderful

"It tells such horrendously wonderful truths—What of your book is fact, and what is fiction."

♑ ♋ ♌ ♈

N. Horrendously wonderful.

The rest of this reader's letter went on to describe how as an orthodox Catholic, they found *The Story of Q.* riveting—not because of the controversial center of the tale, but because in everything, in the very center of the controversial center, he could see himself.

The characters think everything I've ever thought. They wonder and say so much of what I, myself, have never have the courage to say (nor will I ever to others … your book has taught me that I don't need to).

But still, he wanted to know, what is fact and what is fiction.

This goes back to a very important decision I made about the 'layout' of the book (answered in The Rules did not Know Me). References.

The hard facts about biblical history, lost meanings, lost gospels, historical anomalies, missing philosophical accuracies are all referenced. These are true.

The story built around it, *The Story of Q.*, was created to tell the truth found within and maybe even hidden by, those hard facts.

It's a weaving of what it would mean if we all discovered a lost truth that speaks beyond the borders of religion to teach us something we've known all along but have been disallowed the gift of understanding, simply because of an order of historical events.

Farah, Rose, Roger, and Mateo are fictional characters whose experiences mirror our own to some degree—whose hopes, fears, religious suspicions, religious glories, God seeking, and debate invoking queries reflect the most hidden wonderings of our hearts and minds.

The Q-document was a real document, but I've taken its historical existence one step further by suggesting its original meaning was misinterpreted. The original meaning then is revealed via the characters experiences—which themselves link up all the missing theosophical aspects so heatedly debated in academic and theological circles, ending the divisive argument over 'whose religion is right'?

This original meaning then, becomes the horrendously wonderful answer some people fear and others have been so desperately waiting for.

To pull a quote I gave in an interview, "*The Story of Q.* addresses some of the most controversial and thought provoking topics of our time, as well as some of the deepest philosophical wonderings of the human heart."

Horrendously wonderful … I suppose because it challenges everything we ever thought was true about life, death, and the meaning of being human (by revealing a lost meaning of an ancient text … the basis of the Bible), but wonderful because this lost meaning can be seen a true, living, breathing link between us all.

Recognizable.

Ancient.

Relevant.

Always.

Perhaps just how some of us expect God might be.

(Horrendously wonderful too perhaps, because *The Story of Q.* reminds us that we are the only ones who stop ourselves from knowing the godly truths we seek.)

On Writing ...

What you noticed

"How is it possible you wrote an entire book without describing the way any of your characters look? As a writing student I found this an incredible feat. Was it intentional?"

♑ ♋ ♌ ♈

N. I love that you noticed this.

It was indeed intentional.

I was lucky to be writing about a topic that is generally so visceral to people, how they look is largely irrelevant to how they cope with the experiences they are having.

I also find that the only people overly concerned with how the characters might 'look' are those feeling a need to categorize them in a way that will reinforce any potential judgments they want to maintain about the characters actions or reactions to the content of the tale, as it unfolds.

It is, after all, a story about a lost meaning of the Bible (verified by ancient and modern Biblical scholarship) that completely contradicts everything we've been told is true about life, death, and the meaning of being human.

I always thought that how the characters cope with discovering this information was far more important than how they looked, so made every effort to maintain ambiguity about specifics.

The Rules Did Not Know Me

"You've written *The Story of Q.* in an usual format for fiction using references and footnotes at the end of the book, as well as a complete bibliography. Why do this? Why not just write the story as a complete fictional tale?"

♑ ♋ ♌ ♈

N. The references are necessary—not just as an homage to the wonderful academic writers whose works are mentioned, but because, as you will have seen, while *The Story of Q.* is indeed about the experiences of four characters, it is just as much a story about us—every single one of us, whether we go to church or not, whether we believe or not, whether we are seeking, or quietly curious about discovering a relationship between ourselves and some idea of God.

Also, it was important to me to be responsible for the information.

I have too much respect for the impact of these topics in people's lives, not to provide an actual context for people to learn more about where the information came from that builds the foundation of *The Story of Q.*, or where they can learn more about it should they so choose.

For some the impact is confrontational, for others, delicious life-altering revelation.

Either way, the references are about respect, context, information, and strength of the foundation—the reality behind the story.

I had some industry backlash about the format, but it was very important to me to stick to the vision I had for the story, even if it was unconventional.

The saying goes, "Just because it's tradition, doesn't mean it's right". This applies to industry convention—just because it's there, doesn't mean it's the only way to tell a story.

Or it's as Eddie Vedder says, "I knew all the rules, but the rules did not know me."

Tricks of the Trade

"Writing process—any special tricks of the trade?"

♑ ♋ ♌ ♈

N. The only trick I know is work *hard*. Work, work, work.

You have to be able to pull it out on your own. No one else can help you or get it done but you. So many people say they would like to write a book one day, and while anyone can put a pen to paper, it takes something else to actually sit down and do it, start to finish. To edit it a hundred times, to re-read and be honest about your work. As soon as you think you have nothing left to give, you have to work harder. That was my biggest trick.

Second trick is honesty. There is a difference between honesty and self-deprecation. Honesty involves humility—meaning you can look at your work and see when it needs work, as in, you're not happy with it purely because you know you can do a better job. Self-deprecation involves ego, insecurity, and even self-loathing. That won't help you get your work done, but it, coupled with fear, will feed the procrastination monster until it becomes a complete accomplishment inhibitor.

As a part of honesty, in my opinion, you need to be able to take constructive criticism. Professional, neutral, constructive criticism can help you see things about your work that maybe you can't see. You should then take that criticism and filter it through your writing identity—be able to change what really does need changing (and drop your ego about it), and use the opportunity to strengthen your talent. It is always my goal to take editorial comments on board, but keep my writing identity when I implement them. Being honest about my work allowed me to take professional criticism without taking it personally, and that only made me feel stronger in my craft.

That said, I wouldn't recommend letting friends or random people/writer's groups assess your work. If you're serious about it, you need a professional opinion. Someone from within the industry—there is no other way. The rest are just random opinions. The only thing stopping you from getting professional feedback is fear. And fear is just a moveable reality, a perception.

The Smile

"Water is a significant theme in your book. Was this intentional?"

♑ ♋ ♌ ♈

N. Yes.

Sort of.

The linguistic, symbolic, and metaphorical links were indeed intentional.

I wanted to connect everything back to the central tenets of the lessons and what was appearing to become a lost meaning of the actual Bible.

But there were times (and I only realized this afterward, reading the final draft before it went to print) that water emerged in places I hadn't 'expected'.

This to me is the mystery at the heart of writing—of any creative process really.

There is the part of us thinking and planning our way through a book, and then the part that just listens, expresses, composes, lets flow whatever it is that seems to be flowing through our thoughts that creates them into stories. It's a huge, wonder-filled mystery how this works.

So when I saw water in places I didn't perhaps plan for it to be, and that these places often bolstered—somehow cinched—the edges of the story together tighter, more powerfully, I smiled.

What else was there to do, but that.

Book Club

The Dinner Party Sessions
&
Gnothi Seauton (the Private Sessions)

For gathered friends, for groups, for yourself

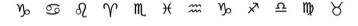

www.thestoryofQ.com
www.nmfreeman.wordpress.com

The Dinner Party Sessions

1. How did you feel when you finished the book? Relieved? Joyful? Nervous? Why?

2. Pious Fraud: discuss

3. By the end of the book, you are left to question whether or not the infallibility of the Bible really matters. Does it?

4. Many readers have written in saying the story made them feel like they weren't alone, or as if *The Story of Q* said things they had been thinking their whole life, but didn't know how to put into words—if you felt any of these things, which characters brought out those thoughts most in you—why?

5. Who is Sophia?

6. Discuss the 'original' meaning of the Christ and Jesus stories, versus the orthodox meaning.

7. For the women in the group what impact, if any, did the revelations regarding women and changes made to scripture have on your personally. Do the changes matter? Why or why not?

8. For the men: same question.

9. *The Story of Q* consistently plays with the idea that only through recognition of the invisible and the physical will you experience the whole of reality. Can you relate to this description of reality? How so?

10. The definition of Christ and Christmas are forever altered in *The Story of Q*. Discuss the pros and cons of this 'new'/original definition. (Expansion: on a local and on a global scale)

♑ ♋ ♌ ♈ ♏ ♓ ♒ ♑ ♐ ♎ ♍ ♉

Gnothi Seauton: Know Thyself (the Private Sessions)

1. Many readers have written in saying the story made them feel like they weren't alone, or as if it said things they had been thinking their whole life, but didn't know how to put into words—if you felt any of these things, which characters brought out those thoughts most in you—why?

2. How often does self-created fear stand in the way of your own personal growth?

3. When you read *The Story of Q.* and learned what the characters were learning, as a direct challenge to the church and religion in general, how did you feel in your heart? Why do you think you felt that way? How do you feel now? Is there any fear, and if so, where do you think it came from? Does it need to be there?

4. The book closes with the quote, "Come unto me all you that labour and are heavy laden, and I will give you rest"—Jesus

5. How does the meaning of these words change from the start of *The Story of Q.* through to the finish?

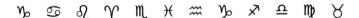

Natasha Freeman authors under the initials N.M.Freeman.

Born and raised in Canada, she departed her home country in 2001 to take up residence in the UK before moving to South Africa for an extended period. From there, she explored New Zealand for six or so years (where *The Story of Q.* was written).

She currently resides in Australia with her husband and son.

*

More officially, N.M.Freeman is a Rhodes University Alumna with a post-graduate diploma in Journalism and a BA in English (cum laude).

Her other areas of study include political science and women's studies, but she has always maintained a personal interest in theology - in particular, the many ways in which people are affected by religion.

To interact with the author,
and for access to exclusive blogs and discussions related to *the story of Q.*,
updates, information, and intimate book signing venues visit:

www.nmfreeman.wordpress.com

or join her writer's profile page on Facebook: N. M. Freeman / author

www.thestoryofQ.com

CPSIA information can be obtained at www.ICGtesting.com
Printed in the USA
LVOW052233280513

335808LV00002B/440/P